High Andes

High Andes

Wylie Cypher fights his way across the White Mountains of Peru with his daughter, Mercy, to protect a vital international secret. Featuring torture, mayhem, international smuggling, the ancient goddess, Pachamama, a child mummy, and the CIA.

BY ROLF MARGENAU

PUBLISHED BY FROGWORKS PUBLISHING

High Andes is a work of fiction.

Names, characters, incidents, places, and organizations are the product of the author's imagination or are used fictitiously. Any resemblance to actual persons, living or dead, events, organizations or locales are entirely coincidental.

Published in the United States by Frogworks Publishing

ISBN-13: 978-0-9882311-3-9
ISBN-10: 0988231131
EBook ISBN 978-0-9882311-4-6

www.frogworks.com

First Edition
Library of Congress Control Number: 2014913564
CreateSpace Independent Publishing Platform
North Charleston, South Carolina

By Rolf Margenau

PISTILS AND POETRY
PUBLIC INFORMATION
MASTER GARDENER

PREFACE AND ACKNOWLEDGMENT

If the description in this novel of the situation in Peru in the early 1980s conjures up a not so distant mirror of the United States now, it is not accidental.

I find disturbing our current dysfunctional United States government and the large and growing gap between rich and poor, the inequality of which is receiving only lip service by pundits and legislators. I believe these elements represent a danger to our nation, and I wanted to create a cautionary tale that relates to those elements.

Rather than invent a dystopian world, I cast about for historical examples of what happens when administrative timidity and legislative incompetence are coupled with disregard for the most vulnerable members of a society.

I focused on a time and place that I know. I had the opportunity to spend time in Peru on business and personal quests for four decades. The geography and culture of the country fascinate me, and I consider the people warm, gracious, and generous. During those years, members of my family and I trekked the Andes on Inca trails, rafted wild rivers, visited remote archeological sites and lived in jungle huts along tributaries to the Amazon River. High mountains and deserts were traversed, condors tracked, and ancient artifacts examined. I fell in love with the country and its people, and observed the joys and frustrations of their lives.

I also gained insight into the political environment, dealing not only with members of various administrations, both military and democratic, but also with business people who worked closely with government officials. I observed that, for one reason or another, full use of the country's riches always seemed to elude the government's grasp.

I wanted to expand the horizons of Wylie Cypher, the reluctant hero of two other of my novels, and examine his journey through a series of pitfalls. Accordingly, I insinuated Wylie into the fabric of a deteriorating Peruvian social and economic environment and tasked him with thwarting various bloodthirsty villains. In his mid-forties, suffering from a mid-life crisis, his relationship with his wife deteriorating, he seeks to bond with his only daughter on a trek through the Andes. Things go awry as the story unfolds.

As I researched the historical incidents that I hoped would provide verisimilitude to the story, I came across a photograph of a child mummy recently exhumed from a niche in the thin air of the Andes. I found the picture unsettling, not for the deformities visited on the child by time, but because I felt she should not have been disturbed from her eternal slumber. That led to a sub-plot involving the child mummy, Cocohuay, and Gaspar, the epitome of a modern Inca. My favorite Incan deity, Pachamama, has a strong supporting role.

For purposes of story telling, I have taken liberties with some distances involved. For example, the trip to the Lagoon of the Condors from the main highway involves a twelve- to fifteen- hour trip on horseback. The Cypher group finds its way to the amazing underground mummy display after a short truck trip and brief hike.

Otherwise, the trek over the Cordillera Blanca is an honest description. I have included what I felt were basic details about mountain trekking, but resisted the urge to add more particulars.

I acknowledge, with thanks, the help and support of my editor, Tiffany Yates Martin, FoxPrint Editorial, who helped create a more rounded and vivid hero, challenged my poor choices in words, explanations and plot, and prodded me to focus on the story and eliminate digressions.

Ahni Kruger, fine artist and art professor, created the striking cover for the book using a photograph of the Kuelap Fortress as a background for the ominous condors that appear throughout the story. Susan Haake, graphic designer for all my books, employed her formidable skills to complete the cover design.

And to literary friends who nurtured, commented and improved the narrative, I offer heartfelt thanks.

1

The special child seemed almost weightless in his arms as he approached the niche in the rocks where he intended to place her. Ayar continued to gauge his ascent carefully, constantly scanning the path below and the horizon. Special concern was necessary, as the Chimu had not yet settled the war between their nations. They still sent out raiding parties even as far south as Huaraz.

The body of the four-year-old girl he carried was the daughter of Cuca, wife of Maita Capac. Cuca herself was now sick with the plague that lay like a dark hand on the people of the White Mountains. That disease had quickly taken the life of her firstborn, the lively and adored Cocohuay, named for the turtledoves kept in a dovecote outside her window.

The sickness spread almost faster than the noble runners could report. There was news about strange white people at Tumbes in the north. They wore silver jackets and sat on four-legged beasts three times the size of the largest llama. They had huge wooden houses that went on the sea, and sticks that carried thunder.

The plague began at Tumbes, and the wooden houses left two of the strange men there and sailed away. Huayna Capac sent to have them brought to him, but they were lost along the way. Now the ruler's people in Chavín de Huántar were dying. The embalmer's services were in high demand.

Cuca called Ayar when her little daughter died. As wife of the regional administrator, Cuca was highly placed and her demands took priority. Not that the embalmer would have denied her. Once he saw the frail little child carefully arranged on the low table among sweet-smelling grasses and flowers, and noted the florid flush of her face and body, his heart went out to the grieving mother. He would do all he could to prepare the little girl.

It took him two days. First he selected a series of elongated hooks that he inserted into her anus to remove her internal organs. Ayar placed them in a finely made pottery jar to accompany her to the place of eternal sunshine. Then he carefully began to treat the skin. Slowly he rubbed a balm of oil from llama wool, beeswax and a bit of wood ash onto the skin with a pad of alpaca hair. He paid particular attention to her head, and treated her still-glossy black hair with this unction. Once the skin was treated, he placed cotton in her facial cavities. She retained her childlike features, except for the dark marks from the disease.

Her body was free of rigor, so he carefully moved her limbs so that she was in a sitting position and placed flat, thin boards at each side to keep her upright. Later, as Ayar wrapped the first layer of fine cloth around her little body, he would remove the boards. First, however, he placed a necklace with three silver triangles around her neck and slipped a silver bracelet adorned with doves on a tiny wrist. Cuca had sent cloths for her daughter decorated with birds and pumas, and he bundled her in those fabrics. Her mother had ordered that she not be placed in a pottery urn. She wanted her daughter to experience the clear radiance of the high mountains on her journey to everlasting light.

Ayar stepped back from the wooden table where Cocohuay rested to examine his handiwork in the soft light coming through the entryway. He could do no better; she was ready for her new life. He picked her up gently, surprised, as always, how little she weighed, perhaps no more than a melon. Pressing her to his chest with one hand, he gathered a leather bag of corn, a little fur jacket, the ceramic vessel with her organs, and a water gourd. On his belt he carried a small pot with brilliant red paint.

It was early morning, still cold and damp. He could see mists rising from the valley below as he began his ascent to the sacred place, the high peak among the highest mountains of the white *cordillera*. They called it Huallpa, Sun of Joy. Completely adapted to the thin air of the mountains with his barrel chest and short, sturdy legs, he carried his bundle upward. When he felt the sun fully on his shoulders, he surveyed the snow-capped peak ahead. Ayar could see the plateau just below the sacred place of the mummies. He would be there when the sun reached its zenith.

The embalmer climbed carefully between boulders to the opening of a large cave, home to ancestors from a time before time, before the puma that bore his tribe. The little bundle might fit there, but he knew of a better location, a place that would please Cuca.

He picked his way to a shelf of rock where the last snow of winter yet remained in the shadow of a stone promontory. He placed her on the shelf and began to remove loose stones and shale from the mountain's face, creating a little niche for the dove girl. When he was satisfied, he dipped the fingers of his eating hand into the little pot of paint and traced outlines of a bird, a deer, and a llama on the clean stone. They would be companions to his small charge. The bag of corn, pottery jar, and drinking gourd were there to help on her journey.

Satisfied that all needful things had been supplied, Ayar placed Cocohuay in the niche so her face was turned to the east, where she would see the rising sun. He used the stones removed from the side of the mountain to build a wall around the small bundle, filling the chinks with dirt and pebbles. He left the top open. He did not want to obstruct her view.

The embalmer descended from the sacred place soon afterward.

Cocohuay remained undisturbed in her aerie for centuries, untouched by anything other than the sun and thin air of the High Andes.

Then she began a journey unimaginable by any of the people of the White Mountains.

2

Gaspar watched as the smaller of the two police officers killed the chicken that he had just taken from a corner of his tiny yard. The officer absentmindedly twisted its head around until the bird became motionless, and tucked its feet under his belt so it hung at his side like part of his dusty uniform.

Gaspar no longer felt outraged at this casual theft. It was common practice endured along with all the other hard aspects of trying to make a living and survive with his family in his small pueblo. The police missed the shoat hidden under the outcrop behind his home and had no interest in the two scruffy llamas munching short grass down the hill. They did not care to snatch guinea pigs from their runways in the adobe walls of Gaspar's home, but a chicken was an easy conquest. For a while now the policemen from the *comisario* in the valley below had puffed their way up the mountain to talk with the campesinos about infiltration by dangerous rebels from Ayacucho, the Sendero Luminoso. In spite of efforts by the military and police, the insurrectionists were gaining strength and challenging the government forces throughout the highlands of the Andes, the Cordilleras Blanca and Negra, from Ayacucho to north of Huaraz.

The rebels' basic strategy was to enlist the poor people of the mountains in their cause by promising them a better life under a communist regime modeled on that of Chairman Mao in China. The idea of confiscating properties of large landowners and redistributing parcels to the poor campesinos initially generated great support from the people of the highlands.

The officers and men of the Sendero Luminoso understood that their revolution would be a long time coming, and they chose to live in the towns and villages of the mountains to learn the ways of, and become part of the life of, the campesinos. They married local women and spoke the native language, Quechua. It was an effective strategy. The people of the mountains were impressed, at least at first, that the bearers of the news of the revolution chose to share their lives and work with them. The ranks of the Sendero Luminoso grew. As they did, the leaders grew bolder, more aggressive, and bloodthirsty. That intensified government efforts to corral them.

The officers' questions this time were more specific than during their last visit. They began the usual way—the weather, the health of his family, the acceptance of a little coca tea. With the tea, the two moved outside to a crude bench to warm themselves in the afternoon sun. Evening's chill came fast even in the valley below. Enrique stretched his short legs, digging his heels into the powdery dust in front of the bench. The other officer (Gaspar did not remember his name) leaned against the door, marking the dust with brown spittle.

—Any new ones coming through? Any young ones visiting? People from the city perhaps?

Gaspar slowly shook his head.

—You remember our understanding. For your own protection, for the family, you let us know when strangers come.

Gaspar confirmed that obligation solemnly. There had been no strangers in his village. He had no choice but to answer that way.

During the last harvest festival, his cousin visited from Ayacucho, the stronghold of the insurrectionists. He explained to Gaspar and his neighbors how it was there.

—They come to the village, he said, to see whether someone has had conversation with the police. If they suspect someone has done so, he is beaten. His wife is beaten. Sometimes they break bones or cut you. Then the police come another time. If they suspect anyone has aided the Sendero Luminoso, that person is taken to jail, where he is beaten. Some do not return. They join the ranks of the "disappeared."

—Aiii, said the cousin, we are like corn ready to be ground. Above and below, there is nothing but a hard place. Up there they call us tamales, mashed corn. Thanks be to God, they are not here yet.

But they were, sometimes.

Gaspar repeated that there were no strangers in their village. He felt certain that these lazy policemen were not prepared to beat anyone unless there was sincere provocation, which he would not offer.

He watched the policemen pull themselves up from the bench and begin the descent among the raised stone terraces below the village. They should be used to it by now, Gaspar thought, but they still grabbed their chests and wheezed when they climbed the mountain from their nice adobe office in the valley. He did not know what region they came from, but they were not his people. He was glad to see them begin their descent.

Gaspar turned his attention to other plans he had for that day.

A temblor had shaken his mountains two days before. As usual, the dogs gave early warning, whining and crouching against thick stone walls. The earthquake came with a low rumble, shaking the ground of his pueblo, causing some pots to fall from shelves to earthen floors. It lasted perhaps two minutes.

Gaspar searched for evidence of damage along the sides of the surrounding mountains, looking for cracks and signs of landslides, but saw nothing. It was like almost all the movements of the mountains he experienced during his life, a shrug of the shoulders, a clearing of the throat, an adjustment of the buttocks for comfort. It was a bother to be tolerated and endured, an integral part of life in the Cordillera Blanca.

Every time his mountains shook themselves, he recalled when his father took him, along with one of their donkeys, not so far away to the base of Huascarán Mountain, to what remained of the town of Yungay. He was young then. He had not even met his wife.

His father explained that it was important for him to know how it was when the mountains became angry. Gaspar was young and careless and took many things for granted. He did not then have proper respect for the mountains. He understood their beauty, but did not associate it with danger, like a snake hiding among the branches of the *gantu*, the Cantuta bush. There, in that place, he could see the mighty scar on the north side of the mountain where the eight-hundred-meter-wide slab of glacial ice and debris slid away and caromed toward the town of Yungay.

From the knoll where they had stood, Gaspar could see a vast plain stretching toward the foot of the mountain. He led the donkey and followed his father to the single, surprisingly short palm tree standing lonely near the edge of the plain.

It was, his father said, the tall tree standing near the house of the alcalde by the town square. Now the town and the alcalde were buried below, and the miniature palm tree was all that remained. Gaspar reached up as far as he could and almost touched the lowest branch of the tree. From his angle, he again saw where the missing part of the mountain had been.

They let the donkey forage for young grass on the plain and sat by the palm tree. His father handed him cracked corn and cheese and passed over a jug of water. His father was not hungry; he rolled a cigarette, and narrated the story of the disaster.

—The people here were not afraid of the mountain. They saw the glacier and they saw dark cracks where the glacier was pushing against the side of Huascarán. But they said to themselves, look how far away that is, and look at the valley and the steep slopes that separate us from the mountain. We will be safe.

Father looked at Gaspar, exhaled smoke and continued.

—On that day in late spring, when ice was melting, that side of the mountain collapsed. They say that fifty million cubic meters of ice and dirt and stone slid down at speeds of up to four hundred kilometers an hour. The only ones who saw the avalanche and survived were visiting relatives in the cemetery, back over there on the high ground. They were very lucky. In three minutes, the avalanche traveled fifteen kilometers, more than twice the distance we went all morning. No one is certain, but the government says twenty-five thousand people died that day.

Gaspar could not comprehend all the things that his father said to him. He lived in a village of fewer than three hundred people. He could not imagine how many people twenty-five thousand were. Nor could he understand cubic meters. However, he could understand the massive scar on the mountain and the pygmy palm tree. Ever since, when he heard the mountains rumble and felt movement beneath his feet, he saw the palm tree and the missing part of the mountain.

Nowadays he was not fearful, but he was cautious. It was a defensive attitude necessary for all those living with the mountains.

Long-distance examination of the highlands surrounding his village would disclose only the most obvious disturbances of land, rocks, or vegetation. In his experience, only careful and close inspection of the crags, crevices, and looming peaks was required to show potentially rewarding changes to his surroundings.

Sometimes disturbances exposed formerly unknown mineral deposits of copper and silver, even gold. Openings to caves suddenly appeared, and scientists from Lima came to gawk at mysterious things discovered there. Sometimes they hired campesinos to cook, carry, or dig. Gaspar himself had worked for two months last year near the Veronica peak hauling supplies for the camp of some red-faced scientists. They were surprisingly excited about finding worthless pieces of pots, bones, and hair. They paid well, and he was sorry when they returned to Lima.

Now the call of the mountains was strong—and urgent. He needed to begin his journey before the snow moved down to cover mountain passes and obliterate known trails among trees and meadows. He explained to his wife that he would not be gone long, perhaps no more than a week or so.

She did not understand why her husband needed to climb up into the mountains, although other women said it was because of the noble blood of the ancestors, undiluted by conquistadors' blood. Gaspar had the look of an Inca, with high cheekbones, a nose like a hawk's beak, and a receding chin.

The things he carried were few. A slingshot for small game, a little sack of cracked corn, a dented steel cup, two sheets of plastic, his freshly sharpened machete, some braided rope, coca leaves for tea, cheese, tissues and matches. He wore canvas trousers, a shirt covered with a tattered alpaca sweater and a faded denim jacket. He cut a new pair of sandals from the used tire leaning against the back wall of his home and secured it with cords. He chose a colorful native wool hat with earflaps and tucked it along with other items into the rolled blanket slung across his chest. For added safety, he grasped one of the stout sticks resting by the front door. There was no wood like that at high altitude.

Ready for the ascent, he kissed his little son and daughter and caressed his wife. She was reluctant to release him, grasping his strong shoulders, hugging him and slipping a little sack of sugar into his pack.

He climbed east from his home and felt the sun on his forehead. He realized there were not enough daylight hours left to reach the place he had hoped to spend the night. It was on the banks of the Laguna Conococha, the mountain lake glistening between the Cordilleras Negra and Blanca. He intended to follow the ridgeline above the north-flowing Río Santa to the perennially cold lake at an altitude of four thousand meters. He would reach his favorite spot the next day, where the view across the lake in the early hours always lifted his heart.

He searched for changes along a familiar path, discovering the earth had stirred only slightly nearby. He saw the remains of a few small avalanches that covered low vegetation, and some new hills, hummocks and gullies. The big rocks that he knew well were steadfast, and the jagged peaks had not changed. As he climbed higher to crest the ridge above the Río Santa, he noticed larger disturbances. Unfamiliar boulders pushed against the current of the river far below, and new openings appeared on some of the steep slopes. Raw ochre gashes showed along the gray slopes of the Cordillera Negro.

At dusk, he found himself on the ridgeline, looking down at rushing waters. To get there, he had traversed new areas of scree, loose rock fragments slippery and treacherous as quicksand. Now he was on firm footing. He spied a grey squirrel scratching under a shrub and dispatched him with his slingshot. Dry leaves and litter around the shrubs fueled his fire, and he dined on roasted squirrel and cracked corn. Patches of snow scraped into his cup became clear water for his coca tea. He found a comfortable spot, covered himself with his blanket, and was soon asleep under the brilliant stars.

The afternoon of the following day, he reached the familiar brown sandy beach on the east side of the Laguna Conococha. He had taken numerous detours since setting out early that morning, searching disturbed areas of the mountains for newly revealed treasures. The only discovery of note was an arm of one of the glaciers covering the peaks of the Cordillera Blanca that had poked through the lower wall of the mountain, sending rocks and debris cascading down, narrowly missing a farmer's hut in the valley. Lucky farmer, he thought.

He intended to sleep on the beach that night, and decided to try for a meal of fresh fish that evening. He wandered along the edge of the lake watching the horned coots cruising across the surface of the water and disappearing to forage for food below. Gaspar sharpened a branch for a spear and approached the place where the Río Santa originated, where the water ran swiftly. He hoped for something better than a small pupfish—a pike or a catfish.

The brilliant reflection of the afternoon sun off the snow- and ice-covered peaks obscured his view underwater, and he made numerous unsuccessful tries to spear what he thought were fish. Finally, the sun moved below the distant peaks and the clear water revealed its bounty. He caught two catfish, shoved the spear through their gills, and carried them back to his place on the beach. Under the light of the moon rising above the snowcapped mountains, Gaspar prepared another meal. The sand yielded as he moved his hips to form a fitting resting place. He pulled his blanket to his chin and felt a chill breeze from the lake. Tomorrow morning, he hoped, he would experience again the sight that drew him here.

He awakened under the luster of the North Star. It was well before dawn, but the mountains to the east and west of the lake stood out clearly against the myriad lights of the Milky Way. He sat up and searched for clouds in the night sky. There were none. Good, he thought. Nothing to spoil the light.

As the darkness slowly receded, he turned his attention to a cluster of high peaks pushing northward in the Cordillera Blanca. He saw their east faces from where he stood—obscure, brooding monoliths. That was where he hoped to find the ancient Pachamama, the goddess of natural things. Nowhere else in the mountains had he experienced her closeness, her glory, as in this place. Here she became real, and when it happened, he felt invigorated, hopeful, and peaceful. It was a feeling the padre said he should have when he was with the saints, the Savior and the Virgin. But he never did. He felt it here, alone with the ancient deity, on a morning like this.

The sun was still below the horizon as the first faint hues of pink illuminated the distant peaks. The color on their icy cliffs intensified, deepening to maroon and then crimson, rich and dark as a dove's blood. The deep red contrasted with the midnight blue of the opening sky, where stars still glittered like dew on pine needles. Next, as the first rays of sun crested the mountaintops, a brilliant halo of golden light surrounded the wide crimson band below the peaks. The mountains glowed with ethereal illumination.

It lasted but a moment but, in that moment, Gaspar believed he was in the presence of Pachamama. Her luminosity was more blessed and real than any light pouring through a stained-glass window. She was his pathway to his ancestors; she renewed the intangible bonds to the ancient ones that sustained him through adversity and self-doubt.

He was now ready for whatever the mountains had in store for him. Once again, he was blessed. He was ready to go back home.

3

Wylie made the usual visitor's mistake as he prepared to cross the street and looked the wrong way for oncoming cars. A maroon taxi avoided him as he stepped from the curb, and the driver reminded him of traffic patterns in London with a rude universal gesture. Admonished, Wylie walked past the well-preserved row of Georgian houses on a street leading toward Picadilly.

Seeing the well-ordered buildings, he recalled the weekend many years ago when he and Mavis visited London together. It was the first time in months they had been able to escape the demands of two small children, long hours of work, and the stress of being newcomers to the social structure of Middletown. Wylie arranged for Mavis to meet him as he concluded some legal business, and they spent a weekend in a small hotel created from three Georgian row houses.

Despite good intentions of absorbing London's historical, theatrical, and cultural offerings, their weekend became a liberating experiment in the joys of sex, using the Victorian *The Pearl* as their guidebook. With no infant demands or whiny voices to distract them, they spent most of the weekend in bed, on the ottoman, and at the local pub refreshing themselves for yet unexplored activities. On the flight back to New York Mavis snuggled up to Wylie and purred that she was very happy to learn what the English meant by a "dirty weekend."

Wylie sighed at that recollection, and looked down London's cobbled walkways, noting attractive young women in light spring dresses moving briskly along, their skirts swishing invitingly, their hair backlit and glowing before the midmorning sun. Mavis, he thought, was like that back then – slim, active, warm and sexy. Now it was like breaking into Fort Knox to gain her sexual favors. What had it been, five – no, six – months since they made love?

Looking again at what seemed to Wylie a parade of nubile young women, he wondered if all couples in their mid forties suffered from sexual ennui. Admittedly, his sporadic squash games did little to diminish the love handles pressing against his belt or the little apron of fat spreading above his penis, but Mavis was no longer in her prime either. On the rare occasion that he caught a glimpse of her breasts, they seemed to be pointing toward her navel, and her former hourglass figure was tending toward pear-shape.

Perhaps it was sour grapes, but since Mavis seemed little interested in sex he adopted the same attitude. Neither one initiated moments of intimacy nor, as time went on, were they able to convert the pleasure of sexual contact to the less intense but equally important enjoyment of companionship. They were drifting apart, and the recollection of that dirty weekend in London faded. Wylie felt that his marriage was slipping into a dark and gloomy pit, which he could neither understand nor resolve.

The sight of all the young women only enhanced his misery; as solace, he planned to walk part way to his appointment down his favorite street. It was like stepping into another, simpler time that he found soothing. He intended to walk down Old Bond to Jermyn Street, and then take the underground from Piccadilly to Aldwych, a short walk from the solicitor's office in the business district known as the City. The old-fashioned style of the underground cars and their cleanliness were a satisfying contrast to the dirty and graffiti-laden subway cars in New York. The clever billboard advertisements along the escalators amused him, and the almost hushed sound of approaching cars was soothing compared with the metallic clanking and screeching heard when he traveled under Manhattan. He appreciated the history commemorated by the various stops: Waterloo, Westminster, Victoria, Tower Hill, Blackfriars, and Covent Garden. When the escalators carried him to places far under the city and river above, he recalled how these stations had protected Londoners during the Blitz. He always felt peculiarly comforted when he waited for the underground train.

Wylie made his way across Piccadilly, walked around the corner of Duke Street, and stood on the corner of Jermyn, facing Alfred Dunhill. He was not a smoker, but, as a daring exploit, he occasionally purchased Club Havana cigars there to smuggle back home for a favored client. Wylie liked Jermyn Street because it represented the essence of the British upper crust, a high-style fashion center for gentlemen originating in 1664. Whether clothing, footwear, perfume, groceries, tobacco, antiques or dining, the best available was found along this quiet byway stretching from St. James's to Regent streets.

This morning he made his way to Floris, the oldest shop on the street. He needed to replenish his Elite cologne, sold at eight pounds for three ounces. As he left the shop, he imagined himself a proper English gentleman and strolled past shirt makers Hawes & Curtis, Hilditch & Key, Turnbull & Asser, and Harvie & Hudson. He wondered why it always took two tailors to make men's shirts, and gawked at Harvie & Hudson's shop front, with its concentration of stripes in every color, shape, and form. He marveled at the most widely spread Windsor collar he had ever seen, and fingered his pedestrian button-down guiltily. Brooks Brothers suddenly felt common.

He glanced at Burberry, housed in the Simpsons of Piccadilly department store and the little antique shops fitting themselves into narrow spaces along the street. Wylie considered rewarding himself for the successful conclusion to another acquisition with four-hundred-dollar handmade shoes from Trickler's.

During his early years at the New York law firm of Biddle and Ofstrosky, the exhilaration of completing a complicated business acquisition would be its own reward. Now Wylie needed to mark the event with a fancy souvenir. It helped allay the feeling, lately, that there was a sameness about his work, a plodding reenactment of much he had done before. He specialized in helping large American corporations make foreign acquisitions.

He shrugged his shoulders, entered the Piccadilly line at the corner of Haymarket, and was at Aldwych in two stops. He crossed the Strand to Melbone Place and turned left along the great arc of Aldwych to the polished oak doors of the solicitors' offices. A discreet but gleaming brass plaque read, "Bimble & Squire, Solicitors. Founded 1842."

Peter Pender, local counsel for a number of deals Wylie had worked on in London, awaited him. The two men worked well together and enjoyed each other's company. Peter confirmed that almost all needed parties were waiting to execute the papers. Missing were Corwin Handleberry III, great-grandson of the founder, and Mathew Finch, the investment banker. Not to worry, said Peter. Corwin was perennially late, and Finch had just called to say he was on his way.

Corwin soon arrived. He was in his mid-thirties, dressed in faded jeans, polo shirt, a knitted scarf, and sandals. A soon-to-be wealthy rebel, Wylie thought. They shook hands and Corwin left, waving to a cousin seated in the conference room. Then Finch entered the antechamber. He clutched a large file folder and looked unhappy.

—A word in your ear, gentlemen?

Peter motioned Finch and Wylie to a corner of the antechamber,

—Um, you recall I advised yesterday that the required number of shareholder agreements approving the sale were in hand.

Peter and Wylie were immediately on the alert. They nodded.

—It appears that statement was, um, slightly premature. We re-counted the forms and shares tendered last evening and it appears we are short a handful of approvals.

—A handful?

—Um, yes. To be precise, we are missing—he peered into the file folder—confirmation for fifty shares. That represents, let me see, a tiny fraction of a percent of outstanding shares.

—Bloody hell, muttered Peter. You have been working for months to contact family and public shareholders to grant approval for the sale of Handleberry shares. Now you say you are fifty short of the ninety-five percent needed to proceed! Moments before the closing. Bloody hell!

Wylie swallowed hard and tried to remain composed. The prospect of postponing the closing and recalling all the people assembled in the conference room later was devastating. Such a misstep would compromise his reputation and that of Biddle and Ofstrosky. The financial press would have a heyday poking fun at the Yankees who could not manage a simple purchase agreement. Red-faced and with heart pounding he approached Finch. He tried to appear calm.

—Yesterday you believed all necessary approvals had been obtained. How many remain outstanding—that you know of?

—There are, um, dozens, representing thousands of shares. It is just that many holders are tardy, forgetful or cannot locate our request letter. That is why we have five percent leeway in rounding up the approvals. But, you know, new forms arrive daily. No doubt, approvals for many times fifty shares will arrive today and tomorrow—if past experience is any guide.

Wylie continued.

—You are absolutely certain of that? That after all this time and expense and the best efforts of your highly respected firm, you have failed to produce the necessary number of approvals—contrary to your contractual obligations.

Finch bristled and attempted to interrupt, but no words came out.

—Would you say that a concerted effort by your firm to reach out today, by all means possible, to obtain approvals for fifty more shares would be successful?

—Um.

—Thereby avoiding potential unpleasantness.

—Um.

—Put another way, assuming the necessary approvals are "in hand" by today's date, being a moment before midnight, would you feel at all uncomfortable certifying that the necessary number of shares approving the sale have been gathered?

—Yes, but . . . No, I mean . . .

—Comfortable?

—I suppose I could certify to that at this closing and issue written confirmation later.

—Of course. The documents have to be vetted and proofed before they are printed in any case. Your written confirmation might not be needed for days.

Wylie placed his hand on Finch's shoulder and smiled at him.

—Shall we go in?

There was cheery banter among the Handleberry descendants gathered around the large table as papers were passed around to be signed. A banker made a telephone call authorizing the transfer of a large sum of pounds to the escrow account established for the shareholders. Within a day or so, many of the people around the table would be wealthy, and Biddle and Ofstrosky would collect a substantial fee.

Wylie visited Tricker's on his way back to the hotel and arranged to have custom shoe lasts made. He paused in front of Simpsons' window and bought the cashmere sport coat displayed in the window as well.

That evening as he examined the sport coat, finishing his second glass of whisky, seeing himself wearing the buttery jacket in the mirror, he flashed back to the day's events. When was it, he wondered, that he traded the ethical certitude gained in law school for the need to make a deal at any cost?

Two days later, when printed copies of closing documents reached all participants and financial pundits analyzed the deal, Finch's firm had received and collated approval of the purchase by holders of an additional eight hundred shares.

Since Swallow Street was just a few blocks from his hotel, Wylie decided to walk to Bentley's for dinner that evening with Peter Pender, QC. Peter had been appointed Queen's Counsel that year, a signal honor known as "taking the silk." Wylie was pleased for his friend and wished that New York conferred similar honors. He could imagine himself in a black robe with chevrons and a horsehair wig, standing before the bar.

The elderly hostess at the entrance motioned him to the upstairs dining room, where Peter waited. Bentley's was Peter's favorite place for oysters and beef. Oak accents emphasized creamy walls, and the servers acted like everyone's favorite aunt. The comfortably upholstered woman who brought the menu asked Wylie,

—Now what would you like to drink, dear?

His favorite, Glenmorangie, neat. Peter joined him.

A large platter heaped with crushed ice, shucked oysters from Whitstable, and lemon halves cloaked in porous cloth diapers appeared. As expected, they were delicious.

As they scooped out the bivalves, the conversation turned to family matters, then American politics.

—The situation in Iran certainly won't help President Carter. He is a good and sensible man but circumstances are playing against him. What do you think of this Reagan character, Wylie? Does he have a chance?

—We have a joke that Sam Goldwyn is in heaven when he hears that Ronnie is running for president. No, he yells. Hank Fonda for president, Ronnie as his best friend.

—I see.

—Actually, he was a very effective governor of California, and he is reputed to be a talented leader. He certainly has excellent speaking experience—and it looks as though he has managed to distance himself from some real movie clunkers, like *Bedtime for Bonzo*.

—*Bedtime for Bonzo*?

—Bonzo is a chimpanzee.

—Oh.

—Nevertheless, I believe Reagan has a solid chance. Carter seems to be flailing. In a way, I suppose, Reagan is more politically aligned with your Margaret Thatcher. Very impressive, that woman. First female prime minister for England.

—Just so.

Conversation halted as one of the servers arrived with a cart concealing under its domed silver lid what appeared to be half a cow. They chose their favorite cuts, added pearl onions and peas along with roasted potatoes, and requested bitter ale to accompany their meal. Only after they had ordered profiteroles for dessert did Peter resume serious conversation.

—Wylie, are you still making frequent journeys to South America?

—Yes, fairly often.

—Any visits scheduled for Peru?

—I think I am going to be in Lima the middle of next month. I am working on a mining joint venture and visiting with one of my local clients. Why do you ask?

—One of my friends at the club has an interest in Peru. He is Percy Walsham, Earl of Wimsey—a very engaging chap. Business is antiquities, fine art, that sort of thing. Percy was bemoaning the fact that he couldn't find anyone in London with contacts in Lima, and I thought of you.

—That is flattering. But does he need legal help?

—Not sure. Perhaps you could meet him and discuss.

—With pleasure, but I am planning to return to New York Thursday. I could make time the next two days.

—I will arrange something.

The profiteroles arrived, oozing creamy chocolate.

Boodle's was located just around the corner from Jermyn Street, on St. James's. Wylie was enthralled with its location and exterior architecture. For the members of the private club, change was anathema and the interior of the building seemed to be as it had looked in 1782. Wylie felt awkward in its hallowed but somewhat musty chambers. No one seemed to speak above a hushed whisper.

Peter would not be there; he had an important client meeting and could not be there to make introductions.

—You don't need me, he had said. Percy is a good chap. You will get along famously.

An official in starched collar and brass-buttoned navy suit directed Wylie to a high-ceilinged library filled with leather-bound books and upholstered leather chairs, comfortable but worn. Wylie felt he was entering the set of a Hitchcock film. Awaiting him in a sitting area in a corner of the room sat a dapper man about his age. He rose, revealing his diminutive stature, and clasped Wylie's hand.

—So good of you to come. Peter speaks so highly of you. May I call you Wylie? Would you like a drink? Graves, please get Mr. Cypher a drink. Glenmorangie, isn't it? Please sit, sit.

Percy beamed at Wylie. He took his hand again.

—Yes. Yes. Can't thank you enough.

The whiskey arrived, and Percy confirmed that Wylie was indeed the famous lawyer from the silk stocking New York Biddle and Ofstrosky firm. Wylie shook his head to correct the "famous" part, but Percy chattered on in his charming fashion, dribbling little tidbits of praise as he referred to Wylie's curriculum vitae. Percy even knew where he had gone to school.

Wylie was interested that this aristocratic little man had learned so much about his background. Wylie was familiar with the use of insincere flattery as a way to ingratiate himself to potential clients and was on his guard. Nevertheless, the Englishman's patter and aristocratic tones intrigued him. During a momentary pause in Percy's encomium, Wylie decided to cut through the opening gambit and said that Peter had spoken of Percy's business interests in Peru. Was there some way he could be of service?

—Dear boy, yes, there is. As Peter probably mentioned, I deal in various antique artifacts and recently was approached by a friend in Lima who has some attractive items available. Permit me to show you some photographs of those ornaments.

Percy reached into a briefcase beside his chair and pulled out an envelope holding a number of glossy photographs, which he spread out in the table beside them. His gaze lingered over each picture as he lovingly passed them over to Wylie.

Wylie was no expert in Peruvian antiquities, but he had seen earpieces, breastplates, and necklaces worn by members of ancient Peruvian cultures at the University museum in Lima. The photographs showed similar items, as well as some whose purpose he could only surmise. It seemed to him that the pieces in the photographs were exquisite - earpieces and chest plates with jade, rock crystals, amethyst, silver and gold. Percy's eyes were shining when Wylie looked from the pictures back to the art dealer.

—These and others, he said, are in demand from many of my European customers. These items are very popular now.

—That is easily understood, offered Wylie. They are beautiful things.

Now Wylie was curious. Was Percy going to suggest he become involved in transporting these items to the United Kingdom? As a legal matter that was out of the question.

Percy began to discuss his problem.

—I am sure you are aware, Wylie, how difficult it is to arrange for the transfer of funds to less developed countries.

Percy paused, probing Wylie's reaction to his statement.

Wylie knew of the difficulty of managing international currency transfers, especially to less-developed countries with questionable banking infrastructures. Even Citibank had misplaced for days a wire transfer from its offices in New York to Lima. Such delay made business dealings difficult, but he resolved that issue by establishing proxy accounts in the United States.

Wylie suggested that might apply to Percy's problem. Percy said his solicitors had already reviewed that solution and discovered it would not provide for a timely and reliable transfer of funds.

Percy ordered more whiskey and Wylie watched as he reached forward to put his hand on Wylie's knee. Wylie categorized this as akin to the two-handed handshake he employed to simulate sincerity and good fellowship. Something interesting was coming; it was like watching a tennis match at Wimbledon. Maybe Percy's forehand smash was on its way.

—I understand, began Percy, that you will soon be returning to Lima. Peter confirms that you are a person of integrity, which emboldens me to ask if I may retain you to deliver a small package to the person who has offered to provide me with the objects in these photographs.

Wylie paused to consider as Percy withdrew his hand from his knee. First, he needed to assess Percy as a potential client, an important concern in maintaining his reputation as a rainmaker at his law firm and as a source of continuing fees. Second, he quickly reviewed the legal ramifications of Percy's request. Most likely Percy wanted him to deliver negotiable instruments to his dealer in Lima — either currency in large denominations or bearer bonds. Unlike some other countries, Peru's immigration forms did not ask whether the traveler was carrying large sums of money. There was no legal prohibition to acting as a courier. In fact, he had previously provided such a service for existing clients in Peru.

The potential for Percy's continuing legal business or representation was unclear. Wylie decided at ask a blunt question.

—May I ask, Percy, do you have many business dealings in the United States?

—Ah, of course, you want to know if there are other areas where you might provide service.

The smaller man leaned toward Wylie with a conspiratorial air.

—Not only do I have numerous contacts across the pond, but my friends in London do as well. I am sure we could be of benefit to each other.

Wylie placed his empty glass on the table beside them and decided to use the move recently employed by Percy. He placed his hand on the dealer's knee and said

—Percy, I would be pleased to deliver a parcel to your contact in Lima — as a courtesy.

Percy smiled broadly.

—How splendid! I will have it sent over to your hotel straightaway, along with Señor Hernandez's particulars. I can't thank you enough, old man.

Business accomplished, Wylie soon took his leave. Percy Walsham, Earl of Wimsey, settled back into his large chair and complimented himself on persuading Wylie to deliver the bearer bonds needed to conclude the acquisition of the Lima artifacts. The exportation of Indian artifacts was illegal, but poorly enforced under the current ineffectual government regime. Nevertheless, significant cash payments to the proper government officials assured no interference. Also costly were dependable transfer agents who could assure the surreptitious arrival of the artifacts at Heathrow under manifests listing leather goods, alpaca scarves or carved magnolia amazonica utensils. The invoice for his most recent shipment showed "various alpaca throw rugs."

For all his questionable maneuvers, Percy never engaged in sharp trading with his clients. They knew he dealt only in genuine articles, never a questionable artifact or counterfeit. There was an unwritten rule that no one demanded proof of provenance. His clients relied on their own research and expertise to confirm the value of their purchases. In many cases, the innate beauty of the piece was sufficient in itself. On the rare occasion that one of his imports found its way into a museum, curators agreed they were authentic and unique finds. In short, Percy was an honorable crook. A wealthy honorable crook.

He reviewed his meeting with Wylie. He enjoyed the give and take of their conversation, believing that Wylie was an astute resource who understood the intricacies of international trade.

He called Graves to his side and asked for pen and paper. He needed to draft a cable for Señor Hernandez to let him know funds were on the way.

Wylie was pleased to discover that the steward on the Pan Am flight to Kennedy offered a generous dollop of his favorite whisky before the afternoon meal. The aromatic liquor should have comforted him as he reclined on his seat on the second floor of the 747 but it seemed to heighten his discontent. Aside from his increasing distance from Mavis, he was troubled by what he perceived as the boring sameness of his work. He knew that tomorrow he would meet with clients who needed his help in merging, acquiring, or selling businesses – a field in which he was expert. However, one deal seemed more and more like all the others. The businesses involved might as well have been grapefruits or overstuffed couches.

He stared out the window at the bank of clouds below and fantasized about skimming over them on a surfboard or day sailer. Soaring. Carefree. Young.

His drink made him sleepy, and he decided to take a nap before touching down at Kennedy. The afternoon traffic from the airport to his home in Middletown was sure to be a bitch.

4

Gaspar returned by the same route that he used to reach the lake. As always, it seemed changed from before, affected by shifting light. He continued to look carefully for disturbances brought about by the recent earthquake, but almost failed to notice a tiny opening beneath a rock ledge some distance above his path. What caught his eye was a slim shaft of sunlight illuminating a tuft of grass clinging to the black stone. From where he stood, he saw a fresh mound of debris at the edge of a large, flat boulder, and sunlight blinking through an opening a meter or so above the ledge.

There was a brownish-orange stone lodged in the opening. He had never seen an orange stone in the mountains before. It was worth investigating. Loose pebbles and dirt made his climb awkward, but he soon reached the outcrop. In a niche under a protecting ledge, protruding above a small rock cairn was the orange stone. It grinned at Gaspar.

Gaspar had never seen anything like it before. Carefully he reached out and touched what he now realized was a tiny head above a body and limbs exposed to wind and sun for eons that turned shriveled limbs the color of *café con leche*. Hints of their original colors remained in the cloths that swaddled the child, and black hair still fell to its tiny shoulders. From the long hair and type of clothing, Gaspar assumed the child was a girl. Her head and face, carefully attended by the embalmer, had a golden orange hue, but time had drawn back her lips and exposed her teeth in a perpetual grin. As Gaspar approached, he first saw her large forehead, then her grinning mouth. He was rooted to the spot. Pachamama, he thought, why have you brought me here?

He squatted on the rock ledge looking up at the little mummy and considered that question. Curiosity overwhelmed him, and he climbed up to the ledge and carefully removed the stones and pebbles that had protected her.

He marveled that the wind or a curious condor had not dislodged the tiny creature during the many years she had rested in her niche. He touched a shriveled arm. It felt like the paper used to wrap parcels at the *mercado* in the valley. The two bones in her forearm were clearly outlined under the skin. They looked like twigs. He reached out to pick her up, to feel her weight, but reconsidered. Instead, he returned to the ledge below.

The situation was puzzling. He believed this discovery was no chance occurrence, and credited Pachamama for drawing his attention to the place where the little mummy rested. The deity no doubt intended him to find her, but then what? He cursed himself for being too dull to understand the next step. Absentmindedly, he reached for a handful of coca leaves from the pocket of his jacket and tucked them into his mouth. At this high altitude, he soon felt the invigorating effect of the leaves. Shadows on the mountain walls brightened and he felt he could evaluate his position more clearly.

The choice was simple: either let the little mummy continue her eternal rest where she was found or take her away. But why take her away? He did not need an ancient baby to decorate his home and scare his little children. Nor, he was sure, would his wife appreciate such a guest. However, was it likely Pachamama directed him here just to have a look? If the goddess wanted her left alone, there was no need to involve Gaspar. Things were pointing toward taking her with him.

He looked to the mountain peaks for inspiration. He recalled a photograph of adult mummies he had seen years ago in *El Comercio*, the newspaper he occasionally read to see football scores. They were in a museum, with uniformed officers in attendance. If they are guarded, he thought, they have value, but how much he could not guess. He glanced at his find again. She was very small. That probably meant she would not be as expensive as large mummies, if value was based on weight, like maize and charcoal. However, she would certainly be easy to carry back to his home, where he could discuss his find with those who might know, like the *proprietario* in the valley. There was no reason not to believe that Pachamama intended him to have a good future. He was due.

The little mummy weighed no more than a few potatoes. The concretion of her body over that long time resulted in a surprisingly solid, tough and durable little being. Nevertheless, Gaspar treated her with great care, packing leaves around her as he placed her in a sling he made from his blanket. He placed the little pot and a stick figurine he found next to her in a fold of his blanket. There were also wisps of some kind of fur next to her body. He left those.

Before retreating down the mountain, he placed rocks in a natural position on the ledge where he found her. Should he need to find this place again, the rocks would signal its location, but in a way others would not notice. He balanced the blanket sling so the tiny girl rested in the small of his back, placed his machete through the thong on his belt, gathered his staff and began the return trip home. He estimated he would be there tomorrow, midday.

That night he camped amid scrub pines and woke refreshed at dawn. His breakfast was eggs from a ground dove found the previous afternoon, and he drank clear water from a glacial stream to hydrate himself. He was very thirsty after a night's sleep in the mountain air.

After eating, he descended through thick clouds. The moist air caused a strange singing in power lines stretching through the valley below, like a poorly tuned E string on a guitar. The singing continued as the cloud sank lower into the valley and sunlight penetrated the mists surrounding Gaspar.

His route took him along a trail on the ridge overlooking the Río Santa, and he looked down the steep sides of the mountain descending toward the river. The river itself was unseen beneath the low clouds, but he could hear the rushing waters along with the singing of the wires. He had experienced those sounds and sights before, and appreciated their mystery. It gave him an eerie feeling of isolation in a strange world where he was master of the mountains. He continued along the slick path, checking that his bundle was secure behind him.

The master of the mountains forgot about the recently uncovered patch of scree along his path and stepped onto it at the same pace he used on firm ground. He might as well have stepped onto a waterslide. The loose stones beneath his feet gave way and he scrambled upward, searching for better footing. There was none, and he lost his balance as he began a dangerous descent down the mountain. He sat down, lowering his center of gravity, and used his stick as either a rudder or an oar to guide and slow the rapid slide toward the river and the rocks below.

It was a long way, and he became the center of a little avalanche, with loose rocks, pebbles and dirt surrounding him and hastening his swift descent. Yet he managed to keep from tumbling, and searched through the enveloping mist for a handhold or outcrop or anything to break his fall. He saw a large Puya raimondii shrub directly below, its six-foot-long leaves rushing toward him, its huge flower spike not yet in bloom. He slowed himself with the stick and grabbed at the leaves with his left hand. He stopped, and his body spun under the bush.

The sharp edges of the leaves sliced into his hand and quickly flowing blood made it too slippery to sustain his grip. He placed both hands on his stick and dug its end into the mucky soil, hoping to wedge himself to the side of the mountain. He sat, motionless, breathless, gauging the distance to the river below from the sound of rushing waters. It was far, still far.

After a few moments, he attempted to adjust his stance by slowly moving his feet for better purchase on the slippery mountainside. It was the wrong thing to do. The tip of his stick began to slip, as stones and dirt came away from the incline on either side. He reached back in another attempt to grab the shrub, but that movement caused his bottom to shift forward. Suddenly there was no resistance to either feet or bottom and he renewed his descent toward the river. He focused all his attention on surviving this fall.

Gaspar felt almost as though he were floating, slowly taking in the sights around him. The cloud dissipated about one hundred meters above the river, and he zoomed through the hazy light toward the rocks and water below. In a heightened state of awareness, he could count the sharp stones below, see beige foam in the lee of large boulders, and count the reeds growing on the far side of the river.

He remained in a sitting position as his body slid toward the river's edge. Matted reeds, stones, and the water itself broke his fall, but his right foot became wedged into a crevice of rock below the water. He experienced sharp pain as the current turned him and something happened to his foot. The hydraulics of the river caught and trapped him, pushed him underneath the surface and then up again, just long enough for him to gasp air. The cold water numbed the throbbing ache and he fought the current to work his foot loose. The rocks did not want to release him, although he pulled with all his might. Something gave way and he experienced a surge of agony that coursed up his leg and seemed to lodge behind his eyes. He lost consciousness, and the river took him.

5

—Dammit, Wylie, you parked so I have to step right into the middle of this stupid puddle! intoned Mavis as she pushed open the passenger door of the Buick and surveyed the three-foot-wide moat of dewy grass separating her from the dry pavement beyond. She muttered curses at Wylie as he arranged his tie in the rearview mirror, watching Brooks exit the Buick on the side away from Mavis, tuning out his wife's verbal abuse, hoping she would not spoil another family celebration.

Their trip from Middletown to Bryn Mawr on a splendid June morning had been quick and uneventful, except that Wylie sensed, as the miles clicked along, a spreading web of hostility emanating from the passenger seat where Mavis stubbed out one Pall Mall cigarette after another. In Wylie's view, Mavis gave new life to the meaning of "change of life" that he and his partners sometimes ruefully considered over drinks after Thursday afternoon meetings in the office. His life was changing – and not for the better. He glanced toward his wife as she raised her foot to crush the glowing ember of a cigarette into the dewy grass before maneuvering from the car to the sidewalk.

—Hold on, honey, he said, let me give you a hand.

Wylie moved to the side of the passenger door and took her arm, permitting her to imprint one toe tip on the manicured grass before the three stood on the sidewalk, looking upward toward neat University buildings, close-cropped grass, and the area prepared for the day's events. White wooden chairs were arrayed like military crosses at Arlington cemetery, awaiting the backsides of proud parents, siblings and friends. All were prepared to commemorate the escape of this year's graduating class into the great good world awaiting them, a world where they could follow their dreams and make a difference.

Brooks took his mother's arm as they joined the stream of well-dressed people finding their way to their seats, boldly marked by placards showing row and seat numbers. Wylie saw his son's gesture of support for Mavis both as a rebuke to himself for some unremembered offense against either or both, and as evidence of Brooks' decision to join his mother's side on the widening chasm that separated his parents.

Physically, Brooks resembled his father, tall and blandly handsome with sandy hair and blue eyes. Yet, Wylie believed his strong sense of entitlement, ability to bend facts to suit his demands, and slippery moral sense confirmed Brooks as Mavis' offspring. For years, Wylie hoped to find evidence of Wylieness in his only son, a basis for fraternal connection, a chink to allow a loving relationship. He discovered none. The compass of Brooks' affection pointed always in one direction – toward Mavis.

They found their seats, not too far from the stage and podium, and saw the eager graduates in unaccustomed robes shuffling in their places. Brooks pointed out his sister's location, but Wylie could not see her; it seemed a flowering dogwood blocked his view. Brooks' college graduation, four years earlier, had been much grander and involved, requiring binoculars to see him receive his diploma. He exchanged that diploma for a junior management position at Lehman Brothers, where his character traits allowed him to flourish. Wylie made it a point to invite his son to lunch at his club in the city at least twice a year.

A college orchestra began playing a vaguely familiar march and the audience settled down. The parade of dignitaries, laden with flowing robes, hoods, chevrons, shining necklaces, and instruments more reminiscent of battle and heraldry than education filled the center aisle and flowed, like unconstrained mercury, to their assigned places on the stage. The Cypher family prepared itself to be enlightened by the flow of erudition to be offered by the assembly of luminaries.

Wylie stretched his lanky frame for comfort in the hard wood chair; Brooks awaited words of guidance from the main speaker, a graduate and Academy Award winning actress; Mavis allowed discreet periods during which she did not puff on a cigarette. Bees buzzed among the azaleas, Kousa dogwoods, and early clover blossoms, and Wylie allowed the warm sun and soporific natural melodies to induce a pleasurable muzzy semi-sleep where the promises of the day might be fulfilled.

—Dad, Dad, there she is! announced Brooks as the main speaker withdrew from the podium amid generous applause.

Mercy, tall, tawny-haired, robust and smiling, stood with the other students in her row as they prepared to file to the stage and receive their awards. At first, Wylie did not recognize her, perhaps because of his abrupt arousal, perhaps because of the unfamiliar cap and gown. Then she responded to another student's comment and laughed, head back, shaking her hair, the sun emphasizing light brown strands against the dark gown.

Wylie blinked his eyes as though to refresh the image of his daughter. His first impression remained; she was a beautiful young woman, transformed during the recent passage of time through emphasis on her best qualities. Blotchy freckles that crowded her forehead and nose (when was that, last Easter?) were gone, blended to a rosy hue that complimented her hazel eyes. She stood straight and poised - the slouch that Mavis kept complaining about a distant memory. She moved gracefully forward, taller than most of the other students, and ascended the podium.

Wylie looked quickly toward Mavis who was busy brushing gray ashes from her lap and then focused on his daughter as she stood by the podium listening to the Dean recite her accomplishments and awards. To his great surprise, Wylie felt tightness in the back of his throat that, when he tried to clear it, only grew more pronounced. His chest expanded involuntarily and tears welled in his eyes. My God, he thought, look at her – my little girl.

He wiped his eyes and paid attention to the Dean's words as she smiled at Mercy and brandished a wooden plaque.

—...Proctor prize for excellence in literary criticism for her senior honors essay, *Emily Dickinson's Undiscovered Continent*.

Then the Dean referred to her leadership of the undefeated Martial Arts team, her captaincy of the Varsity Lacrosse team, and other achievements such as her involvement in a program for unwed mothers in north Philadelphia. As she turned from the podium, with scrolls and the large plaque, she dramatically moved the tassel of her cap to the other side. Her classmates cheered as she floated back to her seat.

Brooks and Wylie helped Mercy fill the trunk of the Buick to overflowing with detritus remaining after four years of active college life. Since she did not plan to return to her parents' home for some months, Wylie and Mavis agreed to store her things in their basement – next to Brooks' stuff that, by now, had achieved a patina of dust and permanence. At dinner, they joked about having to move to an old folks' home finally to rid themselves of their children's memorabilia. Mercy and Brooks advised against that.

—We intend to become famous, noted Brooks, and all that stuff will be fantastically valuable. Don't even think of donating it to the Salvation Army!

The evening is going well, thought Wylie. Mavis, moved by the occasion, hugged her daughter for an over-extended time as they met just after the graduation ceremony and promised they would soon be doing something "very special" (mysteriously undefined) together just as soon as Mercy made her way back to Middletown. Mavis helped carry Mercy's stuff to the Buick and sat in the back with her daughter as they drove to the restaurant for dinner.

As the waiter cleared the entrees and they sipped the remains of the second bottle of Bordeaux, Brooks asked about his sister's immediate plans.

—Well, Brooksy, it's probably dreadful that I have no firm plans in place, but I am going to consider various options for the future this year and try to figure out what I want to do. Take a year off. I will spend the summer just like the last couple of years, as chief counselor at Camp Upnoweegon in the Poconos. Then, we'll see.

—Awesome, said Brooks. What every girl wants - a life of leisure. Way to go!

The words were neutral, but his tone was not. Envy sprinkled with sarcasm; a pouty mouth. Brooks realized inner feelings had tainted his comment; his ears reddened slightly.

Mercy looked closely at her brother and Wylie realized that his independent, feminist daughter was calculating her need for assertiveness versus continuing family harmony. It had happened before.

—Sure, Brooksy, a nice year-long vacation – like the two times you were booted from prep school for smoking pot and dealing drugs.

Harmony left the table as the waiter approached with the bill.

Mavis and Brooks sat in the Buick smoking as Wylie and Mercy exchanged a few last words at the entrance to her dormitory. No mention was made of their abbreviated dinner conversation.

—Listen, Dad, I have a number of options I need to consider, and I intend to take your advice about not making hasty decisions. One is going to law school...

—Well, I...

—Another is joining the Peace Corps and traveling at the government's expense to some of the exotic places you visit. That would be at least a two-year commitment and a break from college that most employers or Universities understand. I also have two job offers – one is with a non-profit in New York working on affordable housing, and the other is as editorial assistant for Ms. Magazine. Neither one offers much money, but I don't need that much anyway.

She looked at her father with a quizzical expression, awaiting his comments. Wylie, feeling ambushed, leaned against the porch railing and fiddled with some coins in his pocket.

—Sweetie, you are fortunate to have such wonderful choices, and I think it is a very good idea to gather yourself and your resources for a year or so to consider next steps. I wish I had that luxury when I graduated. Things were less complicated then; we just moved...

Wylie paused, realizing this was not about him, trying to respond appropriately, wishing to offer wise guidance. He tried again.

—Of course, don't worry about money. Mom and I will support you as you make the right decision.

—Thanks, Dad, and I don't want to appear ungrateful, but I think it is about time I struck out on my own. I do not intend to become the daughter/wife cliché - moving from dependence on father to dependence on husband.

That tidbit of insight was novel to Wylie, but he absorbed and accepted it quickly. He understood yearning for independence, more so lately as the pressure of sameness pushed at his edges and fingertips, quietly demanding something else, something more.

As though prompted by an alarm, they joined in a brief embrace of farewell, and agreed to meet again soon, quietly, away from pressure of family and the excitement of the day, to discuss in detail Mercy's options.

As Wylie turned toward the Buick, Mercy touched his sleeve.

—Do you remember, Daddy, some time ago you promised to take me on one of your foreign trips, just the two of us. I would love to do that now – I really would.

6

In 1974, when Fredo was in his third year of studies, he had two great passions. Principally he was deeply in love with his classmate, Claudia, whose supple body, raspberry nipples, luxurious silky pubic hair, and sexual abandon drove him nearly to distraction. By contrast, the Maoist philosophy taught by charismatic professor Abimael Guzmán Reynoso at his university in Ayacucho captivated him intellectually.

Claudia, also a good student, was more interested in the historical evolution of communism in China under Mao, while Fredo believed fervently that a peasant revolution was just what Peru needed to overcome its inept and oppressive military administration.

The military regime of General Juan Velasco Alvarado controlled Peru. His economic mismanagement, corruption at top levels of government, and abuse of human rights devastated the Peruvian economy. People with Spanish or European backgrounds were favored in employment, education and social standing. Those with dark skin were ignored or repressed. The natives of the highlands, scornfully called *"los indios"* by the city dwellers, suffered.

When Fredo was thirteen, his father decided to leave a medical practice in Ayacucho and move to San Miguel, in the highlands some kilometers east of the main city. There he worked in a small clinic with another doctor and a veterinarian who attended to the medical needs of the mountain folk and their animals. Fredo's parents were happy in a practice comprised mainly of campesinos and their families. They loved the simpler life, the splendor of the mountains, and the feeling that they were having a positive impact on a distressed population.

At first Fredo was unhappy with the move. However, he soon made new friends in San Miguel who tutored him in mountain traditions. As he grew taller and stronger, he learned how to work with llamas and donkeys, how to handle a machete, and how to judge weather in the high *cordilleras*.

Fredo excelled in school and won easy admission to the university when he was eighteen. He knew little of politics, philosophy or economics when he arrived at the University of San Cristóbal but was soon fascinated by the teachings of Professor Guzmán. A leader of the Communist Party of Peru who had witnessed the Cultural Revolution in China, Guzmán believed armed struggle was the only way to create real political change. When the communist party gained control of the university council, Guzmán used his position to promote his revolutionary agenda and ridicule the government. The Velasco regime briefly jailed Guzmán and other teachers.

Soon after, Guzmán gained leadership of the Bandera Roja and renamed the Communist Party of Peru the Sendero Luminoso—the Shining Path. Its goal was to establish Maoist communism as the government of Peru—through armed struggle that justified any means, including terror tactics, to obtain communist domination.

From his days in San Miguel, Fredo recognized that the villagers of the highlands relied mainly on their own devices to survive – with little or no help from government authorities. He sensed that purposeful discrimination against the natives of his country must somehow be wrong. Guzmán framed Fredo's inchoate sense of injustice through the teachings of Marx, Engels, and *The Communist Manifesto*. He used the Bay of Pigs invasion to demonize the United States. He lectured that the coming struggle would free Peru from Yankee domination and the yoke of servitude to that imperialist dominator. Only communism would create a superior state and equality among the common people. Guzmán was a mesmerizing speaker and persuasive pedagogue.

Fredo, Claudia and his best friend, Lucho, with other impressionable young students, were in an environment dominated by members and supporters of the Sendero Luminoso, so opposing political or economic philosophies were either denigrated or ignored. After more than two years of exposure to these teachings, it was not surprising that all three of them volunteered to join Sendero Luminoso. Late-night debates centered not on the philosophical differences among capitalism, socialism and communism, but on the most effective way to bring down the current government headquartered in Lima. Students began to search for weapons to arm themselves with for the cause when the time came. Old rifles, pistols, machetes, and ammunition were gathered and cached in secret places. It was important work. It was very exciting.

Lucho had two bottles of good Chilean red wine to share with Fredo and Claudia. Near sunset, the three arrived at a favorite place by the ancient aqueduct in town. They settled against the crumbling wall on parched grass that smelled sweetly like fodder beginning to ferment. Fredo passed the bottle and they savored the taste of wild black fruit and spices.

In a month or so they would graduate. The three had shared their hopes and desires for the future during the past year, but now it was time to decide on new paths to take. They realized the choice would not be easy. Their shiny new degrees did not offer a route to fame and riches. In cities of the lowlands, like Lima, which offered good jobs, graduates from the communist university in Ayacucho faced suspicion, disdain or fear. Their future employment was not secure. Claudia might work in her family's hotel business, but scorned the prospect of serving hotel guests. In any case, she intended to match her plans to Fredo's.

Lucho poured from the first bottle. He was large and burly, not a typical man of the mountains. His exterior matched his personality. He was rough-and-tumble and loved sports. He was the highest-scoring forward on the university football team and loved the physicality of the game. When he checked an opposing player he invariably stole the ball, and the player could be bruised and dazed. His footwork was clever and precise, and he frequently scored with headers. He took crazy risks that enthralled spectators and earned him the nickname of "Lucho Loco." Of the three, he had solid job prospects. Two teams from Peru's Primera División, Sport Huancayo and Melgar in Arequipa, offered him a position with generous salary and benefits. He had mentioned this development to Fredo the week before. Fredo was pleased and excited for his friend. Claudia teased him about using his head for hitting balls.

The evening darkened and the three friends leaned back on their elbows — silent for a while. Lucho poured from the second bottle.

—So, Fredo, have you come closer to finding work after you graduate?

—Yes, I think so. I talked with a member of the Huánuco regional committee who visited last week. He was looking for teachers to work in the villages near Huaraz, and liked that I know some Quechua. He says we can make a real difference by educating the peasants so they can be effective members of the revolution.

Claudia interrupted.

—I think Fredo would be a fine teacher. I do not see him attacking military outposts with a rifle or explosives. Fredo, he is a lover, not fighter.

She kissed his cheek.

—So, it is settled then? asked Lucho.

—Not yet. I need to seek my mother's advice. She is a teacher, as you know.

—*Claro.*

—And you, Lucho. All settled?

The last of the wine was poured into their glasses. He grinned at them both.

—Not in the way you think.

He saw the consternation on their faces and enjoyed their confusion.

—I had a meeting two days ago with Chairman Gonzalo himself. The leader put his hand on my shoulder and looked in my eyes. It was a great moment. He said that he saw me as a leader of the People's Guerrilla Army and offered me a captaincy. He knew about the football clubs and said I was too serious a person to go and play games when I could lead my country to a glowing future. I tell you, he is a most persuasive man. He never let go of my shoulder until I said yes.

His friends were stunned.

—I don't know exactly what happened, Lucho went on. He has this attitude, this machismo that just makes me want to do as he asks. Now I am committed. I am excited to be a soldier for the cause.

All three stretched out on the burned grass and stared at the stars, considering their own fantasies. The new world promised by Chairman Gonzalo. Their next steps into what they knew would be a bright and exciting future. The stories of the ancestors, Pachamama, Catequil, Ch'aska, and all the spirits of the past and of the mountains. The wine, the crisp night air, the comfort of their friendship. It was exhilarating stuff.

The two young men parted company after graduation, each beginning an apprenticeship with an arm of Sendero Luminoso.

Fredo became the schoolmaster in a highland pueblo of about five hundred people located many kilometers north of Ayacucho, in Huánuco Province. It was a three-day bus ride to Huaraz, followed by a three-hour pickup drive to a place in the valley below the pueblo. A mule carried Fredo's belongings and school supplies from there up to the little village. The pueblo lay in the shadow of the Cordillera Negra, and the white peaks of the Andes stretched out to the east. A mountain pass, at almost three thousand meters, provided access to a fertile valley surrounded by terraced fields.

There the villagers farmed and bred llamas with exceptionally fine hair. Their knowledge of and association with matters beyond the mountains was limited. They met Fredo's arrival with curiosity and bemusement—a young man with soft hands and strange books whose rudimentary Quechua was that of a young child. Nevertheless, they greeted him with the rough hospitality of the mountains and made him welcome. That is, until he might prove himself to be undesirable.

Fredo carried with him enough Sendero Luminoso money to construct a small schoolhouse and dwelling for himself and Claudia, who was eager to join him as soon as arrangements were completed. There were two abandoned houses at the south end of the pueblo, too damaged by an earthquake to be habitable. Fredo offered to rent the houses, but no one claimed ownership. The alcalde said they were his to use, and the villagers helped him repurpose the crumbled stones into the walls for the new school. When the corrugated galvanized-steel panels Fredo ordered for the roof arrived from Huaraz on the backs of a train of llamas, it caused a sensation. All the other roofs in the village were of grass or thatch. This young man was building a fine school for them. The men were eager to complete the roof. Women scolded him for being so thin; they brought him food—maize, chicken, and chilies. They called him *maestro*.

In a month, the school was completed. It was the best building in the pueblo. The cistern on the roof provided running water, and flat stones set in mortar paved the floor. Rude desks awaited students, and a large white board with multihued crayons hung against the north wall. Big window openings provided bright light and, when they were shuttered, kerosene lamps lit the interior.

A separate apartment attached to the schoolhouse would house Claudia and Fredo. Although Claudia said she looked forward to the adventure of living in rustic conditions, Fredo was not sure how well the daughter of a hotelier in Ayacucho would acclimate to stone walls and a toilet in a hut with a view of the mountains. However, their rooms did have running water, a kerosene stove and a large bed with a commercial mattress delivered almost to his door by a creaky pickup that labored from Huaraz. Fredo and two helpers from the pueblo whitewashed the interior, and he placed colorful mountain wool and alpaca blankets on the handmade furniture in the rooms. The helpers said

—*Se está bien aquí.*

He hoped Claudia would agree. She planned to arrive in early August.

Fredo explained to the alcalde and the older members of the pueblo that the Sendero Luminoso sponsored him and the school, that they would have a better life under communism. Since the village already operated somewhat as a commune, it seemed to the village elders little would change, but Fredo emphasized that the government in Lima also would change, and that the people of the mountains would have greater power and support from their leaders. The elders were skeptical that any good could ever come their way from Lima and debated the matter for many evenings as the school neared completion. Eventually, the alcalde had this conversation with Fredo.

—We are very proud for the new school and we thank the Shining Path for offering it to us. It is a fine school.

—Many thanks.

—Now, this talk about fighting for new power is troubling.

—How is that?

—Things as they are, we are left alone. No taxes, no help. We follow the old ways and we like that. The last time we saw the government was a soldier running through the valley looking for a lost horse. Perhaps two years ago.

Fredo was about to explain that they paid taxes in their meager purchases, but the alcalde continued.

—Life is not easy, but change may be more difficult. We will listen, but we are always suspicious of help.

—Why?

—We are not sophisticated, but we are not stupid. We may not know exactly how it is, but we know that no one gives without benefiting in return. So, tell me: What does the Shining Path expect to gain from us?

Fredo began to talk about altruism, common good, and taking from the few to give to the many, but the alcalde cut him short.

—Maestro, you have done a fine service with the new school. We thank you.

Fredo returned to his apartment along the steep and rocky path from the alcalde's home. He decided that explaining the noble principles of the Sendero Luminoso to the children could wait. Change, as always, would be difficult to accomplish. School began in July, when the noonday sun cleanly bisected the azure sky above the mountains. Well-scrubbed children with glistening black hair and ruddy cheeks came across steep rocky paths to the new schoolhouse. Girls wore colorful blouses and dark skirts, and boys arrived in shirts, some frayed and worn, with shorts or pantaloons. Most were barefoot, though some older boys wore sandals cut from used truck tires. They hesitated at the entrance, and Fredo ushered them in, pointing out the neatly aligned desks. There were twenty-three children, none older than ten or eleven. Of course, he thought. The older ones are working.

The Cuban told Lucho to breathe normally and slowly squeeze the trigger of the M-16 rifle. After almost a week of training he no longer flinched in anticipation of the recoil and, on discharge, the round sped into the concrete block two hundred meters ahead and shattered it completely.

—*Bueno.* Had that been a Yankee dog he would never go home again. Your aim is improving. You are doing well.

Lucho grunted acceptance of the compliment. The Cuban officer had been instructing his group for almost two weeks. He had helped defeat the invasion at the Bay of Pigs in the spring of 1961 and had fought in Angola in 1975, a seasoned warrior with no love for Yankee imperialism. He was the sort of fighter Fidel Castro exported to help the cause of exploited minorities. Che Guevara was among those sent to help and, if anything, his execution at the hands of

CIA and Green Beret–trained Bolivian soldiers at La Higuera in the fall of 1967 intensified Castro's desire to support the growth of communism anywhere in the world. Naturally, he wished to help Chairman Gonzalo, so he sent a select cadre of trainers to Peru to help prepare for the overthrow of the inept government.

Lucho and other young men classified as officer material comprised the company led by the Cuban. He was glad to have bright and motivated recruits eager to learn the craft of combat. It was unnecessary to subject the group to harsh discipline, as imposed on the peons who were "enlisted" for the cause. In addition to teaching his men to use the weapons of war and guerrilla tactics, he explained techniques to win the "hearts and minds" that the Yankees failed to win during the Vietnam War. It was important to respect the culture of the Indians of the highlands, to speak with them in Quechua if possible, and to assist with the redistribution of property liberated from large landowners and the government. Lucho's indoctrination included studying the organization of the Sendero Luminoso. He learned that the five-member Politburo was the decision-making division of the party. The Politburo gave orders to and received support from the People's Guerrilla Army and the Popular Front. As a member of the guerrilla army, Lucho recognized that the Popular Front helped with recruiting, legal defense for arrested members, and family support for members killed in action or imprisoned. Of course, he did not plan to require such support. Being killed happened to other people.

Chairman Gonzalo structured the army as groups of cells. There were five to ten members with specialized duties in each cell, with little contact among cells. That minimized damage should the government capture a cell member. The cell leader received orders from a commander, who reported to a company commander. Lucho expected his first assignment would be as a cell leader.

After six weeks of training, the members of Lucho's group began to receive assignments. Many left to join operations in the Upper Huallaga Valley, the largest coca-growing area in the world, and Huanta Province, all in the country's Andean region. Each morning Lucho waited for word of his assignment and said farewell to the other members of his group as they departed to the highlands. The Cuban pointedly ignored him.

Had Lucho done so poorly in his training? His natural athletic ability let him dominate the others in the physical aspects of their training, so perhaps it was something else. His cursed inability to read a topographical map? The time he forgot to tighten the wires from the claymore mine to the charger?

He felt discouraged that evening when the Cuban came to his hut and offered him a drink of rum.

They sat on the rough wooden bench in front of the hut, and an unopened bottle of golden Ron Mulata appeared from the Cuban's pack. He twisted the bottle open and passed it to Lucho, who took a mouthful and let the liquor abrade the inside of his mouth before swallowing it. He coughed lightly as the Cuban swallowed a formidable slug. Immediate warmth softened the evening chill of the training camp.

—Lucho, I need to ask something of you.

He waited.

—Lucho, *mi compadre*, there will be many new recruits coming here for training in the next months. You know that.

—*Es verdad.*

—But these are not like your group. Many have been recruited with a rifle and may not be eager to serve the cause. They are farmers and shepherds. They can handle a machete, but know nothing about fighting. Or, if they do, it is when they have a skin full of *chicha*.

—What is that to me?

—You are much admired for your athletic talents and you have excelled in your training. I would consider it a great honor if you would stay here with me.

So, this is what it is all about, thought Lucho, both relieved and disappointed.

—Stay here? I thought I was training to lead a cell of fighters! I want to combat the corrupt *ladrones* who are ruining this country. I want to blow things up! I don't want to wipe the asses of recruits. Please let me fight.

The Cuban lit a little brown cigar and offered one to Lucho, who refused.

—Take my word: You will have many opportunities to fight. But right now, it is my judgment and that of our superiors that you would be most valuable training new fighters. I like you, Lucho, but understand that what may seem a request is an order. The matter is settled.

Lucho let that sink in. It was sometimes difficult for him to acknowledge the command structure of the People's Army.

—I mean no disrespect. How long is it that you expect me to train these Indians?

—Some months, at least. I know you will do it well. These young men will respect you. That will help motivate them. After all, they have little and know little or nothing of our enemy. The government is just a vague thought that hardly touches their lives. Making these peons into guerrilla fighters will be a great challenge and an important thing.

During the next week, about forty recruits arrived, and Lucho soon learned how great the challenge really was.

By the time Claudia arrived in August, Fredo was beginning to appreciate the joys of teaching eager children. They had overcome their earlier fear of the Maestro and with it their timidity. Fredo was definitely not a strict disciplinarian and encouraged the children to go beyond rote learning and to listen to one another tell stories. The smaller ones clung to his hands and pulled on his trousers for attention. Fredo felt a strong affection for his stocky and rambunctious charges. He wondered whether all teachers felt that way. He had not expected it. Sometime during his first weeks as a teacher, he began his love affair with his students and the art of teaching.

Claudia made an enthusiastic point of praising Fredo for the "beautiful little hacienda" he created from the abandoned buildings. She enjoyed herself for a few weeks, adding the material touches she felt Fredo had neglected—curtains, a tablecloth, soft towels, found art (like dried flowers and artistically weathered wood from high above the village) on the walls, and the tableware she had shipped from Ayacucho.

After a separation of two months, their lovemaking was spectacular and exhausting. Villagers tittered at Fredo as he dragged himself wearily those early mornings from the doorway of their apartment to the schoolhouse door—only a few meters away. Claudia appeared sometime later, bright and refreshed. She enjoyed interacting with the women of the village and prided herself on using expertise gained from working in her father's hotel to select the best vegetables and meats (mainly chicken and guinea pig) offered in the village's daily market. She befriended many of the women in the little village, who referred to her at first as "La Gringa" because she had white skin and came from the city. As the weeks passed, she became "La Maestra," in reference to her man's position in the village, and to her own ability to teach the women of the village about things happening in the great world beyond the mountains.

In October, she decided to establish a simple medical office in her apartment, offering first aid, medications and supplies she ordered through her parents in Ayacucho. Among other things, she sheepishly provided advice about birth control. That caused an ironic buzz among the villagers when it became clear in January that she was pregnant.

7

Rojo, iridescent red, was his first hazy thought as consciousness returned. The Andean sun inflamed his eyelids, which he did not have the wit to open. He felt his blood coursing through the thin membranes, and his eyes hurt. As he opened them, his eyes hurt more from the brilliant light reflected on the surface of the water around him. A cloudy film dissolved and he could make out rocks and greenery above the water. He made the mistake of moving.

The pain in his left leg was overpowering. He forgot the pain in his eyes and the icy chill from the river. He was momentarily consumed by an agony that attached itself to all his senses. He could hear the pain. He could smell the pain. The pain danced in sheets of brilliance before his eyes. It was as though hundreds of blunt needles had been pounded through his flesh into the bone. It was as though—

He lost consciousness again.

Later, he awakened as his head slipped and he choked as water filled his nose and mouth. This time he worked through the pain, reached behind, and dragged himself along the smooth stones until he rested on the river's bank, his legs stretched out in the still rushing waters. He noticed that his left foot wobbled back and forth as it was caught and released by the current. His pain increased and receded with the motion of the foot. He was fascinated by the experience and fought to hold back nausea as he watched his foot flopping in the water. Then he saw a sharp white bone pushing through jagged flesh. He had seen that before, both in animals and people. It was not something he could repair himself.

Slowly he pulled himself upward, away from the river, until he rested on a grassy hummock. He was thinking more clearly now, and, as he searched for his machete, he felt the sling he had arranged to carry Cocohuay. He pulled the sling forward and saw that the little mummy had survived the onslaught of the river. Her skin still looked like parchment, and her hair was wet and glossy. Perhaps a wisp or two was missing, but she still looked at him with her perpetual grin, as though unperturbed by her contact with the rushing waters of the Río Santa. Gingerly, he placed her on a soft, dry spot on the hummock, and twisted himself into position to cut two stout branches from a nearby shrub. He loosened the coiled rope at his waist and, with teeth clenched against a twig, cut from the same shrub and fastened his foot to his ankle and shin by wrapping the rope around the two crude splints. At least, he thought, it keeps the foot from dragging along the trail. He quickly realized his left leg could bear no weight, so he crawled to a sapling and shaped it into a workable crutch with his machete.

He took inventory. There were many other cuts and bruises, and his sandals now belonged to the river. His hat was gone along with most of his food, but knife, machete and rope remained, along with the things he carried in his pockets. He practiced hobbling along with his crutch and experienced some very painful moments as his left foot hit rocks and branches. Soon, however, he felt ready to go forward, to descend the remaining five or six kilometers to his pueblo. Carefully he gathered Cocohuay and adjusted her sling.

It was late in the day. Too late to make the journey before nightfall. He resigned himself to spending another night under the clear sky. He shifted the bundle on his back to accommodate his awkward movements with the crutch, and picked his way along the trails he encountered just below the ridgeline. He was exhausted well before dark and rested in a bed of dry grass, waiting for morning. He could not sleep.

After Gaspar hobbled down the path to his home, his wife took one look at Gaspar's wound and realized he would require professional attention. She sent for the bonesetter, then made Gaspar as comfortable as possible and cleaned the smaller wounds she found on his body—but the leg and foot, that was bad. The bonesetter probably had a formal name, but all called him Cirujano, the surgeon. He was not from their village, and the boy sent to fetch him had to travel deep into the valley before he found him. He arrived at Gaspar's village at midday on the day after the day the boy left to search for him.

Cirujano was leathery and old, with crisp white hair that curled over his ears, a tuft of a mustache and a few long chin hairs that wiggled when he talked. He carried his instruments and medicines in a grimy pack, now dusty from travel. Cirujano walked to the cot where Gaspar lay and inspected the wound.

—I must go into the leg, which will cause much pain. Gaspar, you found your way home with great bravery, so I know you are a strong man. I will give you tea to help with the pain.

Cirujano extracted a glass jar filled with greenish-brown wrinkled leaves and asked Gaspar's woman to boil a handful of leaves and strain the liquid through cloth. She did as asked and cooled the liquid on stones in the north corner of their house. The patient became woozy moments after drinking the tea and felt happier than he had for some time.

Cirujano asked waiting neighbors to carry Gaspar and his cot out into bright daylight so he could attend to the broken bone. It seemed to Gaspar that he floated out of the room onto the path in front of his house. He smiled at the neighbors attending the al fresco surgery. The smile turned into a grimace as Cirujano applied a tourniquet and pulled on his ankle. He pushed the shard of bone back inside the leg, deftly fitting with the jagged piece he found there. Not satisfied, he used a razor to enlarge the wound and cut away bits of bone. Sweat glistened on Gaspar's face, and his wife refused to watch any more.

The bonesetter used a clean twig to extract some paste from a glass jar and gently applied it to the inside of the wound, around the bone. As the surgery progressed, he had been humming to himself in a low monotone. Now he spoke to the paste he spread in the wound. It seemed like an incantation.

—Fedegoso, Fedegoso, root of the Amazon. Cleanse the blood, purge all evil things from this good man and relieve his pain. Make him whole again!

Carefully, using needle and cotton thread, he sewed the layers of the wound together with precise stitches. Then he applied more Fedegoso paste. He asked one of the neighbors to light a cigarette and place it between his lips. He drew the smoke deeply into his lungs and blew it slowly over the now-closed wound.

Gaspar experienced a sense of cooling and loosening as the smoke passed over his leg.

Cirujano then placed bamboo strips like a cage around the leg, using cotton strips to hold them tightly in place. Finally, he pulled a bright maroon ribbon from his pack and tied it around the leg cage.

—That, my friend, is to remind you which leg was hurt, and let the good spirits easily know where it is.

In time, Gaspar's leg knit itself together, his body absorbed the cotton threads, and the ruddy incision became a slender pink scar. However, his leg was not as before. In healing the bone, his body created a knob where it had broken and, thought Gaspar, borrowed more bone from elsewhere to complete the process. His leg was as strong as ever, but it was a bit shorter. He moved without pain, but listed to one side until his wife doubled the thickness of his tire sandal on that side and he walked with only a slight limp.

—Thanks be. You live, you can walk, *tonto*, she said, and cuffed his ear gently.

The little mummy, all this time, rested on a high shelf above the bed in which Gaspar and his wife slept. His wife wrapped her in a rough wool blanket, protecting her from prying eyes and the attention of curious rats and mice. The ancient child filled her with wonder, and she asked Gaspar repeatedly to retell the story of how he found her. She did not say it to Gaspar, but she believed the mummy had protected him against the wrath of the river. She and her husband kept to themselves the presence of their special visitor.

He saw her every morning, as slanting rays of sunlight from the window moved downward from the top of the wall to their bed. For a moment, they highlighted the threads of her dark hair that protruded from the blanket. Unsaid to his wife, he also considered his discovery a talisman, an omen of good fortune, and ascribed to her the kind powers that allowed the spirits to heal his leg.

By the following spring, his belief had changed. That winter his goats refused to give milk, and unusually heavy rains washed out all the plantings on his terraces. His best llama ate cocklebur seedlings, resisted all his efforts to make her throw them up, and died the next day. His little boy developed a cough that would not go away, no matter what the elders prescribed. His wife became sad.

One evening they took the mummy from her place on the shelf and examined her carefully by the light of the lantern. Gaspar, noticing the decorations on her neck and wrist, pointed them out to his wife.

—Look, there is a bracelet and a charm here. It could be gold.

—No, it is too dark. Silver, maybe.

—Not much.

He held the lantern higher.

—When you move the light, her mouth and teeth are so ugly.

—*Sí*, his wife agreed.

—The little one seems different. I don't know.

—She does not please me anymore.

— *Igualmente.*

—Do you believe she carries bad spirits?

—It is possible.

They sat together, frowning, and Gaspar wrapped the little one in her blanket and placed her back on the shelf. Husband and wife had reached an understanding.

Two days later, Gaspar fashioned his blanket into a sling and carried the mummy, as though she were a basket of corn, down the steep trail from his village to the proprietor of the *tienda* located at the far end of the valley below, near the rutted road that led to Huaraz. People called the owner "El Gordo." He was that fat.

—I have seen one like this before—not so small, though, he said.

—It was from over there, near where the large ones were found. Gaspar pointed toward the mountains.

—It is necessary for me to carry this on to Huaraz when I go there next week. I know someone.

—Good.

—Right now I have no understanding of what value this little thing might have. I know there are collectors of such things, but it may be *poco valiosa*. My friend in Huaraz is understanding and fair. He will not cheat us.

—Good.

—Now, as I know you and your family are well, is there something you would like for your wife, your children?

—Do I have credit? For the mummy?

—Certainly.

Gaspar picked out some things he knew would please his wife and children, found some medicine for his son's cough, and selected stiff blue jeans for himself. As he carried the bundle of items back up the trail to his pueblo, he felt relieved. The little one would no longer be a benefit or a burden. She was gone. Surely their luck would change.

El Gordo carefully unwrapped the little mummy and displayed it to his friend who owned and operated a souvenir store, mainly for tourists, in Huaraz. Being in commerce, Lopes had connections in Lima and, El Gordo believed, was the most knowledgeable among his friends about how to enter a little mummy into commerce.

Lopes examined the prize very carefully under bright sunlight, noting her features, the remnants of clothing and the pieces of silver jewelry.

—I believe it is a girl, almost a baby. That is rare. And the condition—that is very good. You say she fell into a river? It seems to have done her no harm.

Lopes found some clean cloths and wrapped the mummy carefully before placing her in a battered leather case.

—I will keep her by my side when I take the bus to Lima next week. I will take her to a man of some importance who deals in things like this. That is better than going to the university with her. They would take her and say *gracias*, and that would be the end of it.

—I understand. We must be careful with the law.

El Gordo referred to the legislation that prohibited the trade in and export of ancient artifacts, whether of Spanish or Peruvian origin. Fortunately, for the two businessmen, it was honored more in the breach by Peruvian authorities. If honored at all, a small payment assured temporary blindness.

About two weeks later, a dusty Señor Lopes carrying an equally dusty leather case admitted himself to the fashionable jewelry emporium called Casa Hernandez. It was located across from the venerable Gran Hotel Bolívar on the

Plaza San Martín. In the back of the store, sitting at an ornate desk in an office surrounded by glass walls, was Gustavo Hernandez, the proprietor.

On seeing Lopes, he rose to greet the dusty traveler and offered him refreshment. They took tea in his office and spoke of renewing their friendship, the perennially cloudy winter skies, and the difficulty of making an honest living under such deplorable business conditions. The new president had not repaired the mismanagement of the national economy by the recently deposed left-wing military junta.

Eventually Lopes mentioned that he had come across something that might be of interest to his friend. He opened the leather case and began to remove the cloths that protected the mummified child. Hernandez motioned him to place the object on his desk as he removed the final layers. The proprietor prided himself on maintaining an inscrutable expression in business dealings, but Lopes caught him blinking his eyes as the object's head appeared.

—Interesting, said Hernandez, regaining his composure.

Lopes told him what he knew of the mummy's provenance as the other man examined her, finally reaching for a jeweler's loupe to study the silver around her neck and wrist. Hernandez pursed his lips and settled back in his desk chair, looking all the while at the object on his desk.

—Without doubt, this is an unusual artifact. I have heard of only one other such in all my time in Lima. I believe I know of one or two who would be interested in protecting her. As we both know, the matter must be handled delicately.

—Yes.

There was a pause. Lopes spoke.

—And do you have an idea of how much money would be involved? I ask it not for myself, but for those who brought her to me.

—That is difficult to say. If I am fortunate enough to attract two bidders, the object will become more valuable. The last one I heard of—a full-grown woman and thus more difficult to arrange transport—netted, I believe, over one hundred and fifty thousand pounds sterling.

It was Lopes's turn to try to conceal his amazement. He attempted to swallow and nearly choked on his cold tea.

—And I will receive my customary finder's fee? he asked.

—Of course—the usual five percent.

—And you will retain the handling fee plus expenses?

—I will be fair.

—Of course, Señor Hernandez.

Lopes was eager to leave. He wanted to make the calculation of the amount of his fee in pounds and correlate that to *soles*. The way the *sol* was devaluing on an almost daily basis, better to keep his fee in pounds. He left Hernandez's shop and walked slowly under the open archways surrounding the Plaza San Martín. Unburdened by the leather case he carried into the store, he had a light step light and high spirits. He could do much with more than seven thousand pounds sterling. He enjoyed contemplating all the things he could do with new wealth. Then he thought of El Gordo and the Indian. Certainly Hernandez would take care of them as well. But it would be wrong to overwhelm them with too much money.

A grubby stranger in ill-fitting clothes arrived in the Port of Callao in the summer of 1946 on a decrepit freighter flying the Panamanian flag. The Lithuanian passport he carried was in the name of Gustav Hochbein, but the clean shaven person in the photograph bore only slight resemblance to the figure standing before the customs officer clutching a tattered carpet bag. Herr Hochbein was abruptly ushered into the office of the port's chief administrator who looked disapprovingly at this possibly unwanted immigrant and began a close examination of his stained papers. His finger paused as he noted another Germanic name on a Soviet passport. He was dubious that the man before him who supported himself by leaning on his desk would contribute to the future of Peru.

Nevertheless, a few minutes later, as if by magic, the administrator smilingly ushered the scruffy Herr Hochbein from his office, bade him a sincere farewell and arranged for a taxi to take him to a hotel.

By some legal alchemy, the Lithuanian immigrant soon became Gustavo Hernandez. He purchased a small home on a bluff overlooking the ocean in Miraflores and a somewhat run-down emporium by the Plaza San Martín. The refurbished emporium became the finest jewelry store in Lima. In the 1950s, he branched out and became a dealer in antiquities, specializing in silver stirrups from the Spanish Conquest and antique armaments.

There were rumors that he also traded in illegal Incan and pre-Incan artifacts, but they were but rumors, in the same category as the one about the black velvet bag full of diamonds that arrived with him in the Port of Callao.

Now Hernandez was a civilian member of the Lima aristocracy, and he held forth almost daily at the National Club a few doors down from the Gran Hotel Bolívar. He appreciated the club's long-standing tradition of excluding women. He arranged intimate lunches and dinner meetings with local and visiting dignitaries, and he could always be counted on to support good causes and charities. Whether it would have been too difficult to nationalize a jewelry store or that his influence prevented it, the military junta, so recently deposed, let him and his business be. He never married. It was more agreeable, though costly, to exchange mistresses every year or so.

Hernandez carefully placed the swaddled mummy into one of the large safes concealed behind sliding panels in his office. He was certain she was a very important artifact that would require astute marketing. Because of unsophisticated local buyers and those annoying regulations about exporting antiquities, he planned to move the little mummy out of the country into the hands of a renowned foreign dealer.

Much as he would have liked to inform that person of the availability of a delightful new acquisition by telex, he was always concerned about the many prying eyes that might review such a message. As in past practice, he would take pictures of the new find and mail them from Miami. It was standard business practice to rely on the United States postal service for such matters. He always managed to find a traveler who was willing to accommodate his simple need of posting a letter in the United States. That evening he began to pen the letter to his contact in the United Kingdom. It began, "Dear Lord Wimsey."

8

Claudia grasped her swollen belly in both hands as she navigated the cobble path from her apartment to the section of the village square designated as the morning market, a place where gossip, fresh produce, local news, chickens, eggs, guinea pigs, hardware, clothing and items Claudia had never seen before were exchanged. She placed her feet carefully on the potentially treacherous stones descending to the square. Her balance was precarious as she leaned slightly backward to counter the weight of new life. She had slipped two days before, fell and bruised her thigh. To complicate matters, the baby moved unpredictably, challenging her equilibrium, pushing on her bladder.

She greeted many of the women sitting next to their tables of produce or wares by name, and they reciprocated, pleased to talk with the Maestro's wife who helped with medical problems. To many of the women of the village she was an exotic being, fresh faced, tall and slender who came from the big city. When she spoke Spanish they were impressed by her cultivated accent; when she tried their native language, they praised her effort, offered mild corrections and loved her for trying.

As Claudia picked out some green vegetables for their evening meal she grimaced as the baby turned, causing concern by the woman, Rosalita, who tended the table.

—Does it hurt? she asked. That is a sign that you must take care.

—A little, confessed Claudia, especially at night just as I go to bed.

Rosalita assembled an impromptu conclave of other woman vendors who clucked together as they observed Claudia, embarrassed, standing alone clutching an armful of vegetables. Finally, Rosalita, as spokeswoman, said

—With the first baby it is sometimes necessary to rest, to conserve your energy. We can see there is some difficulty.

Rosalita nodded to the other women who, with almost military precision, established a new routine for Claudia and her baby involving their providing meals for her and the Maestro, and helping about the apartment. The sturdy women of her village insisted, and Claudia accepted their help gratefully.

Unfortunately, Claudia discovered that the elimination of many chores associated with her daily life in the village emphasized her growing sense of tedium and dislocation. One afternoon, as she sat in her chair, fidgeting with the alpaca blanket on her lap, staring blankly out the window at sun baked snowcapped mountains, she made a frank assessment of her new life. Compared with the vibrant activity at her family's hotel and the intellectual stimulation of the university, life in the mountain village was dull. Friendly and kind as the villagers were, she could not share their concerns with the minutiae of their hard lives. Former avenues of diversion were unavailable. With her swollen belly, lovemaking was either perfunctory or avoided. Without electricity, there was no radio, television or telephone. She read by the light of lanterns, repelled by the smell of kerosene and unable to avoid the buildup of soot on the glass chimney.

She recalled the looks of concern from the village women. What if something went wrong? Who would care for her and her baby in a tiny village at the end of a pitted dirt road miles from Hauraz? She clenched her jaw at the thought and loosened a small flap of skin inside her cheek, and the rusty taste of blood flooded her mouth.

Concern followed concern. What would it be like for two college-educated young people to raise a child in a village where few people could read or write— in spite of Fredo's dedicated teaching efforts. Fredo was maddeningly noncommittal about when his assignment would be completed—probably because he did not know himself.

She fingered a recently arrived little cross on the chain around her neck— an unsubtle gift from her mother. At the university, Claudia and Fredo agreed not to honor such bourgeois conventions as marriage. Claudia, raised in the

Catholic faith, now felt guilty about denying herself that important sacrament. Unfortunately, she had staunchly declared only twelve months ago, when Fredo raised the subject, that there was no need for a wedding or a ring. What kind of a person would she be to renege on her former position?

She was the kind of person who would soon bear a bastard child if she refused to remedy her situation.

Her eyes reddened and she banged her small fist onto the wooden arm of her chair. The thump of impact acted as a signal; the door opened and Fredo entered their apartment, fresh from a meeting with village elders where his opinion about various matters had been required.

Even in the dim light in the apartment, Fredo recognized something was amiss as Claudia turned toward him, holding her belly, eyes glistening, tears welling in their corners. He kneeled beside her and held her in a gentle embrace, stroking her hair, brushing the tears from her eyes. She heard him say that everything would be all right and vowed to fix it —whatever it was.

He coaxed her to the edge of their bed and sat beside her, hugging her shoulders. She wiped her eyes and began to pour out her fears and frustrations, ever more rapidly, like spring runoff from the mountains around them. Fredo was slack-jawed, overwhelmed. He simply had no idea how disaffected she had become with their life in the village. Under the onslaught of her words, he felt cowed and guilty that he had not realized how unhappy she was.

Claudia soon focused on the impending birth of their child. Fredo had thought, somewhat vaguely, that they would arrange for the delivery in Huaraz. He believed that babies came on a prescribed timetable. There would be plenty of warning to make the bumpy trip in the battered pickup truck belonging to El Gordo at the foot of the valley. Claudia swiftly disabused him of that idea, and reminded him that this was not exactly a robust pregnancy.

—The care I need is in Ayacucho, she blurted out.

There was a pause as Fredo digested this suggestion. He nodded in agreement. —*Claro.*

The discussion turned to the practical aspects of transporting Claudia and their child-to-be to her parents in Ayacucho as she completed her pregnancy. He was certain he could arrange a leave from teaching for a week or so to be with her on the trip south. When advised of the situation, his mentor in the Sendero

Luminoso provided airplane tickets for a flight from Lima to Ayacucho, sparing them the long and unpleasant bus trip to Claudia's hometown.

As the two experienced their first flight, thrilled by the vistas along the Pacific coast, the towering cumulus clouds over the foothill to the Andes, and the craggy ice valleys at the top of the mountains, Claudia sighed deeply, leaned toward Fredo and clasped both his hands.

—I was just thinking. I will probably be spending a few months with my parents, and I know how happy it would make them if we were married before the baby comes. I know we agreed not to bother with a meaningless spiritual ceremony, but it would please them. What do you think?

He leaned toward his wife, put his lips to her ear and whispered loudly enough to be heard above the roar of the engines,

—*Desde luego que vamos hacerlo lo más rápido posible.*

They shared a kiss just as the baby delivered a strong kick.

The Cuban was not mistaken about the quality of recruits arriving at the training camp in the high valley of the Cordillera. They were Indians, peasants with little or no schooling, and not exactly burning with zeal to follow the Sendero Luminoso. The recruiters promised they would have the basics: *comida*, *bebida* and *dinero*, and would become macho warriors, firing rifles, handling dynamite and blowing things up. The recruits were not sure about the need to follow military discipline, whatever that was, and they refused to accept the notion that they could not always go home to help with the harvest.

At least they are reasonably clean, thought the Cuban, woefully scrutinizing the ragged bunch. He drew them together and, in time-honored military fashion, suggested that they represented a large pile of excrement, probably had no idea who their fathers were, and had spent the best part of their post puberty lives screwing sheep, llamas or their sisters. Lucho, standing at his side, noted that that seemed to get their attention. One of the recruits protested and the Cuban walked to him, grasped his nose between thumb and forefinger and squeezed until the hapless recruit was on his knees, tears streaming from his eyes. Training had commenced.

The next day the recruits received new dark green tennis shoes to replace their sandals, baggy camouflage fatigues, and thick branches that resembled rifles. As people of the high mountains, they were in uniformly excellent physical condition except for the few who coughed too much. Lucho adopted the role of drill instructor, and gradually managed to get the recruits to follow his directions and begin to carry packs instead of blankets filled with daily needs.

Other instructors showed them how to use various types of explosives, and how to assemble and use the small arms provided by the Cuban government and other nations friendly to their cause. There were surplus M16 and AK-47 assault rifles acquired from various war zones, including Vietnam; small mortars and rocket launchers; some fifty-caliber machine guns; and explosive materials ranging from black powder to plastique—C-4—from Algeria. Chairman Gonzalo was particularly interested in using explosives to wage guerrilla war, and subsequent successes supported his belief as he blew up civilian and military infrastructure around Peru's major cities.

After four weeks of training, the recruits were given their own weapons, with the three most talented marksmen receiving a Dragunov SVD sniper rifle from the Soviet Union. With that rifle, the Cuban claimed, they should be able to light a kitchen match at five hundred yards. Or separate a fly from its genitals. Ammunition was limited, however, so target practice was rudimentary. Lucho and the Cuban wanted to be sure the recruits could at least function as riflemen, keep their weapons clean, and come close to hitting a target. The Cuban surprised Lucho by saying that many soldiers failed to aim or even pull the trigger in the heat of battle. As an officer, he would have the responsibility of stepping on their *cojones* to encourage participation in any firefight. The image amused Lucho.

One afternoon, as the recruits learned to use knives and machetes for unaccustomed purposes, such a slitting throats, the Cuban discovered a cache of hand grenades—fragmentation, incendiary, phosphorus and concussion—in the back of the armaments bunker. There were enough to include them in the training curriculum. Lucho ordered the troops to construct semicircular sandbag bunkers to shield themselves from blasts.Lucho experimented with some fragmentation grenades the afternoon before the day of training. He could not read the Cyrillic letters on the wooden box holding the grenades, but they seemed old to him. His tests confirmed that the fuses were not uniformly timed but, so long as the grenades were thrown quickly after the pin was pulled, there was no danger. He discovered that the sandbag bunkers were critical. Little shards of metal forced their way into the face of the bags as he crouched behind them.

The Cuban was right: Lucho was popular among the recruits. He was easygoing and reasonable—not a stickler for military discipline like the Cuban. He played football with the recruits and immediately won their admiration. A few noted that they learned more from him about football than about being a soldier. By the second week of training, Lucho not only knew all their names, but their home villages or regions. He made a habit of visiting on occasional evenings one or two of the eight-man tents the recruits used. In the first tent he visited he spotted Enrique, one of the younger recruits, playing cards by lantern light. He reached across the cot and tousled the soldier's hair.

—So, Enrique, have you stopped wetting your cot?

There was instant laughter from the other men. Enrique had been subjected to a standard military prank two nights before. Others in the tent had waited until he slept soundly and immersed his hand in a cup of warm water, producing almost instant urination, a sodden cot and an embarrassed Enrique.

The young soldier smiled ruefully, focused on Lucho, grasped his right biceps in his left hand, raising his fist. Lucho threw back his head and laughed at his obscene gesture, the cue for the rest of the recruits to relax and join in.

—Come here you poor baby, and let me diaper you, one of them shouted. Enrique grinned, dropped his cards, sailed across the cot and tackled him, head in his stomach. They both fell to the dirt floor, and Lucho pretended to try to separate them, only to involve himself in the fray as well. The three rolled among the cots on the dark mountain dirt until fits of sneezing and laughter ended the exercise. Lucho vainly brushed at the dirt on his uniform.

—Looks like we'll all need cold showers, again, in the morning. Get some rest, men. We'll be doing grenade practice in the morning.

He gave Enrique and his wrestling adversary pats on their dusty backs and moved on to the next tent. As he returned to the shack he shared with the Cuban, he stood for a few moments in the chill winter night and stared at the stars. He enjoyed the camaraderie he shared with his company of men, but it was not the career he had envisaged when he agreed to join the Sendero Luminoso. He saw himself as a fighter, not a wet nurse to recruits from the highlands. It was difficult to reconcile the lofty principles he learned at the university with the reality of teaching uneducated young men to fight in the dirt, cold and squalor of their camp. His prior goals, expectations and needs had diminished to the simple desire for a hot shower.

The next morning Lucho saw that Cuban had removed the explosive material from a few grenades so the young men could practice in the open.

—Pull the pin, aim, prepare to throw, release the handle, *throw*.

They all repeated that litany and tried to hurl the grenades into the mouth of an oil drum twenty meters away. When Lucho and the Cuban were satisfied with their efforts, practice began in earnest. The recruit, with his partner—either Lucho or the Cuban—crouched behind the sandbag bunker, received his live grenade, stood, followed the cadence of the litany, threw and crouched behind the bunker as the grenade exploded. The mentors were pleased with the accuracy of some of their soldiers.

Enrique plopped down next to Lucho. He seemed nervous, so Lucho calmed him, explaining he could wait for another turn if he wanted to.

—No. I can do it. *Momentito, por favor.*

—Take some deep breaths. Look up at the sky. Remember what it was like the first time you got laid.

Enrique laughed.

—*Vámonos*, Lucho said.

—*Sí*.

Lucho removed a fragmentation grenade from the wooden case and passed the egg-shaped explosive to Enrique. He held it in his right hand so that the ring on the pin faced him. He prepared to pull the pin and glanced at Lucho, who nodded encouragingly. Enrique rose from behind the bunker, pulled the pin and extended his arm behind him, ready to throw the grenade. They both heard the distinctive *ping* as he released the handle and armed the grenade. He leaned forward and unimaginable happened.

The grenade slipped through his fingers. They both stared as it descended as though in slow motion, landed on the compacted dirt by Lucho's feet and rolled to a rest between his legs. The fuse hissed. They both scrambled, Enrique moving away from the grenade to the rear of the bunker, Lucho on his knees trying to scoop it up as it slipped through his dusty fingers. He cursed as the grenade, demonstrating a perverse life of its own, rolled away from his hand. Finally, he held it firmly, rose to a crouch, extended his arm over the top of the sandbag bunker and tossed it away with a flick of his wrist.

The grenade fell about a meter and exploded just as Lucho withdrew his hand. Hot gases and shards of metal flew in all directions. Lucho felt the impact of the explosion rock the ground at his feet and heard bits of hot metal strike the sand bags in front of him. Adrenaline immediately coursed through his body, all his senses alert, his heart beating so fast that he feared it would burst from his chest. He forced his eyes open, concentrated on the blue sky above, and breathed deeply, to calm himself. Realizing he was on his back, he instinctively leaned forward and reached behind with his right hand to push himself to a sitting position. That simple movement failed. He remained on his back.

From the corner of his eye, Lucho saw that Enrique had overcome his initial terror and was approaching him from the back of the bunker. Enrique kneeled, reached around his shoulders, and raised Lucho to a sitting position. He moved his right arm and rested his hand on his lap, adrenaline still pumping through his body and masking pain. The lack of pain confused Lucho as he examined the remains of his right hand, staring in disbelief.

His hand was covered in fine black dust and the thumb and little finger were intact, but the middle three fingers had disappeared. Jagged bits of flesh stood like little pink crowns poking through the dirt, surrounding the stumps where his fingers had been moments before. He raised his hand for closer examination and saw there was not much blood, but that action overpowered the numbing effect of adrenaline and what had been a dull ache at the end of his arm became searing, unremitting pain, blinding him, causing him to fall backwards again onto his side. He retched, covering Enrique's green tennis shoes with puce vomit and dark bile. Finally, dark nothingness overcame him.

The Cuban attended to his wound, cauterizing the stumps and applying antibiotic and dressings. There was no pain medication, but there was rum. For two days, Lucho remained in an inebriated state. By the third day, he felt well enough to join the Cuban for a meal. Afterward, they sat together outside on a bench and Lucho accepted one of the Cuban's little cigars. Exhaled smoke expanded in the cold night air. Lucho looked down at his bandaged hand, which was now shaped like a giant letter "C." Musing, he addressed the Cuban

—I just wonder what happened to them.

—Them?

—The fingers.

—Oh. The fingers.

—*Sí*. No point in looking for them, of course.

—No point at all. Flesh and bone are atomized. Where I have been in battle they say the birds eat the bits of flesh and little creatures gnaw on the bones to get minerals. Nothing goes to waste.

—Birds do?

—*Sí. Las aves.*

For all the misery Claudia suffered in bringing her child to term, the delivery was without consequence. She and Fredo had a perfect baby girl, and Claudia regained her strength as she luxuriated in the attentive care she and the baby received during her weeklong stay in the hospital in Ayacucho.

Fredo beamed at his infant daughter: perfect tiny fingernails translucent as opal, dark eyebrows, iridescent blue eyes, and facial features that belonged to him. Until then, he had not given much thought to the responsibilities of fatherhood. Now, as he gazed at his daughter, sleeping cradled in the crook of his arm, he understood that he was accountable not only for creating this little creature, but for her care, her future. That thought returned to him some days later, on the bus, when he returned to his pueblo.

He was gazing idly at the dun-colored rocks east of the Pacific coast on the highway to Lima. The monotonous scenery and the constant rumble from the bus caused a mild torpor, and the sudden recollection of his daughter in Claudia's arms as he left her with her parents wakened him with a start. He became aware of a conflict between his work as a teacher and promoter of armed insurrection against a corrupt and inept government and the responsibilities of fatherhood. Where, he considered, would he be five years from now? The prospect of remaining in his little village and commuting once or twice a year to Ayacucho was unthinkable. He had not considered the prospect of fatherhood and a family when he agreed to join the Sendero Luminoso. It was all about changing the world, establishing new glories, sacrificing himself for the greater good. But now he was responsible for an infant daughter and Claudia. How was he to support them on the occasional meager distribution of cash from his superior in Huaraz? No answer came to mind.

Fredo chewed on this worrisome bone for a few hours. He decided to demand from his superiors more responsibility, higher wages and reassignment to a more cosmopolitan place. Let some unmarried idealist take his place. He hated to admit it, but he had not been very successful in persuading the people in his village to embrace the ideals of his employer. They were always willing to listen attentively and politely, and ask questions, but no one moved to action. It occurred to him that newfound demands of family life may have dampened his ardor for the goals of Sendero Luminoso, but he let that become but a passing thought. He needed to concentrate on improving his financial position. He planned to stop in Huaraz to discuss his needs with his superior. Surely, he would not refuse such a simple request.

El Jefe greeted Fredo in the anteroom of his dusty office on the second floor of an office building near the central square of Huaraz. The collar of his shirt was tight, and he punctuated his comments by hooking a finger over it and pulling it outward. That caused the folds of fat at the back of his neck to bulge. El Jefe wore a pince-nez. As Fredo began to outline his demands, the other man polished the glasses with a well-worn handkerchief and occasionally held them up to the window for inspection. He nodded pleasantly as Fredo spoke about his family and his delightful little daughter, but pursed his lips as Fredo moved on to what was really on his mind: more pay and relocation to a more cosmopolitan area.

El Jefe referred to a manila file folder at his side.

—My information is that you volunteered to become a teacher for two years. Is that not so?

—*Claro*, but—

—There seem to be no exceptions for fatherhood. Has anything caused you to question your mission, or the need to pursue the cause of the revolution selflessly, and sacrifice yourself nobly for the greater good?

—No, Fredo said hesitantly.

—Well, then.

El Jefe continued to smile at him, as though the matter were settled. Fredo made no move from his chair. Since one aspect of his concerns seemed blocked,

Fredo asked about his wages. Yes, an increase would be appropriate, under the circumstances.

—As to the other, the relocation, I will look into it. We are very busy now, as you know. It will take some time.

Fredo expressed mild thanks and shook El Jefe's hand weakly. He scurried down the stairs to the street, muttering "*mierda*" under his breath, and searched for a bar. Once he found one, he ordered Pisco straight. It did not help.

Lucho received word at his new office in Ayacucho from Claudia that Fredo had returned for a visit. An orderly delivered the message to *el capitán* Garra— Captain Claw—as the members of his unit called him. He held the note in his right hand, now encased in a dark brown leather glove that covered his missing fingers. As he pinched the note with thumb and little finger, it was clear where his nom de guerre originated.

Lucho was delighted by the news since he missed Fredo greatly and wanted to tell his friend about his new responsibilities and assignment in the city. Reaching him by telephone was difficult, so Claudia relied on a messenger to communicate. Lucho immediately dialed her number on his telephone, and waited while a servant searched for Claudia.

—*Sí*. He's just arrived and will be in Ayacucho for a month or so, and then we will be going to Huaraz as a family. He has been promoted to replace the *jefe* there, who suffered a stroke last month. We both want to see you. You are well, I hope?

—Fabulous. This work is more interesting than training recruits—and a bit less dangerous. When can I come by and see my goddaughter? And Fredo?

—Tomorrow night at the hotel?

—Perfect!

The two friends embraced, pounding each other's backs—a true Peruvian *abrazo*. As they untwined, Fredo saw Lucho's injured hand for the first time. A look of surprise, followed by concern, crossed his face. Lucho responded by squeezing the muscles atop his friend's shoulder between his two remaining fingers. Fredo winced.

—See, just as good as ever. I still have an opposable thumb.

Claudia quickly changed the subject.

—She will probably be asleep, but we can look in on Marie after dinner if that would please you.

As the drinks came, Fredo said he would like that very much. A few more awkward moments passed before the imponderable elements that cemented their friendship reasserted themselves. Claudia threw back her head and laughed as Lucho tried to pull a gray hair from her husband's temple. Fredo displayed his bright new wedding band. Lucho grinned his approval.

—It appears that both our hands have changed. So, how long have you two enjoyed the state of matrimony?

Claudia responded teasingly:

—The way Fredo looks, perhaps "enjoy" is a bit too strong a word. However, he gallantly offered to marry me about the same time Marie was kicking the daylights out of me.

The married couple brought Lucho up-to-date on the less obvious changes to their lives since they left the university. Fredo sat on the arm of Claudia's chair and touched her hair as she spoke. She held his hand.

Lucho explained about his transfer from the Sendero Luminoso training camp to new, undisclosed military offices in Ayacucho.

—I believe the higher-ups thought it might be discouraging to have a one-handed training officer teaching new recruits. My new assignment is much more interesting and exciting. There is much discussion and planning about the opening phases of armed conflict with the oppressive current regime. Chairman Gonzalo believes we are now prepared to initiate our broader mission. You would be surprised at how our military organization has grown—and the support we are receiving from foreign allies.

Fredo and Claudia pressed him for details, but he was unwilling to speak more on the subject. Instead, he told them about his mentor, the Cuban.

—You know, he was the one who salvaged my hand after the accident. We worked together for more than a year, and then he joined the twenty-five thousand Cuban troops in Angola. He sent me letters. He is a funny guy. He claims he drank a quart of rum a day to avoid disease, but got hepatitis anyway. He is back in Peru now, up in the mountains. I saw him two weeks ago. He is the color of a lemon, and he is called El Chino now.

His audience seemed befuddled.

—How interesting, said Claudia.

Lucho realized his friends missed the point.

—Here is a man so dedicated to the cause we follow that he is willing to leave his home and expose himself to terrible dangers and diseases. He is a complete patriot and an example for us all. He is a true communist hero.

Fredo paused a moment to absorb his friend's fervor.

—*Sí, un héroe. ¡Claro que sí!*

Claudia nodded in agreement. The conversation turned to other things, but during its course, the young married couple exchanged a confirming look. A fleeting glance conveyed a volume of information. Unlike Lucho, their passion for the cause had waned; they had no regrets about that, and wasn't it scary that Lucho, the easygoing, funny football star, had become a fervid communist warrior. Had they changed as much?

On the evening of May 17, 1980, Lucho and Fredo sat casually on one of the wooden benches located in the village square of Chuschi, a small town on the outskirts of Ayacucho. Lucho's suggestion that he join him that afternoon and evening for a "very important" action on the part of the Sendero Luminoso intrigued Fredo.

—What does that mean—'an important action'? Are you going to blow something up? Fredo asked.

—No. We have not been authorized to do anything as extravagant as that. However, this will be our first bold step in the campaign to thwart the authorities. We will not be directly involved. If you come, you and I will act as lookouts. Without a doubt, it will be interesting.

During their bus trip from the hotel in Ayacucho where Fredo and Claudia lived, Lucho had explained that the leadership planned a raid on the government offices and *consejo* in Chuschi to burn the boxes holding ballots from the election that took place that day. It was important, he said, to begin their campaign in Ayacucho, in the place where Antonio José de Sucre crushed Spanish forces in 1824 and secured Peruvian independence from Spain. The plan was to create an overt act of terrorism to announce the beginning of the long campaign to convert Peru to communism.

—Burning ballot boxes? That is the bold new step?

—Yes. That and hanging dogs from lampposts.

Fredo was confused. He stared out the bus window before turning to his friend.

—What is that about? Hanging dogs. Is the party declaring war on dogs as well?

—No. I think it's a metaphor. Hanging the running dogs of capitalism. Yes, I think that is what it means.

—And that is something you plan to do.

—With your help, of course, Lucho had added.

Fredo did not speak again until they reached the stop in Chuschi.

As daylight began to fade, Fredo returned to their bench with food he had purchased at the cantina on the corner of the square. Lucho and Fredo observed the five young men who were Sendero Luminoso operatives leave various places around the square, walk casually to the entrance of the consejo, and quickly covered their faces with knitted balaclavas. Two of them burst into the office with drawn guns and demanded that the clerk show them the ballot boxes.

The clerk seemed unsurprised, as though masked men routinely demanded his ballot boxes. He pointed them out to the invaders and asked whether he could leave. One of the men shoved him out the door, after the man gathered his hat and keys. Lucho and Fredo watched him wander to a far corner of the square, light a cigarette and await further proceedings.

The five young men dragged the ballot boxes out to the square, doused them with kerosene and lit them on fire. The yellow flames illuminated the white buildings around the square, and Fredo noted that more flames were leaping from the windows of the *consejo*. The office of the registry and *consejo* were reduced quickly to charred and glowing embers.

In the glow of the fires, two of the young men raised the flag of the Sendero Luminoso. The wind rushing to fuel the fires caught the bright red rectangle with the yellow hammer and sickle. It fluttered for a while above the little square. The clerk crushed his third cigarette out under his heel and began to walk home. The five young men disbanded, scurrying down the narrow streets of the village.

—They must be looking for dogs. We should do the same, said Lucho.

Fredo moved reluctantly from their bench. He replied sardonically:

—What, you didn't bring along a couple of dead dogs?

Lucho chose not to reply. They moved away from the square. After ten minutes of wandering, it became clear that one of the young men from the ballot-burning party had found his quarry. A wire noose suspended a small gray bitch with distended nipples from a lamppost. The yellow light showed her long tongue dangling between discolored teeth. Flies gathered on an open wound on one of her legs.

Fredo and Lucho moved on. Never persuaded that hanging dogs was a good idea in the first place, Fredo thought that continuing to hunt for stray dogs in the village in the dark of night was brainless. However, as they approached an area the village used as a landfill, a dark shape materialized from the ditch beside their path. It was a typical Peruvian dog—uncared for, mangy, wary and ill fed. It had been foraging in the garbage dump.

The townspeople located the dump with great care. It was on the down slope of a long hill located on the eastern side of the village. There winds from the west carried away offensive smells from rotting vegetation dumped by the many farmers in the region. The compost generated by the natural decomposition of the plant materials was later harvested for use in the fields but, as that process occurred, fearsome odors surrounded the landfill. Apparently, the dog had become accustomed to those surroundings.

—It's a dog! Get it!

Reluctantly, Fredo ran beside Lucho as he chased the animal. The dog loped down the narrow alley toward the dump, leaped over the fetid ditch and slunk behind vibrant shrubbery nourished by the decomposing vegetation. Lucho reached in his pocket with his injured hand for a length of rope he had brought for the occasion as he stumbled toward the ditch separating him from the dog. Fredo decided to move to his friend's left side to avoid a collision. Lucho was unsteady and cursed as he realized his right hand was not up to the task of fishing out the rope. Distracted, he misjudged the width of the ditch, caught the toe of his boot on the far edge, tripped and fell forward, sliding downward through the weeds and debris surrounding the landfill. Fredo stumbled through the gloom of last light, trying to grab his friend's arm. He missed and caught the back of Lucho's jacket, braced himself and held tight. He pitched forward and they both began to slide downward toward the hectare-wide mass of fermenting vegetation. The dog remained motionless, listening to the sound of two bodies striking the surface of the stagnant pool below, like a bucket hitting water in a deep well

Within a week the police caught the five young men who had foolishly removed their masks as they pranced around the burning ballot boxes, exposing themselves to onlookers and particularly the clerk they had threatened with their weapons. Additional ballots replaced the burned ballots, and the elections proceeded without further incident. Their action received little attention by the Peruvian press, and the government regarded it as a pitiful amateur attempt by a communist fringe group. The five young men languished in jail for a while, but were soon released. It was an inauspicious beginning as a planned act of terrorism.

Chairman Gonzalo was not disheartened. He reminded his followers that Chairman Mao, when he started the Long March, quoted Lao-tzu, the ancient Chinese philosopher: "The journey of a thousand miles begins with a single step."

—This is our single step, said Guzmán. It is a solid beginning.

9

On this visit to Lima Wylie helped conclude a manufacturing agreement favorable to his clients, the Weschler family. Their supplier of feminine hygiene products in the United States, tired of restrictions on the repatriation of profits and painful inflation, agreed, with Wylie's prodding, to let the Weschlers manufacture and sell those products in a territory that included Peru and its bordering countries. The royalty payments were fair and the arrangement provided broad new markets for the Weschlers.

After the documents were signed, Don Weschler, the family patriarch, asked Wylie to join him in his ornate office overlooking the dusty Avenida below. Wylie smiled to see that his old friend, Weschler's son Rodrigo, awaited him there. Friends for more than twenty years, they embraced and began roughhousing as they had at college. Rod punched Wylie in the right bicep, which Wylie answered by pretending to poke at his eye with a middle finger. They finally settled down, and, more calmly, brought each other up to date on their personal affairs.

Their friendship began when Rodrigo and Wylie met by literally bumping into each other at the squash courts at Harvard, when Wylie was in law school. After graduation, while Rodrigo worked to succeed his father in managing the family business, he called on Wylie, still an associate at Biddle and Ofstrosky, for needed legal assistance. Wylie, now a partner at that firm, grateful for business provided by a large Peruvian company, visited Rod and his father at least twice a year in Lima—more frequently if deals such as the one just completed required his talents.

With a promise of joining Wylie at a family dinner later in the week, Rodrigo excused himself, and his father insisted that Wylie join him for a meal at the National Club. Although Wylie always felt uneasy when he visited the club, he would not reject the older man's offer. A chauffeur helped the arthritic man down the staircase to the street and maneuvered him into the Lincoln waiting at the curb. Wylie slid onto the leather seat beside him, and they pulled out into the mild rush-hour traffic. It was not long before they arrived at the National Club.

The burnished wooden walls, soft leather furniture in the anteroom, high ceilings accompanied by massive glass doors, crisp linens on dark tables festooned with crystal and silver, solemn serving people blending into the surroundings, the hushed gentility all seemed anachronistic to Wylie —an oasis of splendor in a third world city beset by poverty, corruption and mismanagement.

The maître d' approached Don Weschler with open arms and clasped the guest's right hand with both of his. He led them to a secluded dining table in an alcove and beckoned to a waiter to help the older man to his chair. For Wylie's benefit, he announced the chef's special meals in English and motioned the waiter to deliver an aperitif of Lillet while the guests decided on the evening meal. Wylie sipped his aperitif, trying to overcome a feeling that the massive curtains and dark wood of the room were closing in on him.

There was a pause in their conversation as they studied the leather-bound menus offered by the waiter—in case the special dishes already noted did not suit their fancies. From their window in the dining room, Wylie looked down upon the Plaza San Martin. There unkempt little boys offered to shine shoes for a single *sol*, hawkers promoted lottery tickets for instant wealth, women carried trays of dust-encrusted candy and Chiclets for sale, itinerant photographers offered Polaroid photos of tourists standing in front of the fountain in the center of the square.

Shops selling cheap trinkets and shoddy leather goods clustered around the arcade surrounding the square, marred by uncut grass and dirt paths. Customers sat on rickety chairs in front of little restaurants, drinking, eating and watching the flow of traffic as a single policeman vainly attempted to control the cars and trucks maneuvering around the square. The heavy drapes in the dining room muffled the sound of the vehicles below. Blue-gray diesel fumes wafted toward strollers, and pyramids of trash rose from gutters on all sides of the square. Pickpockets clustered in the square, well prepared to separate visitors from their valuables.

Wylie compared the hubbub and energy he saw in the square below with his funereal surroundings. He looked at his host examining the menu with a magnifying glass supplied by the waiter. He respected the older man and enjoyed his company. However, for the first of the many times he had dined at the National Club, he thought he would prefer to stroll in the square below, hoping some of the vigor and excitement might rub off.

The both dined on seafood ceviche: sea bass, scallops, octopus and sea cucumber marinated in the juice of Peruvian lemons, which Wylie thought looked like key limes. He agreed with Don Weschler once again that the ceviche at the National Club was the best in Lima, probably the best anywhere. As the waiter delivered coffee and Hennessy cognac, Don Weschler turned to Wylie.

—So, my friend, will you be able to join me for dinner at home tomorrow? Rodrigo and his wife will be with us. He is eager to see you again.

—Certainly. I fly back to the States day after tomorrow, and I have only a little bit of business to deal with tomorrow.

—May I be of help? Would you like to use the car tomorrow? My driver will be at your disposal.

—Generous, as always, but my brief meeting is just around the corner from the hotel. I plan to use the rest of the day to work on some of the legal loose ends from the agreement just concluded.

—So, we will pick you up at the hotel at six?

Before Wylie could respond, all the lights in the building cut off. They looked out the window and saw a wave of darkness envelop buildings along the main avenue leading east toward Miraflores. In moments, the darkened buildings stood out against the rosy purple haze of dusk. The only light was from vehicles rushing along the *avenida*.

In a few minutes, a recently installed diesel generator coughed to life and the lights in the club glowed deep orange and gradually brightened to illuminate the room.

Don Weschler threw down his napkin,

—*¡Está la puta Sendero Luminoso!* Those bastards have done it again!

—The Shining Path is responsible for the power failure?

—Yes. That is their latest trick. They blow up the transmission towers around the city. And while they are at it, they shoot the guards and any police who stand in their way. And that asshole Belaunde seems powerless to stop them. He wasn't any good as president the first time, and he is even worse now.

The older man fumed on. Wylie understood his frustration. The communist group was successfully targeting major cities—disrupting power and communications. Powerful businesspeople like the Weschlers were accustomed to dealing with such problems directly, forcefully and quickly. However, Wylie thought, its was ironic that the same lax administration approach that benefited their business rankled when it failed to halt threats to stability and order.

Don Wechsler was winding down. He completed his diatribe.

—Wylie, we should just kill all those communist bastards, no questions asked. And while we are at it, exterminate all the Indians, too. They contribute nothing!

They left the club, entering on to the dark avenue. Wylie helped Weschler into the Lincoln and decided to walk from the National Club to his hotel. Although risky, a stroll through the darkened city would be exciting, daring. It would also provide quiet moments to consider Weschler's bloodthirsty and shocking desire to eliminate all communists and Indians. He had heard similar statements from members of the Lima aristocracy during other visits to that city, and they always conjured up images of the Holocaust, images that were just as disturbing now as they had been when he first saw them as a boy of twelve. He knew that contradicting the Peruvian believers in manifest destiny would be a fruitless exercise, although the queasy feeling in his stomach suggested self-criticism for not trying. He navigated the four blocks to the hotel without incident. He stopped at the notions shop in the lobby, looking for Pepto Bismol.

Lucho shot the surprised guard directly through the left eye. His knees buckled and he fell softly to the heavy grass beside the wooden shack, his rifle scraping along the raised shingles. Lucho noticed that one of the guard's faded tennis shoes had a frayed hole over the little toe. His lieutenant reached for the guard's rifle and slung it over his left shoulder, still pointing his own weapon at the fallen soldier. They moved down the slope to the concrete pillars under the massive steel girders supporting the transmission cables.

The other member of Lucho's team collected the brick-orange packets of Semtex explosive, and the three began placing the material carefully around the north leg of the tower. Experience had taught them that they needed to destroy only one part of the tower. Instability after the explosion caused it to topple, pulling and then breaking the cables, which shattered amid spectacular fireworks. The team always looked forward to those special effects.

The lieutenant shoved projectile fuses into three blocks of the explosive, checked the time delay, and snapped the igniter. As the fuses hissed into life, the three ran toward the earthen depression behind the shack, safely beyond the reach of the coming explosion. From this position, they could see a series of transmission towers marching eastward toward the foothills of the Andes. They were burnished by slanting rays of sunlight coming across the Pacific, golden against the dark shadows of the mountains beyond.

Lucho turned to face the setting sun and could see Lima and, beyond, the Port of Callao outlined against the bright ocean. You are in for another surprise, he thought, as lights twinkled in the capital city. A few more moments and the transmission tower was engulfed in the brilliant yellow explosion that was Semtex's signature. It shuddered and began to crumble. The demolition team could hear the groaning sounds made by the sudden stretching of the cables, followed by new explosions as the cables snapped and showered the countryside with luminous white sparks.

Apparently, the military regime neglected proper maintenance of the towers. The force of one tower descending unseated the tower directly above it and it, too, crumbled and fell, repeating the spectacular death throes. Lucho and his team watched, fascinated, hoping for a domino effect, but two towers were all that fell. The men embraced. Not a bad evening's work. It would be days before those inefficient *cabrones* in Lima could make necessary repairs. Clearly, the invincible Sendero Luminoso would prevail. Lucho pulled three of the last of the Cuban's little cigars from his jacket pocket and handed them around. Aromatic smoke followed them as they worked their way down the hill to the battered Ford pickup that was their military vehicle.

There were kerosene lanterns sitting atop the glass cases inside Casa Hernandez highlighting the many pieces of jewelry below, but the high ceilings of the building seemed to absorb and diminish the light. Moments after Wylie entered, the proprietor walked quickly toward Wylie and offered an effusive welcome.

—Ah, this must be Dr. Cypher, Hernandez exclaimed, squeezing Wylie's free hand. Thank you so much for making this visit. Many thanks.

Wylie recognized the South American honorific for members of the legal profession, conferred based on his *Juris Doctor* degree. His elevated title amused him, but the overenthusiastic welcome by the oily proprietor put him on his guard. He offered his card as confirmation of his identity, and Hernandez motioned him to a comfortable chair in his glass-enclosed office, more brightly lit than the rest of the area. A staffer entered to offer cups of strong coffee. Hernandez waved toward the dimly lit interior.

—Damn insurrectionists— hanging would be too good for them! This loss of electricity is a tremendous inconvenience. I hope you were comfortable in your hotel last night.

By local custom, the men exchanged pleasantries as they sipped coffee, and Wylie explained how much he enjoyed visiting Peru with all its natural splendors, to say nothing of its ancient cultures. And the people—how friendly and generous.

The staffer returned with fresh coffee and, having exchanged a sufficient number of platitudes, both men bent toward business. Wylie began.

—Our mutual friend, Lord Wimsey, has entrusted me with the errand of delivering some papers to you, as I believe you are aware.

Wylie opened his briefcase and extracted a manila envelope sealed with red wax.

—Here are the documents.

Hernandez saw that the envelope was just the right size to enclose bearer bonds. Casually he reached for the package, which quickly disappeared into the lower drawer of his desk. He thanked Wylie profusely, noting how problematic it was to entrust documents to the mercies of international post, and how unreliable to deal with couriers.

As Wylie finished his coffee and rose to leave, the other man asked,

—Tell me, my friend, do you have a wife, daughters?

Wylie admitted to one of each.

—Perhaps you would like to return with a little gift for them. Women always appreciate a well-chosen piece of jewelry. It would please me greatly to give you a small token of my gratitude.

Wylie understood the Peruvian etiquette of gift giving. It was not unlike bringing along a bottle of wine to a friend's home for dinner in the States. It was a cultural nicety observed by the business aristocracy. Unfortunately, when pushed to its extreme, gift giving amounted to bribery that supported the endemic corruption of recent and current government administrations in Peru. Wylie was torn between offending the merchant by refusing a small gift and becoming indebted for accepting an unearned reward – a bribe of sorts.

Señor Hernandez took Wylie by the arm and led him into the store, stopping in front of a display case containing an array of silver trinkets with bold designs – bracelets, rings, necklaces, earrings, and peculiar pipe-like items. The jeweler stepped behind the counter and pulled out a few trays lined with dark baize, holding them under lantern light so the items sparkled. He selected a few items that he placed on the counter top in front of Wylie.

— Our own craftsmen make these pieces, and we are careful to incorporate Inca and pre-Inca design elements, said the jeweler with pride. Here, what do you think of this bracelet with the set in amethyst stones?

Wylie genuinely admired the subtle workmanship and dramatic design. He calculated from the little tag showing the price in *soles* that the price was under forty dollars, well below the amount the United States government officially categorized as a bribe.

—-I think my wife would love these amethyst earrings, and I am sure this bracelet with the bold designs would suit my daughter very well.

—That bracelet is very unusual, said the jeweler. The designs are from stellae located in an ancient pyramid in Chavin de Huantar. It is a place near Huaraz, north of Lima in the mountains. Do you know of it?

—I think I have heard of it, but I don't recall it being noted as a tourist attraction.

—Yes, that is so. One must cross mountains to get there. But it is of great interest to archaeologists. They say that the pyramid there is older than a thousand years before Christ. Just a moment, I think I may have photographs of the site.

Hernandez quickly returned to his office, pulled something from a drawer, returned to Wylie, and handed him a creased and faded brochure showing a large black basalt pyramid boldly etched against a background of snow-covered peaks. Inside were somewhat faded photographs of large white monoliths covered with peculiar symbols along with stone skulls and crossbones.

—See, said Hernandez, we used these design elements in this very bracelet.

Wylie studied the fanciful characters embedded in the bracelet. Among them were little skulls and crossbones that he had overlooked. Now he had a story to go with the bracelet for Mercy. He slipped the brochure into his briefcase.

—These are very beautiful, and I am certain my women will love them, said Wylie. Now, I appreciate your generous offer, but I insist that I pay for them.

A comical Mutt and Jeff argument ensued, with the jeweler insisting the trinkets were his gift and Wylie insisting that he pay for them. It ended in a compromise; Wylie paid for the earrings and accepted the bracelet as a gift.

An assistant buffed the jewelry pieces, wrapped them in gold foil paper, and placed them in a little soft leather pouch. The store's owner placed the pouch in a small silver box and tied it with a ribbon. He placed the box in Wylie's hand.

—Go with God, my friend.

Wylie expressed his thanks and, as he was about to leave the store, the proprietor, as though a sudden thought struck him, asked

—Let me ask—do you fly to Miami tomorrow on your way back to the United States?

—Yes.

—I hate to impose but, if it wouldn't be too much trouble, could you post a letter for me at Miami International?

—Of course.

Hernandez scurried back to his office and returned with a large manila envelope festooned with appropriate United States postage, and another silver box, slightly larger than the one Wylie held.

—Since you are being so kind, I have another favor to ask. This is a gift for my sister, a little token for her birthday that I forgot to send earlier. I can arrange for her to be waiting for it, and you, right after customs in the Miami airport. Then she could pick it up directly.

Wylie hesitated. Hernandez was inches away from over stepping the bounds of propriety. Dropping off a letter was simple, but delivering another parcel for someone he had just met…

However, Wylie knew that in the tightly knit upper crust of Lima inhabited by both the Weschlers and Señor Hernandez little slights could take on a malicious life of their own. Why risk it? He nodded to the jeweler.

—I suppose that would be all right. But how will I recognize her?

—I will call her. She will be holding a sign with your name on it—like the airport chauffeurs. Ha, ha.

His broad smile exposed gold-rimmed teeth Wylie had not noticed before.

—Fortunately, she doesn't look like me. She is slender with blond hair.

Wylie accepted the other silver box and placed it in his briefcase. He and Señor Hernandez parted.

The Lincoln stopped in the portico next to the main entrance of Don Wechsler's home. It was of Spanish style, with buildings surrounding a central courtyard, beautifully landscaped, with flowers offering bright splashes of color to contrast with a lush green background of palm trees, bromeliads, and jungle vegetation. Since the house was located in the city, a high wall crowned with broken glass defended it. Steel gates closed behind the Lincoln as Wylie stepped out. The blue-suited man by the gate carried a sidearm.

Rod and his wife, Sarah, were already there. Wylie enjoyed their effusive greeting and was pleased to see his old friend again. It had been what, since Christmas, that he had last seen Sarah?

As night fell, soft lights illuminated the patio, and music from a concert of flutes and pipes from the Andes floated from speakers hidden in shrubs. Wylie caressed his third Pisco sour and decided it was a perfect evening. Cosseted, isolated in this island of privilege and comfort, separated from the rude sounds and frantic activity of the city, he envied the life his friends had created for themselves. Yet, as he looked across the manicured lawn at the high fence surrounding the estate and saw the broken shards of glass gleaming in kaleidoscope patterns from the just reactivated street lamps, he felt a chill. Probably it was the Pisco; what else could it be?

As his morning flight to Miami reached altitude, Wylie's sensitivity to the lower amount of oxygen in the air kicked in and he began to feel drowsy. He asked for a vodka Bloody Mary, his customary antidote. He knew alcohol was no cure for oxygen deficiency, but it made him feel better nonetheless. As he swallowed the last of the drink, he looked out the window and discovered that the airplane was cruising atop the spine of the Andes, with unforgettable vistas of craggy, snow and ice-covered mountains stretching away forever beneath indigo skies. He stared out the window for a long time.

He was transported to the mountaintops, a sturdy hiker in mountaineering kit, strong leather boots, rip stop shorts, flannel shirt, red bandana, rucksack filled with important things, sunglasses, and a floppy hat that blocked strong sunrays and served as a pail and drinking basin as well. He could see his breath in the thin air and feel the heft of a walking staff in his hand. As he moved along the ill-marked trail, he felt invigorated, buoyant, striding purposefully toward a well-defined goal. This was the life, he thought, this...

The attendant, reaching for his empty glass, wakened him.

—Would you care for a refill?

He declined and tried to sleep again, to find that wonderful place where life was fresh and full of unanticipated wonder.

That did not happen. Wylie reached for his briefcase to pull out some papers that required attention. The faded brochure of Chavin fell out and fluttered to the floor. He reached down to pick it up.

10

Wylie located a mailbox and posted Señor Hernandez's letter while waiting for his bag in Miami. He rushed out of the international section of the airport believing he would be late for his flight back to Newark. In vain, he searched for his name among the placards and signs held by those in the crowd awaiting travelers. He took a deep breath and looked more carefully for a slender blond woman holding a sign with his name on it. There was no one like that there, no "Cypher" on any name card. He looked at his watch. Okay, he thought, I can give it another five minutes.

The terminal speakers announced his flight to Newark. No sign of a thin blond woman. He hurried to the departure gate and found his seat, ordered a drink, and searched for his sleep mask. He was tired and planned to slumber during the three-hour flight to Newark.

His driver dropped him at his home in New Anglia late in the evening. Mavis called out to him from the study, where she was watching television, and Wylie left his bags in the foyer. He decided to remove his passport and a few other papers from his briefcase for safekeeping and noticed the two silver packages there. Absentmindedly, he placed them on the Hepplewhite side table in the foyer, removed his jacket, loosened his tie and went into the study to greet his wife.

Gudrun Kelly was unable to keep her appointment at the Miami airport with Wylie, posing as Hernandez's sister, because she was, at that time, a guest of the

Miami police languishing in a holding cell. That unfortunate circumstance kept her from following Hernandez' orders to collect a package from Wylie Cypher and deliver it to a local collector of Peruvian antiquities.

Her current disposition also prohibited her from advising Hernandez of her difficulties or, perhaps more importantly, that the valuable package entrusted to Wylie was now out of their control. As she paced a corner of the cell, however, other things were on her mind. She would worry about Hernandez later; now, she was cursing her lawyer and the fact that she was not yet there.

In alternate breaths she cursed Mose Herrington, her partner in their current, very remunerative confidence scheme. Refusing to consider herself at fault, she thought he had to be the one who alerted the Miami bunco squad to their latest moneymaking endeavor. He was an old man and talked too much, either in the bar or to the latest cute young thing that attracted his attention. He was probably in the same building. If so, that meant the end to the very sweet con they had enjoyed for the last few months.

It was a variation of the fiddle game, with a fancy gold pocket watch substituted for the fiddle. Mose, wearing slightly shabby clothes, would enter an upscale restaurant and eat dinner. When the bill arrived, he would go to the owner to explain that he left his wallet back in his hotel. He promises to go back and get it and, as collateral, offers to let the owner hold his grandfather's gold watch—the watch he was planning to have appraised tomorrow.

After he leaves, Gudrun, sitting at a nearby table, approaches the owner, says she overheard the conversation about the watch, and asks if she can have a look at it. She explains she is a dealer in rare timepieces and, although she just had a glimpse of the watch, it might be of interest. If she remembered to put it in her purse, she uses a jeweler's loupe to examine the watch. Otherwise, she looks at it under a bright light. She looks excited and tells the owner,

—I haven't seen one of these for a while. The black edging gives it away, though. It is a Lange and Söhne pocket watch, probably from the early twenties. They are going at auction for thirty-five to forty thousand dollars these days.

Gudrun would then consult her own watch and declare she had to go, but not before giving the owner her impressively embossed business card.

—Please call me if the old man is interested in selling the watch.

Then she rushes out the door.

Soon Mose returns with his money for the meal. The owner, four out of five times, will ask Mose if he would like to sell the watch, expecting in his larcenous heart to cheat the old man and sell the watch to the bogus dealer for a huge profit. Mose ultimately agrees to accept a couple thousand dollars and a free dinner, and shambles out the door. The telephone number on the business card is, of course, nonexistent and the pocket watch was cobbled together last month in China. Gudrun and Mose buy the watches by the dozen.

Her lawyer made her belated appearance, and Gudrun complained of some terrible mix-up that must have occurred to place her in these current circumstances. Surely, it was a mistake and—

Her lawyer interrupted.

—Cut the crap, Gudrun. What is this—your third arrest this year? Are you still working the fiddle con?

Chastened, Gudrun admitted that, yes, she and Mose were still working the fiddle con. It was a cherished moneymaker.

—Well, if I can get you off again, you had better fly straight or fly to another city. I can't keep working my magic here forever.

Gudrun regretted that the good times in Miami probably had ended. She discussed the distasteful subject of the lawyer's retainer, and asked her to convey to her contact in Lima, Señor Hernandez, that the package had not been picked up.

—Hernandez will understand that message?

—Yes, said Gudrun, he will. But he won't be happy.

—Wylie, it's beautiful, but I have no idea what it is! Mavis called up the stairway.

She held two packages in her hand. There was no response from Wylie, so she climbed the stairs and entered his bedroom. He was still in bed, his nose pressed into the pillow. She prodded his back twice before his eyes fluttered open and he turned to look at Mavis. Her face wore a quizzical expression. He propped himself up on his elbows and focused on what she held in her hand. He recognized the two little leather pouches containing the earrings and bracelet received from Señor Hernandez, but the other object was unknown. It was an ornate silver rectangle with a stylized human figure at its center. Its design reminded him vaguely of the characters on the silver bracelet he had selected for Mercy.

He raised himself from the bed to stand closer to Mavis and look at the mysterious object. It was of burnished silver, about five inches square, and decorated with fanciful little figures around the figure in the center. This was what he saw:

Mavis had mistakenly opened the package intended for Hernandez's sister. Before she could ask more questions, he raised his hand as if to stop her words in midair.

—Honey, it's a mistake. I'll explain it over coffee—for which I have a desperate need.

In slippers and robe he followed Mavis to the kitchen, poured ten fingers of coffee and explained the events that led up to the appearance of two silver-wrapped packages in their foyer. His wife was pleased with the amethyst earrings and modeled them for Wylie. They both examined the "silver thing," as they called it, but could not deduce its origin or use. Mavis examined it closely, front and back.

—Looks pretty old, she said.

—Definitely. But what is it for? There's just this little raised band on the back with the heart-shaped hole in it. You can't pin it to anything, or wear it like a bracelet.

They both stared at the object as though further scrutiny would reveal its use. It did not.

—Well, this belongs to Hernandez. I'll just take it along and return it to him on my next trip to Lima. Unfortunately, I don't have a telex number for him. But I suppose I could get a message to him through Rod Weschler.

They put the silver thing to one side as they finished their breakfast and brought each other up-to-date on what happened in their lives while Wylie was out of the country.

Unsolved mysteries sometimes gnaw at little corners of the psyche, unrelieved as dreams, unresolved by action. So it was with the silver thing, carefully rewrapped and put aside on the middle shelf of the Chippendale corner cupboard. For the next week or so, every time Wylie walked near the cupboard he visualized the strange silver object, his curiosity rearoused. His internal dialogue went like this:

—What *is* the damn thing? But it belongs to Hernandez. None of my business. Strange gift for a sister. It really looks old. None of my business. What *is* the damn thing?

Two weeks after he returned from Lima, he explained to Mavis over breakfast,

—I would really like to know what that silver thing is. I was thinking of taking it to the office and letting Bob have a look at it. What do you think?

Bob Flanders was a partner at his law firm whose specialty was museum law. His familiarity with objets d'art was legendary. Although Mavis did not share Wylie's deep curiosity about the silver thing, she understood his need to analyze and understand all matters that touched upon his work and life. She sometimes teased him about applying "due diligence" too thoroughly to trifling matters.

—Wylie, you don't always need to give a five-dollar answer to a nickel question, she would say, and Wylie would smile. In this case, she simply agreed that Bob Flanders would be the right person to approach about the silver thing.

Wylie unwrapped the little package and placed the silver object on Flanders's mahogany desk. The lawyer pulled a flannel cloth from a desk drawer and cradled the piece as he held it to the strong light from the window.

—Wylie, this certainly looks authentic, not some recently manufactured rip-off. And it definitely has artistic value, to say nothing of its potential worth to collectors. My guess is that it came from the Andean region, probably Peru. It is a very nice piece.

Wylie asked whether he knew its purpose or use.

—Well, most of these things came from funeral bundles or graves, so it could be a decorative item. On the other hand, I don't know what this strip in back with the hole is for. By the way, how did you come across it?

Wylie explained its origin. Flanders reexamined the object and reminded Wylie

—You know, of course, that Peru like many countries has laws that prohibit the exportation of important archeological objects unless rigorous requirements are met. Also, as in many less developed countries, those laws are easily ignored or avoided—especially if a little money changes hands. Part of my practice is dealing with demands from various countries that my museums repatriate artworks removed from their borders. You know, like Greece demanding the return of the Elgin Marbles. I can assure you the British Museum would not be pleased to deal with that hot potato.

Flanders warmed to the subject and lectured his partner about the intricacies of his practice. Wylie was listened attentively. As he came to the end of his monologue, Flanders brightened, as though a new thought had crossed his mind.

—I just recalled that I do know a person who would know a great deal more about this little artifact. He is a professor at George Mason University, near DC. He was once rotating chair of the archaeology department, and his main interest is Peru. Down there two or three times a year. Let's see . . .

Flanders riffled through the Rolodex on the credenza.

—Yes, here it is. Lawrence Kuitkowski. Let me write down his address and number.

Two weeks later, Wylie found himself meeting with two officers of the United States Agency for International Development (USAID) in Washington. They worked together on the details of a private/public venture in India for the manufacture of Picolines, an industrial solvent derived from coal tar, horse urine and bone oil. The Indian government requested his client, a pharmaceutical company, to set up a Picolines production facility in exchange for permission to establish a generic drug manufacturing business. USAID was interested in adding its influence and finances to the venture, since it would employ numerous people collecting horse urine. Wylie tried not to think about how that would work.

Expecting the USAID meeting to end before noon, he arranged to meet Professor Kuitkowski at his university office that afternoon. During their telephone conversation, the professor said he would be pleased to examine the artifact and explain, to the best of his knowledge, what it was. The packaged silver thing was in Wylie's briefcase.

Unlike Wylie's office, with carefully arranged files on his mahogany desk and imposing legal tomes marching across polished shelves, the professor's workplace looked as though a paper tornado came to rest in the general vicinity of the battered oak desk behind which the professor was almost visible. Tall piles of books, files, manuscripts and paper coffee cups pushed away from the center of the desk, threatening to plummet to the floor. The floor, in turn, was covered with columns of paper debris that created two colonnaded pathways from the office door—one to the desk, the other to a battered leather chair that rose like a pinnacle from the debris. A few books leaning against an arm and a tiger-striped cat occupied the seat of the chair. The cat hissed softly at Wylie's entrance and bounded from the chair to the nearby bookcase, on which hundreds of books rested, all in the horizontal position. A tuft of ginger hair appeared above the stacks of paper on the desk, followed by the professor himself as he rose to greet his guest.

—Cypher, is it? he said as he worked his way around the corner of the desk and took Wylie's hand.

Larry Kuitkowski was about Wylie's age, shorter, stockier, with a slightly rumpled look. An unruly cowlick of ginger hair adorned his head and eyebrows, and glasses secured by a leather band around his neck hung at his chest. He smiled broadly as he pumped Wylie's hand.

The professor removed books from the leather chair, magically found an open space on his desk to park his body, and asked Wylie to have a seat. Their conversation quickly turned to the silver thing. Wylie unpacked it and they found a spot on the professor's desk where he could examine it. Kuitkowski looked at it for a few moments and prodded it with a pencil. He turned to Wylie.

—Nice piece. Too bad one of the disks is missing, but overall, it is in excellent condition and very representative of the period.

He smiled at Wylie again, as though his explanation covered the subject entirely. Wylie waited.

—Ah, you want to know what it is. It's a Chimú silver nose ornament from the Imperial Epoch—around fourteen hundred, I suppose. The Chimú were located on the northern coast of Peru, subservient to the Incas—until the conquest, of course, in 1532. I have seen many of these nose ornaments on my visits to Peru, but never in the United States. How did you manage to come by this?

Wylie avoided the question. Instead, he asked,

—What is a nose ornament used for?

—For the rulers of the period, the headdress, nose and ear ornaments, necklaces, belts and bracelets had ceremonial and funerary functions. In death, the rulers were adorned with these items in their funeral bundles. In ceremonies during their lives, the rulers represented themselves as deities, and these gaudy decorations reinforced their divinity.

Kuitkowski turned over the ornament and pointed to the heart-shaped opening in the back.

—That narrow opening fitted the nasal septum, which held the piece in place and covered the mouth. By speaking behind this mask, the ruler enforced his awe-inspiring deity. His voice seemed to come from the heavens. It was a Wizard of Oz conceit.

The professor pointed to the central figure on the ornament.

—Actually, this is the guy who wore it. He must have been pretty hot stuff—with two crowns over his head!

To divert the scholar further from the question of how Wylie came to possess the item, he asked many more questions about the meaning of the other decorations, which the professor answered in detail. There was much the silver figure revealed about the lives of the Chimú elite and the culture of the people of northern Peru. Then as now, Wylie observed, the elite had power and wealth, and everyone else scrabbled around for scraps and crumbs.

Kuitkowski placed the nose ornament back on his desk and smiled at his guest.

—So, Wylie, how did you acquire this ornament?

During the course of his legal practice, Wylie had learned two essential lessons: one, assume a lie will be discovered eventually, and two, an answer based on truth avoids the necessity to remember untruths. So, without emphasizing how he had been taken in by Señor Hernandez, he explained how the recipient of the intended gift had not appeared and how Mavis had mistakenly opened the box. His curiosity led him to the Professor. Kuitkowski steepled his hands under his chin and considered Wylie's situation. He looked from the nose ornament on his desk to Wylie.

—Looks like this guy in Lima is unlawfully trading in archeological artifacts and exporting his country's patrimony. I know enforcement is lax in this area, both here and in Peru, but I hate when that happens. This item is an important part of ancient Peruvian culture and should be available to the people of that country. Yeah, this pisses me off.

Wylie smiled at the professor's colloquialism; he was warming to the archaeologist. Kuitkowski patted his desk with the palms of both hands and stood.

—I'll tell you what. You keep the ornament for now and I will get in touch with my good friend at the Universidad Nacional Mayor de San Marcos for advice on how to deal with this situation. I will call you after I hear from him.

Wylie worked his way among the columns of paper to the door and waved good-bye. He was outside the building before he remembered the other thing he intended to ask the professor. It was about the ancient pyramid at Chavin de Huantar.

They met again two weeks later at the Oyster Bar in Grand Central Station. Larry had taken the train to Manhattan for a business meeting, and Wylie's office was only a few blocks away from the station. Larry had only a half hour or so before his train for DC departed, so they skipped small talk and came directly to the various points under discussion. Larry began.

—I had two long conversations with Jorge Benson, my friend at the university in Peru. If you agree, he is willing to arrange for the repatriation of the nose ornament to their collection of Chimú artifacts that, it turns out, is one of the more extensive ones in the country. His plan is to send me an "official" letter explaining that the ornament was on loan to me for research purposes and that I am returning it to the university collection, in case I am discovered bringing it into the country. That is unlikely, but I prefer to eliminate risk wherever possible. I am planning another trip in about three months and could return it then.

Wylie readily agreed. He wondered whether Larry had asked his friend if he knew anything about the activities of Señor Hernandez. That question was not germane to the disposition of the nose ornament, but Wylie had two weeks to consider how naive he had been, how easily he had been taken in by the jeweler, and was searching for a way to salve his wounded pride. Either knowledge that others had also been fooled by Hernandez or appropriate retribution would do.

—No, Larry said, but I have given some thought to the appropriate way to deal with your deceiver.

What, wondered Wylie, would that be.

—Well, I wouldn't exactly seek him out when you return to Lima but, should you happen to meet, you might ask how his "sister" enjoyed the gift you passed on to her.

Conversation paused as Wylie absorbed the devious suggestion of his new friend. He savored the dilemma that Hernandez would face. Either Wylie or his contact in Miami was lying. Was it more likely that this regarded lawyer or Hernandez' supposed sister was untruthful? A conundrum, thought Wylie, a delicious conundrum.

Like a cloud briefly passing before the sun, a shadowed thought occurred to Wylie. It seemed completely out of character for this roly-poly archaeologist, so knowledgeable of Peruvian antiquity, and so disorganized, to hatch this Machiavellian ploy.

He saw his companion glance at his watch, so Wylie quickly raised the other thing on his mind.

—Larry, are you familiar with the area around Chavin de Huantar?

—Familiar? I spent a year and a half doing graduate studies there—helping clear out rubble from the 1945 earthquake and documenting the location of the various temples. I also charted the tunnels under the main temple, the one they call the Castillo. The trip I mentioned is to return there. Why do you ask?

Wylie admitted only that he had read about the ruins during his last visit to Lima and was mildly interested in a visit. What he did not mention was that he had concocted a fantasy, over the past month, of trekking bravely to Chavin de Huantar, of becoming one with the mountains. Recently, the fantasy had expanded to include Mercy in a long-awaited bonding experience. However, he did not feel comfortable in exposing his middle-aged daydream just then.

Kuitkowski placed his empty beer glass on their table and grabbed his bag.

-—Wylie, it's been good to see you again. We need to arrange the transfer of the silver ornament, so I can deliver it to my friend in Lima when I visit. I will be in touch.

He paused before he turned to go.

—I'm going to send you some materials about Chavin de Huantar. I think you would find it an excellent place to visit – even for a lawyer.

The following week a bundle arrived from the professor. It contained his personal journal from a number of years ago entitled *Field Notes from Chavin de Huantar*, detailed photographs of the ruins and some snapshots of a younger professor posing with large carved stone skulls. His brief note said simply that he hoped Wylie enjoyed "the enclosed."

Friendship between Wylie and Larry Kuitkowski developed during the following weeks, as Wylie called to express his pleasure and thanks for the information about ruins at Chavin and to arrange a meeting where Wylie could hand over the silver nose ornament. In turn, Wylie's quick grasp of arcane archaeological data and his thoughtful questions about mountain trekking and pre-Inca cultures impressed Kuitkowski. Each had an interest in the other's chosen profession, so different from his own, and they were soon exchanging bad lawyer and archaeologist jokes.

Wylie had given the silver nose ornament to Larry during a previous visit to Washington, but, upon hearing that Wylie had business in the city a few weeks later, Kuitkowski invited Wylie to dinner at his bachelor apartment near the university. Expecting a cluttered abode similar to the professor's office, Wylie was surprised to discover a neat and spacious apartment, the walls decorated with beautiful photographs of remote places, views from picture windows of classic monuments.

Wylie accepted a glass of red wine and they settled into easy chairs in a large L-shaped room that was for living, dining and watching television.

—Listen, I don't want to create the impression that I actually make anything other than breakfast here. I have a long-standing arrangement with Luigi's, around the corner, to cater anything more sophisticated than a toasted bagel. I have learned how to keep my oven at three hundred degrees, and that is where the Capellini, veal stuffed with crabmeat, garlic bread, and spinach await. Salad with Luigi's special dressing, I have learned, is best kept in the refrigerator. So, anytime you are hungry we can serve it up.

Wylie preferred to savor the wine and take surreptitious inventory of his friend's tasteful home. So different from his office, it seemed that dissimilar people inhabited each space. Wylie complimented him on how peaceful and refined his apartment was. Larry guessed at Wylie's thoughts.

—Yes, this place is different from my man cave of an office. However, I am comfortable in both places, and my students seem to get a kick out of having a teacher who lives in a rat hole.

They both laughed, a cue to begin loading plates with Luigi's fine Italian food.

The dinner conversation, at Wylie's prodding, turned to Larry's visits to archaeological sites in Peru and what it was like to follow high altitude paths across the white mountains.

—Trekkers experience a mountain high that comes when the body manufactures endorphins, either to reward strenuous physical activity or to alleviate the pain that activity causes. It doesn't happen on every trek but I have experienced that high a few times. The sensation is like an out of body experience, as though you were looking down at yourself from above, and is very pleasurable. Combine that with finding an important archaeological artifact or a previously unknown site, and it's a double whammy of feel-good experience.

Larry seemed lost in thought for a moment and, from his expression, Wylie guessed he was reliving one of those exceptional experiences.

Larry recovered himself and grinned at Wylie.

—Looks as though I was on a mini mountain high —sorry.

They worked their way through the meal and the bottle of red wine, continuing the talk about mountain trekking. Larry worked magic with his kitchen espresso machine and they savored the dark, rich liquid.

—Listen, Wylie, with all your questions and the stuff I sent you, you could probably find your way across the Cordillera Blanca on your own. It occurs to me that it might be amusing to invite a greenhorn lawyer along on a visit to Chavin. Interested?

Interested? Wylie flashed back to the image of himself as noble conqueror of the high Andes, defeating the malignant forces of middle age, strong and resilient, a man out of the ordinary, like his friend Larry. He beamed at his friend.

—I think I could be persuaded to come.

During the course of the remainder of the evening and telephone conversations the next few days, Wylie confirmed that Mercy would join the excursion, arranged to coordinate his next visit to Lima with the beginning of the trek, ordered catalogs from outfitters to find the proper gear for Mercy and himself, and worried about finding a proper guide and porters for the excursion. Larry explained

—Look, just be ready for the trek; I suggest you begin taking long walks to prepare. I have a trusted guide who will handle the local details, and he will let us know what to expect in the way of expenses.

The next morning Wylie rose early and began to jog through the quiet streets of Middletown. He returned sooner than expected with a stitch in his side and a resolution to be a little less aggressive about his training for the wonderful trip to the southern mountains.

11

He returned his gaze to his favorite image of the little mummy. It was the close-up of the mummy's tiny face, with sallow skin, sunken cheekbones and an eternal grin. He found it poignant and endearing. In his imagination, it generated images of a little child at play in an ancient time, and produced questions about the cause of her early death and what her status was, that she was so honored by mummification. Of course, Lord Wimsey knew more than most about the culture and practices of the pre-Columbian era in Peru. It was knowledge necessary to his business of trading in authentic antiquities.

The photograph was included among the materials received from Hernandez in Peru. Another picture that held his attention was of a Moche gold-and-silver breastplate formed in a yin-and-yang pattern. Wimsey was fascinated with the quality of workmanship existing at the time of Christ, as well as the deep symbolic power of the two precious metals. Gold represented the sun, silver the moon. These two heavenly bodies dominated the skies and, for the Moche and other ancient societies in Peru, they were major gods. Both metals conveyed the power of these deities as well as the duality of nature, a concept central to the thinking of the people of the Andes.

Lesser deities such as Pachamama, goddess of the earth, were not often represented with precious metals; they appeared on items of pottery. However, the ancient people believed fervently in their power, and developed strong attachments to their personal deities. Violence frequently resulted from threats to that attachment. The most tangible evidence of that was the practice of human sacrifice to appease the deities. Wimsey chuckled to himself and thought, it gives fresh meaning to "don't mess with Mother Nature."

He pushed back from his elegant regency desk and moved his head from side to side, as though to clear it of cobwebs. The various items identified in the letter from Hernandez represented the finest and most original pieces he had seen in a long while. Their disposition would require utmost tact and discretion, which meant he must search his mental list of potential buyers to qualify those with the appropriate wealth, sophistication and, most important, lack of ostentation. It would not do to release one of these pieces to someone who would brag to the members of his club about his latest acquisition.

His energetic mind was also considering the logistics of transporting the items from Peru to the United Kingdom. His most recent efforts in that regard were not without problems. The ancient amphorae shipped from Piraeus in barrels of olive oil had been left with a distinctive residue that required hours of painstaking labor to eliminate. The Bulgarian driver hired to transport fourteenth-century icons in a moving van stuffed with furniture from IKEA suffered a panic attack on the cross-channel ferry, and nearly gave the game away. Wimsey's was a risky business. He decided to wait for Hernandez's suggestion about conveying the pieces to the UK.

The ring of the door buzzer to his Kensington apartment interrupted his thoughts. Peter, Wylie's solicitor friend, was there.

—What a delightful surprise, said Percy.

He had not expected his lover until the following evening.

During the course of the next three weeks, Walsham narrowed his list of potential purchasers for the child mummy to three collectors of South American antiquities. In qualifying them as potential buyers, Walsham knew they belonged to that rare subset of assiduous creators of personal wealth for whom possession of a unique item was enough. They had long ago established their self-worth; it was unnecessary to show off their wealth. Moreover, they trusted Lord Wimsey about the provenance of an item.

After two weeks of discrete bidding, a Scot with substantial interests in North Sea oil became the future caretaker of the child mummy—a privilege obtained for more than one million pounds. Walsham consummated the arrangement at one of his distilleries east of the Golden Mile in Edinburgh.

Now Walsham reverted to the problem of transport. How to arrange for the delivery of the little bundle from Lima to the United Kingdom? It was time to advise Hernandez that a sale had been completed.

12

The skeptical Weschlers, Rod and Don, offered only grudging approval to Wylie's report that he was excited to begin a trek in a few days from Huaraz to Chavin de Huantar with his daughter, Mercy, led by a renowned archaeologist. It would never have occurred to members of the aristocracy to venture away from the comforts of home without the availability of similar comforts. Sleeping in a tent on hard ground, eating food prepared in the open on a wood or propane fire, walking for hours at a time, or, worse, mingling with the natives—it simple was not done. However, Wylie was an American and, accordingly, deserved some latitude. The Weschlers patted him on the back and wished him a pleasant walk in the wilderness. Their lack of enthusiasm did not dampen Wylie's keenness. He chided them for not taking advantage of their country's natural beauty. The call to dinner interrupted their conversation. Wylie sat next to Marie Weschler, Don's wife, and across the table from a white-uniformed naval officer. He had introduced himself during the cocktail hour, but Wylie did not catch all five Spanish names and was relieved to address the officer by what others called him—"Admiral."

The dinner banter began blandly enough with reports about what family members were doing, the Weschlers' plans to visit the just-opened EPCOT Center in Orlando, Florida, and congratulations to the Admiral for his prestigious assignment to lead the Ministry of the Interior. Don Weschler expressed confidence that the Admiral had the needed qualities to resolve the very difficult problems facing the ministry.

—President Belaunde is wise to promote you, Admiral. His administration is not exactly robust, and the recent flooding, earthquakes and other natural disasters, along with plummeting international commodity prices, are ruining us economically. Our businesses are certainly feeling the pinch, I can tell you that!

The Admiral understood all that. He added,

—As if that weren't enough, that damned Sendero Luminoso is a serious problem. Not only are they killing people and blowing things up, they are funding their "revolution" through alliances with drug cartels. Peru is becoming one of the largest coca producers in the world. I feel my most important mission is to stop those communist *cabrones*!

His emotion was apparent; his face was bright red against the white collar of his uniform.

Those around the table offered their own stories about the depredations caused by the Shining Path. There were muttered comments about how "we ought to kill them all!" As before, Wylie held his tongue. There was no way allusions to the Holocaust would influence these people.

After the meal, the Admiral sat next to Wylie, warming his after-dinner liqueur glass in his hands.

—And you, Dr. Cypher, you make many visits to Lima, I understand. Do you like out city?

—Very much. It is so much older and more historically important than American cities. And I enjoy working with the Weschler family. It is a privilege to assist them in their legal and business dealings. In addition, I do have other clients with Peruvian interests.

The Admiral appeared unusually interested in Wylie's business, and Wylie could not resist telling this charming man about some of his dealings in Peru. Obviously, the Admiral was a man of powerful influence; it could do no harm to mention his legal capabilities. When Wylie noted his difficulties in protecting his clients' industrial property rights in Peru during the previous left-leaning military leadership, the Admiral asked,

—You do not believe that things such as patents, trademarks, and designs should have a very limited international monopoly? That, after a short while, they should be made freely available to all?

Wylie warmed to one of his favorite legal topics, and held forth on the need to protect such rights for a considerable period to encourage innovation and development. To him, patent protection for seventeen years was almost too brief a period to reward the time, money, and effort that went into creating something new.

The Admiral, on the other hand, believed it was important to limit those protections, especially in less developed countries, to allow the free exchange of new ideas.

Wylie truculently defended his argument and the Admiral seemed to enjoy the exchange. Finally, he sipped the last of his drink, rose, and patted Wylie on the shoulder, saying it had been a pleasure to talk with him. His aide joined him as he departed.

Wylie was about to leave his chair when Rod appeared at his side with a young man Wylie had not noticed before.

—Wylie, I want you to meet my young cousin, Raoul de Sousa. He is studying law at the university, and is very interested in meeting such a famous international lawyer as yourself. He just arrived.

Raoul was slender, darkly handsome, with a thin mustache. He looked to Wylie like the quintessential Latin lover, the sort of young man whom Wylie would have discouraged Mercy from spending much time with.

Nevertheless, Rod's cousin was polite and engaging. He spoke excellent English and had obviously looked Wylie up in Martindale-Hubble, the lawyers' reference book. From his bearing and his references to visits in the States, he appeared ready to join the Lima aristocracy after he passed the bar. As their conversation continued, Wylie knew that this was a business meeting—there would be future connections.

As his aide held open the limousine door, the Admiral said,

—That Dr. Cypher—I think there is more to him than meets the eye. He may be working for someone else. An American who spends so much time in Lima is always worth a closer look. It is just a hunch, but let's keep an eye on him.

At about the same time, Raoul de Sousa discussed Wylie with Rod Weschler.

—Unquestionably, Dr. Cypher is very experienced in foreign matters. Do you know if he every uses local attorneys in working on his transactions?

Rod considered.

—Yes, he does confer with one or two Lima lawyers that I know of.

He smiled at his young cousin, clapped him on the shoulder, and laughed.

—Raoul, you are not yet out of law school and you are angling for work? No question about it, you have the makings of a successful lawyer!

As they walked away to refresh their drinks, Raoul asked,

—You have known Dr. Cypher a long time. Men of his importance sometimes have hidden agendas. Do you think he might have contacts in Washington?

Rod considered.

—Well, I know that he makes frequent visits to Washington to work with government agencies.

Raoul nodded slightly.

Wylie had a few free days in Lima before Mercy's and Professor Kuitkowski's arrival in Lima. They planned to rest for one night at the Lima Sheraton with Wylie. Their adventure would begin on Sunday. To fill part of his free time, Wylie made a courtesy visit to Larry's archaeologist friend in Lima who provided a tour of ancient artifacts in the university collection: pottery, Incan "huacos," and silver from the time after the conquest. They were pieces not normally on display and very beautiful. Wylie thanked Larry's friend profusely for the visit. His head was still filled with images of ancient art as he left the building and oriented himself on the street.

Wylie looked both ways down the avenue and was about to move along the sidewalk when Raoul de Sousa seemed to appear out of nowhere. The boy glanced furtively over his shoulder and motioned Wylie back into the alcove shielding the entrance to the building where they were not visible from the street.

Like the Admiral, Raoul had mistakenly imbued Wylie with characteristics and capabilities he did not possess. Raoul saw a well-educated, well-traveled and successful lawyer who was a partner in a major New York law firm. Were it Peru, a man like Wylie would certainly have friends and influence in very high places. . It must be the same in the United States. Surely, he believed, Dr. Cypher must have important United States government connections

Raoul was a member of the intelligence arm of the Sendero Luminoso and had been entrusted with very sensitive and dangerous information. He was tasked with passing it on to foreign governments, the most important being the United States. The Sendero Luminoso leadership hoped that information would blacken the reputation of the Peruvian administration and offer justification for their acts of violence and sabotage. Contacting the United States embassy was impossible. Peruvian security people monitored comings and goings there, and Raoul had no innocent reason for visiting. Rod's confirmation that Wylie frequently worked with government agencies in Washington suggested that he might be an appropriate conduit for the inflammatory information. In his view, it was worth a try. Other avenues might arise later, but Wylie was the prospect of the moment.

—Raoul, how nice to see you again! Is this where you have your classes?

Raoul explained that the law school had its campus in another part of the university, and that he had noticed the doctor entering the archeological building on his way to class. Rod had mentioned the doctor's intended trip to Huaraz, and Raoul wanted to give him a little gift—a guide to that area.

—Please forgive me; it is in Spanish. I could find no English guides to the pyramids at Chavin.

Raoul handed him a slender volume wrapped in the same kind of silver paper Hernandez used.

—I hope you will find it useful, he said.

Wylie thanked him for the gift. It was very thoughtful, he said. They shook hands and Raoul walked from the alcove and along the sidewalk to the corner of the building. Wylie walked in the other direction.

Two of the Admiral's men had been lounging and smoking diagonally across the street from the alcove where Raoul and Wylie talked. They quickly ground out their cigarettes, one ambled in the direction Wylie was taking, and the other hurried down the street after Raoul.

Wylie looked through the glass bottom of the elevator at the Sheraton Hotel as it ascended to his floor. He enjoyed the sensation of movement as he watched the lobby floor move away under his feet. He did not notice the man who followed him from the university, who had settled in a comfortable chair in the lobby and pulled a copy of *La República* from his pocket.

It was Wylie's habit to empty his pockets on the desk in his room and inventory the contents of his briefcase before taking a shower. He decided to unwrap Raoul's book. It looked as though it had been found in a used bookstall, a bit tattered, but with a good photograph of the main temple on its cover, and a comprehensive map of the ruins. With his improving Spanish, he was able to translate most of the introduction. As he replaced the book on the desk, something slipped from between the pages. He pulled it from the book and discovered two black plastic rectangles, about five inches square. At first he was confused, but then he recalled seeing them before—on his secretary's desk. What was it she called them? "Floppies"—that was it. But what the hell were they doing in this guidebook?

He sat on the bed to consider the sudden appearance of the floppies. It was unlikely that Raoul had put them in the guidebook by accident and forgotten to remove them before wrapping the present. Wylie recalled that the black rectangles contained some sort of disk that was used to store and transfer information on computers. The secretaries in the law office used them for making legal documents and favored the computers greatly over their Selectric typewriters. Apparently, their use avoided having to retype lengthy documents, but he was only vaguely aware how that worked.

So, if those floppies were conveyors of information and writing, he assumed that there was something on them that Raoul wanted him to see. However, he had no access to a machine that could decode the disks. The best he could do, he believed, was to hold them until his return to New York in about three weeks' time, when he would ask his secretary to figure out what the floppies contained. That decided, he dropped them into a file folder containing his to-do lists and slid it into the top section of his briefcase.

As he stepped out of the shower, the telephone on the desk was ringing. A heavily accented woman's voice announced that he had a call from Rodrigo Weschler. Should she put him through? Slightly wet and wrapped in his towel, Wylie answered.

—Sorry to bother you, Wylie, but I was wondering if you had Raoul with you. His girlfriend said he was planning to visit you this afternoon, and he never showed up for dinner with us tonight. It is unlike him, so I thought maybe you had met and had drinks or something.

—That's right; Raoul found me at the university this afternoon, but he just wanted to give me a guidebook—a thoughtful gift. Our meeting didn't last more than a couple of minutes, though. He left in the direction of the law school.

Wylie heard Rod pass that information on to someone else by the telephone. There was a pause.

—All right. We will look elsewhere for him. Did he seem okay to you?

Wylie recalled that he seemed a little nervous. Suddenly he connected that with the discovery of the floppies in the guidebook. He told Rod about that.

—Raoul is taken with all this computer stuff. I keep telling him that it is simply an office tool, but he keeps talking about a digital future. You know how young people are. But it is possible he meant to give you some special information. He thinks very highly of you, Wylie.

Flattered, Wylie agreed that learning what that information was might be important, but how?

Rod thought for a moment, then recalled,

—We have a couple of new Commodore computers in the office here. I think I can figure out how to use them. Want me to pick you up and go over there? We can have dinner later.

Wylie was waiting in the hotel lobby when Rod arrived. He sat in an overstuffed chair across from a sallow young man reading a *La República* newspaper.

They arrived at the Rod's office at dusk, and Rod had to find the night sentry to turn on the lights. He ushered Wylie to a large office near the back of the building, but stopped at the desk just outside the office door. There was one of the Commodore computers. It looked like a large beige typewriter supporting a small television screen. There was a slotted beige box attached to the machine. Rod pressed a button and flicked a switch; a bright dot appeared in the middle of the screen and a green light glowed. The dot expanded into a sky-blue screen, and small columns of white letters flicked across the blue background. Wylie fished the floppies from his briefcase, and Rod slipped one of them into the box beside the computer. The box whirred and the screen turned black. A moment of panic seized the two men. Had Rod managed to break the machine?

Slowly an image began to form at the top of the screen. It was a negative view of a typed memorandum. The distinctive letterhead of the Ministry of the Interior appeared, followed by a jagged *"Ultrasecreto"* written by hand in block letters. Someone had crudely blacked out the recipients' names, which appeared as a white smear, and the opening paragraph, in Spanish, seemed to contain bureaucratic preamble language. Wylie could not translate the other words that quickly filled the screen. He glanced at Rod, who was staring at the screen in shocked fascination. The white letters quickly tumbled to the bottom, where they disappeared, momentarily leaving the screen dark before a new page opened and more rows of white letters danced in front of their eyes. The letters finally stopped, and the final screen glowed brightly in front of them. A scrawled signature stood out at the bottom. Wylie turned questioningly toward Rod, his drawn face ashen, reflecting the garish light.

—My God, Wylie, this is unbelievable. Raoul gave you a copy of a secret memorandum in which the Admiral authorized what they call "extreme measures" in dealing with all "insurrectionists"—principally, I guess, the members of the Sendero Luminoso. This part here sanctions the use of horrific torture techniques like blowtorches and pliers, electric shock to the genitals and nipples, sleep deprivation, extreme temperatures, slamming bodies against walls, hanging by the elbows, inserting foreign objects into the body . . .

Rod was unable to continue. He looked away from the screen, his jaw clenched, his eyes red-rimmed. After taking some deep breaths, he returned his gaze to the screen.

—Burning slivers of wood under fingernails…it goes on . . . and what is this? I don't understand. Water boarding?

Wylie had no idea what that was. He asked Rod to repeat what he had said, because Wylie found it incomprehensible that an agency of the Peruvian government would condone such brutal treatment of other human beings—other Peruvians. Was this the Middle Ages?

Rod reluctantly reread the disgusting litany, and Wylie absorbed the impact of the document unfurled on the computer screen.

Rod added,

—That is the Admiral's signature at the end of the document. So that is what he was alluding to the other night. The challenges facing his administration of the agency.

Wylie handed over the other floppy, which Rod inserted in the computer slot. A new document, also under the letterhead of the Ministry of Interior, began to form on the little screen. Wylie could tell it was different.

Rod pulled over his secretary's chair, sat down, and stared as the screen. Wylie suspected Rod was preparing for fresh horrors to scroll across the little screen and stood beside his friend.

Rod explained that this memorandum authorized the use of "final rendition." It described approved methods and techniques for disposing of people who had succumbed to "extreme measures" or simply were required to "disappear." In principle, most bodies were to be disposed of in a public manner to exemplify the futility of challenging the administration. On the other hand, secrecy was in order for "disappearances." No martyrs and no bodies. Comrades and family should never know what happened to friends and loved ones. Rod described a few of the approved ways to manage disappearances. The one that stuck in Wylie's mind was drugging the victim and tossing him or her, still alive, from a helicopter or cargo plane far out over the Pacific.

Wylie found another chair and sat beside Rod. They both looked at the final screen. There was the Admiral's signature again.

—Jesus! said Rod. I don't know how to make copies these memos. I don't know how to make copies of those floppies either.

Frustrated and disgusted, they replaced the disks in Wylie's briefcase, and walked solemnly from the building. Wylie had a new problem.

What the hell was *he* supposed to do with these floppies?

Two aides stood before the Admiral's desk late Friday afternoon. They had just completed their report about the outcome of their interview with the detained Raoul de Sousa.

—Your Excellency, your instincts are, as usual, splendid. Under intense questioning, the de Sousa boy confirmed not only that he had passed on floppy disks containing sensitive information to Dr. Cypher, but also that he trusted the Yankee to pass that information on to United States government agencies. Later, he remembered the gist of the information on the disks, even the dates and code numbers of the documents recorded there.

The aide pointed to the folder on the Admiral's desk holding copies of the secret papers. The Admiral had already reviewed its contents, seething about the peril their disclosure would offer to his administration and himself, preparing to disembowel whoever provided copies to the Sendero Luminoso. Containment and revenge flooded his thoughts, but containing this potential disaster had priority. He focused on his aide again.

—So, based on your own observations and that boy's interrogation, there is little or no doubt that Dr. Cypher possesses this damning information.

In unison, both men before his desk said

—No doubt.

The Admiral leaned back in his chair, placing both hands on the soft leather arms. Looking at the ceiling, he asked

—What is your most recent information about Cypher?

The aide reported that the lawyer had left the hotel last night with one of the Weschler sons and visited their office in Lima for a while. This morning he sent two faxes from the hotel that they were unable to recover. He was now visiting with the jeweler, Hernandez.

—Very well, said the Admiral, maintain close surveillance. We must devise ways of recovering those documents, those floppy disks.

—Of course, Excellency.

Wylie had looked forward to his next meeting with Hernandez for over two months. He called on the jeweler ostensibly to thank him for selecting such lovely pieces for Mavis and Mercy, but his main reason was to carry out Larry's plan of revenge.

He confirmed to Hernandez how pleased the women were with their gifts.

He added that he hoped his sister had enjoyed her gift as well. He regretted he had not had the opportunity to spend more time with her at the airport, but he had to rush to catch the Newark plane.

Hernandez charmingly replied that yes, she had, and hoped that she and Wylie could meet once again under less hurried circumstances. Disheartened that Hernandez had not risen to the bait, Wylie prepared to leave, but then noticed a steely look in the man's eyes not seen before and an almost imperceptible tic at the left corner of is mouth. The seasoned negotiator knew he had hit the target.

By Saturday afternoon, Lucho received a report at his headquarters in Ayacucho that Raoul de Sousa was dead. His girlfriend confirmed that the last person he had seen was a Dr. Cypher and that De Sousa intended to deliver important documents to him. Later telephone calls confirmed that the Lima police discovered his naked body in a ditch beside the main highway to the airport. There were clear signs of torture.

Lucho puzzled over this information. He knew Raoul de Sousa to be a passionate but clear-headed revolutionary, bright and careful, and especially valuable as a scion of the aristocracy. Yet, for reasons yet unknown, he was tortured to death soon after contacting this Cypher person. Since Raoul could not explain recent events, the logical person to question was Cypher. Most likely it was an innocent meeting—a coincidence.

The warrior scratched his head with his damaged hand. A few years ago, he might have believed in coincidence. Now Lucho, battle-hardened for more than two years, believed there were no coincidences, no innocent bystanders. When it came to understanding events in a civil war, cynicism was an ally.

Cypher could be an agent of the administration who turned de Sousa over to the detested Ministry of the Interior. It would not be the first time that a supposed ally was unmasked as a traitor. Furthermore, Cypher was a gringo, a hated Yankee from the land of capitalist oppressors. As a minimum, it was his duty to interview the Yankee. The revolution could not afford to ignore Dr. Cypher.

It took a long time to get a telephone connection to Lima. Lucho smiled grimly. The delay was probably because we blew up a transmission tower.

Wylie was horrified to learn of Raoul de Sousa's death when Rod called him at the Sheraton with the sad news.

—The family is devastated. He was such a lively and charming boy, with a bright future ahead. And such a horrible, nasty way to find him—dumped along the road like a sack of garbage. Terribly mutilated. I weep every time of think of his wounds. It is unbearable.

Rod's voice broke. Wylie took the moment to recall his brief association with the handsome and charming young man. Visualizing his body, broken and bleeding in a ditch, caused tightening in his throat and the taste of bile. He could only guess how his friend felt and wished he had the words to offer comfort. Finally, Rod spoke again, in hushed tones.

—I know this had to do with those floppies he gave you. I have been searching my mind to understand how Raoul had them. His girlfriend says she believes he was involved with the Sendero Luminoso, which I first thought was preposterous. Even if we believe her, how can it be that a boy of good family, well educated, could be associated with that rabble? It is unthinkable.

Wylie offered condolences, commiseration. After a few more moments, he picked up the thread of Rod's conversation and said

—For the life of me, I don't understand why he gave me the floppies. I haven't slept, thinking about the disgusting stuff in those memos, and I still don't have any idea how to deal with them. I thought I might discuss them with my partners, but I am leaving for Huaraz tomorrow, and I don't plan to be back home for three weeks. What do you think? Should I turn them over to you?

Rod responded immediately:

—No. Raoul could have given them to me or another member of the family, but he chose you. Someone in your country needs to know about those memos, if for no other reason than for Raoul's sake. Your embassy in Lima, perhaps?

That's possible, thought Wylie, though it would certainly delay his vacation plans with Mercy and Kuitkowski. In any event, there was no time now. He had to find a taxi to the airport. Every hour seemed to be rush hour on the way to Callao.

He promised to call Rod tomorrow.

The crowd awaiting arrivals at the airport was larger than Wylie expected. Amid the bobbing heads and signs lining the path from the customs exit to the interior of the four-story airport lobby he missed Mercy until she stood ten feet away, clutching the straps of her backpack and smiling broadly.

—Hello, Daddy!

She pushed through the people blocking her father and kissed him on the cheek, adding an awkward hug impeded by the backpack. A warm bronze tan from summer at camp covered exposed flesh, emphasizing her extremely fit condition. Her calves resembled bricks under mocha skin. Wylie was extremely happy to see her. He kissed her back. She held the hug, then broke off and looked toward the exit door from customs.

—The professor should be right behind me. We flew down next to each other; he is a very interesting man.

Kuitkowski pushed through the door. He had grown a scruffy beard since Wylie last saw him and carried a hiker's backpack with a rolled Ensolite pad strapped on top. Worn hiking boots dangled from one side of the pack, a faded campaign hat from the other. With a checkered shirt and canvas vest, he looked the essence of a vagabond trekker, certainly not like a respected professor of anthropology. He slapped Wylie's hand in greeting.

—Well, here we all are! Nice daughter you have there, Wylie. I am betting she holds up well on our trip.

Mercy flushed. She was not sure whether it was because of the compliment or irritation at Kuitkowski's offhand condescension, mixed with male chauvinism.

They collected Mercy's bag and found Wylie's taxi, which trundled them from the airport to the Sheraton hotel in the old city. Kuitkowski sat in the passenger seat and enjoyed an animated conversation in Spanish with the driver. Mercy, with her three years of college Spanish, understood about fifty percent of the dialogue, but the rapid-fire flow of words baffled Wylie. He heard "Belaunde" two or three times and guessed that the professor was catching up on the political scene.

Kuitkowski graciously refused to join Wylie and Mercy for a drink in the Sheraton bar. He assumed that father and daughter would enjoy some private time together, and he was right.

They relaxed on easy chairs in the bar off the lobby and ordered drinks. Mercy chatted about her still unresolved plans, confirming that she decided not to join MS magazine. She concluded that long hours at minimum wages and dealing with the gritty aspects of living in a big city outweighed the glamour of working for such an icon. She paused to swallow her drink and noticed that her father seemed lost in other thoughts.

—Dad, you all right?

—Well, honey, I had a shock today. A young man I knew, a relative of the Weschlers, was brutally murdered. Right here in Lima. I did not know him well, but it's always horrifying when a young person dies, especially in such a cruel way.

He said no more, nothing about the documents, nothing about his connection to Raoul. Nothing about his growing concern that unknown malignant forces might interfere with their plans.

Mercy expressed her concern but sensed her father had said all he intended to say about the matter. They sipped their drinks.

—I'm really pumped about our adventure, Dad. I've been walking four or five miles every day and working out. But I have never been at such a high altitude before. I hope I will be okay.

Wylie involuntarily tightened his stomach muscles, but that had little effect on the insidious little pouches of fat trying to flow over his belt. He offered Mercy a rueful smile.

—You look to be in excellent shape, sweetheart. I'm the one who should be worried.

His comment, which Mercy graciously but without sincerity rejected, reflected a twinge of conscience. Work always seemed to interrupt his good intentions of getting more exercise, knocking off those love handles, eating more sensibly. He weighed twenty pounds more than what he referred to as his "fighting weight"—what he weighed when in combat in Korea.

It was past midnight when they finished their drinks. Wylie kissed his daughter good night and went to his room. The elation from seeing Mercy again and engaging in caring conversation was tempered by thoughts about the sad business with Raoul and the problem of the floppies. He hoped that the arrangement he made with Rod Weschler and the result of the faxes he sent that morning would help resolve the situation.

13

Zorro turned the corner sharply, crossed quickly under the portico and slid the van into a parking space just to the left of the Sheraton hotel entrance. He decided to save the empty bottle of Inca Cola beside the driver's seat for later during the trip north, opened the door and leaned over the macadam, spitting out a sturdy stream of viscous greenish brown liquid tainted with bits of soggy coca leaves. Having prepared his mouth for a fresh charge, he reached into a leather pouch at his side and stuffed a generous portion of tender young leaves into the side of his mouth. Thus prepared, he looked toward the hotel entrance and spotted the guide, a tall, dark-haired young man carrying a heavy pack.

—Hey, Pedro, he called, over here. Good to see you, man. Looks like you are ready for the trip north.

The two young men exchanged a stiff embrace, the masculine equivalent of the double air kiss favored by Latin women.

—Right. We are just about ready to go. I think they are settling their accounts and having a last bit of coffee. Any reports on the weather in the mountains?

Zorro had called a friend in Huaraz earlier. Clear. Cool. Sunny. But it was a mountain weather report. We know how that is.

Pedro motioned toward the hotel entrance. Porters were helping an attractive woman and two middle-aged men with their bags and packs, heading toward the van. It seemed, to Zorro, like a lot of luggage for their short trip.

Even when he was young, people called him Zorro. It may have been his narrow ferret-like features and sharp nose, or his cautious manner. As he matured, he grew into his nickname—he was devious and cunning, a person who always seemed to have the biggest slice of the pie, the prettiest girl on his arm, money when he had no apparent source of income. He lived in Huaraz, where he operated as an intermediary between porters, guides, cooks, and muleteers, and the various parties that used Huaraz as a base for adventures in the mountains. He received a fee from the travelers as well as the laborers. He had friends and acquaintances in many places, and they said of him *"Se sabe que la gente."* He was adept in working his connections; *propinas* would come his way. Conflicting ideologies never bothered him, so long as money was involved.

For example, through one of his uncles he had a contact in the Ministry of the Interior who rewarded him for the answers to difficult questions from time to time. On his mother's side, a cousin believed fervently in the mission of the Sendero Luminoso and needed his help on occasion. Zorro was pleased to oblige. Today, however, was unusual. Contacts in both the administration and the insurrection asked him to perform the same service. There was a certain person they both were interested in and, by lucky circumstance, he had been hired to drive the van that was to carry that person to Huaraz. One trip and three paychecks. It was certain that Inti, his most revered god, was shedding his grace on him today.

Pedro hurried to the three travelers and greeted Larry with a warm embrace, after which Larry introduced him to Mercy and Wylie.

—This is Pedro de la Hoya, a friend and excellent guide who has been on three of my expeditions over the past two years. He made most of the arrangements for our visit to Chavin. But you also need to know that he just finished his second year of medical school and, I guess, will not be in the guide business for much longer.

Pedro shook hands with the other two travelers, said how happy he was to meet them, and promised them a safe but exciting trip across the mountains. Then he busied himself with arranging bags and luggage. Wylie and Larry helped load the baggage and Wylie, in the process, slipped something into Mercy's backpack. No one noticed.

The triumvirate stood beside the van awaiting further direction from Pedro. Mercy and Larry were dressed as the night before, but Wylie sported multi-zippered rambling trousers from the U.K., along with a plaid Viyella shirt. He tucked his trousers into polypropylene socks protruding from stiff leather climbing boots. Mercy was accustomed to seeing her father in dark suits, button-down shirts, and paisley ties. This more rugged look intrigued her, but she teased her father nonetheless.

—My, those are rad duds, Daddy.

Feigning shock, he turned to the professor.

—How about that! Four years of college and she talks like a valley girl.

He leaned forward, kissed her on the forehead and added,

—But she has other good qualities.

Their banter continued until Pedro said they were ready to board the van. He introduced Zorro to the travelers, and Mercy grinned at the slender young man and flashed an imaginary sword to carve a "Z" in the air. Apparently, the driver had not spent time during his formative years watching the masked swashbuckler on television. But Pedro understood Mercy's reference and laughed at her jest.

—Yes, the hero Zorro. But that is our driver's *apodo*—what you call a "nackname"? In Spanish *zorro* means fox. You are a foxy one, right, Zorro?

Pedro punched Zorro lightly in his biceps. Zorro smiled—weakly.

Pedro checked the bags lashed to the roof and made certain the travelers were comfortable in the back seats of the van. Zorro put it in gear and the vehicle began the eight-hour trip from sea level to ten-thousand-foot-high Huaraz. Early fog cleared by the time they reached the Pacific Highway by the ocean at Callao. They could see the gleaming highlights of the Cordillera Blanca in the far distance. Pedro slipped a cassette of flute and guitar music from the highlands into the player and they listened to the haunting tunes as the van sped along the highway.

It was Mercy's first visit to the Pacific coast of either of the Americas, and she gazed at the expansive ocean dissolving into distant fog, the spires, and bluffs rising from the shoreline, the massive ocean-facing dunes, and the powdery white-sand beaches as they drove north from Lima. She began to understand her father's fascination with the geography of Peru; this scenery was spectacular.

Kuitkowski sat diagonally behind Pedro and engaged in animated Spanish conversation with him as the van rumbled along the Pacific highway. He told Wylie and Mercy interesting tidbits of Pedro's background.

—Our medical student comes from Trujillo—an old Spanish city on the coast well north of where we will be heading. He finds time during the tourist season to guide tailored expeditions like ours. He likes Americans; they tip well. He is one of the few English-speaking guides who know the trails around the Huascarán National Park. He finds it unusual that we want to trek to Chavin de Huantar. Only students and what he calls "hippies" go there. Not often either.

The highway began to turn inland after they passed Chancay. Pedro confirmed with Zorro that they were ahead of schedule and could make a stop at the salt fields near the Bahía Salinas. Pedro explained that it would be an interesting rest stop. Soon they stretched their legs at the edge of what seemed to be endless fields of gleaming white salt slurry, drying in the warm sunlight.

—They sell it as "sea salt," said Pedro. For some reason, people in *el norte* pay much more for it when it has that name.

They wandered along the border of one of the fields for a while before Zorro called them back to the van. They needed to arrive in Barranca by noon, so he could refuel the van and the passengers before the swift ascent to the mountains. At Barranca, Pedro recommended a light lunch of cheese, bread, oranges, and beer. He cautioned the travelers not to drink anything but bottled water and beer, and not to order ice for their drinks.

Zorro returned with a full tank of diesel, and they began the ascent from Barranca to Huaraz. Pedro showed them their route on a tattered road map. Huaraz was situated in a valley between the Cordilleras Negra and Blanco, with the immense white mountains to the east. He pointed to the 13,500-foot pass they must cross before descending to Huaraz.

—You have probably heard this from our professor, but I need to remind you that the temperature drops more than three degrees Fahrenheit for every thousand feet we climb.

He pulled a worn blue wool sweater from his pack, as did the others.

—If the weather holds, I plan to make two stops. The first is at Rumi Siki, a great dark brown rock formation that looks like its name. Then I would like to show you the Puya raimondii, just before we pull into Huaraz.

Mercy was the first to ask.

—What does "Rumi Siki" mean?

—In English, it is "rump rock," but some American tourists call it "hard ass." You will see for yourselves.

Wylie and the professor enjoyed the definition, and Mercy resolved not to ask about the Puya raimondii.

As the road climbed gradually from the coast, the view of the ocean remained clear. The Pacific was even more impressive from a perspective that included the foothills to the Andes in the foreground and the curves of the roadway. Soon the "rump rock" came into view and Zorro shifted into lower gear as the climb steepened. The van lumbered slowly to the highest pass, and the passengers had their first unobstructed view of the great valley below and Lake Conococha, from which the Río Santa rises. Their sweaters barely kept out the cold, and their breathing quickened. Mercy and Wylie felt light-headed, while the professor seemed unaffected by the high altitude. Of course, thought Wylie, he'd lived up here for a year and a half.

A few miles farther, and they saw their first Puya raimondii, the thirty-foot-high bromeliad called the "Queen of the Andes." The first ten or so feet of the plant resembled a ball-shaped bush of spiky dark green leaves, like a well-manicured topiary of a golf ball on a tee. The rest of the plant was a twenty-foot-high bright green flower stalk shaped like an elongated pineapple stretched by giant hands. There were dozens of them on the hillside. Wylie persuaded the professor to photograph Mercy and him standing arm in arm in front of one of the giants.

As they began their descent into Huaraz, Kuitkowski explained that the plant was unique to the Andes at elevations of about thirteen thousand feet and bloomed only once, when cascades of thousands of creamy white flowers covered the tall stalk. Like most bromeliads, it died after it bloomed.

That information troubled Mercy. She was accustomed to the annual resurrection of flowers, and the idea of a glorious flower display followed by death seemed unnatural. She thought little of mortality; was it the unexpected confrontation of death in such a wild and exotic place that unnerved her? She looked back at the tall sentinels guarding the entrance to the snowy peaks beyond. A bank of clouds suddenly covered the sun, and the Puya raimondii darkened and became slate shafts protruding from umber bases, like a fire-blasted forest. Mercy was cold beneath her sweater.

Pedro assured them that their hotel was the best available in Huaraz, but that they should not expect accommodations equivalent to those in Lima. Huaraz was not a major tourist destination. As they drove through the central square, they saw a number of stone buildings with obvious cracks and broken corners. Kuitkowski explained that Huaraz was a city always close to the brink of disaster. In 1941, floodwaters and avalanche debris from a broken dam smashed a major part of its center. Then, in May 1970, the Ancash earthquake, which registered almost eight on the Richter scale, destroyed every significant building in the city center in forty-five seconds. Minutes later, a wall of icy mud carrying boulders and other debris rushed through and destroyed the north half of the city. Of a city population of twenty thousand, less than two hundred survived.

As the enormity of the disaster, still commemorated by the broken walls and bits of rubble surrounding them, sank in, Pedro told them the story of Yungay, the village not far from Huaraz, the one they would visit before beginning their trek. The quake broke off part of the north wall of Mount Huascarán, causing an avalanche of glacial ice and rock half a mile wide and a mile long. It cascaded for eleven miles at over three hundred miles an hour. Moments later the entire village was covered. A handful of residents who had climbed to the hillside cemetery survived.

—Wow! Mother Nature is harsh in these mountains, Mercy said.

The van completed its tour of the central square and pulled into a side street. Their hotel was a two-story wooden structure surrounded by smaller homes. There were windows around the entrance with an interior of varnished local woods. Small dining areas were located on each side of the entrance, a reception desk opposite, and a long flight of stairs led to bedrooms. They were relieved to discover a crude but functioning bathroom with each bedroom.

The thin mattress on Wylie's bed slid through the gaps between slats and offered a corrugated sleeping surface. That did not help the pounding headache that developed while it was still dark outside. The rooster with the defective internal timer who crowed at the North Star thwarted further attempts at sleep, and Wylie was not at his best as he labored down the wooden stairs to breakfast. He sorely missed the Sheraton hotel in Lima.

Mercy and Pedro sat at a table by a window, silhouetted against sharp morning light that affected Wylie's red-rimmed eyes like a paper cut. He mumbled a morning greeting to the young people and sat in a rustic chair next to them. Kuitkowski was not in sight. Pedro looked solicitously at Wylie and asked,

—Headache?

—Like you wouldn't believe!

Pedro motioned to the server, a woman dressed in bright clothing and a felt hat. She scurried over to Wylie and offered him a large cup filled with steaming tan liquid. It smelled slightly rancid.

—It is coca tea, said Pedro, a mild narcotic. It will help clear the cobwebs, especially if you take these with the tea.

Pedro offered two white tablets he took from a pill bottle in his pocket.

—This is Motrin, a form of ibuprofen. It is usually taken for things like joint pain, but I have found it is quite effective for *soroche*—altitude sickness. The altitude—it affects people differently, but everyone notices something above nine thousand feet, even if it is only shortness of breath.

Mercy nodded agreement.

—That's right, Daddy. I don't have a headache, but climbing a flight of stairs makes me a bit dizzy.

Wylie took the pills with his tea. The warm liquid soothed, and he began to feel better after a few minutes. Another cup of tea arrived.

Pedro spoke of their trip.

—The professor is wandering around the town now. He said he wanted to revisit some places he knew from his last time here. He and I talked about places to visit last night.

He went on to explain that it was necessary to spend at least three days in Huaraz to acclimate to the ten-thousand-foot altitude. Mercy wanted to know more about the "thin air." Pedro obliged.

—The amount of oxygen in air is about twenty-one percent, no matter what the altitude. As we move higher the pressure of the air drops, so the air gets "thinner," and the total amount of available oxygen lessens. We need to stay at this altitude while our bodies generate more red blood cells that absorb more oxygen.

Mercy, the liberal arts major, wanted to know how her body made more red blood cells. Wylie was not sure he needed to know. Pedro, the medical student, was eager to explain.

He pointed to his left rib cage to show the location of his spleen and said the organ stored a supply of red blood cells. As the spleen emptied of blood, the marrow of certain bones created more blood cells, but the process was slow. Three or four days would be needed before they could continue to higher altitudes and the high pass on the way to Chavin. Even then, they would notice fatigue and possibly dizziness. Mountain climbers called it the high-altitude "bends."

Kuitkowski pushed through the outside door into the dining room. Wylie was relieved to see that he was short of breath and moving slowly. The adventuresome professor was not superman after all. He offered a morning greeting and pulled out a chair next to Wylie. The morning was spectacular, he said. Crisp and clear. The white mountains were brilliant. Was there coffee?

Coffee interested Wylie as well, until he saw the lightly rusted tin of Nescafé appear on the table next to a pot of boiling water. Unfazed, the professor took a heaping spoonful of the brown stuff and stirred it into his cup. He sat back in his chair and asked Pedro about the day's itinerary.

Zorro would be with them for two more days before he had to return to Lima, so they would use the van to explore areas south and north of Huaraz for two days. On the third day, they would gather their mule driver and porters, collect the needed gear, and camp out their first night in an open area just above the city. Their trek would begin in earnest the next day. For today, Pedro planned to return to Lake Conococha for a lunch of fresh trout at the village there. Then they could look at the remains of Yungay and wander along the Río Santa to see the waterfalls and spectacular views of the river gorge.

It was so, except that an afternoon rainsquall descended as they walked along the river's edge, and the scramble up the bank to the van tired them quickly. They discovered the healing qualities of local beer at their hotel and everyone slept better that night.

The following morning, Pedro explained that north of Huaraz the black and white mountain ranges converged at a place called Cañón del Pato. Yes, it was the duck canyon, but no one knew why it had that name. The Río Santa coursed through that place between the canyons, at one point no more than six meters wide, with the dark crests of the *cordilleras* looming high above. Nearby was a swinging bridge that offered views of the formations caused by the eons of rushing waters carving away the crust of the mountains.

On their way to the canyon, Zorro stopped at a number of pre-Incan ruins that fascinated Kuitkowski. After visiting half a dozen, Mercy and Wylie suffered information overload from the professor's description of the differences among the represented cultures. Did the Chimú precede the Moche, or the other way around? Both were relieved when Pedro announced the next stop would be at the canyon.

Zorro had not only advised his contacts in Huaraz of the arrival of the person he had been asked to identify, but also of his daily itinerary. Consequently, he was not surprised to see a dusty police car parked beside the road a few hundred yards from the gravel parking area for the canyon. The parking area itself contained a bright green Chevrolet with "Taxi" painted on its sides, and a battered pickup that belonged to workers for the nearby hydroelectric facility. Near the trailhead leading to the canyon, two barrel-chested Indians stood beside mules with colorful saddles and wooden stirrups—in case one of the few tourists arriving would like to ride down the trail. It was a sunny day, but the ridges above cast much of the canyon in shadow.

They walked slowly down the trail because of the altitude. They were not acclimated yet. As promised, the multihued high walls of the canyon had an ethereal beauty, rugged and sinuous. The walls were too steep to support either agriculture or livestock, but swallows and other canyon birds were evident. Pedro laughed as he watched a flight of swallows cascade through the air.

—No ducks, he said.

They continued on the path to the swinging bridge. The professor and Mercy walked happily across, permitting the bridge to sway just a bit. That motion, the altitude, and the long distance from the bridge to the river gave Wylie a queasy feeling. He was grateful to return to the security of land.

They climbed the gently sloping path back to the parking area. As they reached the trailhead, they noticed two policemen in blue jackets with large pistols displayed on black leather belts. The taxi had disappeared, the police car parked in its place. They seemed to be waiting for them.

The larger of the two pointed toward Wylie.

—Dr. Cypher.

It was not a question. It sounded more like an accusation.

Wylie nodded in confusion. How could these men know his name? He looked at Mercy, who echoed his bewilderment. Kuitkowski stepped forward and began speaking to the men in Spanish, as did Pedro. They might as well have been talking to the canyon walls. The police officer brushed them aside and stood directly in front of Wylie.

—There is a problem with papers. You will come with us.

—What papers? demanded Wylie.

—Papers.

A large brown hand clasped Wylie's arm and propelled him toward the police car. The other travelers stepped forward to complain, and the other officer confronted them, legs apart and hand on his holster. He did not look as though he would entertain any questions. Helplessly, Pedro, Kuitkowski, and Mercy watched as a police officer shoved Wylie into the back seat, gravel spewed from the tires and the car worked its way to the highway.

Zorro waited for them in the van. They are going to be worried, he thought.

The two men with mules observed the police car struggle up the hill. Tall grasses and brush had obscured their view of the proceedings, and they were not sure whether Wylie voluntarily accompanied the police. They were sure he had not attempted to escape, however. The information they received about the suspect gringo was not clear. They stared thoughtfully after the police car.

—So, said one, it is possible the Yankee works with the police.

—*Si.*

—We know for certain that he is with them now.

— *Claro.*

—They will want to know this.

—I will take the message tonight, but it will take some time to find its way to Ayacucho.

14

Mercy's eyes blazed with impotent fury as she watched the police car disappear around a curve in the road leading to Huaraz. She was overwhelmed emotionally and intellectually. She feared for Wylie as she replayed the bizarre scene of his abduction—two untidy policemen in a third world country who knew his name ramming him into the back of their car—no word of their destination, nothing said about the reason for his arrest. "Documents." What did that mean? She considered the numerous levels on which the entire episode made no sense. Ultimately, the brazen injustice of it dominated her feelings. Her jaw stiffened; she held back tears, and turned to the professor, also staring after the police car.

—Do you have any idea what's going on? You've been in Peru a lot...she choked back a sob...do you have any idea what the hell is going on?

—I'm sorry. I don't have a clue, he said, in Mercy's opinion, too calmly.

Wylie told her that Larry was now a good friend. She did not understand why he was not more agitated.

—Look, we need to keep our wits about us and concentrate on finding your dad. We can get emotional later, after we locate him.

The professor offered her water from his canteen and turned to Zorro and Pedro, both waiting by the van.

—You both got a good look at those cops. Have you ever seen them before or know where their precinct was located?

Zorro was spared the need to lie; although he lived in Huaraz most of his life, he had not seen them before. Likewise, Pedro could offer no help.

Mercy was still fuming as they left the parking area, and did not calm down until they reached their hotel.

Kuitkowski went directly to the woman behind the reception desk and spread out a pocket map of the city. He and the receptionist bent their heads over the map, and the woman called over a porter and waiter from the little restaurant. They conferred and pointed; the professor made notes on the map. He soon marked the location of all the police stations and offices in the city.

For a town of almost one hundred thousand inhabitants, Huaraz was compact, a large rectangle of city blocks squeezed into a valley bounded on the north by the Río Santa and the base of the Cordillera Negro on the south. The Cordillera Blanca was to the east. Their hotel stood on an elevated point looking toward the river.

The professor and Pedro stood at the entrance, trying to guess how long it would take to visit each of the places marked on the professor's map. Mercy stood with them. She decided to accompany Pedro and Zorro during that afternoon's quest around the city center, while the Professor followed his own inquiries.

Tomorrow Zorro needed to return the van to Lima. Local transportation would be available if Wylie was not found before then. They would postpone plans to begin their trek. Zorro confirmed that the porters and helpers already hired would wait a bit longer before beginning the trip across the mountains.

Now that they had established a plan with the clear purpose of finding her father, Mercy felt relieved.

—It must be some kind of misunderstanding, she said as half a question to Pedro, who nodded in approval.

—Most likely. The police up here are not a well-trained bunch and they sometimes overreact to whatever orders they are given. Your father is probably waiting for us right now.

That was not so. Just then Wylie was sitting in a cell with adobe walls, staring at two soggy quesadillas in a tarnished metal dish and a cup of warm water. That was his dinner. His guards had removed all his valuables—watch, wallet, glasses, daypack and boots— and his requests to contact the hotel, his daughter or superior officers had been rebuffed. With his halting Spanish, he managed to understand from overheard conversation that his captors needed to consult with *el jefe* in the morning. Apparently, *el jefe* had left for the day. Wylie prepared himself for a disturbed and sleepless night on the steel cot next to the inedible food.

Wylie Cypher, Korean War veteran, distinguished graduate of Princeton and Harvard Law School, partner in the renowned law firm of Biddle and Ofstrosky, and model citizen, sat on a hard wooden chair in a dank adobe-walled room in his undershorts, his hands tied behind his back, the tip of a machete prodding the soft and tender flesh of his scrotum. He tried to avoid looking at the little splotches of blood on his shorts caused by careless probing with the machete.

The larger of the two police officers who had detained Wylie at the Cañón de Pato wielded the machete. Ernesto entered law enforcement obliquely by marrying the alcalde's daughter, and the alcalde recommended his new son-in-law to the prefecture for service in the police force. He had served for five years, and was the senior member of the five-man team in his precinct of Huaraz.

After Zorro reported Wylie's presence to the assistant chief in his office by the central square, he selected Ernesto to detain and interview the gringo. Ernesto had demonstrated very persuasive interview techniques in the past and, since the police in Huaraz were not sure about exactly what the gringo had done, it would be up to Ernesto to pry out that information. Accordingly, after *el jefe* arrived that morning and Ernesto advised him about their prisoner, *el jefe* immediately provided authority for his interrogation. Ernesto and an assistant promptly hustled Wylie from his cell, stripped him, and tied him to a wooden chair in the interview chamber adjacent to the large room that served as entrance, office, and conference area. Ernesto straddled another chair in the small room and hit Wylie in the face a few times to gain his attention.

It had not occurred to Ernesto that his prisoner would not be conversant in Spanish. The interrogator knew only a few English words, mainly from watching undubbed television programs from the United States. His adjutant, however, recalled some English from a winter spent in Florida many years ago. So the adjutant stood in the doorway to the room, holding a worn English–Spanish dictionary to the light, trying to make sense of the conversation in the room. The situation was rife for failure in communication.

—*¡Documentos!* demanded Ernesto. This was after a thorough search of Wylie's backpack and clothing had disclosed nothing.

By now, Wylie had reached the inescapable conclusion that his present situation had something to do with the floppy disks that Raoul had passed on to him. Certainly, were it known to them, the authorities must be interested in assuring their retrieval. What he could not understand was how those authorities were even aware that he possessed them. Until now, it had not occurred to him there might be a connection between Raoul's execution and the transfer of those damning documents. However, with the taste of his own blood in his mouth and the Ernesto's pitiless eyes staring from his face to his genitals, the association became clear.

Under ordinary circumstances, Wylie would have relied on cogent arguments and rhetoric to seek resolution to his dilemma. Or, as demonstrated during his military service, he would fight with whatever weapons were at hand. These were not ordinary circumstances, however.

—*No entiendo*, he managed to say.

Ernesto was not pleased. He spoke more slowly and loudly in an effort to penetrate the language barrier. As he did so, he raised his machete and sliced a two-inch gash under Wylie's left rib cage.

—*¡Docu . . . men . . . tos!* he roared.

—*Shit!* Wylie replied.

Both men glared at each other for long moments. Ernesto turned to his adjutant and, although his victim's reply was abundantly clear, requested a translation.

—*Mierda*, the adjutant offered.

—*Claro*, said Ernesto, and pushed his lips tightly together. The tip of his machete wavered again over Wylie's private parts. He asked something of the adjutant. The policeman seemed to Wylie to be demanding a translation of something he intended to say to his victim. Many words came quickly, and Wylie caught only *gringo*, *huevos*, and *corto*. None of it sounded good.

As the adjutant strained to find the correct English phrases, he turned toward the anteroom to find stronger light. He was surprised to see a large, dark object crash through a pane of glass in the door, roll across the floor, and come to rest a few feet in front *el jefe's* desk. *El jefe* leaned over his desk to peer at the object with a look of mild surprise. The bomb, a makeshift affair of black powder, dynamite, ball bearings and six penny nails encased in the top half of a double boiler, exploded, ripping upward through *el jefe's* desk, permanently freezing his face in that look of mild surprise. Moments later two men in balaclavas crashed through the door, guns drawn, and surveyed the damage. The bottom half of *el jefe*, like most of his desk, was missing. The two other officers in the room suffered from shrapnel wounds and were groggy with concussions from the force of the explosion. Pistol shots rang out and they fell, sprawling, to the floor. One held both hands to his throat; his cries degenerating into a ghastly bubbling sound, like smoke drawn through a hookah pipe.

The force of the explosion funneled into the interrogation room. The adjutant fell backward, saving himself from hitting the floor by grabbing the doorsill. Ernesto rocked sideways in his chair, losing his balance. In an instinctive reaction, fueled by fear, adrenaline and cortisol, and the chaos of the moment, Wylie kicked upward with his left foot, trying to unseat Ernesto, rising up on his right leg to pull his hands up over the back of his chair. As Wylie's left foot rose, Ernesto fell backward from his chair, trying to regain his balance by thrusting his machete forward, like a tightrope walker's pole. Wylie's foot moved up, the machete out and down. The razor-sharp blade cleanly sliced off Wylie's little toe, and the blade followed the severed digit to the dusty floor of the room. Blood began to flow immediately, but Wylie felt no pain.

Then the following things happened simultaneously in that little room.

The adjutant, still clutching his dictionary, turned to face the intruders from the door way to the anteroom, a look of disbelief on his face. He dropped the dictionary to reach for his pistol and discovered his holster was empty. The pistol was in a drawer in the desk in the other room. He moved slowly into the room, his hands chest-high, palms open—a supplication to the two masked men who turned toward him. It happened so quickly, he almost did not hear the shotgun blast. An incarnadine blotch of brightest pink appeared on his chest, between his palms. He was dead before his knees hit the floor.

Wylie stumbled backward over his chair, but failed to pull his hands above the back. Half in the chair, he crashed to the floor, crushing his hands on the stone pavement, breaking two knuckles of his right hand. The pain soared from his hand to neural receptors like wildfire; his hand was an inferno. In an effort to relieve his agony, he wrenched his arms free of the chair, facing the doorway to the anteroom, where he saw the adjutant had already sagged to his knees. He saw that Ernesto was on the floor, still tangled in his chair, struggling to recover his machete, trying to draw his pistol at the same time.

Wylie looked desperately around the little room. Escape through the anteroom? Impossible.

Behind him, he discovered another door that seemed to show bright light around its frame. He hobbled to it, hands still secured behind his back, and saw that it opened in. He turned around to grasp the handle, soon slick with blood flowing from his hand. The handle might as well have been covered with grease; it would not budge. He stumbled and began to slide down the front of the door.

Ernesto, wild-eyed, glared in his direction and raised his pistol. In desperation, Wylie pushed against the door with his shoulder. The bottom panel broke away and he fell through, hitting cobbled pavement in bright afternoon sunlight. Ernesto managed one shot that dug harmlessly into an upper door panel. His instinct was to pursue his prisoner. He finally untangled himself from the broken chair, found his pistol, and began to crawl to the broken door, brilliant sunlight playing across his features, emphasizing the beads of sweat dripping from nose and eyebrows.

He thought he heard a noise behind him, from the anteroom, and paused, looking over his shoulder, over the body of the adjutant, into the dark stillness of the room. All was quiet. Then slow footsteps moved toward the doorway. Ernesto rolled onto his elbows and pointed his pistol toward the anteroom.

—Ernesto? a familiar voice called out.

He was too shocked to answer, but he lowered his guard. His wife's brother peered around the doorframe.

—There you are, he said.

He pointed the shotgun at Ernesto and pulled the trigger to discharge both barrels simultaneously.

The Sendero Luminoso lookout for the terrorist attack stood facing the square in front of the Huaraz police station. He held an AK-47 casually at his side and watched diligently for any sign of enemy activity. That was unlikely. The communist forces, now experienced in raiding police stations, carefully planned their attack, which they executed swiftly seconds after companions cut communication lines. From the sounds in the building, all must have gone well. Shots and cries had ceased. The door behind him opened slowly and the first of his comrades slipped out. With his attention focused elsewhere, he did not notice the bizarre sight of half-naked Wylie Cypher stumbling from the back of the building and trying to navigate a side street.

Completely disoriented, Wylie squinted at the bright light reflected from the whitewashed walls of the alleyway. He swayed at the curb, hands still bound behind his back, blood oozing onto his polka-dot Brooks Brothers shorts. Where the little toe had been, the bleeding lessened and the area crusted over with a slurry of dirt and blood. As he stumbled over the cobblestones, two little children sitting in doorways rose. One ran away, the other toward him, seeking to help. Wylie stepped forward and raked the open wound on his foot against a raised stone. The pain literally took his breath away. He raised his foot in anguish and stumbled, falling against the curb, striking his shoulder and smashing his temple. The brightness of the walls above him slowly faded, followed by an explosion of light and then . . . complete darkness. The child prodded his shoulder, but Wylie did not move. A low moan escaped his lips and he was silent.

"*Enfermera, enfermera*," cried the child as he poked his head through Claudia's front door. Even though she was busy with her two small children, managing the affairs of her household, and supporting Fredo who was now an area superintendent, Claudia continued her practice of providing rudimentary medical help to neighbors in need.

By the time Claudia arrived at the street behind the police station, the attackers had vanished and a knot of confused and angry people had gathered in front. The carnage was brutal, and the foul smell of sudden death reached into the square. Clearly, there were no survivors, yet the curious peered in for a glance at the five bodies. One of the officers' wives, surrounded by friends, collapsed on a bench, keening high-pitched wails of grief. The ones who first arrived at the scene after the attackers left called an ambulance and police in another district, but no one expected a rapid response.

Claudia took all this in as she rushed to the strange body in the back alley. At first she supposed the man was another officer who managed to escape the killing zone. However, this man was tall and very fair with light brown hair—and the most peculiar undershorts she had ever seen. Also, his hands were bound behind him with some kind of tape. He must have been a prisoner. All this she concluded as she examined the wounded man. His breathing was shallow but his pulse held steady. The cut in his side was not as deep as she first thought, but matted hair and blood obscured the wound at his temple. Blood covered both hands. His pupils seemed normal, though it was difficult to tell in the strong afternoon light. Altogether, he did not seem in critical condition, but his injuries definitely needed attention. She cut the tape securing his hands with scissors from her first-aid kit and rolled him onto his back. Not a bad-looking gringo, she thought.

She considered next steps. If the wounded man was a prisoner, it probably was not because he was a petty thief or criminal offender. More likely he was a political prisoner—the police were picking up many of them as the Sendero Luminoso intensified its attacks on the administration's infrastructure. If he was an enemy of the administration, did that mean he was a friend of the Shining Path? Should she risk turning him over to the local medical teams, who would deliver him to the hospital and inform the authorities? She checked his pulse again—still strong. She decided to have him carried to her home and tend to his immediate needs. She sent one of the children standing nearby to tell Fredo at his office of the day's events. He would help her decide what to do about the gringo.

By now, some of those gathered in front of the building had noticed the activity down the street. Claudia motioned for a man with a mule cart to approach and others helped her load the injured man onto it. The cart bumped its way along the cobbled streets and carried the unconscious Wylie to her home, where neighbors moved him to a leather couch in Fredo's study.

Many terrible things had happened that afternoon. Allegiances, responsibility, and outcomes were unclear. It would be unwise to gossip too soon about anything they had seen. The townspeople would quietly ignore Wylie's journey to the Maestro's house for a day or two. Even then, there had to be a very good reason to squander such a valuable thing as the truth.

Claudia washed his wounds and applied antibiotic ointment—the best she could manage now. There was a deep cut where he hit his temple, but the bleeding had stopped. She decided to repair the gash where the little toe had been by drawing the flesh together with thread and needle. Gauze and tape protected the wounds in his side and on his hands. She did not know how to deal with his two depressed and wobbly knuckles. She turned his head so the blood collecting under the skin by his ear was visible. It was a very angry bruise.

Pedro, Mercy, and Kuitkowski continued their visits to police stations and the administrative headquarters in Huaraz the next day. "*Lo siento*," was the uniform reply to their questions.

—Very sorry, but we do not know of Señor Cypher, your father, or anyone resembling the gringo you describe. We will look into it. Try again tomorrow.

They discovered there were gaps in their list of police stations, and they experienced numerous delays. By the day after Wylie's abduction, they had visited fewer than half the places on their map, and Mercy was becoming frantic. This situation was bordering on the surreal.

On that same day, a garbled message reached Lucho at his office in Ayacucho. It seemed to confirm that Cypher had met with the police in Huaraz the previous afternoon. He deliberated whether such sketchy information warranted continuing their investigation of the man. He decided he could not ignore a confirmed meeting with the police. If they did and it was later discovered that Dr. Cypher was an agent of the administration his rising star in the party would be extinguished. His superior agreed it was a serious matter. Among other things, the Sendero Luminoso was in the retribution business. If this Yankee had a hand in Raoul's death, he would be eliminated.

Lucho gladly accepted the assignment of discovering the truth. All flights to Huaraz were canceled that day because of weather, but he could be there tomorrow. It took almost two hours to connect a scratchy telephone call to his man in Huaraz. Lucho would arrive on tomorrow's afternoon flight.

Pedro banged heavily on Kuitkowski's door, loud enough to arouse Mercy in her room down the hall. He shoved the local newspaper at the professor and pointed to one of the five photographs on the front page.

—Wasn't he the one who picked up Dr. Cypher?

Kuitkowski stared at the photograph of a burly man with a Zapata mustache.

—It certainly looks like him.

He straightened out the paper, read the story of the attack on the police station, and studied again the photographs of the five slain officers. The article stated that the Shining Path accepted responsibility for the assault. He reread the story. There was no mention of a prisoner, no report of additional fatalities.

The professor was grim faced as Mercy rushed toward them down the hall, buttoning her sweater.

—There is some information, Kuitkowski began.

He reviewed the article in the newspaper for her and showed her the photographs. She studied them carefully, torn between elation and despair, relieved that Pedro had discovered a possible way to find Wylie, distressed that there was no mention of her father in the newspaper account of the attack. She looked at the two men and pointed to the slain officer who looked like the one who led her father away. There was a numbed silence as the three stood together in the entrance to Kuitkowski's room.

Pedro led them downstairs to weak coffee, huevos rancheros, and refried beans. Kuitkowski suggested that they should reconsider their approach to finding Wylie.

—We now have a good idea where the police took Wylie. We can forget about making more fruitless visits to other police stations.

—Yes, agreed Pedro. And there may be other information that the press can provide.

They decided that Pedro would go to the newspaper office and talk with the reporters who had written the article. His objective was to discover whether there was any sign of a prisoner.

Mercy and the professor would visit the area of the attack on the police station and talk with people who might have seen something. They understood that the residents there might be suspicious of a gringo and gringa asking questions, but they needed to take action of some kind—especially Mercy, whose concern for her father, now missing two days, fanned her internal flames of guilt for having suggested this adventure with Wylie in the first place.

Pedro joined them near the destroyed police station later that morning, having learned nothing about a prisoner from the reporters who wrote about the attack. They questioned passersby in the central square and talked with shop owners around the plaza. Their inquiries received blank looks, requests for money and open hostility. They received no helpful information.

Fredo was surprised by the message from Claudia. A wounded gringo taken to their home? That was the ultimate personification of Claudia's penchant for taking in strays. He guessed it had something to do with the attack on the police station, but he had no foreknowledge of it. By design, there was no communication among cells. He left his office earlier than usual and walked the seven or eight blocks to their home. He diverted his usual route to walk by the police station. It showed signs of the attack— the front door was smashed, broken frames hung from windows, and there was medical detritus on the pavement—left over, he guessed, from failed attempts to revive the slain officers.

Claudia had washed Wylie's body and was refreshing the antibiotic salve on his wounds as Fredo entered the room to look at the unconscious man. Except for the bloody undershorts that lay on the floor near the couch, there was no indication of his origins. The only thing Claudia could confirm was that he was not Jewish. Claudia recounted in detail the events of the afternoon, and Fredo agreed that the stranger must have been a prisoner. He agreed also that turning him over to the authorities, even those as benign as the ambulance staff, was a mistake.

—I know it is a cliché, he said, but until I get more information from our people, let's assume that the enemy of our enemy is our friend.

He looked more closely at the man on the couch.

—That is an ugly bruise. When do you think he will wake up?

Claudia said that his vital signs were strong. She thought she noticed that one of his pupils responded only sluggishly to bright light, but she could not be sure. The fall on the curbstone probably shook his brain a bit, but sleep was a great healer.

—Let's see how he is in the morning.

Fredo agreed. In the meantime, he would make a few calls. Perhaps the raiders knew something about the prisoner in the police station.

The next day Fredo discovered that the raiders were unaware of any prisoner when they made their attack. Their perception was perhaps clouded by their excitement about and single-minded concentration on slaughtering the hated police.

The prisoner, meanwhile, had developed a chill and was sleeping fitfully under winter blankets. Claudia was concerned. She had Fredo contact a trusted medical doctor who treated wounded members of the cause. He arrived mid-morning, examined the wounded man, and praised Claudia's suturing of Wylie's foot. He pumped two ampoules of antibiotic into the man's veins and left two more for Claudia to administer. A few hours later, the man breathed more slowly and began to sweat under the heavy blankets. Claudia took that as a good sign. By the next morning, color had returned to the man's face and, although he still slept, he began to swallow water when Claudia held up his head and placed a cup to his lips. He was murmuring unintelligible things.

Late on the second afternoon since Wylie's arrest, Pedro stood on the corner of the plaza diagonally across from the ruined police station, waving to the taxi Larry and Mercy were taking to their hotel. Discouraged by almost a full day of disappointing interviews, Mercy gave in to a growing feeling of sickness, reluctantly asking to return to the hotel. Larry went with her.

It seemed to Pedro that the presence of the bombed station, unchanged except that someone had boarded up the entranceway, cast a pall on the vibrant activity normally associated with life around the plaza. No laughter; no games; no men drinking in the shade of a Pisco bar awning. Instead, a few dogs scratched themselves in the dust of the road, two old men played cards on a wooden bench, a man pushed a card laden with pots and pans. In the afternoon shade from a tall building a child vendor stood, holding a dusty tray with combs, lighters, Chiclets, and candy.

Pedro had not noticed him before; perhaps he came to the plaza after school to try to earn a few *soles*. The boy picked at a scab on his neck as Pedro approached. The guide selected some chewing gum from the tray and casually asked if the boy was nearby when the bandits attacked the station. Warily, the boy cocked his head and looked up at Pedro, faintly nodded his head in affirmation, then looked at his feet. Pedro regained his attention by dropping two *soles* on the tray, kneeled down so his eyes were on the same level as the boy's, and said

—You seem like a very clever boy who knows what goes on here. Tell me, did you see a gringo near the station when it was attacked?

The boy picked up the coins and scuffled his feet. He pointed over his shoulder and smirked.

— *Dónde.*

In a low voice, the boy confirmed that he had seen a tall, near-naked gringo stagger from the police station.

Pedro now held out two five-*sol* silver pieces and demanded to know more. The boy showed Pedro where he had been watching as the attack began. He had seen the entire incident from a half a block away. He told Pedro that the gringo fell down and stopped moving, and then some people carted him away.

—*¿Dónde?* asked Pedro.

—*La casa de Maestro.*

The silver pieces fell onto the boy's tray, and Pedro asked where was the *casa de Maestro.* It was a short distance, and the boy took him there.

Pedro stood in the street a few houses away and examined the modest home carefully, noting entrances, its distance from adjoining buildings, and the swing set at the rear. He walked quickly to the central square and found an ancient taxi to take him to the hotel.

Heavy storms over the Cordillera Central diverted his plane, and Lucho arrived at the little airport in Huaraz more than an hour late. His contact had nothing new to report. The Cypher person was last seen getting into a police car, destination unknown, and inquiries about his present location produced no results. There was, however, a photograph of him and his daughter standing by a mule at the entrance to the Cañón de Pato. The mule driver assigned to watch for him had taken it surreptitiously as the gringo posed for his guide. Lucho praised him for that and examined the picture—a tall, light-haired gringo with a pretty blond gringa. It certainly would be helpful to their search, though he wondered why all these gringos looked so much alike.

His contact had a telephone in his home that Lucho used to speak with two other contacts in Huaraz and arrange to continue the search for the Cypher person tomorrow. There was excited discussion about the success of their raid on the police station. All the other stations in the city were now on high alert, and police activity in the city was limited to guarding other police officers and stations. Not only had the raid succeeded in killing police, it succeeded in destabilizing the city. It was a perfect result of Chairman Gonzalo's classic tactical plan.

Lucho planned to assist in the search tomorrow, but also make time for a visit to Fredo and Claudia. He had not been with them for many months and was eager to see their new baby and their eldest, his goddaughter. He brought along a Minnie Mouse doll for her.

In the meantime, they planned to canvass hotels, tourist offices, outfitters, and guides, looking for the gringos Zorro had brought to their attention. If he guessed correctly, the Cypher person had not spent much time with the police and was now planning to do what tourists here did—go trekking in the Cordillera Blanca.

The stars were out when Pedro returned to the hotel. Mercy and the professor awaited him in the bar off the lobby, Larry nursing a large Cristal beer and Mercy sipping a Coke that, with coca tea, was supposed to help her upset stomach. They brightened immediately when they saw the huge grin on Pedro's face.

—I am almost certain I know where he is, he announced in a stage whisper.

The guide recounted his conversation with the boy, which he later confirmed with another older, more reliable resident. It seemed that the Maestro's wife provided first aid to people in the neighborhood. She had taken a wounded gringo to her home directly after the attack on the police station. Pedro was uncertain why she chose to do that instead of waiting for an ambulance—perhaps the delay involved. No one had seen the gringo for two days; he was probably still there.

Mercy was so relieved she hugged Pedro, and said,

—So, let's go!

—Perhaps we should consider this for a few moments before rushing off, suggested the professor. Banging on a strange door in the middle of the night might not be the smartest thing to do right now. Maybe we could find out more about this situation tomorrow and approach the woman then.

After further discussion, Mercy reluctantly agreed. They would hurry to the casa de Maestro tomorrow morning.

There was, however, a delay. Mercy suffered severe intestinal discomfort. She tried to ignore the problem so she could continue the search for Wylie, but the professor and Pedro convinced her to rest, take healing medicine, and join the search later in the day.

—Look, everything will be all right. Those pills will help a great deal. Just keep drinking bottled water, and you should be feeling better by noon. Pedro and I will go to the *casa de Maestro* and look around—whatever the result, I will come back to see how you are around noon and we will find your dad.

As promised, Kuitkowski returned at noon, found Mercy waiting in the lobby, nervously tapping her heels on the stone floor. Kuitkowski said there was nothing to report and they took a taxi to meet Pedro at the plaza nearest the *casa de Maestro* where they met Pedro and strolled to a position across from the home. Mercy discovered that one of the hardest things she ever did was to engage in a pretend conversation while her insides were raw with concern for his father. They moved from time to time, and Pedro wandered to the end of the block and back.

Soon a large young man wearing a dark coat and carrying a stuffed animal came around the corner and bounded up the steps to the front door. He knocked with the heel of a strangely shaped hand. The door quickly opened and another young man greeted him warmly. They embraced and entered the house. Before the door closed, Mercy caught a glimpse of a young woman rising from a chair to greet the newcomer.

There was no sign of her father.

The slamming of the front door caused Wylie to stir. His first sensation was of a headache of gargantuan proportions, caused by a combination of high altitude and the blow to his head. Afternoon light pouring through a window was like glass spears flung into his eyes. Aside from the headache, pockets of pain called his attention to other parts of his body, the most pronounced on his left foot, which throbbed in synchronization with his heartbeat. He groaned, then found internal resources to raise himself on his elbows and looked around.

He was on a leather couch in a small room with faded flowery wallpaper, a single window, a wooden desk, and a couple of chairs. A sheet and thin blankets covered him, and when he looked under the sheet, he discovered he was buck-naked. As he struggled to raise himself higher on the couch, the door to the little room opened and three people, two men and a woman, stared at him.

Lucho knew immediately that the wounded man was the Cypher person in the photograph from the Cañón del Pato. However, the story Claudia told of rescuing him from the police station and the presumption that the police tortured him challenged his supposition that this person collaborated with the administration—that he was somehow responsible for Raoul's death. The way Cypher looked now— pale, confused, and disoriented— reinforced the idea that he was harmless. Also, finding this wanted man in his best friend's study was co-incidental beyond belief. It was too easy; guilty people were much more elusive.

Claudia approached Wylie, and he involuntarily drew the thin blankets to cover himself. She smiled in relief that her patient was conscious and seemed to be aware of his surroundings. She touched his forehead and examined the cut at his temple. No fever, and a clean scab covered the wound. Wylie remained confused but made no attempt to resist her care.

—*¿Quieres algo de comer o beber?* she asked, but received only a befuddled gaze. She made motions of drinking and eating and Wylie nodded.

In a weak voice, he said,

—*Sí.*

As Claudia hurried to find sustenance for her patient, Lucho and Fredo withdrew from the doorway to confer in the next room. Fredo was as incredu-lous as his friend to discover that his Good Samaritan wife had rescued a man wanted by the Shining Path—for complicity in murder, no less. Lucho asked for his friend's advice.

—Obviously, the idea that he is an agent of the administration does not sup-port his being tortured by the police—unless there was some sort of falling-out or double-dealing. You know, as I do, that there are people who work for both sides. But this one hardly looks clever enough for that.

Lucho shook his head and replied,

—Looks can be deceiving, but in this case, I agree. Nevertheless, we need to verify his involvement. Will you help me question him later? I have no English.

Fredo smiled ruefully.

—And what makes you think I know English? I know more Chinese than English. The English I have is from subtitles on American movies.

They looked at each other.

—This could be a problem. How about Claudia?

—The same as me—and I don't think she would relish interrogating this man the way we usually do it.

—Yes, this could be a problem.

Twenty minutes after the young man with the stiffed animal entered the house the three watchers decided they had waited long enough. Larry agreed to wait in the street while Mercy and Pedro knocked on the door. Mercy could hardly contain her excitement at the thought of seeing Wylie again.

The two men stopped talking as they heard the rapping on the door. Fredo uttered a mild curse and wondered who the hell that could be. He opened the door to two strangers—a vaguely familiar young blond woman and a dark-haired young man in a leather jacket. He asked them what they wanted, but before they could answer, a commotion occurred behind him. Claudia was entering the study with a plate of warm food and a glass of milk as a still-confused Wylie, lightly clad in a thin blanket, stumbled through the door. Claudia dropped what she was carrying to steady her patient, and they both collapsed to the floor. Mercy saw all this.

—Daddy! she screamed as she bolted through the door to her father.

15

The large, red, tattered vinyl suitcase seemed to glower at him from the corner of the room. It had a sad, poverty-stricken look of desperation—patched with duct tape, two hemp cords pulled around its middle, a cracked seam showing red fabric. It also appeared unbalanced, ready to tip forward from the wall at any moment. Señor Hernandez smiled as he observed the young man's reaction to the decrepit bag.

—Not exactly your style, eh, Zorro?

—Very ugly, if I may say so.

—That is the idea, and be assured, you will have to make yourself look as though this bag belongs to you.

—Have a bar fight and roll in the dust before entering the airport?

—A bit extreme, but you get the idea all right.

Zorro had arrived in the merchant's office in Lima soon after turning in the van that had transported the Cypher group to Huaraz. Pedro and the two Yankees decided to let him return to Huaraz, according to the rental agreement, while they looked for the gringo detained by the police.

There was a message from Hernandez in the auto rental office, which was not far from the store near the Plaza San Martín. He had an opportunity for Zorro that involved travel. The young man would have preferred to stay in Lima for a while, enjoying his three paychecks, before returning to Huaraz but it was not good policy to ignore a request from Hernandez. The jeweler led him into a back room that contained a battered desk, a couple of chairs and a green-shaded light suspended from the ceiling. The suitcase rested near the desk.

—My boy, I propose a simple arrangement. You take this bag as your luggage to London the day after tomorrow, hand it over to a gentleman who will meet you at the Heathrow airport, and receive a *propina* of five hundred British pounds. You can return here the same day.

Zorro was not convinced the offer represented a simple arrangement. Clearly, he would be smuggling something valuable if Hernandez was involved, and he could anticipate years in an English prison if something went wrong.

Zorro examined the bag more closely, and then sat on the chair next to Hernandez.

—Tell me truly that there are no drugs or weapons in that bag.

—As a man of honor, I swear to you there is nothing like that in the bag. Trust me, it contains antique artifacts that are a little difficult to export, and I have a customer in London who needs them now.

So, thought Zorro, if I believe him and something goes wrong it will be less time in prison over there. However, the young man had accepted similar assignments in the past, all completed without difficulty. Suckers and fools might be caught at customs—not Zorro. He thought about ways to sweeten the deal.

—Since I am not a traveler like you, please inform me as to the flights from here to London.

Hernandez called in a woman who worked in his office and asked for flight schedules. She quickly returned and he dragged a forefinger down the columns.

—Usually, we fly from here to Miami and then take an onward flight to London. Also, there are…

Zorro interrupted.

— Good. Good. I would like to stop over in Miami. My cousin and his family are there and I have not seen him for a year.

Zorro smiled at the jeweler.

—My cousin jokes that the streets in Miami are paved with platinum and the girls are more beautiful and willing than flamenco dancers. How long could I be in Miami?

Hernandez flipped a page in the guide, sighed, and ground his teeth. How had this cabrón managed to make him his travel agent?

Finally, Zorro was satisfied with the travel arrangements—a mid- morning flight to Miami and an evening departure for London—with five hours to visit with his cousin. He arranged a quick return flight, non-stop from London to Lima. Eager to move on to other business, Hernandez agreed to let Zorro call his cousin from his office.

Hernandez rose to dismiss his new courier, but Zorro settled in his chair and said

—Let us consider the *propina* you suggested.

At mid-day, two days later, a rumpled and unshaven Zorro with his first installment of five hundred dollars in his pocket stood at the meeting point in the Miami airport, a daypack over his shoulder and the disreputable bag at his feet. His cousin, boyhood confidant, partner in small crimes, good friend and companion rushed toward him and smothered him in a solid embrace.

The contrast between the two men was remarkable. Zorro looked as though he had just surfaced from a cardboard shack under a Miami bridge, his meager belongings in the bag at his feet. Juan, clean-shaven except for a well-trimmed moustache, wore an expensive white linen suit, alligator shoes, dark silk shirt, and a gold chain around his neck that threatened to pull him to his knees.

—How are you doing, asshole?

—From the looks of it, a lot better than you, dickhead.

They found two chairs in a waiting area and Zorro explained that he was acting as a courier and needed to look shabby.

—You should be proud. You are so much more than shabby.

Through jibes and insults, the conversation carried on. Soon not a single family member had gone unmentioned and they began to discuss their own business affairs. Juan paused.

—I have a membership in the General's Club here. Since you have more time, why don't we go there? It is private and the drinks are free. It would be a better place to talk.

Dark glances followed them as they entered the club. Fortunately, shabbiness did not disqualify attendance.

—Zorro, you don't know how glad I am to see you! We had such good times together and your luck always rubbed off on me. Other people would step in shit, but you always found roses for us. There are many opportunities here in Miami. It would be so great if you could join me.

His saying that pried open the chamber in the back of Zorro's mind that contained all his secret wishes. Being a big shot in Miami popped out first.

They sat opposite, leaning toward each other. Juan explained that he had become an executive in a large importing operation. Zorro demanded particulars and Juan soon translated that generality to his specific position—lieutenant in a large Miami based drug cartel dealing mainly in cocaine and heroin. He confessed he had to rent out storage lockers to contain the bricks of one hundred dollar bills that came his way.

—*Mira, pata*, lets go to one of the conference rooms. Like the gringos say, I'm going to blow your mind!

He pulled a plastic envelope from an inside pocket and spread white powder on the Formica table top, skillfully created lines with the edge of a credit card, and offered Zorro a rolled up fifty dollar bill to sniff up the cocaine. Zorro hesitated. So far, his exposure to the drug had been by masticating coca leaves. Snorting the stuff directly into his nostrils would be a new experience. His cousin noted his hesitation.

—This is the best stuff we have—not cut with any of that crap like baking soda, baby laxative, meth or other shit. Here, I'll go first.

Juan snorted a line into each nostril and rubbed the bottom of his nose to collect residue. He sucked in air until Zorro thought his lungs would burst, then exhaled hugely and beamed a beatific smile at his cousin.

—Man, that is GOOD shit!

Zorro tried to imitate Juan, but managed to irritate his eyes and cough before delivering a full ration of good shit into his lungs.

Zorro was torn between wanting to sit down, relax and enjoy the delicious sense of wellbeing that overwhelmed him and a need to still his beating heart and relieve the urge to race from one wall of the room to the other. Juan, more accustomed to the powerful effects of the drug, settled into his chair and stared at the ceiling, enjoying what he saw as shards of colored light pulsing outward from a center of radiance. His head drooped, and he noticed Zorro's bag next to the table.

—Whass in de bag? he demanded.

—Dunno, Zorro offered. Art shit or something.

—Let's see, said Juan and moved toward the bag.

After fifteen minutes of misdirected effort, they managed to expose the contents of the bag. Silver stirrups from the time of the conquest, sophisticated metal work in gold and silver; ornate nosepieces, earrings, necklaces, and breast-plates lay carelessly strewn on the floor of the conference room. They greeted each new discovery with expressions of awe and delight and, as their work continued, the room became very warm. Both men removed articles of clothing. They were in their underwear when Zorro discovered a small parcel carefully wrapped in a metal cage and protected by tissue paper and plastic foam.

By now, the almost pure cocaine had a firm grip on Zorro's central nervous system, conditioned by years of continuous exposure to the powerful alkaloid through his habit of chewing coca leaves. He began to hallucinate, hearing colors and seeing sounds. He thought he saw tiny shafts of light peeking through folds in the wrappings of the unopened package. Guiding his fingers to unwrap the package seemed suddenly difficult. He paused, took deep breaths, concentrated on his fingers, his hands, and slowly peeled away the sturdy wrappings, opened the wire mesh cage, and uncovered the little mummy. He stared at the wizened face, the lopsided grin, and the sticklike arms and decided this was the most beautiful thing he had ever seen.

He was right about the light emanating from the tiny figure; she contained an unearthly radiance, and beams of golden light haloed her head and body. It was so lovely that Zorro began to weep, taking a step back more fully to absorb her ethereal quality. Slowly she straightened her body, sat up and turned her head to face him. She raised her shriveled arms toward him—in supplication. Her voice, high-pitched, reverberating, filled the little conference room.

—*Ayudarme. Ayudarme,* she called, a sound like silver bells in the breeze.

Zorro looked toward Juan, sleeping at the table with his head in his arms, to confirm the magical utterance. Juan seemed not to have heard the plea for help.

She said it again, more plaintive, more insistent.

Zorro fell to his knees before the speaker,

—*Si. Si. Si. Si* .he cried and kissed the tiny creature on what remained of her mouth.

He rewrapped her with great care and slid her into his backpack.

Juan awakened to Zorro's announcement that he thought he had less than an hour before his flight to London. Fortunately, he was looking at Juan's Rolex upside down; they had more than two hours to repack and prepare the shabby bag for its flight to London. They managed to protect the metal objects scattered on the floor with their original wrappings and were about to close the bag when Juan noticed the little metal cage hidden under the bag's lid.

—Look around. We missed something!

—No, I have her, said Zorro. I accept the responsibility.

Juan had no idea what his cousin was talking about and stuffed the little cage into the bag, secured its outer bindings and pulled it toward the door.

They exchanged long embraces before Zorro left the waiting area. Juan slipped another plastic envelope with white powder into Zorro's shirt pocket.

—Think about what I said, cousin. You can have a good life in Miami. No grubbing for soles up there in Huaraz. No running errands like this. You could be a man of importance here—I would see to it.

Zorro leaned forward to kiss his cousin on the cheek, hefted his backpack, turned down the tunnel to his plane, and called back

—I will come. Be assured, I will come.

As soon as the cabin crew dimmed the lights on the aircraft, Zorro managed to inhale more of the white powder. He soon entered another world where his infallibility was assured.

Walsham awaited the courier just beyond the baggage claim area at Heathrow's terminal three. He looked for the man who would pick up the scruffy red bag festooned with "Visit Peru" stickers bumping along the baggage conveyor. Lord Wimsey was accompanied by a large man in a blue serge suit.

Soon Zorro, rumpled, red eyed and unshaven, appeared, worked his way to the conveyer belt, pulled the bag off, and turned to look for a sign of recognition from someone in the waiting crowd. He felt a tap on his shoulder and saw the large man in the blue serge suit offer to carry the bag. The courier followed blue serge along a corridor to a vacant table in the fast food area where Walsham was just taking a seat. Blue serge prodded Zorro to sit next to the dapper Englishman.

They shook hands and began a brief conversation. It was quickly clear that Zorro understood little English, so Walsham spoke in his rudimentary Spanish. He smiled at Zorro, thanked him for his help and placed an envelope thick with ten-pound notes into his hand. Zorro acknowledged the money, and then pointed back toward the airline counters to explain that his onward flight would soon be leaving.

—Sorry you won't be able to visit our lovely city, perhaps next time.

Walsham patted Zorro's arm and the scruffy young man hurried toward the American Airlines counter.

16

—Lost? *Lost?* demanded the Admiral of the two aides who stood stiffly before his desk.

—You are telling me that a man who was in custody has simply disappeared? *¡Coño carajo!* I am surrounded by an impenetrable morass of imbecility! If this keeps up you will be eating your own livers.

The Admiral stood to reinforce his next words.

—This Dr. Cypher possesses supremely sensitive information that could embarrass our nation in the eyes of the world. He is not lost—he is somewhere up there in Huaraz, or in the Cordillera, or some other godforsaken place. Lost is not an option! You will find him, and you will find him now. We have the military; we have the police; we have helicopters; we have paratroopers, we have missiles. *Find* him.

The Admiral inhaled and returned to his seat. His words were threatening enough, but what really intimidated his aides was his face. It was the color of venous blood.

The Admiral's senior aide immediately called the garrison that housed the special missions group known as *tropa entrenados especialmente para misiones difícil— comandos* for short. These were elite troops known for their daring, cruelty, and knowledge of the highlands. If Dr. Cypher was in the Huaraz area, they would ferret him out. He arranged for them to be on the ground in the high Andes by the next day.

Three men stood temporarily frozen, watching the strange tableau by the entrance to Fredo's little study. Mercy was kneeling next to her father, weeping and holding him, and unwittingly keeping him from raising himself from the floor. Claudia tried to extract herself from under Wylie, who had fallen on top of her when he stumbled while navigating his exit from the study. A slippery pool of milk from the dropped glass inhibited Claudia's efforts to regain her footing. Wylie gasped in pain as Mercy pressed on his wounded temple with her forearm.

Finally recognizing that the situation called for their help, Pedro rushed to assist Mercy, Fredo knelt next to Claudia and pulled her upright, and Lucho assisted Pedro in guiding Mercy to her feet and placing Wylie in a sitting position against the wall—properly covered with a blanket. Meanwhile, the professor appeared in the entranceway. He had run to the house after hearing Mercy's cries. The little front room of the house suddenly filled with seven people, most of whom were very confused.

Kuitkowski was the first one to speak, in formal Spanish with a Castilian lilt.

—I am sorry for the intrusion. This young woman has been searching for her father for two days. We were informed he might be here. This young man is our guide and has been helping us. I am also, in a sense, a guide—a doctor of archeology revisiting the ruins at Chavin. Again, I apologize for our stormy entrance.

The professor made a little bow of contrition. Fredo accepted the man's explanation at face value. Lucho, more attuned to human treachery, carefully reviewed the man's statement. It was plausible on its surface. There was clearly a connection between the girl and their patient. That the professor was a Yankee militated against his being truthful. Yet it seemed unlikely that these two soft Yankees, in particular, were part of a cabal associated with the administration. However, questions remained. Why was the gringo of such interest to the police? And how had these strangers located him here? He stepped forward into the room, closer to the man who called himself a professor.

Claudia broke the silence, not with the question she wanted to ask—*¿cómo lo averiguaron?*—how did you find out?—but with a statement that reflected her upbringing:

—You are welcome in our house.

Fredo, as man of the house, felt obligated to welcome them as well.

Lucho remained skeptical of the professor's story and recognized that this sudden incursion threatened his plans to confirm the gringo's involvement in Raoul's death. His warrior's eye assessed the potential enemy. The girl—a chop to the neck would dispose of her quickly. The pudgy, middle-aged professor—probably a blow to the stomach would immobilize him. The dark-haired guide looked fit; shoot him. Involuntarily, he felt for the automatic pistol wedged in his waistband. He decided to remain quiet and observe developments.

Claudia picked up the glass and dish on the floor and placed them aside to help Mercy move Wylie to a more comfortable chair in the little room. When settled, he took his daughter's hand.

—Mercy, you have no idea how glad I am to see you!

A few tears escaped as she bent down to kiss Wylie's cheek.

Meanwhile, the professor explained how grateful they were for the couple's kind care, and suggested they let him call for a taxi to take the patient back to his hotel.

Fredo began to sputter an objection, hastily pointing out that the patient was under a doctor's care in their home and probably was not ready to travel. Kuitkowski spread his hands and prepared to rebut that statement, but, before he could speak, Lucho addressed him.

—No, he cannot go now, he said abruptly, as though his authority were beyond question.

The professor looked more closely at Lucho, who emphasized his statement by pointing toward the front door with his ruined hand.

—You should all leave now, he added. Claudia will care for the gringo and you can come back tomorrow.

Mercy overheard, left Wylie's side, and moved to confront the large man with the claw like hand. Her Spanish was imperfect, but her meaning was clear.

—That is ridiculous. If you think I am going to abandon my father just because you say so, you are crazy. We will take care of him at out hotel!

Lucho was not accustomed to being contradicted, especially by some blond gringa. He grabbed her arm and began to propel her toward the door. Mercy was grimly determined not to let that happen. Although she felt fully confident of her martial arts training, there was something fearsome about this man with the deformed hand. She refused to panic and briefly let herself go limp, offering no resistance. Lucho responded by trying to hold her upright, causing him to go slightly off balance. Mercy took a deep breath, felt a rush of adrenaline, and crouched slightly, causing Lucho to bend down, and tripped him as she leaned forward so that he lost his balance and fell headlong to the floor. On his way down, she raised her knee with all her power and struck him in the groin. The big man lay stunned and groaning on the floor. Mercy, red faced and excited, turned toward Wylie as Fredo moved aggressively toward her. He stopped when the professor called out.

Kuitkowski was standing spread legged and rock solid a few feet from Lucho, holding a .38-caliber Smith & Wesson semiautomatic pistol in both hands, pointing it at Fredo's nose. As Fredo backed away, Mercy stared dumbfounded at the cheerful archaeologist, while Lucho began to recover and instinctively reach for his pistol. Kuitkowski pulled it away and kicked the man on the floor in the head without malice or expression, as though it were simply the ordinary course of business. He knocked the pistol toward Pedro and asked him to secure it.

The two women in the room stared at the professor.

Claudia was afraid for Fredo and moved toward his side. She had no previous experience with archaeologists other than seeing Indiana Jones in a movie the year before, so she was not completely astounded to see the professor with a pistol in his hand, incongruous as that seemed.

Wylie, Mercy at his side, looked with wonderment across the room seeing the motionless man on the floor, the couple who cared for him, his friend Larry, and their guide. For some reason Larry and the guide held pistols. He wondered if he had gone back to hallucinating.

In a calm voice, Kuitkowski said,

—We will be taking our leave now. Again, thank you for your care of our friend. Mercy, would you and Pedro help Wylie get to a taxi in the square? I will stay here with these people and join you soon.

Mercy and Pedro reached for Wylie who managed to stand up and, with their help, hobble toward the door. They wrapped him in the thin blankets, placed his arms around their shoulders, and carried him from the room to the street.

Larry stood at the doorway where he could see both the occupants of the room and the departing trio. Once they boarded a taxi and sped away from the main square he reached down to feel for Lucho's pulse. It was steady. Good, it would have served no purpose to kill him.

The professor reached into his pocket and unfolded some large-denomination dollar bills, which he placed on a table by the front door.

With sincerity he said,

—I hope this will help pay for your trouble—the medicines, bandages and such. Thank you again for your kindness, and please explain to your friend that it was not my intention to harm him.

Lucho moved slightly and groaned.

—I trust we will not meet again.

He made a slight bow in Claudia's direction, backed out the door and hurried to the square.

The doctor arrived at Fredo's residence the next morning to examine his patient. He learned that the gringo was gone, but that their friend required assistance. He had an accident the day before and had hit his head. There was something wrong with his hearing. The doctor prudently accepted their story, although he wondered what kind of accident left the purple imprint of a boot on the side of a man's head. Lucho winced as the doctor examined his left ear canal and then looked into the other ear. He changed the eyepiece and reexamined his left ear. He muttered an ominous,

—Hmmm. — the eardrum is not normal, torn away from its fastening. That is different from a puncture. A tear is serious, not easily repaired, if at all. You need to go to the hospital in Lima for examination. I can do nothing for you here.

Lucho cursed. The oath resounded in his right ear, but was a muffled blur on the other side. Fresh awareness of his injury mingled with murderous thoughts about the polite gringo who kicked him in the head. He cursed again.

—*Puñeta, coño.*

It was disorienting. When he lost three fingers, it took some time for his mind to accept the visual evidence that they were no longer there. Now his mind expected sounds to pour into his left ear, but no noise came. He wanted to turn his head to capture the sounds that should be there. When he did, he felt unbalanced. Fredo noticed that and held his friend as he tried to rise from the chair where the doctor examined him. Lucho stood and held the doorjamb with his left hand. He thanked the doctor, who seemed eager to leave.

Fredo placed the bottle of Johnnie Walker Black on the dining table and poured for both of them. Claudia was attending to their two little children. She would drink wine with the men later. The whiskey soothed, and Lucho, with moistened eyes, talked about their college days, their friendship, and the splendid future of the revolution. Fredo replied in kind.

The invasion of her home and the rude extraction of the gringo still upset Claudia. Even though she provided his care for just a few days, she developed a bond with her patient and was concerned for him. She tried to explain this as she joined Lucho and Fredo.

— Do you think that really was the gringo's daughter? I don't know about those men. They needed guns to take him away—like the police. They didn't have any medicine...

—Good riddance! exclaimed Fredo, disturbed that their maudlin pledges of undying friendship and eternal brotherhood had been interrupted. Claudia was irritated at being cut off and poured herself whisky instead of wine.

Later, Lucho occupied the couch where Wylie recently reclined. Claudia paused on her way to bed to wish him a good night. Lucho raised himself to respond, and thanked her for her kindness. He was about to lie back when a new thought formed itself and penetrated his whiskey haze. To his friend's wife, silhouetted against the light behind the doorway, he said,

—Tomorrow I will find that *chingado* gringo. I will find him and cut off his balls.

Claudia was not sure which gringo Lucho had in mind.

—*Claro*, she said.

The five men in battle fatigues all carried sidearms. Heavier weapons remained in the dusty vehicles parked in front of the office of the deputy to the police administrator, the official to whom Zorro had reported the arrival of the Dr. Cypher party. The deputy was a small, balding man, wary of the burly soldiers crowding his office. As the interview progressed, he used the handkerchief stuffed into his left sleeve to wipe small beads of perspiration that formed, unbidden, above his brow where his hairline formerly existed.

The leader glanced at the passport photographs of a middle-aged man and a blond girl smiling brightly at the camera. He understood they were quarry, the individuals his team was assigned to find and recover. He knew also that the man carried sensitive information on floppy disks. It was imperative they be recovered also. Well, he thought, if we find one we will have the other. And we will certainly find this gringo.

The deputy explained that Dr. Cypher had been in custody when the Sendero Luminoso attacked the station. There had been no time to discuss his interrogation, and after the attack, he disappeared. There was some confusion at that point, and the deputy had not yet located the other members of the doctor's party. In fact, he was not exactly sure who was in the party. There was the girl, of course, but his informant confirmed that they were a party of four, including the doctor. Surely, there was a guide, but so far, he had not turned up.

The little man mopped his head. The leader confirmed the location of the Sendero Luminoso attack, and the team of *comandos* departed.

As they approached their vehicles, the leader spit out a wad of coca leaves and glanced back at the office they'd just left.

—Stupid amateur—dumb as a sack of dried peas.

He put some fresh green leaves inside his cheek and boarded the first truck. They were on their way to the plaza where the attack had occurred.

Pedro arranged for a sudden departure from their hotel and told the young woman at the desk that they were leaving immediately for their trek to Chavin de Huantar. As Wylie sat bundled in a taxi, the others collected all their gear. They departed not for a trek, but to a seedy hotel near the river, the Casa Andeana, where Wylie could convalesce. The hotel catered to amorous local couples and business visitors from outlying villages. No gringo tourists stayed there, which was exactly why the hotel was attractive to Kuitkowski and Pedro. They assured themselves that Wylie had a clean bed and necessary bandages and medicines, and Mercy stayed by his side and saw to his needs.

Mercy tried to concentrate on caring for Wylie, but the numerous contradictions to her sense of order and reality bothered her. As Wylie recovered, she went over them with her father, who was equally confused by what she told him. He understood how his possession of the damning documents on the floppy disks put him at risk, but this business about the professor becoming an armed avenging angel and extracting him from the Casa de Maestro seemed totally out of character. His prior observations supported the view of an academic who was expert in his field, engaging and very bright. With his ready smile and portly build, Kuitkowski was an unlikely action hero. Yet Mercy reported that he'd played that role five days ago, glossing over her role in subduing a large and aggressive young man. It was puzzling indeed.

Now Wylie was on the mend. A week after his interrogation, his head was clear, probably from acclimation to the altitude and the reduction of his concussion. The cut on his side, not as deep as originally thought, was healing, and flesh accumulated around the flaps of skin over his missing toe was knitting together. Unless he disturbed the area of the cut on his foot, he felt no pain. Mercy devised padding for his hiking boot to cradle the injured area, and Wylie practiced walking on a foot with four toes. It was going well.

During Wylie's recuperation, the professor visited repeatedly to see how his friend was progressing. Every time Wylie attempted to shift their conversation to the events surrounding his arrest and liberation, Larry patted his shoulder and said they would discuss it later, when Wylie felt better. In the meantime, Larry and Pedro arranged for their departure from Huaraz. As Pedro was asking about porters and other helpers for the trek across the mountains, he discovered Zorro, just returned from abroad, was an effective resource. He hired him to recruit needed workers. Today, as those arrangements neared completion, both Larry and Pedro entered Wylie's room as Mercy guided him from his chair to the window and back again. Both men wore serious expressions.

—Looking good there, Wylie, said Kuitkowski, commenting on Wylie's improving gait.

—Thanks. I am feeling good. I believe I am ready to move on.

Larry settled into a wooden chair as Wylie returned to the edge of his bed. Pedro leaned against the wall by the window and Mercy found another chair in the corner. Without a word being uttered, they all knew that it was time for a serious conversation. Larry spoke.

—I guess the most important thing to understand is how you managed to come to the attention of the police, be arrested, and be interrogated so brutally.

Tourists do not get that kind of attention. Right or wrong, bad people think they have a reason to question you. You must have some idea why you were targeted.

Wylie decided to confide the story of the floppy disks to Mercy and Larry. Pedro was an unknown, although he sensed that Larry trusted him. What the hell, he thought, might as well just tell it all.

He did, leaving nothing out. He told them how concerned he was that he had somehow precipitated Raoul's death, and that he had unknowingly put his daughter and friend, Larry, in danger. The idea that unknown men hunted him terrified him almost as much as thinking what they might do to Mercy. He ended his monolog by describing in detail the contents of the two memoranda.

When he finished, there was a brief, numbed silence. Mercy looked at Wylie with disbelief. How could her innocent father have become involved in such a perilous mess? Larry was the first to ask the important question.

—Where are the floppy disks now?

—For your own protection, I would rather not say, Wylie responded.

The lawyerly part of his brain was functioning again. He was certain that the disks were in a safe location and saw no need to disclose to his comrades where. Such knowledge probably would do them more harm than good.

Larry rose from his chair abruptly, excused himself, and motioned that Pedro should follow him from the room, leaving a befuddled Wylie and Mercy wondering whether their friend and their guide were deliberating whether to disown this messy business and leave the Cyphers to their own devices. It was a reasonable but disturbing thought.

Mercy sprang to attention as the two returned to the room and Larry stood beside Wylie's bed, saying

—Pedro and I have been discussing logistics, ways and means of getting us all the hell out of here and back home.

Mercy sat down, immense relief in her eyes. Wylie silently took Larry's hand and said simple thanks.

—There are at least three reasons why we need to do this, Larry announced. First, I would never turn away from a good friend in need. Second, Pedro and I believe it is vitally important to deliver the information on those floppy disks to appropriate agencies in the United States government. And, finally, we have the training and resources to make that happen.

Larry's statement raised questions for Wylie. Why "Pedro and I"? What "training and resources" was he talking about? The professor continued.

—Perhaps I should explain that Pedro and I have worked together on a number of missions in Peru…

Missions? thought Wylie. *Missions?*

—…because we both have the same employer from time to time.

—What do you mean, the same employer? What damn employer is that?

—We call it "the company."

—There are lots of companies. What company was it? Perhaps I know of it.

—I suppose you do. It is the Central Intelligence Agency.

—The CIA? Bullshit! Take my right leg and pull that one too! Come on— the CIA? Cut the crap!

—Sorry, Wylie, but it is true. The reason we decided to explain our affiliation is that, to get us out of here, we probably will need do things not typical of a guide or humble archaeologist. This will avoid awkward explanations later.

It was evident that Wylie and Mercy already were having difficulty absorbing this latest bit of information. Mercy shook her head as though she had a hearing problem and Wylie moved slightly back into his bed. Kuitkowski turned so he could have eye contact with both Wylie and Mercy.

—I think a little background would be helpful. You understand it is in our national interest to know as much as possible about a communist-dominated insurrection in the Americas. Especially in the middle of a cold war. Naturally, the CIA has attempted to infiltrate the Sendero Luminoso movement—with little success, I'm afraid. Failing that, the agency has employed traditional intelligence-gathering techniques to monitor and assess the threat posed by the guerrillas. Guzmán, their leader, uses anti-American rhetoric all the time to rally his followers.

He paused as Wylie and Mercy absorbed his information. Wylie responded,

—I understand. What do you do with the information you gather? Do you involve the Peruvian government?

Larry answered.

—Unfortunately, they have not proved to be a reliable partner when it comes to sharing intelligence. Corruption is so serious that we cannot trust the ministries to keep information confidential. That is not surprising, since they spy on their own people, listen to private telephone conversations, monitor mail and make warrantless arrests.

The professor continued.

—Unauthorized disclosures by the administration have placed our contacts in serious danger. Unfortunately, some of our own local people have been "disappeared"—as in the documents that Wylie just told us about.

—Terrible! said Wylie, but please tell me how you and Pedro became involved in all this.

—I was recruited soon after I obtained my doctorate. As you know, I did much of my graduate work in Peru and I was a prime asset, as far as the agency was concerned, to gather information as part of my archaeological research in the country. It is, as they say, an excellent cover. It works out well for me. I engage in legitimate scientific explorations and obtain intelligence without calling attention to myself. Pedro was recruited locally, a couple of years ago, when one of our agents heard some of his anti-government comments. He is a "stringer" who can be called upon as needed.

Larry grinned at Pedro, and changed to a bantering tone.

—Pedro is basically in it for the money, the excitement and to help get through med school. *Claro*, Pedro?

The guide answered,

—Of course. I am ideology free, except that I hate the communist bastards more than the incompetents running our government. It is a hard choice, though. I hope, as a doctor, to help—medically and politically.

Wylie and Mercy took a few moments to digest this information. They were greatly relieved. Confused, yes, that an adventurous lark for father and daughter could degenerate into a perilous need to escape from lethal pursuers, but thankful that Kuitkowski and Pedro had become unlikely rescuers— and employees of the CIA no less.

Wylie asked the professor,

—How do you recommend we proceed?

—Pedro and I both believe it would be very dangerous to return to Lima and try to get home from there. We think a better escape route is over the Cordillera Blanca and then north to any number of locations where a plane might pick us up. So long as I can get to a telephone, there are ways of contacting people who can help us. Right now Pedro is working on a plan to disguise our travel plans.

That sounded sensible and professional to the Cyphers. Larry turned to Wylie.

—Put into agency terms, our pleasurable trek to an archaeological site has changed into a mission to get those floppy disks and ourselves safely home— and not to place Pedro in jeopardy. That being said, I hope you will understand why I need to know where those disks are.

Wylie decided to provide certain information.

—I put them in a book that I slipped into a zippered pocket of Mercy's backpack.

She was sure her father had considered that step carefully, but it shocked Mercy nonetheless.

A week after his altercation with the professor, Lucho remained in Huaraz. Although his contacts had not located any of the members in the Dr. Cypher party, he believed they were still in the city. The only road in and out of the city was monitored by Sendero Luminoso agents, as were the customary departure points for treks into the mountains above. It had been easy to persuade the clerk at the hotel where the gringos originally stayed to confirm they planned to trek to Chavin de Huantar, although he did not think the doctor was physically in condition to climb any Andes mountain.

Lucho's wounded pride and eardrum prompted reborn anger each morning. He burned for a chance to do serious damage not only to Dr. Cypher, but to the so-called professor as well. Surveillance continued. They would be found.

The *comandos* also believed their quarry remained in Huaraz. They persuaded the police to assist them in monitoring routes of egress from the city, without results. Their questioning of residents around the square where the police station was attacked drew them to Claudia and the *casa de Maestro*. Observations confirmed that the gringo was no longer there, and questions of the teacher and his wife suggested she had only acted as a Good Samaritan, and that her patient was long departed. Why, wondered the leader, had she taken on such a responsibility when she could easily have waited for an ambulance to take him for medical treatment? Rather than draw a line through their names on his list of witnesses, he scribbled two large question marks. What began as a straightforward recovery mission was becoming a bit complicated.

However, the *comandos* were determined not to let anything sidetrack their search for the gringo and the floppy disks. Their leader temporarily set aside such niggling concerns and intensified the hunt of potential hiding places. Hostels and low-end hotels were at the top of their list.

17

Zorro returned to Huaraz via a bumpy truck ride from the Lima airport during which the residual effects of the good shit provided by Juan gradually wore off. Now he sat in his little apartment, head in hands, trying to reduce his fear by a comforting maintenance dose of cocoa leaf extract. It was not working.

Soon after he returned, the owner of the shop below his apartment called up the stairs to say he had a telephone call. Still exhausted from his long airplane trips, Zorro navigated the stairs and took the telephone. It was from one of his good friends in Lima.

—Man, what did you do?

—What? What?

But he knew. *He knew.* It was that thing—that little mummy. He felt his testicles ascending, seeking to escape upward pointing icicles of dread.

—Hernandez has sent out word that he needs to talk with you about something you forgot to deliver. He needs to hear from you urgently.

—When did he say this?

—This morning. You know, when he asks for someone, we all notice. I have not seen Hernandez myself, but one of my friends has. He is very angry, although he says he is mainly disappointed. Zorro, this is serious.

—*Claro.* Many thanks for the call. I will be in touch with Hernandez right away,

He replaced the telephone and leaned against the banister. He had expected this kind of news, but not so soon. After all, he had left London only the previous noon. Slowly climbing the stairs, he considered the strength of his friendship with the caller. Not true brotherhood. There was an even chance his friend called to see whether he was in Huaraz, information of interest to Hernandez. The call reinforced his need to leave Huaraz as soon as possible—and not to return to Lima. His goal was to return to Miami and begin living the life he deserved.

Entering his room, he saw his backpack on the corner of the bed, untouched since he dropped it there last night. The little mummy was inside. He tried to solve the puzzle of her future disposition as he sat in his room, chewing cocoa leaves, rubbing his head as though to soothe the demons within.

The hallucination he experienced on discovering the mummy was so powerful that he refused to abandon completely his fantasy of rescuing this grinning damsel in distress. Now, however, the repercussions of his rash act became clear as the fog from using the good shit cleared. One did not cross Hernandez without suffering serious punishment. Mutilation, even death, had occurred in the past to provide an example to others. Zorro could not resolve the idiotic thing he had done by simply returning the mummy to Hernandez. The best solution was to leave Peru, go to Miami. Not that Miami was out of Hernandez' reach, but Zorro hoped his chances would be better there.

Not knowing what else to do, Zorro decided to carry the little mummy with him.

Considering Wylie's disclosure of the contents of the floppy disks and the fact of his detention by the police, Kuitkowski and Pedro were certain that elements of the administration would continue to hunt for Wylie. The also reviewed the interaction at the *casa de Maestro*. Kuitkowski concluded that the large man with the damaged hand was probably involved with the Shining Path. He shielded Wylie from the authorities, but was unprepared to let him leave his control. There was good reason to suspect that the man with the ruined hand intended to continue his pursuit of Wylie—and now the professor himself.

—Not exactly what I signed on for this time, noted Pedro, smiling ruefully at his mentor.

—Are you having any doubts about his mission— making sure we get that devastating information back to the agency?

—Not at all! Who could pass up the challenge of having two sets of villains chase us across frozen mountaintops chaperoning a girl and her disabled father. If it was easy, anyone could do it.

Larry passed Pedro another Cristal beer. They clinked the necks together in a mock toast.

—That's the spirit from one I know and love. Now, let's figure out how to confuse the bastards and keep them off our track.

Later that day, Pedro asked a man leaving their hotel and returning to Lima by car if he would be willing to participate in a practical joke, telling him that a friend intended to stay in Huaraz to visit his mistress, but wanted other guests to believe he was on his way home. The man found the idea appealing and, in return for a new jacket and Wylie's prized Tilly Endurable hat, the traveler bundled himself in Wylie's coat and the hat and allowed himself to be escorted to a waiting hired car by Mercy and Pedro.

As his car left the hotel, Mercy and Pedro stood on the curb and made a grand show of bidding "Daddy" and "Dr. Cypher" a fond farewell. Mercy even managed a few tears. They stood and waved as the car turned onto the main highway to Lima. Pedro overacted a bit by waving his handkerchief to be certain that none of the hotel employees missed the show.

The workers hired for their originally planned trip had dispersed and, as Pedro tried to assemble two new teams, local merchants suggested he contact Zorro, just returned from Lima, to locate needed helpers.

—Is that the same Zorro who drives the van from Lima to Huaraz? asked Pedro.

—He does many things, but mainly he picks the best people for you to take on your journey. You know him, do you not? His place is over there.

Pedro recalled that he had relied on an agency in Lima to find the original team of helpers for the trip to Chavin. Perhaps Zorro was the local contact who assembled them. He walked to the repair shop where, the merchants told him, Zorro had a little office, and almost bumped into him as he entered the shop. They exchanged surprised greetings.

—Still here? I thought you would be in Chavin by now.

—We were delayed…and lost our team of porters. We plan to begin again in two or three days. Dr. Cypher had an accident and needs to rest a bit more. Will you help us organize reliable people?

—Of course! With great pleasure.

—This time we will need two teams.

—*Dos*?

—Yes— I will explain later.

Larry had made contact with agency members in both Peru and the United States, explained in general terms the importance of the documents he intended to preserve, and received approval and support for his new "mission." A benefit of that approval was the availability of a seemingly inexhaustible supply of dollars, which Pedro employed to hire the two teams of porters, cooks, and muleteers to make the trek from Huaraz to Chavin de Huantar, the place of the ancient pyramids.

He told Zorro that one team was to meet a group of travelers who had journeyed to the archaeological site by four-wheeled vehicles and now intended to enjoy the mountain trek back to Huaraz. The other team was to prepare for a nighttime departure to Chavin, so that the travelers could experience the crystalline skies and the luminescent Milky Way without ambient light as they made their way to the foothills of the mountains.

None of it seemed plausible to Zorro.

—I know about groups that travel to the ruins by foot, donkey or vehicle, and I have heard of no one leaving for Chavin within the past week.

—They probably left while you were away from Huaraz.

Zorro had to agree it was possible, though unlikely, that his contacts had failed to inform him about such a departure, though he remained skeptical.

—Pedro, you have asked me to provide supplies for your visit to Chavin sufficient for almost three weeks, yet, even if you take the route that skirts the highest pass, it never takes more than five days to reach Chavin. Tell me why that is.

Pedro drew close to Zorro and said, almost in a whisper,

—I will tell you something in strictest confidence—something you can never repeat to another soul.

Zorro's eyes glistened and he licked his lips.

—*Claro.*

—You know that the professor is a renowned archaeologist, with a reputation for making important discoveries in Peru.

Zorro did not actually know that, although he knew the chubby, sandy haired man was a professor. He waited for further disclosures.

—Remember to keep this in utmost secrecy! The professor has received word that local people have stumbled on ancient ruins, long hidden in the jungle, in Yarowilca, on the eastern slope of the Cordillera Blanca. That is our actual destination; we are pretending to go to Chavin in case others of his profession are watching. According to the professor, you would be surprised how much cutthroat competition there is among archaeologists.

Given his current paranoid state about what Hernandez might have in store for him if their paths crossed, Zorro was primed to believe Pedro's story. His nose twitched as he assessed this information, looking for ways to use it for personal gain, finding one almost immediately.

—Pedro, do you know the way across the mountains to Yarowilca?

—I have a good geological survey map that will show me the way.

—Has it been updated since last fall when an earthquake and landslide wiped away the approach to the most accessible pass?

—Perhaps not.

—The trail is poorly marked as well. Trust me; you will need a guide who is familiar with the route.

Pedro weighed the prospect of adding another stranger to their expedition against the chance that Zorro was right—they might become lost in the mountains.

—Did you have someone in mind to guide us?

Zorro drew himself up and smiled at Pedro.

—None other than myself!

Soon, the two men confirmed that arrangement and money exchanged hands. Pedro was content because he believed Zorro had swallowed the story about the undiscovered ruins, he had gained a competent guide across unknown territory, and a person who could disclose information about them would be with them—under their control. Zorro was happy that he had found an untraceable way out of Huaraz to the east of the mountains where there were numerous routes north, ultimately to Miami.

Zorro had recommended Gaspar, a reliable muleteer with two animals and an intimate knowledge of the mountains, to carry the heavier gear required by the Cypher group. Pedro readily hired him; he had a positive feeling about this weather-beaten man with a limp who treated his mules like his children. On the evening that they prepared to leave for the trek, he stood in a meadow on the northeastern border of Huaraz with the other *indios* hired for the trek. Gaspar checked the panniers strapped to his mules, seeing that the cooking utensils, food supplies, and canisters of fuel were secure. He saw the two gringos, the young gringa, Pedro, and Zorro slipping on their daypacks, checking canteens. The tall gringo used a walking stick. Something seemed wrong with his foot. Pedro said something to Zorro, and the two walked to Gaspar to make sure he and his mules were ready.

The professor spread out a map on the ground, pointing with his flashlight.

—It is awkward having Zorro with us, but Pedro is convinced we are better off with him than without him, and I agree. We just have to careful what we say.

He turned his attention to the map.

—Our goal at this point is to cross the mountains and make our way to Cajamarca. The diversions we have set up and taking this little-used route across the cordillera should buy us some time. Once Zorro has delivered us safely to the area near Yarowilca, he will leave us and we will make our way north to Cajamarca.

The professor straightened the map and pointed to their current location and the city of Cajamarca, approximately three hundred miles due north of Huaraz.

—That's a very long way to walk with a couple of mules, said Mercy. You are planning on wheeled transport, I hope.

—Yes. The usual way to go from here to Cajamarca is to take the good highways up the coast and cut back to Cajamarca on the new road across the mountains. Obviously, that route is easily monitored and not for us. We will work our way north on the eastern side of the cordillera and then cut west to Cajamarca.

Wylie leaned in to get a better view of the hodgepodge of narrow roads and unpaved arteries on the map.

—Tell me again why we need to go to Cajamarca. I think I missed that memo.

—Sorry, said Larry. I think you were resting when I reviewed this with Mercy and Pedro. I was finally able to contact one of our people in that city yesterday afternoon.

"Our people" had a vaguely ominous ring to Wylie. Did the CIA have "people" everywhere in Peru?

Larry continued.

—The nearest secure small airport is in Cajamarca, and I have arranged to fly us from there to a place in Ecuador where we will be safe. It will be a small propjet that experienced friends operate. Our challenge is to get there within the next eleven days. After that, the plane must complete another mission that seems to be more vital than getting us out of Peru. But we should be able to get there in time. Let me show you the proposed route.

The professor traced with his finger the route he and Pedro planned. It involved trekking northeast across the Huascarán National Park, descending to the foothills of the Cordillera Central and crossing its lower mountains before dropping down to the Marañón River and following it north to the intersection of two roads near Huancaspata. There they would find motor transportation to Cajamarca.

Pedro returned without Zorro, who was talking with their cook. He confirmed that the trip would take perhaps a full week on the trail. That accounted for the extra supplies and having Gaspar with his two mules available: first, to carry Wylie if needed and, second, to pack additional food and equipment for a longer trek. Santiago, the cook, demanded porterage of large iron cookware and numerous utensils and plates to prepare food for the ten travelers. Wylie looked at the mules and their packs and the five people hired to provide for them. He smiled at Pedro.

—So, in addition to becoming a doctor, you are a logistics expert as well. Looks like we are ready to take an expedition to the poles. My compliments.

Pedro shrugged off the praise. He and Mercy walked over to the mules so Gaspar could introduce them by name. Wylie stood up next to the professor and took a few tentative steps to test the wrappings Pedro had devised for his injured foot. He experienced tightness, but no pain. This is going to work, he thought.

—Larry, I am sorry you became involved in this crazy mess, but I am so glad you are here with us. No telling where I might be without your help. Mercy and I are extremely grateful.

The professor offered his arm, but Wylie demurred. He was pleased with his freedom of motion.

—Well, we're not out of the woods yet. Pedro says that, in addition to Zorro, Gaspar, the mule driver, knows these mountains well, but Gaspar says the trek may be a little difficult for gringos. The highest pass is over seventeen thousand feet, and we will be there in four days. Fortunately, we've all been in Huaraz for more than a week. I think we are well acclimated now to this twelve-thousand-foot altitude.

They both took deep breaths of the chill evening air, exhaling frosty clouds, and walked to the others in the group. Pedro was testing the fastenings for the tents and sleeping bags while Zorro and the cook sampled his cache of coca leaves. Gaspar checked the panniers once again.

—We are ready to go. How do you feel, Dr. Cypher? asked Pedro.

—Fine and dandy—and let's make it Wylie, please.

The moon was rising as the small army of travelers and their helpers moved east across the wide meadow to a trail leading upward in the direction of Huascarán Mountain. Pedro, with Mercy at his side, took point, with the cook, Zorro and three porters packing needed supplies directly behind. The light from a full moon in a cloudless sky, reflecting off the shimmering snowcapped mountains, was more than sufficient light by which to proceed.

Wylie and Larry walked together, with Gaspar driving his mules in the rear. After a while, Larry moved to Gaspar's side and engaged him in conversation, partly in Quechua but mainly in Spanish. Later, as they stopped for the first night's bivouac, the professor said to Wylie,

—Wylie, this Gaspar is a very interesting person. He has always lived in the mountains and knows them like the back of his hand—and he knows about mummies, too.

The leader of the *comandos* returned to the main police headquarters in Huaraz with what amounted to a "wanted" poster for Wylie and Mercy, complete with their photographs. He faxed the poster to every police office in Ancash,

Cajamarca, and San Martín provinces. His team would remain at their command post in Huaraz, awaiting news of sightings. He was convinced the quarry had not headed west toward the coastal highway making for Trujillo or Lima. Two of his men had stopped the car carrying the Cypher decoy yesterday and let the man, somewhat the worse for wear, go. The local police, prodded to help in the search, contacted tour agencies and independent operators, asking about this group of gringos.

The news would soon filter back to the leader that it was likely the party was on its way to Chavin de Huantar. The fact that gear, guides and porters for two similar groups had left for those ruins, one in the morning, and the other in the evening of the same day confused matters. The leader decided to split his team so two men could stay in Huaraz to monitor information from outlying stations, while he and two others pursued the travelers on their way to Chavin. He wished they could use horses to initiate the chase, but they were unreliable on narrow and treacherous mountain trails. He had no fondness for mules or donkeys, but they were needed to traverse the high mountains.

He assigned two men to requisition animals for the chase. It was not the easiest task, since the government usually did not pay when items were appropriated from the "Indian" population. They knew there would be a dearth of suitable animals as soon as the locals found out they were for government use. Their departure was delayed.

As a more effective alternative than mules to search the mountains, the leader contacted Lima to request use of a helicopter to facilitate the chase. He asked to speak directly with the Admiral.

Lucho did not need modern communication techniques to help him find the elusive gringos. There were enough locals either favorably inclined toward the Sendero Luminoso or appropriately intimidated by their cruelty that informants could be relied on. He soon knew that a car with a male passenger had been stopped by men in uniform, beaten, and let go. He was amused at the crude deception, and wondered whether Dr. Cypher had allies in Huaraz. Again, he pondered the contradictions surrounding his hunt. If the gringo had delivered Raoul to the authorities, why were they so interested in pursuing him now? And what had he done with the floppy disks at the middle of this mystery? They certainly were not with him when he escaped the police.

The stabbing pain in his ear cut short any deeper examination of such subtleties. He winced and thought about the man who had wounded him. If nothing else, he needed to reason with him again. With a machete or burning cigarette. His time would come.

The next day villagers living near the great meadow north of the town reported that a group of trekkers, which included two gringos and a light-haired young woman, headed into the Cordillera Blanca the previous evening. They seemed to be on their way to Chavin. Lucho called on Fredo and other contacts in Huaraz to help organize a reliable group of searchers to locate the gringos. He was sure the people of the mountains would help in the search.

It was past midnight when Pedro decided to camp for the night. The porters quickly set up tents on the grassy plateau, and Santiago primed his naphtha stove to make tea for the hikers. The porters smoothed thick Ensolite pads and placed zero-degree down sleeping bags on top. Pedro identified the area for the latrine with a little orange fluorescent flag that fluttered in front of a conveniently located screen of brush. The trekkers were in a good mood; there was banter with Mercy about whether ladies went left or right behind the latrine screen.

Santiago produced canvas-covered stools that he placed around his cooking area. Beside the glow of the gas stove and a neon lantern placed on the ground, the trekkers drank hot tea flavored with coca leaves and ate what appeared to be Oreo cookies. Above them, moonlight slightly obscured the Milky Way, and snow-covered peaks seemed to glow with a bluish haze. Such peaceful moments were what Wylie had intended for his trip with Mercy, who sat close and hugged his arm. Larry sat smoking a miniature cigar, and Pedro rested on the ground, propped on his elbows, cataloging the constellations he knew. Zorro did not know the stars above had names; he enjoyed hearing them. Fears and concerns melted away in the hush of the night, under the bright stars and thin chill air. Reluctantly, Wylie moved toward his tent, relieved that there was only slight discomfort in his foot and side. He massaged his calf muscles before crawling into his sleeping bag, and called out a good-night to the other travelers.

The rising sun created a corona around the not-so-distant peaks of the *cordillera*, gradually replacing the violet and cerise hues of the cirrus clouds with startling gold and white that hurt Wylie's eyes as he poked his head from his tent. He woke when the porter placed a porcelain basin of steaming hot water by the flap of his tent and called out in heavily accented English, "Face first, feet last." It was his idea of humor, which he repeated each morning until he left the group.

Wylie saw that Mercy and Pedro were already drinking coffee by Santiago's kitchen and that Larry was in animated conversation with Gaspar, helping feed his mules. He scrubbed face and hands and carefully washed the tender areas on his left foot. It was healing very well, in spite of walking about six miles yesterday evening. He rebandaged the foot, retied his boots and left the tent to wander over to the fluorescent flag fluttering in the morning breeze.

He rubbed a hand across his chin and rummaged in his pack for the properly charged electric razor he carried with him. He greeted his fellow travelers and adjusted the steel mirror attached to a pole by Santiago's kitchen to catch morning light. Santiago and the porters were surprised and amused by the buzzing of the razor. "*Americano loco*," they whispered to one another.

Whiskers gone, Wylie, who had noticed the porters' interest in his shaving exploit, motioned to Santiago with the razor. He asked Pedro to translate.

—*¿Quieres que te dará una afeitada?* asked Pedro.

Santiago laughed and touched the smooth brown skin of his cheek.

—*Sin pelo*, he said, but Wylie approached him anyway and attacked his few black chin hairs and scraggly mustache with the razor. It tickled and Santiago giggled, then rubbed his chin—hairless for the first time in years. He looked at the porters and Gaspar and gave Wylie the thumbs-up sign.

—*Muy liso . . . Gracias*. He took Wylie's hand in both of his. No doubt about it. The *Americano loco* was *muy simpático*. Nevertheless, for the remainder of the trip, the porters referred to Wylie as "*el loco*" among themselves.

Santiago served breakfast to Wylie first: steaming oatmeal with brown sugar, condensed milk, fried plantain, fried meat that resembled Spam, toast with butter and jam, little bananas, and coffee or tea. Seeing his look at surprise at this abundant meal, Pedro urged him to eat as much as he could.

—Food is fuel that you'll need for energy. And you have to drink lots of water, too. We'll be climbing to over fourteen thousand feet today, and you will need protein and water, believe me. Lunch is trail mix and ham sandwiches with tea.

Zorro suddenly appeared around a bend in the trail ahead. He had been scouting the terrain ahead and searching for signs of pursuers that Hernandez might have hired to detain him. In the chilly morning, last night's feelings of comfort and safety evaporated. He was beginning to suspect that Pedro's story about searching for ancient ruins might not be true. There was a peculiar wariness about these gringos, especially the professor, that he had not noted in other trekking parties. He silently held out his mug for some of Santiago's tea.

As they sat together preparing to begin the day's trek, Mercy had a question for Pedro.

—Last night I overheard Larry and the mule driver—I think his name is Jasper—talking about what he called the spirit of the mountains. Do you believe in something like that?

Pedro paused to consider her question. Since childhood, there were elements of mysticism and spirituality in his upbringing. Like all Peruvian schoolchildren, he had memorized the names of all the Incan rulers by heart, and had learned the names of the major deities worshiped not only by the Incas, but by many of the cultures that preceded them. At the same time, the Catholic religion taught him to believe in the Virgin birth, the Resurrection, angels, and miracles. Why not, then, believe in the power of ancient Peruvian gods and goddesses? His answer was:

— I do believe there is something or someone that inhabits the mountains that is not what I call tangible. I have seen things here that have no rational explanation. The people of the old civilizations were pagans and had a large number of gods, beginning with ones associated with the sun and moon. The one I am most interested in is Pachamama, the earth goddess, the one who lives in the mountains and is closely involved in guarding what we now call the environment. The people of these mountains believe she is guarding their heritage and influences the weather, earthquakes and disturbances of any kind. To this day, they make sacrifices to her. She is very powerful. Who am I to say they are wrong?

—Sounds like our concept of Mother Nature.

—Is she a god?

—No—not exactly.

Mercy looked at the not so distant snow-capped peaks. Both Pedro and Gaspar respected Pachamama, the mystical spirit and protector of all this natural beauty. She could understand how exposure to this glorious terrain might foster belief in a deity. Mercy wondered if praying to Pachamama would permit their safe passage over her mountains. She laced her boots tightly.

Before following Gaspar, who would be in the lead, the five huddled to go over the plan for the day. This time Pedro handed the map to Zorro who pointed to the map.

—Dr. Cypher seems to be doing very well, but I think we should avoid the customary route around Alpamayo Mountain and instead head for the village of Yanama on this little-used trail. It is not as beautiful as the usual way, but it cuts a few days off the usual time to reach that village.

Zorro moved his finger across the map.

—Here is the high pass, just west of the Chopicalqui Mountain, and it is over sixteen thousand feet. We will make camp a thousand meters or so from that pass day after tomorrow, and get an early start the next day—when we are fresh. There will be high walls of ice on either side of the pass. We have to cross a glacier to reach the eastern slope.

On the map, the highest mountains appeared in three groups. To the west, containing the Alpamayo peak was a group that resembled a long, slender Rorschach test. Huandoy Mountain dominated the middle group, which looked like a horse with large, swollen feet. Mercy saw the eastern group as a dog crouching atop a large cactus plant. Huascarán towered above the other peaks in this group.

Larry traced the path they would take today, and pointed out that they would be passing two high mountain lakes the following day. He addressed Pedro.

—Is it right that the Incas bathed in those lakes?

—Yes. There are even ruins of what you might call stone "cabanas" along the shore of one of them. Of course, don't plan to spend too much time in the water. The lakes are glacier-fed and the temperature is exactly at the freezing point. We should reach them in early afternoon, when we will be hot and dusty. A quick dip will work well to cool us off.

No one volunteered to be the first in.

Mercy applied sunscreen to Wylie's arms and the back of his neck. The thin atmosphere encouraged sunburn and sun poisoning. Frequent application of sunscreen was mandatory. Wylie did the same for Mercy. He pulled on a felt hat Pedro found for him in a Huaraz market. He sorely missed his favorite Tilly hat that had covered the head of the traveler recruited to resemble him.

Father and daughter stretched and extended their arms and legs. Under a cloudless sky the trek began. For no reason at all, Mercy gave her father a generous hug. They headed eastward, toward the high pass between the Huandoy and Huascarán mountains.

No helicopter would be available for another two days. However, one would definitely arrive at the little airport in Caraz, just north of the city, three days from now. A Bell helicopter, it would accommodate the leader of the *comandos* and three men, plus some of their gear.

Meanwhile, they monitored the reports to the main police station and tried to confirm the route taken by their quarry. Now it seemed clear that they had moved into the mountains. But where? A helicopter search was very difficult without some idea of the right direction. There were so many crags, passes and hollows, you could be right on top of someone and not see them. And the mountain range was one hundred and eighty kilometers long. He experienced a loss of confidence. Talk about finding a particular grain of sand on the beach.

By midday, the gringos experienced the full reality of trekking. Clearly, if they began at an altitude of twelve thousand feet and intended to reach a height of sixteen thousand feet plus by the end of the following day, they needed to ascend four thousand feet in about sixteen or seventeen hours on the trail. As Wylie puffed up another steep slope, he calculated that they had to climb about two hundred and fifty feet an hour. Except, however, that the trail went both up and down, which lengthened the total distance to climb. He felt tightness in his calves and a tickle of pain on both sides that had nothing to do with his wound.

Ahead of him, Zorro took point, and Mercy and Pedro walked easily and chatted as they strode up the mountain trail. Larry, walking beside him, did not seem quite as slow as Wylie felt, although he was succumbing somewhat to the altitude and the strenuous effort of going upward in thin air. They had both earlier handed their backpacks to Gaspar to lighten their overall weight.

Pedro and Mercy looked back at them, smiling brightly. Pedro gestured toward the trail ahead and cheerily called out, "*¡Arriba!*" Dark thoughts crossed Wylie's mind and he mumbled to Larry,

—Wasn't it Shaw who said that youth is wasted on the young?

—*Claro*, said Larry, who appeared to be thinking in Spanish.

A short while later, Pedro signaled to Santiago and the porters that they would take their noon break on a lush grassy slope on the north side of a steep outcrop surrounded by patches of snow. The place seemed isolated from the world, and the two older men gratefully sat on the soft grass and loosened the laces of their boots. Wylie lay back and looked up at the sky beyond the outcrop.

As he remarked to Larry that it seemed unusual that they had not seen a single person the entire morning, an apparition materialized on a ledge directly above him. Since, from his position, he was seeing its head upside down, he did not recognize the strange beast at first. It was in fact a goat, vigorously chewing a clump of grass, wagging its chin hairs and regarding Wylie in a friendly fashion. It felt comfortable enough in his presence to produce a loud belch, followed by a copious discharge of urine. This was a dangerous aspect of trekking that Wylie had not anticipated.

Larry laughed as his friend scurried to a safer place on the grass.

—The people here let their livestock run free. Since there are no fences, cows, goats, sheep, and llamas wander at will. They only go looking for them when it is time to slaughter or shear them. See those little colored strings hanging from the goat's ears? That is how they identify them. It's a bit weird to see domestic livestock at this altitude, but they are better accustomed to it than we are.

The goat endorsed Larry's explanation with a pair of *baas* and another belch and moved down the slope to search for more grass. Mercy approached with cups of tea and sandwiches and sat next to her father.

—The mountain scenery is absolutely breathtaking, she said.

—Nice choice of word. It certainly is taking my breath away. Literally, said Wylie, as he brightened with the pleasure of seeing his daughter so happy.

They looked across the alpine tundra. The snowcapped mountains stood in sharp relief against the cobalt noontime sky. Wylie agreed it was beautiful. Sunlight highlighted glacier ice with sparkling glints of amethyst and aquamarine. The contrast between basalt bases and snowy peaks was like white sheets spread to dry on lava rock. The intricate patterns created by eons of erosion, frozen in the present, hinted at the great power of time and weather. It was beautiful.

Pedro interrupted their reverie with the suggestion that they check their feet before returning to the trail heading around the southern base of Huandoy Mountain. The neophyte trekkers had learned to check their polyester-lined socks for lumps and creases to avoid hot spots for blisters. Wylie removed his boots and heavy wool socks and pulled the liners up, being careful not to stretch the left one too tightly over the healing skin. He pulled up his wool socks— which stayed warm when wet—next, before tightening his bootlaces. Mercy and the professor did the same, scuffing their boots on gravel to test the fit. Raw skin under broken blisters was among the worst of the potential irritations of mountain trekking.

Mercy and Pedro put on their daypacks, but Larry and Wylie were glad to let Gaspar again secure theirs to one of the mules. One of the porters had discovered a small tree that yielded two walking staffs that he presented to the two older men. It felt good in Wylie's hand, and he soon developed a rhythm of walking uphill with the staff, using it to both steady his stride and relieve some strain on his left foot. The professor also developed his personal rhythm, and the two men walked comfortably along the trail, following Pedro and Mercy, who seemed unbothered by the upward climb, chatting and commenting on the passing scenery as they moved on. Santiago and the porters were already far ahead. They would have that night's camp ready when the trekkers arrived.

In midafternoon, a cold wind signaled a change in the weather. Zorro came back from leading the group and suggested they put on rain gear, and they all scrambled to find covering. Wylie was eager to try out his rain jacket—a dark blue item lined with Gore-Tex purchased for this trip. It was supposed to be breathable yet waterproof. He would soon learn how effective it was against an Andean storm.

The westerly wind strengthened, ruffling the grasses and low branches of tundra scrub. The sun disappeared behind a monolithic dark cloud that seemed to stretch across the horizon. They watched the dusty flatlands behind them turn dark brown as moisture from the cloud surged across the open plain. There was no shelter in sight —just a few jutting boulders and brush flattening before the wind.

A powerful gust of air came first, then sharp, stinging tiny icicles unlike anything the Americans had experienced. They pulled their hoods tight against their faces, bent down, and turned their backs to the wind. Pedro looked carefully into the heart of the storm, searching for lightning. Fortunately, it was not an electrical storm; they would not have to lie down on the tundra to avoid becoming lightning rods.

Hammer blows of rain arrived, drilling into the ground around them, and lashing at their clothes. They huddled together as though they were in a rugby scrum as water cascaded from their backs. Wylie ludicrously recalled an army expression from years ago—"coming down like a tall cow pissing on a flat rock." Very apt, he thought, and chuckled. Mercy noticed and wondered what her father found funny about being in the worst storm she had experienced. Howling wind enhanced the cacophony and drove moisture into crevices in their coverings, which were not yet completely sodden. Wylie felt water running down from his boot tops into his boots. Surprisingly, the cool water was at first soothing. Then it added to his overall feeling of weirdness, for it sloshed in his boots as he moved. Considering their awkward movements, the other members in the party had the same experience.

Pedro yelled above the sound of the storm to move away from the culvert that provided small cover from the rain. They scrambled up the side and stood next to a group of boulders. Within moments, a great rush of foaming brown water appeared above them and inundated the culvert. Ten feet of debris-laden water crashed downward, wrenching rocks, brush, and soil from the side of the mountain. Mercy's face was ashen; she realized how close they had come to joining the other elements plucked from this Andean paradise.

Almost as quickly as it arrived, the water in the gully receded, heralding the end of the storm. The cloud dissipated. The afternoon sun shone forth, and the travelers stood in a semicircle by the group of boulders, steam rising from their shoulders. Suddenly a warm breeze helped dry faces and hands. Wylie loosened the seal around his face and peeled off the waterproof jacket. His back and arms were dry, but a dark cascade covered his chest where rain had seeped through his collar. His bottom half, as were those of the others, was thoroughly sodden, and water squirted up through the lace holes of their boots as they walked.

Pedro surveyed his charges and laughed.

—It doesn't look like any of us are going to melt. Our pants will be dry after an hour or so of walking, and we can deal with the other stuff when we make camp. Welcome to mountain weather. If you don't like it, just wait a minute!

They were happy at having survived this mountain squall. It was a victory over nature's onslaught; they had not succumbed. It was empowering, strengthening. Bonding.

Wylie walked to his daughter, kissed the wet curls on top of her head, and squeezed her shoulder. For her benefit, he loudly addressed the mountain.

—Okay, badass mountain, let's see what else you got!

Tension broken, they all laughed at the suddenly comical "group leader."

Wylie offered a silly grin, put his arm around his daughter's waist, and sloshed up the trail with her. She instinctively adjusted her pace to his.

18

Santiago offered them hot tea fortified with local firewater and honey the moment they arrived at camp. They sat in still-damp clothes on the little camp-stools surrounding the cook fire and drank the welcome infusion. In deference to mountain weather, Santiago had erected a lean-to covered by a tarp for protection. The porters had neatly aligned their tents beside a steep berm covered with stubby grass.

Their damp discomfort faded as the soothing liquid warmed their bellies. Only unfamiliar noises from the gathering darkness reminded them about malignant forces dedicated to finding them. For the moment, however, they felt secure. Wylie stretched out on the stool, heels in the dirt, neck thrust back to observe the sun sliding down behind jagged peaks. Larry managed to light a damp little cigar, and aromatic smoke mingled with warm air rising from Santiago's fire. Mercy removed her boots, poured out water, and set them by the fire. She wrung out her socks.

—Put the socks next to your skin when you go to sleep tonight. They will be dry as toast tomorrow, said Pedro.

Wylie decided to follow that advice. He assumed underwear would be dry as well. Conversation faded, and they sat in contented silence, watching Santiago do wonderful things with chicken pieces submerged in an unknown sauce on his large iron skillet. They did not realize how exhausted they were until they needed to move to the little table for their evening meal. Wylie felt as though he carried sacks of sand. Nevertheless, he joined the others in eating cabbage soup, rice, chicken, and soggy oatmeal cookies before crawling into bed. He almost did not hear the professor say they would review their travel plans in the morning.

Patches of the páramo montane grassland that stretched westward from the front of his tent glistened with frost as Wylie pulled back the tent flap and squinted through the steam rising from a pan of hot water. He saw clear sky above the foothills and long shadows flowing across the plain. As he reached for the pan, invisible forces pushed down from above and he groaned involuntarily as he tried to raise the pan and place it inside his tent. Unaccustomed exercise and the almost fifteen-thousand-foot altitude were taking their toll. As his body was creating red blood cells to absorb more oxygen, his brain responded to the "heavy" blood by making almost imperceptible adjustments in the way it worked. The result was a combination of slight euphoria and diminished reaction time to stimuli. In Wylie's case, he felt somewhat sluggish and unmotivated. He had to resist the urge to splash warm water on his face and take a quick nap to recover from the exertion of lifting the pan into the tent. Nevertheless, he soon appeared, bathed and clothed, and applied to Santiago for a cup of Nescafé and condensed milk.

Kuitkowski popped out of his tent. From his tentative movements Wylie guessed he, too, was feeling the effects of the thin air and the previous day's exertions. Mercy followed, skipped to the coffeepot, and wished them a gracious good morning. Pedro appeared from the direction of the fluorescent flag and joined Mercy. Zorro returned from his lookout position to sit with them. To Wylie, their chattering sounded like that of the chinchillas they saw along the trail.

Santiago loaded plastic plates with eggs, roasted purple potatoes and slabs of mystery meat that resembled Spam. Not a scrap was left as they reached for their second cup of coffee, served with stiff sweet bread that resisted breaking until it was dunked in the coffee.

Mercy balanced a cup on her knee as she completed the morning's entry in her journal.

Sunlight scattered the morning haze, and the porters struck the tents while Gaspar loaded heavy utensils on the back of his mules. Pedro and Zorro reviewed their maps and traced the day's route with their fingers. They would be the day's leaders; Wylie and Mercy would walk together.

They glided down the slope from their campsite to the poorly marked trail and followed its rising path with their eyes. The mighty Huascarán Mountain was directly before them—a monolithic slab of gigantic rock, its snowy top golden in the early morning sun.

They hitched up their packs, drew tight the straps. The adventurers were ready for another day.

After about three hours, the gradual upward climb was biting into the gringos' calf and thigh muscles, and they were using their hiking staffs to take a bit of weight off their legs. While Mercy walked lightly beside him, enjoying the spectacular mountain scenery, Wylie concentrated on the placement of each foot as he worked his way up the trail.

They encountered switchbacks almost every hundred yards, and it was difficult to see where the next turn in the trail led. As they reached one obscure corner, they were overwhelmed by the odor of rotting flesh—so strong it was like bumping into a curtain of offal. Involuntarily, they covered their mouths and noses with their hands as they turned the corner. Larry and Pedro were there, handkerchiefs over their faces, as they observed four huge vulture like birds dispatching the rotting remains of a cow that had collapsed a few feet from the trail. Pedro hailed them.

—Andean condors—the biggest land birds alive! They nest at around sixteen thousand feet, so we are now entering their domain.

Mercy observed them closely: large birds with glistening black wings, a fluffy white ruff, and a naked blood red neck. Their beaks had a scimitar curve, and their dark eyes glistened malevolently. They probed the innards of the cow with their ivory beaks, now flecked with blood and fleshy debris. The travelers watched in silence.

The birds took little notice of them. It was as though they graciously tolerated the humans' presence. They quickly exposed the cow's rib cage as they gulped bits of ruby flesh. They worked methodically, occasionally disturbing a neighbor as they hopped about the carcass for a better position.

Pedro walked back to the two Cyphers. They were mesmerized in morbid fascination. Pedro broke the spell as he pointed at other condors soaring above.

—Look, he said, how they don't flap their wings and simply rise on the updrafts. The only feathers they move are their wingtips; they seem to float effortlessly.

He lowered his hand and looked back at the birds feasting on the cow.

—Not everyone gets to see them up this close. It's hard to tell from here, but they have a wingspan of over ten feet.

They all stared silently at the birds, torn between the need to leave and avoid the stench, and fascinated by the businesslike manner in which they dispatched the cow.

The birds finally took notice of the interlopers. Perhaps they were full. One by one, they straightened and extended their wings. As if in formation, they pushed off with two or three light flaps of their wings and a great rushing of air. They soared into the great expanse of the mountains below.

The entertainment over, the trekkers hurried along the trail, catching up with Zorro who chose not to watch the condors. Pedro added a few more tidbits about the life and times of condors.

—Mercy, do you believe that animals and birds have emotions?

—Of course. Anyone who has ever owned a dog or cat knows that.

—That's interesting, because some of the people I have guided think that "dumb animals" don't have feelings. If we are lucky enough to see condors up close, I point out their shiny red necks and tell them that scientists say the condors express their feelings through the color of their necks.

Mercy paused to assess whether this might be another tall tale from the mountains. However, Pedro looked completely sincere, and Wylie seemed to accept the story.

—So, you're saying that a pissed-off condor has a very red neck.

—Pissed off . . . ?

—Angry.

—Oh. Yes, I believe that is so.

The condors had circled back above them at a higher altitude, silhouetted against the sky. One could not see their red necks.

By noon, they reached the first mountain lake on the way to the highest pass. Santiago and the porters had set up a dining area next to the cooking fire—a tarpaulin stretched across a pebble beach surrounded by the canvas stools.

—No samweeches today, said Santiago, as he added a final ingredient to the iron stew pot over the fire and stirred it with a wooden spoon. Stew of the fishes today, he added proudly.

They found plastic bowls and let Santiago fill them with a creamy stew full of translucent pink and ivory chunks of unknown flesh. Flatbread appeared, along with the noon ration of tea. After five hours on the trail, Santiago's lunch was nectar and ambrosia. As Wylie and Larry returned to refill their bowls, Larry asked the cook what was in the stew. He listed basic ingredients, and added,

—Mostly she is *caracol* and feesh.

Wylie misunderstood.

—Charcoal?

—No. *Caracol* are snails. They come in all sizes in these alpine lakes and, as you know, are very tasty.

Wylie, who had avoided snails on his many visits to Paris, was surprised. Damn, he thought, they are tasty.

Lunch concluded. Mercy walked to a cascading stream of icy water that poured into the lake to refill her canteen. As she bent to collect the water, Pedro pulled back her arm.

—Sorry, but we never drink water from streams here—no matter how pure it looks. Santiago and his crew always boil water for ten minutes before letting us use it. The problem is giardia.

—I read about that. But at this altitude it shouldn't be problem, should it?

—So long as an animal can put its waste into the water anywhere upstream, it is a problem. If those tiny parasites infect your intestines, you can get very sick. Let me tell you, I know. I did very stupid things when I was younger.

Mercy decided not to demand details. She recalled her own intestinal discomfort when they arrived in Huaraz.

—Thank you, Pedro. You are taking very good care of us.

Pedro blushed.

Wylie and Larry decided to take a few minutes to cool their feet before proceeding to their evening's campsite. They found a rock jutting out into the lake from which they could dangle their feet into the azure waters. The porters and Gaspar watched, waiting for the expected reaction.

—Christ! That's cold! offered Wylie, as he withdrew his feet.

—Witch's tit! exclaimed Larry, who managed to remain immersed in the freezing water a bit longer.

Pedro, amused, said,

—The water temperature is about half a degree above freezing. The pupfish and escargots enjoy it, but it can be very dangerous for people. If you fall out of a boat here, you will be dead in fifteen minutes if no one rescues you.

Wylie turned to Larry.

—Beautiful but dangerous. Where have I heard that before?

They relaced their boots, grabbed their hiking staffs and followed Pedro and Mercy up the trail.

Larry reported on a conversation he had with Gaspar during their lunch break.

—That Gaspar is a very interesting man—and he knows much about these mountains and has an adventuresome nature. He is fascinated by mummies—*momias*. He told me about a trip he made a few years ago to the Chachapoyas area, where the locals showed him a place that had many mausoleums full of funeral bundles. He knows I am interested in such things and offered, sometime, to show them to me.

Wylie suggested that, with numerous villains after them, this might not be the right time to consider a new archaeological venture. Larry agreed. It was far to the north and distant from the town where their flight to Ecuador awaited. Nevertheless, he said wistfully,

—You are right, of course. It is just that no one has reported anything about mummies in Chachapoyas. Just the way, I suppose, you can't stop being a lawyer, I can't ignore being interested in old cultures and artifacts, especially an unknown tomb with mummies. But, that must be for another time.

Larry shrugged his shoulders, picked up his staff and trudged up the trail with Wylie.

That afternoon they climbed steadily upward toward the highest pass they would be crossing tomorrow. There was no storm, and the slanting rays of sunlight and the clarity of the air permitted astonishingly sharp vistas of the surrounding mountains. Mercy joined her father and Larry as they gazed northward, past Huascarán, beyond Chopicalqui Mountain—perhaps twenty kilometers distant. A major avalanche was in progress. Thousands of tons of snow cascaded down the southern slope of the mountain, sending plumes of icy dust skyward. Even at that distance, they could see a myriad of little rainbows as the ice crystals refracted sunlight. They had the eerie sensation that the snowfall occurred in slow motion. Perhaps it was the distance or a trick of the light. The massive fissure that grew at the top of the cascade disfigured the mountain's former symmetry, and its borders became dotted with tiny black specks. Boulders and brush added to the momentum, and the avalanche plowed downward, pushing a huge breaker of disturbed snow, like roiling surf preceding a hurricane.

Then it was over. The newly configured mountain rested, and the afternoon winds blew the wispy remains of powdery snow down into the valley below.

Through it all, not a sound was heard by the trekkers—no rumble or roar, no ominous boom. Silence. Visualization was enough; a sound track was not required to emphasize the power of nature.

Speaking to no one in particular, Pedro said,

—Too far away to hear it. The wind and the baffles created by mountain airflows and the shape of the mountainsides deflect the sound. It is strange, isn't it?

There was no response. No one thought it possible to improve on the silence of the moment. They squared their shoulders, adjusted their gear and continued on the trail. They were about two hours away from that night's camp.

The following day Wylie woke to a sound that he could not associate with being isolated in high mountains. It penetrated the walls of his tent, lit by morning sunlight. It penetrated the tattered sleeve of sleep he tried to draw about him as he buried his nose in the moist edge of his sleeping bag. The sound could not be ignored.

Wop. Wop . . . Wop. Wop.

A rumbling.

Then, he remembered. During the Korean War, he heard many Bell MEDEVAC helicopters land to pick up wounded comrades. It was unmistakably the sound of a helicopter—but what was it doing here? He poked his head from the tent to see a small helicopter turning above their camp, the sound of its engine echoing from two vertical facades of rock. He stared at an unmarked dusty green aircraft as it made another turn above their camp, wobbled in what seemed like a greeting, proceeded northward, and disappeared below the pass. The sound of its engine quickly faded.

Sleep fogged, Wylie and Mercy stood together looking northward across the high pass, as though they expected the helicopter to bob up again—for their amusement. Zorro, already on lookout, felt relieved; there was no way Hernandez could muster a helicopter. That feeling changed when he looked at Kuitkowski, cursing and kicking a hummock of turf. Pedro went to him, waiting for him to calm himself. They exchanged worried glances. The five travelers gathered at Santiago's makeshift breakfast table and silently accepted morning tea. Mercy spoke first.

—Any chance those aren't bad guys?

Pedro answered.

—That was a military helicopter. I have never seen one of them flying over these mountains before. They are not here for the scenery.

Larry, the cheerful professor, transformed himself into a steely-eyed combatant. He surveyed the route ahead and behind them with great care. A grim expression confirmed his displeasure.

Zorro was confused and very nervous. He had not understood the words of the conversation, but the tone was unmistakable. Somehow, he had joined a group that suddenly was *en serios*. How could this have happened? He snapped out of his self-pity to respond to the question that the professor addressed to him and Pedro.

—Is there any cover near here? Caves, shacks, large boulders, even trees. If we stay on the trail, we might as well pin targets to our backs.

Eager to escape being a target, Zorro answered,

—There are some ice caves among the switchbacks ahead, but no proper cover until we descend from the pass. As you see, we are entering a canyon of ice and snow that goes on for about four kilometers.

Larry considered the information. In his judgment, they were many hours away from finding a defensible position. There were two box canyons at right angles to their present position, but trying to hide there would be foolhardy—a self-imposed trap.

Staying in camp would amount to surrender, and expose them to the whim of their unseen enemy. Backtracking made no sense; they needed to move forward. Larry addressed the other four travelers.

—The terrain here is rough. I haven't seen a clear area big enough for a helicopter to land. And the wind is constantly shifting. It may take them a while to land and work their way back here. Let's see if we can't throw some sand in their gears.

Wylie suggested they use decoys at the present campsite. The idea was adopted and two tents remained after they and the porters packed their gear. Using sticks and spare blankets carried by Santiago, the porters created scarecrows seated near the cook fire, which they replenished with more wood. Once again, Wylie lost his hat; it now adorned one of the scarecrows.

Gaspar agreed to leave one of his mules with the main party and find a parallel route beside the trail until they reached the narrow pass.

As the group prepared to move onward, Pedro removed a sack from one of the mules and extracted sets of crampons for the travelers. He showed how the steel spikes fastened to their boots with leather straps.

—We don't need them quite yet, but when we reach the first ice field we will put them on. The porters manage very well on the ice with their rubber-tire sandals, but we need the extra purchase. The crampons will seem awkward at first, but you will soon get used to them. Just be sure the front one is set before you release the other foot.

He demonstrated on the gravel of the trail. It looked simple enough.

They shouldered their packs and moved up the trail, Zorro once again on point, Larry and Pedro walking together behind Wylie and Mercy. As Wylie glanced back he saw that they were checking the action of their handguns—Larry's automatic and a pistol that Pedro removed from his pack—the one taken from the large man in Huaraz.

Wylie took Mercy's hand and squeezed it reassuringly. She looked at him with worried eyes and tight lips. He did not know exactly what assurance to offer her, but as her father, he had a duty to protect her. And he would. That was certain.

During the two hours it took them to reach the first ice field on the trail, there was no sign of the helicopter or its occupants. Larry refused to accept that as good news.

—That just means they haven't reached us yet. Until we find cover and establish a defensible position, we must assume they are around the next corner. Let's keep eyes and ears open!

They strapped on crampons and began to make their way across the stretch of compacted snow and ice that led to the narrowing walls of the pass—rugged but unstable slabs of rock, ice, and snow. They had climbed into an area of fog and low clouds that added to the ominous appearance of the walls rising around them.

Wylie and the professor had difficulty in adjusting to the use of the crampons. At this altitude it was tough enough to focus on walking, thought Wylie, who was concentrating on the simple act of moving one foot after the other. With crampons, they had to place each foot in a way that the steel barbs did not stick in the ice, requiring extra effort to pull the foot forward. They both looked as though they were struggling through waist-deep water, breathing harder with each step.

Pedro appeared with a cylinder of oxygen and offered each one, in turn, gulps of sustaining fortified air. After a few minutes, they felt rejuvenated. Color returned to their faces, and the burning sensation in thighs and calves subsided. Enlivened, the two older men moved forward around the next switchback toward the narrowest part of the pass. The sheer wall on the west side of the pass gradually receded and, as they navigated the next switchback, fell away completely. They stood on a narrow path of thick, transparent glacial ice with a looming wall of unstable rock, ice and snow to the east, and a precipitous drop to the valley below to the west. Clouds and fog shrouded the valley, shielding the closest peaks from view. Wylie reached up and touched his eyebrows. They were covered with ice. The cold, moist air hurt his lungs. Mercy came forward and stood at his side, resting a hand on his shoulder. Zorro, up ahead, disappeared from time to time as fog enveloped and hid him. Larry and Pedro stood a few feet away, conferring. Larry seemed to have a second wind. He was poised and alert.

—Time for a break and a pit stop, he announced.

Santiago scurried forward with a thermos of hot Nescafé and filled plastic cups. Equilibrium returned. Wylie and Pedro walked away from the others to relieve themselves against the wall of the pass. It took a while to navigate through the many layers of clothing they wore to thwart the cold and damp.

After the break, the group moved forward slowly, impeded by the rough ice beneath their feet and the swirling mists that occasionally cleared to reveal black ice and chunks of debris that had slipped from the eastern wall of ice and rock. Wylie looked ahead and thought he saw the hazy outline of Gaspar approaching. He was about to call out when the curtain of fog parted to reveal three men wearing camouflage field jackets standing twenty meters away. They were armed with stubby rifles sprouting long ammunition clips, which they raised to point at Wylie. The fog closed in again, and the men temporarily disappeared.

Wylie froze as he flashed back to another time and place where armed men sought to take his life. Korea, 1953. He watched Chinese solders, with grease guns ablaze, charging up a hill toward his position. Well trained and armed, his heart pounding with fear and excitement, he fired back at his attackers. Now, unarmed and thirty years later, he felt a cold knot in the pit of his stomach and fear scorch his mouth, which was dry as desert sand. He recovered quickly, stress hormones adrenaline and cortisol providing extra strength, clearing away the pain in his legs. He ran to where he thought he had last seen Mercy.

Disoriented in the fog, he stumbled as he ran, bumping into a porter who was holding Gaspar's mule a few feet from the western edge of the trail. Wylie crouched there, trying to get his bearings.

The other members of the group also glimpsed the ghostly images of the intruders. Pedro, closest to Mercy, pulled her from the middle of the trail toward the steep eastern wall, and Kuitkowski moved farther back along the same wall, where he found a rock outcrop to shield himself. The fog thickened and receded at the whim of the mountain winds, giving the trekkers a stroboscopic view of the intruders, who were moving toward them quickly. Suddenly a brisk southerly wind cleared the pass of fog, and provided a clear view of all the people on the icy trail.

Zorro, farthest along the trail, stood about sixty meters from a curve in the path that disappeared behind a wall of ice and debris. Close to him was one of the soldiers, who pointed his stubby weapon in Zorro's direction. Two more soldiers, one giving orders, apparently the leader, pointed their weapons, first toward Wylie and the porter holding the mule, then toward Pedro and Mercy, then toward the professor and Santiago. The leader demanded that the trekkers place all weapons, packs, and loose items on the ground. When they had done so, he motioned the professor, Pedro and Mercy to move closer to the soldiers, against the east wall of the pass. The soldier closest to Wylie and Zorro prodded

Wylie with the barrel of his weapon and, as Wylie rose to comply, Zorro made a decision.

All three soldiers were facing away from him, and he was unencumbered by his pack. Rubbery fingers of fog were again creeping across the trail, hiding the bottom of the path ahead. In the slightly euphoric and self-confident grip of the plum-sized wad of coca leaves in his cheek, he believed he could slip away, around the corner of the trail, and run for his life. He was so excited, he swallowed much of the coca wad, bit the inside of his cheek, and involuntarily began to cry a high-pitched "Waaaah," that, unfortunately, brought his intended escape to all three soldiers' attention. He ran, making holes in the ankle deep fog.

Large caliber bullets flew after Zorro, chipping large chunks of ice off the eastern wall, smashing into granite boulders, sending shards of stone flying in all directions. The sounds of gunfire echoed along the trail, amplified in the thin mountain air, ending, finally, as they crested the top of the eastern wall.

Mercy, huddled against that same wall, clearly saw that Zorro did not break his stride and slid around the corner of the trail, out of reach from small arms fire.

—I think he made it, she whispered to Pedro beside her—all three kneeling on the ice with their hands behind their heads. Both Pedro and Kuitkowski observed the soldiers as they fired at Zorro and concluded they were experienced men.

Everything had happened so quickly since Mercy spotted the armed men in the fog that fear and instincts of self-preservation controlled her actions. She did as the soldiers ordered; she followed Larry and Pedro's example; she kneeled on the ice, kept her hands behind her head. Now, her arms aching from the unusual position, and her knees cold and painful, she unleashed a hot burst of anger. She unlaced her fingers and waved her arms, attracting the leader's attention.

—I need to stand up, she yelled, beginning to stand upright.

The leader moved toward her, an unpleasant expression on his face, pointing his weapon at her. He was about to speak, but was interrupted by a loud creaking sound from above.

As the noise intensified, all looked upward. A large fissure had formed at the top of the wall of ice and rock, and a portion of the wall was tipping forward, beginning to dislodge car-size chunks of ice and snow. It was a miniature version of the avalanche Mercy had seen days before.

Mercy stood up, little concerned about the menacing soldier who was staring upward, more worried about Wylie, who stood dangerously near the descending mountainside. She saw a little tableau of Wylie, porter, mule and soldier staring upward, frozen as the ice they stood on. A large section of mountain broke off with the sound of a cannon shot and roared toward the trail below.

She ran toward her father, screaming, clouding the cold air.

—Run, Daddy, Run!

Wylie needed no more encouragement. He ran toward his daughter followed by the soldier and the porter. The mule followed behind.

The avalanche of ice, stone, and dirt first hit the mule with a force that quickly sent him off the trail and on his way toward the bottom of the valley. To Mercy's horror, Wylie, the porter and the soldier followed, overwhelmed by a gritty wave of Peruvian mountaintop. Mercy gasped as her father, caught in hip-high slush, struggled to maintain his balance, and suddenly disappeared from the side of the trail. Apparently, the soldier held his weapon's trigger, and a few rounds flashed from the muzzle of his weapon as he tumbled over the side. The porter made himself into a ball and rode atop the wave of slush as it carried him away.

Mercy stared in disbelief at the rubble on what was left of the trail, now still except for the occasional pebble that bounced onto it from above. Her eyes recorded her father's fall into a half-mile abyss, covered with crushing debris, but internal censors delayed her full appreciation of this horror. That came moments later, as she dizzily put her arm on the ice wall in front of her, rested her forehead there, and retched uncontrollably. Then came gasping sobs and tears as she began to understand how devastating the loss of her father was.

Pedro and the professor stared grimly at the trail, trying to decide whether to move against their captors while the rock and icefall distracted them. However, the soldiers quickly regained control and prodded the two men kneeling on the ice with their rifle tips to encourage their continuing cooperation. Mercy crouched beside the wall of ice, sobbing.

The western side of the trail below the site of the rock- and icefall was not a sheer drop to the valley. Rather, it resembled a series of terraces, like giant stair steps leading down to the valley. The steps were not smooth, but offered craggy tops broken here and there by ice caves, crevasses and rocky outcrops modulated by mountain scrub and brush. The heavier objects swept away by the little avalanche tended to fall onto the top of the terraced steps, while particles of ice and snow, as well as smaller stones, continued to bounce down into the valley.

The porter managed to stay atop the fluid material as it fell, but he bounced from step to step and was irretrievably broken by the time his body lodged in a crevasse hundreds of yards below the trail.

Wylie was among the heavier objects that came to rest on the first step, about forty meters below the ruined edge of the trail above. He fell into a cup-shaped depression the width of a condor's wingspan. Wylie was on his back, painfully aware that his head seemed filled with a thousand angry hornets, his body abraded in so many places that it felt like a thumb just hit by a hammer. Blood from his forehead seeped into the corner of his left eye, partially blocking his vision, causing him to see through a reddish hue. His left ankle twisted under him, caught by a rock.

As he reached down to release his ankle he saw, through the rosy covering of his left eye, that the soldier had also landed in this earthen pit. He seemed to be resting comfortably less than two meters away. Wylie took in more of his surroundings. Ahead and above was clear blue sky. He sat at the bottom of a pit partially filled with dirt, rocks and melting ice. To his left sat the soldier holding his weapon pointed directly at Wylie's chest, his finger resting in the trigger guard, millimeters from the trigger, staring at him menacingly.

19

Lucho was in the passenger seat of the Datsun pickup that cruised along the smooth Pacific highway to Lima. Mesmerized by the asphalt rushing toward him, he was of two minds about this trip to the nation's capital: he was annoyed that he had to postpone his inevitable meeting with Dr. Cypher and that bastard who ruined his ear. But he was excited about the coming mission.

Chairman Gonzalo tried to apply the teachings of Chairman Mao to the conflict in Peru. One of the Chinese leader's tenets was to disrupt the enemy's communications. In these early stages of the insurrection, the guerrillas had successfully destroyed telephone and electric lines. They had also been effective in blocking roads and bridges. Now Guzmán intended to strike another blow and destroy the television transmission tower situated north of Lima. It was in a populated area—not like the power lines in the foothills and mountains south of the capital. The chairman needed an experienced team leader and seasoned fighters to achieve his goal.

Lucho's success in destroying transmission lines had not gone unnoticed. Consequently, two days earlier in Huaraz he had received a visitor who announced Lucho's promotion to colonel in the revolutionary army, and explained his new assignment as leader of a unit tasked with the destruction of government communications.

This morning he took leave of Fredo and Claudia and joined his driver for the trip to a safe house in the Barranca district of Lima. The Shining Path had infiltrated numerous areas in and around the capital city, including the slums near the airport—euphemistically called *neuva jóvenes* ("new youth"), as though the ramshackle hovels were a planned community. Two of Lucho's squad members came from that area.

The transmission tower was an integral part of a five-story building, rising more than two hundred meters. It was made of steel lattice and supported by guy wires secured to the base of the building. Dish antennas sprouted from numerous places, and a slender steel transmitter rose from the top. As he drove by for the fourth time, Lucho recognized that this was not a structure that could be toppled by a single charge of high explosive. It would take a commando-type operation to disable the structure. And he would need advice from a structural engineer to know where to place the explosives.

The attack occurred at two o'clock in the morning. A razor across the throat dispatched the dozing night watchman. The team herded the three people in the control room on the second floor into a large closet and barricaded the door. They cut telephone lines, but continued to broadcast the taped replay of football highlights.

The engineer had advised Lucho that he needed to sever two heavy steel legs at the base of the lattice structure to unbalance the tower and cause it to fall. The ten-centimeter steel beams would each require six kilos of C-4 to do the job. Prudently, Lucho requisitioned forty kilos of the explosive, which was carried by one of the squad's burlier men.

Lucho and his men raced through a rooftop door to the base of the tower and hurriedly packed C-4 inside the two northern steel legs of the tower, wrapping them with construction tape to direct the energy wave directly through the metal. The leftover C-4 was set into steel latticework between the two legs. Detonator cords connected all the blasting caps. As the engineer explained, the impact of the energy waves would literally dissolve the steel at the base of the legs, and the tower would topple forward, to the north, into the street and plaza in front of the building.

Lucho carefully inspected the arrangement with a flashlight before unrolling the reel of detonator cord. He passed it on to one of his men, who clambered down the side of the building and attached the end of one cord to the battery in their truck. The detonation would begin when Lucho touched the end of the other cord to exposed metal. The squad withdrew and stood next to their truck, parked on the south side of the tower building. They craned their heads upward to enjoy the results of their handiwork.

Lucho scratched the copper wire along the doorsill of the truck and the northern base of the tower disappeared in a sustained blinding flash of light and the loudest explosion any of the squad had ever heard. Previous explosions Lucho had orchestrated occurred in open areas, so he did not expect the sledge-hammer of air that struck him in the confines of the city. He turned to look down the street and followed the shock waves as they sequentially burst inward all the glass in buildings leading to the square.

The loud creaking of exhausted metal followed the hushed silence after the crash of broken glass. The squad gleefully watched as the tower began to waver and slowly begin its majestic descent. There was, however, a problem. In his ea-gerness to assure proper destruction, Lucho had used overwhelming explosive force. Not only had the C-4 disintegrated the northern legs of the tower, it had created a powerful energy wave that coursed up through the latticework and up toward the steel top of the tower, pushing the tower away from the explosion. The southern legs of the tower buckled and snapped and the tower, loosened from all moorings, twisted from its base as it fell. Lucho's joy at seeing the suc-cess of the operation turned to disbelief as his horrified eyes saw a latticework of steel began its slow descent down the side of the building, heading directly for Lucho, his men and their truck.

In the seconds that remained before a fatal impact, Lucho barked orders at his men. The truck driver leaped into the truck and put it in gear as Lucho and three other men leaped aboard. The truck roared away, escaping the falling steel.

The three remaining men in the squad, too far away for rescue on the truck, raced along the street away from the descending curtain of pockmarked steel. The first two reached the corner of the building, away from the ruined tower. From the back of the moving truck Lucho saw a foot-wide shard of jagged steel impale the last man through the bowels and drag him, screaming, up the side of the building as the rest of the tower fell, seesaw fashion, toward the structures on the other side of the street. Soon the screaming ended and the lifeless body of his comrade hung suspended like an abandoned puppet three stories above the road. Lucho had seen others die, but never like this. The man's screams echoed in his mind for days; the image of him suspended against a backdrop of twisted metal and crimson flames became a recurring nightmare.

Lucho ordered the driver to stop the truck so they could watch as part of the tower made contact with the tallest building opposite. It was as though artillery shells had exploded. Debris flew in all directions. Chunks of rebar and concrete sailed into the back of their truck, hitting the occupants indiscriminately. He had had enough. Lucho ordered a hasty retreat.

The tower continued its descent, causing massive destruction before it finally came to rest. Within minutes, two blocks of structures were aflame, and small explosions racked the building that had supported the tower. Smoke and flames soon appeared there as well, and in the uproar, no one heard the three people trapped inside.

The extent of the fires overwhelmed the *bomberos*, and it was not until the following afternoon that they declared the smoking ruins under control. The transmission tower was a complete loss. It would be weeks before a temporary replacement became effective, months before a new tower was in operation. No one was certain how many had died in the conflagration; the unofficial estimate was more than sixty people.

In spite of the miscalculated application of explosive force and the loss of one warrior, the chairman considered the operation a resounding success—an exciting display of the Sendero Luminoso's expanding power. Lucho received congratulations from many superior officers, and a written commendation from Guzmán himself.

It was not easy to read the chairman's kind words. Lucho's more lasting results from the tower mission were a sunken left cheekbone and a blinded eye—caused by the chunk of rebar that hit his face as he took a last look at his creation.

A peculiar sensation around his middle finally caused Zorro to stop running. He leaned against a boulder in the rock strewn outcrop somewhere, he hoped, a long way from the trail, the soldiers, the danger. He took deep breaths and looked around. Blue sky, fluffy clouds, sun just below its zenith, high peaks still above him, rugged terrain. There was no sign of followers, only a cohort of condors sailing lazily above. Suddenly tired, Zorro slid down the front of the bounder and sat on the turf, wishing he had some water. He was very thirsty.

Looking down, as though there might be a stream at his feet, he was astonished to see a great ivory grub crawling across his stomach. He followed his instincts and tried to brush it away, but it resisted, clinging tight, and, then, it grew longer. The worm fell over on its side, and Zorro saw that it was working its way out of a dark red puddle. What he saw had no meaning for him. Suddenly he felt very tired; he needed to rest his eyes for a moment. His eyelids fluttered closed and he leaned to one side, his back sliding across the boulder, until he came to rest on the turf, slowly bringing his knees toward his chest, cradling his spilled intestines.

A terrible thirst wakened Zorro. That and the severe cold he experienced, even though, as he woke, he felt warm rays of sun fully on his face. He lay with his left ear to the ground, distorting his view of the turf and rocks ahead, the horizon in a vertical position. As he tried to make sense of this illusion, he saw the silhouette of a condor leaning far to the right, not three meters from his outstretched hand .The bird's white ruff glowed in the sun, the top of his scimitar beak reflecting its rays. The condor moved its head to one side, as though giving Zorro an appraising look, then walked stiff-legged toward the dying man.

The condor hopped to Zorro's thigh, then to his wrist and outstretched hand where he shifted position to make a clean initial thrust of his beak into a favorite target—the eye. The last thing Zorro saw was the condor's deep crimson neck as he dipped his head toward Zorro's face.

20

The soldier continued to stare at Wylie, one finger curled around the trigger of the AK-47 on his lap, the gun pointing directly at Wylie's chest. Wylie, his head still throbbing, his body aching, did not move, and the two men remained in suspended animation. Wylie shifted his head slightly to look beyond the corner of his eye occluded by blood. As his vision cleared, he saw that the soldier's head was cocked at a strange angle and that a muddy crimson stain of blood had pooled around the soldier's collar. Wylie's fear dissolved into curiosity. Was the man dead?

Wylie moved his hand as though to scratch his ear. Not a flicker of response from the other man's eyes. He shifted his weight, turned his body sideways to offer a smaller target and gently reached with his right hand for the weapon. There was no opposition. With great care, he lifted the barrel of the weapon from the man's lap and disengaged his finger from the trigger chamber. As he did so, the soldier fell forward to reveal a jagged hole in the back of his head. The creamy folds of tissue visible inside the damaged skull repulsed Wylie. He prodded the soldier, who fell onto his back, still staring, now at the sky above.

Wylie realized that he had been holding his breath during the fearful moments just passed, and he gulped thin air until his heartbeats slowed. He moved forward to the lip of the depression they occupied and oriented himself. Residue from the recent outfall cluttered the jagged terraces below. About forty meters above was the crescent edge of the trail, newly narrowed by the force of the avalanche. A smooth path of scree showed the direction of the falling debris, a path he could follow to the top if he was lucky enough to maneuver it without slipping on the treacherous loose rocks.

He assessed his physical condition. His ankle was strained from being lodged in the rock crevice, but not broken. His torn clothing revealed minor cuts and bruises, and his left side was tender and sore. However, as he slowly rose to a standing position, all bodily parts were functioning. A miracle, he thought—a goddamn miracle.

He held the weapon to examine it. Nothing that he was familiar with. His weapons of choice during the Korean War, almost three decades ago, were the M-1 rifle and the .45-caliber automatic pistol. This stubby assault rifle with the long banana-shaped clip most resembled the .30-caliber carbine he had used on occasion. He hefted the weapon, assessing its balance, seeing how it felt in his hands. He put it to his shoulder and found the pistol grip an improvement over the M-1 rifle. The sights were disappointing, however. They seemed imprecise and clumsy. Perhaps all these guys know how to do is shoot from the hip, he thought.

He listened carefully for any sounds from above. All he heard was the rustle of mountain wind. There were no voices.

He slung the rifle across his back and began to pick his way upward, moving across the loose scree in zigzag fashion and leaning forward as he climbed. His ankle felt like a burning ember by the time he managed to ascend about fifteen feet, and his lungs ached for more oxygen. He rested and began again. Another fifteen feet. Another rest. Halfway up the trail he stumbled and sank to his knees in loose scree, which moved under his body. He slipped downward, but managed to stop his decline by jamming the rifle butt into yielding rock. He crawled on his belly to recover the ten feet lost, stayed in that position as he rested again. He turned over to look upward at intermittent clouds brushing against deep blue sky. The sun shone in his eyes and warmed his face. He moved upward again.

Finally, after what seemed hours, he reached a point where he found a foothold that supported him under the crumbling edge of the trail. Mountain winds blew across the trail above, covering the sound of his feet scratching in the rocks and scree. He looked down, queasily noting the jagged crags and steep drops below, seeing the dead soldier staring sightlessly at him. Involuntarily, his shoulders hunched forward and he shivered, trying to shake off the grip of terror. He calmed and looked again at the edge of the trail, grasped the edge of a large rock that protruded from the side of the trail and slowly raised himself to peer ahead. He saw Santiago and two porters sitting on the ground by their gear almost two hundred meters away. The professor and Pedro now sat next to the sheer rock-and-ice face of the mountain, fifty meters from his position, hands still clasped behind their heads. A short, skinny man who seemed too small for his uniform rummaged through the packs dropped by the travelers, keeping watch over the two men.

A few yards on, a larger soldier faced Mercy, who had pressed her back against the side of the mountain. Her blouse was ripped, and the large soldier was pressing the tip of his rifle into her crotch. Even from that distance, Wylie could see the disgust and hatred in her eyes. Blinding anger gripped Wylie. He had to resist the impulse to leap onto the trail and charge toward the man molesting his daughter. He looked away and took a few deep breaths, calming himself, trying to remember army rifle training.

Now calmer, he carefully unslung the rifle and placed its stubby barrel on the gravel at the edge of the trail. Only the top of the rifle and his anxious eyes were visible, had anyone looked in his direction. He sighted along the barrel and aimed through the cylindrical opening, but put the weapon down again. He had no idea how the sights were calibrated. Even a minute adjustment could send a bullet yards from its mark. Beads of sweat formed along his brow in spite of the chill air. Gratefully, he recalled lessons learned on the rifle range at Fort Dix many years ago.

Wylie replaced the rifle on the edge of the trail and aimed at a yellowing tuft of grass on a ledge well above and to the left of Mercy and her tormentor. He breathed slowly and gradually squeezed the trigger. The recoil surprised him, but he saw where the bullet hit—the point of impact sent a puff of crushed black basalt into the air. It was two feet to the right and four inches below the tuft of grass. He had his aim.

The rifle shot startled everyone on the trail. Since the echo in the thin air obscured its origin the two soldiers quickly looked in all directions and then at each other. The larger man scowled and pointed at the two captives on the ground, who had loosened their hands from behind their heads. Mercy moved slightly away from the wall, away from the rifle still prodding her private area.

Wylie quickly aimed again—two feet to the left and four inches above his target—and squeezed the trigger. The bullet plowed into the left thigh of the large soldier and spun him around as he began to crumple to the gravel. He dropped his rifle as he reached toward the hole in his thigh. The adrenaline coursing through Mercy's body, preparing it for danger, prompted a swift reaction; she grabbed his rifle almost before it hit the ground and turned it toward the large soldier, convulsed on the ground, screaming and holding the ripped flesh on his leg between both hands. Mercy triumphantly stood over him.

The other soldier, mesmerized, his mouth agape, stared at his wounded commander screaming and thrashing on the ice and gravel of the trail. The professor and Pedro seized that moment to subdue him, knocking him to the ground by the judicious application of a rock from the trail to his head.

In seconds, Wylie had orchestrated a complete reversal of fortune.

He pulled himself clumsily onto the trail and ran toward Mercy, forgetting his twisted ankle and shortness of breath. He had tears in his eyes as he embraced his warrior daughter. Mercy was giddy with relief at her father's resurrection. She clung to him like a leech and sobbed into his neck, finally pulling away and looking him fiercely in the eye.

—Don't ever do that to me again! she cried.

Wylie assumed she meant returning from the dead and promised he would never do it again. His daughter smiled through her tears.

Wylie's bullet had missed major arteries, producing a large, open, and extremely painful wound. Pedro fashioned a pressure bandage for the soldier groaning on the gravel, and the professor bound the other soldier with his belt and shoelaces. The professor grasped his hand and looked at Wylie admiringly.

—Not a bad morning's work for an old man, he said.

—Think nothing of it—all in a day's work, said Wylie, still exhilarated by his unexpected return to battle. However, it was thirty years after his last brush with an armed enemy, and his older body had lost resiliency. He was very thirsty, his ankle burned with infernal fire, his body ached, and his arms suddenly felt too weak to support the AK-47 he still carried. He slowly sank down to sit next to his daughter on a boulder dislodged by the avalanche.

—Please let me have some water.

Mercy offered her canteen. As he drank, he saw she had somehow repaired her blouse and her cheeks glowed from the morning's excitement. She carried the rifle she had taken from the wounded soldier with authority, slung over her shoulder. Where, he wondered, had this Amazon of a daughter come from? Though his wife, Mavis, had a black belt in social climbing, she was not otherwise aggressive. Then he remembered the immortal twenty-year-old combat veteran he had been. Could it be that Mercy resembled him? It was a joyful thought.

Larry, who had been conferring with Santiago and Pedro, joined Wylie and Mercy and asked Wylie about what happened after he disappeared over the side of the trail. Wylie explained about the dead soldier, the acquisition of his weapon and the tortuous climb back to the trail.

—Tell me, Wylie, did that dead soldier look as though he piloted a helicopter? Did he have a special hat or communication gear on him? Maybe insignia with wings?

Wylie tried to recall something other than the dead, glazed eyes and the creamy tissue and blood on the back of the man's head.

—I don't think he was anything other than a grunt, he said. No special markings and a sloppy uniform. Officers usually carry sidearms; that one didn't.

—Okay, Larry nodded. Then we may have a problem. That pilot and helicopter must be around here somewhere.

Pedro and two porters scurried up the trail to see what might lie ahead. By now the group was well armed—two AK-47s, an M-16 that Mercy had taken from the leader, two handguns, two bayonets and a number of rounds of ammunition. Pedro carried the M-16 and the gun liberated from Lucho some days before as he strode up the trail with the porters. There were no obstructions along the trail, no sign of a helicopter, no sign of Zorro, the escapee. Blue sky above, bright sunshine, and condors floating among the clouds. They had gone less that half a kilometer when that heard a shout east of the trail.

—*Hola! Hola!*

Gaspar and his mule appeared along the side of the trail and turned toward them. Tied to one of the panniers on the mule's back was a lariat that reached back to the trussed hands of a disheveled soldier. He was doing his best to keep from falling to the ground as the mule pulled him forward. Gaspar walked beside the mule, the soldier's pistol stuck in his waistband. Pedro was elated. Here was the missing pilot. But how was it that Gaspar had captured him?

The soldier caught his breath as Gaspar stopped his mule and came toward Pedro to explain. His wide grin made his ears wiggle.

—This man and his stinking, noisy machine has fouled the air, disturbed the harmony of the mountains, and insulted Pachamama. After I left the camp, she came to me like a vision, she guided me to that polluting helicopter (Over there, pointing) resting on a small meadow. I watched for a while and saw that this *cabrón* was guarding the aircraft with his eyes closed.

Gaspar pointed toward the soldier who looked guiltily away.

—He was alone, so I guessed others on the craft were the ones the professor worried about this morning, ones who might do us all harm. I tapped that one on the head with a rock and trussed him for travel. I am on my way to deliver him to my friend the professor, who should decide what to do with him. So here he is.

Gaspar and Pedro returned to the temporary camp and secured the pilot with the other soldiers. Gaspar learned of the death of his friend, the porter, and his mule. He walked to the narrow section of the trail and looked down the precipice, hoping for a last glimpse of his friend or a sign of the animal he treated like his child. They were not visible. There was nothing below but the jagged giant steps to the valley, the debris from the avalanche, and a corpse in soldier's uniform staring eternally at the sky above. Tears rolled down Gaspar's cheeks as he stood staring downward, wishing the soldiers had not come, worried that bad luck would disrupt their journey.

When he returned, he agreed to guard the captives as the others gathered to review the events of the morning and consider their next steps. Mercy spoke first.

—I saw Zorro race to the switchback and disappear. He didn't stumble or anything, in spite of all the shooting. I think he made it.

—Well, there was no sign of him ahead on the trail—and we looked carefully, said Pedro.

—Maybe he just went farther away, offered Mercy.

More inconclusive guesses about Zorro's fate, then general agreement that they could not afford to search for him. If Zorro was on the mountain, it would be up to him to contact them.

They mourned the loss of the porter, the one who called Wylie *el loco*, and Santiago agreed to make proper arrangements in his memory. Mercy tried to change their sad mood by saying,

—But we have Daddy back—thank God.

Larry and Pedro turned to consult Pedro's map, spoke quietly together, and turned to Mercy and Wylie. Larry said,

—Two days after we come down from this pass we will be at the Marañón River and the town just to the north. Pedro, Gaspar, and Santiago are sure we can hire transport there and make our way to our plane in Cajamarca. It will be close, but I think we will be there on time.

—Certainly that was and should still be our plan, said Wylie. But what about these soldiers?

Larry looked toward the three men against the ice-and-rock wall. In spite of his wound, the leader glared back. The other two looked worried. Wylie suspected that Larry's solution would involve shots to the head. After a few thoughtful moments, Larry said,

—We will disable them and the helicopter, and be on our way. Someone will miss them soon and come after them. If not, the condors will pick their bones.

Pedro and Larry tied the hands of the pilot and soldier together, removed their boots and threw them over the edge of the trail. The wounded leader was about to receive the same treatment, when Mercy suggested he keep his boots because he seemed in no condition to walk.

—You're right, said Larry. But they will get themselves untied soon, and one of the others could use his boots.

Mercy had not considered that. Larry pitched the third set of boots down the side of the mountain and bound the wounded man.

Since Pedro knew the way to the helicopter, Gaspar offered to stay and help Mercy and Santiago collect their remaining gear and prepare for the descent from the mountain. Within twenty minutes the three men found the helicopter, perched a kilometer away on a little plateau. Larry seemed to have recently completed a refresher course on disabling helicopters. He found a set of tools behind the seats and directed Pedro to use them to remove the rotor blade while he siphoned kerosene from one of the fuel tanks into a thermos probably belonging

to the pilot. He poured the fuel over the navigation and communication equipment in the pilot's console, and refilled the thermos as Pedro kicked the rotor
blade down the sheer side of the plateau into the valley below. He cut a slit
through the upholstered seat and poured most of the fuel into it. Finally, he
soaked the fabric seat belt with kerosene and let the belt dangle below the door
of the helicopter. He turned to Wylie and held out the lighter normally used to
ignite his little cigars.

—Care to do the honors? There is something very satisfying about blowing
things up!

Wylie applied the lighter and a reddish yellow flame began to dance up the
seat belt.

They moved back toward the trail as flames puddled under the cockpit and
reached toward the instrument panel, which promptly erupted in a golden detonation. As they turned the corner back to the trail, the entire cockpit blazed.
There were loud popping sounds as integral parts of the aircraft disintegrated.
No more explosions occurred, but acrid black smoke rose behind them.

As Gaspar secured various items to the panniers on his mule, he saw an
unfamiliar pack by the side of the trail. Santiago saw him looking and called out,

—That is Zorro's pack. He dropped it when the soldiers came. Better look
inside to see if there is anything worth keeping. With but one mule and two porters we need to travel light.

Gaspar examined the worn, medium sized, canvas pack and opened one of
the outside flaps to expose a plastic package containing coca leaves, American
dollars wrapped with rubber bands, Zorro's national identity card, other papers,
and Peruvian *soles* . Another exterior pocket held personal hygiene products,
condoms, clean socks and underwear. Gaspar unzipped the top flap of the pack,
lifted it, and pulled away a sweater and a soiled shirt. Then he recoiled from the
pack, dropping it to the ground, staggering backward as though someone had
pole axed him in the chest. His face was ashen as he stared at the open pack, at
the yellow-orange head covered with wisps of black hair, at the eternal grin of
the child mummy.

Dumbfounded, Gaspar could think of no reason why Zorro had the little
mummy in his pack, no explanation why she had returned to him. He tried to

regain his composure, walking slowly back to the pack, risking touching one of the thin arms. It was not a mirage or hallucination—she was the same little thing he had carried down from her place at the top of the mountain. Still confused, he carefully cushioned the little mummy with Zorro's clothing, and placed it with other items Santiago intended to carry with them down from the mountain. Santiago, looking up from his chores, saw that his friend was upset and slightly dazed and asked if he was all right.

—*Si*, was all Gaspar said, and withdrew to stand by his mule, waiting for the others to return. Now, Pachamama dominated his thoughts. He believed the rediscovery of the little mummy was a sign from the earth mother, but he did not know what it meant. As far as Gaspar was concerned, finding the little mummy and bringing her to his home coincided with the beginning of bad luck for him and his family. Once he passed her on to *El Gordo*, his luck changed. He had money; his children were healthy; his wife was happy; he enjoyed working with his mules. Did the reappearance of the child mummy bode ill—once again?

When Pedro, the professor and Wylie returned from dealing with the helicopter, Gaspar immediately went to Kuitkowski and spilled out a torrent of excited words, trying to explain the rediscovery of a little mummy, how it was *mala suerte*, how it must be the work of the gods that it arrived at their camp. Breathless, he dragged the professor to Zorro's pack and revealed the little creature.

The others looked on as Kuitkowski examined the durable little child. None in their group had seen such a thing before; her grotesque beauty drew them in; her arrival at this time and place mystified them.

—Gaspar, said the professor, this is a strange and wonderful thing and, under different circumstances, I would spend most of today asking you all about her. But, my friend, we must leave here urgently to get to Cajamarca. Will you keep her safe until we have more time?

Gaspar agreed, reluctantly; he had only dark thoughts of any further association with the mummy. Mercy looked on as he rewrapped the creature and secured her in Zorro's pack. Gaspar did not seem interested in answering further questions. She understood his warning about *mala suerte*, however. It seemed to her there was already enough bad luck to go around, and she said so to Wylie. What bad luck, he wondered? He had escaped an avalanche, shot a vicious enemy and destroyed a helicopter. A sore ankle and ruined clothes were a small price to pay for becoming a warrior again.

Pedro and Santiago organized what remained of their gear and they began the downward trek toward the Rio Marañón.

The three soldiers watched as the gringos' caravan disappeared around a sharp corner of the trail. They sat in full shadow, and afternoon chill was seeping into their bodies. It would freeze that night. Self-preservation demanded that the uninjured men find a way to undo their bonds. The pilot and the slender soldier whose hands were bound together stood and hopped toward a jagged outcrop of rock where they found a shard of adamantine stone exposed by the recent landslide. The two coordinated their movements to rub the shoelaces that bound their hands against the edge, cursing as the rock cut their flesh along with the fibers of the laces. When the laces broke, blood stained their wrists and the gravel at their feet. They bent to remove the belts that surrounded their legs and walked slowly back to their wounded leader. Sharp gravel cut through their thin socks.

Their leader located the pouch of coca leaves he carried in his jacket, placed a large wad of the drug into his cheek, and waited for the throbbing pain in his thigh to diminish. The other two men moved him away from the shadow of the high wall into the sunlight and made him as comfortable as possible.

The pilot knew his helicopter had been destroyed but returned to its location anyway, hoping there might be something useful there. He found some blackened tools and a knife amid the charred framework of the aircraft. Everything else seemed gone. Dejected, he began to turn back when he noticed a rectangular, fireproof steel box half buried in the weeds at the edge of the scorched grass. He ran to the box, unsealed it and pulled out the ELT, standard equipment on small military aircraft. The pilot extracted the neon yellow plastic unit, known by its English initials for "emergency locator transmitter," from its container and flipped the toggle switch. An indicator light glowed. He attached the antenna and placed the box in the open. The signal had a limited distance. It would certainly not travel to Huaraz. But it would be useful if anyone came to look for them.

By mid-afternoon, their descent toward the Marañón valley slowed. Wylie's pace slackened first. His ankle throbbed and there was residual pain where his little toe had been. Larry began to feel weighed down by his pack and slowed his pace as well. He and Pedro conferred, and Larry convinced the younger man that they had traveled far enough for that day. Pedro was concerned that it might take longer than expected to find transportation near the river, but Larry believed the application of greenbacks would solve that problem.

Mercy readily agreed to make camp for the night. She accompanied her father on the downward trek and questioned him about his use of the attack rifle. How had her occasionally remote father, who spoke little of his military experience and practiced law for a living, been able to pick up a strange weapon and shoot her attacker in the thigh? She wanted to let Wylie rest so she could continue her interrogation. He explained that the army had taught him to use such weapons when he served in Korea during the war there. It happened long before she was born, had faded from his memory and, anyway was too boring. Mercy guessed that was not so.

Santiago opened one of the bottles of Pisco he had nursed through their trek and joined his employers in toasting their narrow escape of the morning. Mercy continued prodding her father with questions about his military service. In the dark night, sitting around the propane light by Santiago's kitchen, she learned he had been a sergeant in the army, had fought invading Chinese troops, and was a correspondent for the Stars and Stripes.

As the Pisco worked to release the day's tensions, Larry's tongue loosened. He told of his military service as intelligence officer and military adviser in Vietnam in 1963, before the large influx of American troops. Wylie countered with references to his "brown shoe" army ten years earlier, and they both entertained Mercy and Pedro with war stories that grew more fanciful as the Pisco flowed. Finally, the group lapsed into silence. No one wanted to be the first to retire, yet they were all ready for sleep. Moments passed.

Wylie stared beyond the flickering shadows cast by Santiago's kerosene lamp. War stories were just that—stories. In truth, they did not convey the numbing fear, passion or moments of elation he'd experienced as a young soldier. It was probably the Pisco; in the dark hollow of the alpine night were ghosts from his time at war. Those blurred recollections mingled with the panic he felt that morning before he realized the soldier was dead. His eyes moistened.

Wylie rose unsteadily and mumbled to Larry, as though continuing their conversation,

—Yeah, three years of war and thirty-five thousand young troopers killed in Korea.

—Over fifty-eight thousand in Vietnam. The first war America lost.

Wylie agreed, and added,

—Well, Korea was the first war we didn't win. I guess it was a draw.

On that somber note, Larry stood and offered Wylie his arm, and the two warriors moved toward their tents. Mercy and Pedro soon followed. Santiago dimmed the light.

By the end of the next day, after a less tiring downhill trek, they camped at a promontory that jutted out from the side of the mountain, overlooking the Marañón River far below. At this lower altitude, grasses and low brush covered their campsite, and they looked forward to softer places for their sleeping bags that evening. As they sat near Santiago's field kitchen, awaiting the evening meal, distant flashes of lightning, so far away they were silent, highlighted the foot-hills to the east. Pedro and Gaspar stood to observe the distant storm, and then returned to the others.

—Bad storm coming, advised Gaspar. Fix the tents better.

Santiago directed the two remaining porters to add more guy ropes to the tents and dig ditches around them to divert storm water. They completed those tasks just as the first fat drops of rain splashed onto the tarp over the cook fire. The travelers gulped the last of their tea and ran for their tents.

Within three hours, the storm reached its full force over their campsite. The sound of wind and rain lashing tent walls, and the continuing rumble of thunder, both near and far, obliterated the sound Gaspar made as he opened the flap of his tent and walked to the sheltered area where Santiago had stowed their gear. Gaspar, unconcerned by the force of the storm, wore no rain gear, letting the rain soak his clothes and water run down his face in rivulets. He wiped his face occasionally with the corner of the blanket he carried. From the promontory he saw the river below, saw clusters of lightning march toward him from the east like aged dancers. Never before had he seen fiery orange explosions of atomized water as the lightning struck the river. It looked like a path of hot coals briefly simmering in the river below, devil's footsteps in the roiling water.

Gaspar almost believed Pachamama had orchestrated this amazing display for his benefit, to reinforce his resolve to settle the matter of the little mummy. All day he had brooded about her reappearance. His head hurt with speculation about how the creature came into Zorro's possession; finally he gave up, simply accepting the fact that she was with him again, a rebuke from the earth goddess for having released her from her mountain aerie months before. He put aside the things he could not understand, such as why Pachamama directed him to the child mummy in the first place. Clearly, he had been wrong to remove her from her home, but now he had the chance to undo his error—and to halt the bad luck she would inevitably bring to him and his companions. Tonight, as the earth goddess reminded him of her power, he would return the mummy to a place in the mountain.

A tremendous thunderclap wakened the professor, lightening strikes all around lighting his tent and the campsite. He undid the flap on his tent, permitting splashes of water to hit his face, and looked out across the promontory. The stroboscopic effects of the lightning showed Gaspar, in flickering motion, reaching down into the pile of gear under the tarp and removing one pack. Kuitkowski had no doubt that the pack was Zorro's, that Gaspar intended, in his own way, to keep the mummy inside safe.

Kuitkowski watched as Gaspar looked back along the trail they had descended that day and began to retrace their steps. He decided not to call out, not to try to stop their valiant muleteer. Why should he interfere with a man who knew the mountains and all the spirits they contained? He understood mysteries at which Kuitkowski could only guess.

Gaspar pulled a waterproof stuff sack from their pile of gear, removed her from Zorro's pack under the covering tarpaulin, and carefully cradled her in his blanket. As on the first day he found her, he converted the blanker into a sling, carrying her in the small of his back, now slightly bent as he pushed his way upward along the precipitous trail, surefooted, in his element, as the storm raged about him.

During their descent from the mountain Gaspar had given up trying to reason out what, if anything, he should do after rediscovering the little mummy. His thought processes were stymied both by wondering how it was possible that she appeared in Zorro's pack, but also by confusion over what Pachamama meant from him to do now. He crawled into his tent as the storm gathered intensity and tried to sleep. Lashing rain, cannonades of thunder, and his fevered brain kept him awake. Lightening struck nearby and he had his epiphany.

—*Devuelve ella. Devuelve ella.*

The command echoed in his head and he obeyed. No deliberation. No reasoning. His mind eased. Pachamama had spoken. He would return the little mummy.

The weather worsened as Gaspar splashed upward through freshets of storm water cascading down the steep trail. Exhilarated by the sudden clarity of his mission, he pushed onward happily, rummaging in his memory for a place to put the child mummy near the summit of the mountain he climbed. He settled on the spot where he and Pedro had paused the afternoon before, on a promontory jutting from the side of the mountain like the sharp tongue of a snake sensing its surroundings. Above the outcrop rose a weathered schist cliff facing east, corrugated and pock marked with little caves. He hoped he could locate the place again amid the wind, noise, and sleet so sharp he could taste blood flowing from his cheeks.

After another hour of climbing through the storm, he became worried that he would not find the location he remembered. The continuing flashes of lightning provided views of the trail quite different from what he recalled. Fleeting shadows stark against bleached rock mocked his recollection of the trail, and he felt his heart beating more quickly—not from his exertion but from rising panic that he would not be able to honor Pachamama's demand. He sank to his knees in the middle of the trail, searching all sides for the promontory, the cliff.

Through the blue glow of ball lightening that settled atop a blasted tree near the trail, he saw the dip in the earth that led to the jutting stone shelf where he had stood with Pedro. Elated, Gaspar almost slipped and tumbled back down the trail, but righted himself and examined the cliff face, searching for the mummy's new home. Shivering in the cold rain and sleet, he discovered an opening in the wall, about thirty feet above where he stood. It would do.

The upward climb scraped his fingers. He suspected they might be painful, but they were so numb he felt nothing. He braced himself on a foothold below the opening and removed the little mummy from her wrappings, replacing her on the schist shelf of the opening, turning her carefully to face the rising sun. Aided by flashes of lightening, he supported and shielded her with a low wall of interlaced stones, permitting her orange brow, wisp of dark hair and eternal grin to peek over the top of the rubble wall.

He descended and looked upward through bright flashes of light to confirm she could not be seen from below. Only the sun and the condors would be her companions as she resumed her ceaseless rest.

Weary, bloody, sodden, and joyous, Gaspar began his descent to their camp, shrugging off the tempest as though it were a shower. He was sure the storm would soon end. He was sure he had satisfied Pachamama.

The next day they crossed the Marañón River and found their way to the town of Huancaspata, a typical Andean village situated on the eastern slopes of the Cordillera Central. The streets were unpaved, but there was electricity and telephone service in the little post office. Larry disappeared into the telephone booth, where he remained for fifteen minutes. He was angry when he emerged.

—There is a problem with the line. The operator tries to place the call to my contact, and the line goes dead. All she can say is, *Más tarde.* I just need to keep trying. Meanwhile, let's see if there is a place we can stay tonight and organize transportation for tomorrow.

Under normal arrangements for a trek across the Cordillera Blanca, porters, the muleteer, and the cook would leave when the group returned to civilization, such as it was. The people hired to assist in the journey would receive their pay and make their way back home. On this trek, however, an unusual bond had formed through their common brush with danger. Their comrade, the porter, had been killed. Gaspar, for reasons he did not clearly understand, had captured a soldier and left him to the mercy of the mountains. They were all involved in defeating the army aggressors, and would be marked men if identified and caught.

As the travelers gathered around Pedro and Santiago, the cook spoke with the professor.

—*Jefe*, with your permission Gaspar and I would like to continue on this journey with you until you are safe.

Mercy was the first one to react. She hugged each man and kissed his cheek. The professor was more circumspect. He rapidly calculated the risks and benefits of accepting Santiago's proposal. If all went according to plan, they would soon be traveling by car or truck to Cajamarca, at most a ten-hour drive, even over bad roads. He planned to travel light and abandon most of their trekking gear, thereby allowing all four to go in the same vehicle. If Santiago and Gaspar joined them, two vehicles would be required. He foresaw no benefit to using two vehicles.

However, Gaspar had proved himself a worthy ally, and he knew the mountains and this side of the Cordillera Blanca. Santiago was a husky jack-of-all-trades, whom Kuitkowski considered a good man to have on his side. Although the cons seemed to outweigh the pros on his hastily assembled scorecard, his instinct, what he referred to as his "gut intelligence," declared otherwise. He stepped to Santiago and offered him a massive hug—a true Peruvian *abrazo*. He signaled Gaspar, standing with his mules, with a thumbs-up.

—*Con mucho gusto, amigos*, he offered, and the two helpers responded with wide grins.

Larry then excused himself to return to the telephone booth at the post office. Gaspar drove his mule to a corral a few blocks away from the bus stop and arranged for its care until he returned. Santiago refused to let Pedro abandon much of their valuable trekking gear: sleeping bags, tents, camp stools, leather boots and such. He solemnly told Wylie and Pedro that he would store them with his cooking gear and await their next trek through the mountains. Mercy and Wylie met his comment with rueful laughter.

They sat on wooden benches placed in shady spots at the periphery of the town square. Pedro kept watch on the post office, awaiting Larry's return, while Santiago busied himself sorting through trekking gear. Mercy helped decide what items could be discarded, which saved. Soon there were carefully packing bundles of equipment that Santiago and the porters carried to a storeroom near the plaza. Bulging backpacks for each of the travelers remained, clustered near Wylie.

It was now late afternoon; Larry had not returned from the post office and the members of the Cypher party were impatient and worried. Pedro rose and walked toward the post office, pausing as Larry finally left the building and walked toward them.

—Still no damned luck, he complained. The local operator is as frustrated as I am. There are no lines open to Cajamarca. I have a date with her to try later tonight.

—We should find a place to stay, said Pedro, and Larry agreed.

Their choices were limited. There was a cement block–and–adobe "tourist" hotel facing the plaza, and a hacienda converted into a local B and B up a steep road toward the mountains. Pedro, Larry, and Gaspar chose to stay near the plaza, and Santiago planned to accept an invitation from a local widow he met that afternoon. Mercy and Wylie stayed at the rustic hacienda. They would meet early the next morning, and Pedro promised to have transportation to Cajamarca ready. They were running out of time. To depart on the promised aircraft, they had to be at the tiny Cajamarca airport the next day for a late-night departure.

After a restless night, Wylie and Mercy picked their way down the rugged path from the hacienda to the plaza. The others were there, loading their packs in the back of two aged pickup trucks fouling the frosty air with diesel fumes. Pedro greeted them.

—Good news! Last night Larry found his contact. The plane is still on for tonight.

Good news indeed, thought Wylie, though he was concerned that the vehicles Pedro hired might not make it up the hill out of town, much less the two hundred and fifty miles to Cajamarca.

Larry noticed Wylie's dubious glance at the trucks.

—They are beat-up, but they are sound, Wylie. Pedro will be driving the first truck with you and Mercy, and the driver for the return trip will be in back with our stuff. Santiago and I will be riding with the other driver. Gaspar has volunteered to ride in back.

That seemed reasonable to Wylie, and he and Mercy squeezed onto the front seat as Pedro climbed in on the driver's side. As he pulled himself up, they saw he had a pistol jammed into his belt. Larry came to the cab and handed up the AK-47 Wylie had used to subdue the lead soldier.

—Hey, marksman, said Larry, you might want to hang on to this. Never can tell, you know.

Wylie checked the safety and carefully placed the weapon on the ledge behind the seat. He could tell from the weight that the clip was full.

With the sound of a blender grinding marbles, the truck lurched into gear and began to climb the hill to the northbound road toward Tayabamba. It was the first little village of a dozen or so they would pass on the way to their destination.

Wylie looked behind and saw the return driver resting comfortably on two sacks of grain, his feet on Mercy's backpack. Larry and Gaspar were barely visible through plumes of dust in the cab of the other truck. By noon, they were more than halfway to their destination, and they stopped for a meal at the crossroads town of Cajabamba. They washed the dust from their faces and rinsed their mouths with cold Cristal beer.

North of Cajabamba the road was better. It was recently graded and sporadically sprayed with oil. The clouds of dust diminished, and forward visibility improved. The afternoon light created a halo above the peaks of the snowcapped mountains to their left, and the truck gained speed.

—That's the town of Namora, said Pedro. The worst part of the trip is behind us. It is less than an hour to the airport from here.

Wylie and Mercy were elated. They roused themselves from the torpor induced by the monotony of the highway and the roar of the engine, and peered out the windows at local landmarks.

As they looked ahead to the long, straight stretch of road running through flat meadows on either side, Wylie noticed an obstruction. As Pedro drove closer, they saw three dark green trucks blocking the roadway behind a police car with flashing lights.

Pedro muttered a curse, and said,

—Get that rifle out of sight. This is probably because the Sendero Luminoso made another raid. Or maybe it is just the local police looking for a *propina*. I have some pesos just in case.

A police officer waved them to a stop. As they did, the other pickup truck pulled up behind them, and Gaspar stood and looked over the cab for a better view. As demanded, Pedro handed over his identity card, which the officer carefully examined. As he returned it to Pedro, he held out his hand for the identification of the two passengers. Their passports were in their backpacks, so Wylie pulled his driver's license from his wallet and handed it over. Mercy pretended to be looking for identification in her pockets.

The officer examined Wylie's license and walked back to the cab of one of the trucks. He handed the license up through the window to an obscured figure. A light flicked on in the cab, and the passenger door opened. The tip of a Lofstrand crutch protruded from the bottom of the door and rested on the step to the cab. A large man maneuvered the crutch to the ground and swung himself after it. It was the leader of the soldiers, the one Wylie had shot in the thigh.

21

The Admiral took a strong personal interest in the hunt for Wylie Cypher. He was particularly irritated that his quarry had twice been under the control of his forces and had eluded them both times. Additionally, Cypher and his group had destroyed an expensive helicopter (the paperwork to justify a replacement would take his adjutant days), caused the death of a highly trained commando, and shot the patrol leader through the leg. If the pilot had not found the homing device, the rescue team might still be searching for his men in the mountains.

They had patched up the patrol leader, who was highly motivated to complete his assignment of capturing and interrogating the gringo and his cohorts, especially his daughter. The Admiral assessed the possibility that the Americans had let the captured soldiers overhear that their destination was Cajamarca as a ruse. He decided that 1) there was no need for them to disguise their objective, since they believed they would be there before their pursuers could be rescued, and 2) gringos were not intelligent enough to be that deceptive. Consequently, he agreed to authorize the immediate departure of a team led by the wounded leader to set up a roadblock on the only road between Huancaspata and Cajamarca.

The team leader supported himself with the help of a crutch, and added a packet of Vicodin and a fresh supply of coca leaves to his pack. He hobbled to the transport vehicle and spoke with the soldiers seated inside, making lewd remarks about what they would do to their quarry. He pulled himself gingerly into the van, careful not to irritate the stitches that throbbed on his thigh. The vehicle ground into gear and began the journey to Cajamarca, where more soldiers and police waited to help them capture the wily gringos.

The trail was cold. There had been no word of the group of Americans after they left Huaraz and headed into the Cordillera Blanca. Lucho had dispatched two agents to Chavin in case that was their actual destination, but they did not come there. Information passed to contacts along the northern route of the Pacific highway, through Trujillo and points north, as well as in Cajamarca Province. Seven days since they left, and not a word.

He was at a base near Ayacucho, where he could continue to monitor his group of special forces known as *carniceros*. Their mission was to gather intelligence from the people of the mountains about interactions they had with the authorities. Initially they induced cooperation by providing medicine, some money, even food when crops failed. They patterned their activities after campaigns in Vietnam. They intended to win the hearts and minds of *los indios*.

Unfortunately, government authorities intended to thwart all collaboration with the guerrillas and employed a heavy hand to discourage it. Beatings were common. Not so common were "disappearances," although they did happen.

As intimidation from both sides intensified, baser aspects of human nature surfaced. Petty arguments among friends escalated. Denunciations to either the police or Sendero Luminoso resulted in severe repercussions for the suspected collaborator. The intensity of punishments increased. Beatings became harsher, and broken bones were routine. Interrogators used hammers and pliers. The *carniceros*, under Lucho's direction, carried bolt cutters with them. Perhaps as a subconscious reference to his own ruined hand, he sanctioned the judicious removal of fingers and toes to assist in information gathering and intimidation. The more sadistic members of the *carniceros* enjoyed tossing severed digits to the always hungry dogs of mountain villages.

A dedicated leader, Lucho decided to join a *carniceros* patrol. As Claudia remarked to Fredo, Lucho the warrior little resembled the easygoing football star they knew at the university. The physical changes were easily recognized— his ruined hand, cloudy eye and need to turn his good ear toward a speaker. However, the changes in his character were more profound. There was darkness in him. It was as though the weight of his growing dedication to the Sendero

Luminoso unbalanced his scale of moral judgment. He was willing to perform any abhorrent act to further the communist cause. People of the mountains unlucky enough to be visited by him and the *carniceros* recalled his earlier nickname of "Capitán Garra"—now with fear and hatred. His notoriety preceded him.

The patrol entered the village at midmorning. They knew that three policemen had visited the week before. Shortly after they left, soldiers arrived and carted off to an unknown location two young men who volunteered for the cause and planned to begin training as soon as the harvest ended. It was beyond coincidence. Someone certainly had cooperated with the authorities.

Lucho and the patrol interrogated a village leader in his hillside home. It was rough-hewn, with a tin roof, with entrance steps raised to counter the steep upward incline. They remained inside for perhaps a quarter hour, but discovered no helpful information. As they left, a small girl aged nine or ten stood beside the steps. There were tears in her eyes and smudges on her cheeks, caused by the screams of her father inside the home. She held a machete more than half her size.

Lucho, his head turned to speak with a comrade, was the first down the steps and, as he descended, the little girl widened her stance and swung the blade forward with all her strength. The sharp edge bit into Lucho's right shin, just above the boot top, and severed his anterior tibia muscle, stopping short of the bone itself. The man behind him saw him crumple and fall, then roll a few meters down the steep slope, stopping against a stone wall. Neither saw the little girl, who immediately disappeared into one of the many alleyways in the village.

Lucho's injury required treatment at the hospital in Ayacucho, but it was almost two days before he arrived there. By then, opportunistic biotic matter from the machete and the earth he rolled over had found his wound a welcoming host. A surgeon's efforts to debride the wound and reattach the severed muscle were only partially successful. Although he was soon able to walk almost normally with the help of a brace, the muscle remained perpetually weakened. Control of his foot was poor. Kicking a football was out of the question.

22

Two boys noticed the early morning arrival of the vehicles blocking the highway on the outskirts of Namora. They ran back to the highland village to announce the unwanted intrusion of the soldiers, which one of the village elders quickly relayed to the agents of the Sendero Luminoso looking for recruits. The boys and a few friends monitored the trucks and police car as a commander of the guerillas considered plans for their disposal.

High grasses in the meadows on either side of the roadway provided excellent cover. The young men in the village who intended to join the insurrection were enthusiastic about proving themselves against the detested military that treated them like dirt and beat them or worse for harboring revolutionary sentiments. Newly available grenade launchers bearing Cyrillic markings were appropriate for the contemplated assault. It would be a while, however, before the necessary armaments arrived. Some of the young men crawled through the tall grass to get a better look.

They saw two plumes of dust in the distance, which materialized into a pair of vintage pickup trucks that approached the roadblock. The trucks stopped, and a soldier using a crutch approached the first pickup. Almost immediately more soldiers jumped from the back of a truck and surrounded both pickups. A soldier yanked open the driver's door of the first truck and forced the driver out and onto his knees on the ground. Two other people, one a young woman, were pulled from the other side and forced to kneel next to the driver. A man in the bed of the pickup was waved to the ground, where he sat, apparently mystified at the proceedings.

As the same scenario was repeated with the second pickup, a handful of Shining Path guerrillas joined the boys in the tall grass with two grenade launchers and enough rifles to pass around. The rifles smelled of Cosmoline. The grenade launchers resembled Thompson submachine guns from the thirties—stubby, oversize rifles with a circular magazine holding a dozen fat grenades. The guerrillas also carried olive-green satchels that held more ammunition for their weapons. The self-appointed squad leader crouched down in the grass and raised his binoculars to peer at the activities ahead through the waving grass. He tried to assess whether the people detained were friend or foe. Finally, he decided it did not matter—they were there to kill soldiers and police. If others got in the way, *mala suerte*. However, he was interested in the goings-on and decided to await further developments.

The leader of the soldiers was elated that he had found his quarry from the mountains, and was so eager to discipline them that he almost forget his mission was to recover the floppy disks containing sensitive information. He hobbled over to the man kneeling on the ground, the one who shot him. He jabbed him hard in the chest with the end of his crutch and sent him sprawling on the ground. A jolt of pain seared his thigh, but he ignored it.

Wylie spit out road dust and stared at his captor. He realized his negotiating skills would be of little use at this point and decided to become meek and obedient. The wounded leader called over a young soldier and spoke to him quickly in Spanish. The soldier leaned over Wylie, who had returned to the kneeling position, smiled and said,

—Hi, there. You're from the States, right? Great place. I spent my sophomore year as an exchange student in Manalapan, New Jersey. Anyway, listen, *jefe*'s really pissed because, you know, you shot him. But he really needs to know where those disks are, and I think you'd better tell him, if you can. He's not really a nice guy.

The young soldier smiled again and confirmed to his leader that he had properly asked the gringo. The leader stood over Wylie and gestured an unmistakable, *Where?* Wylie did his best to look confused and meek and shook his head slightly. The crutch tip swung out and caught him on his left ear. Until then,

Wylie had not realized how many sensitive nerve endings were in his ear. He reached up involuntarily to cup the throbbing flesh.

In the next few minutes, a succession of blows to tender parts of his body challenged Wylie's endurance and acting ability. He managed to absorb the blows and maintain his confused look. The meek look was over. The leader unholstered his pistol, pointed it at Wylie's groin, and fired. A cloud of gravel erupted from the dirt in front of his crotch and an involuntary splotch of urine stained Wylie's trousers. Somehow, he managed to appear calm and looked blankly at his tormentor. The leader decided on a new approach.

Pedro, the professor, Santiago and Gaspar were lined up on their knees in front of the second truck, watching. They saw the limping soldier aim a weak kick at Wylie's stomach and then recoil from the obvious pain it caused him. He moved to Mercy, kneeling a few feet away, and told two soldiers to lift her up. She kicked one of them in the instep. He yelled in pain, then retaliated by punching her hard just below her breasts. She staggered but they managed to stand her upright. The soldiers began dragging her toward the back of one of the covered trucks.

The leader returned to Wylie, pointed toward Mercy and made the unmistakable sign of his forefinger moving in and out of the ring formed by the thumb and forefinger of his other hand. The message was clear.

Wylie could not retain his confused appearance as he glared at the soldier, who placed the muzzle of his pistol a quarter centimeter from his captive's left eye. For an electric, dangerous moment each man's macho impulses ruled. Mercy stared at her father, praying that he would not do something foolish. He did not. Instead, he realized that the soldier had nothing to gain by putting a bullet into his head, but that he might be stupid enough to do it anyway. With great effort, he relaxed his body and lowered his gaze, a signal that prompted the soldier to withdraw the pistol and keep it aimed vaguely at Wylie's chest.

Wylie straightened and pointed toward the rear of the pickup truck, motioning that he needed to go there to collect the . . . What the hell was the word in Spanish? He made a guess. "*Discos*," he said, pointing once more to the rear of the pickup. The soldier understood and waved Wylie to his feet and followed him to the rear of the truck. He clambered into the bed and pulled Mercy's daypack from the various bundles there. Holding it in his hand, he jumped to the ground and began to unzip the utility pocket in back. The soldier motioned to him to stop, reached for the pack, and pulled a guidebook from the zippered compartment. It was his turn to appear confused. He flipped through the pages and discovered two square black plastic disks, one of which fell to the ground. Wylie looked at him and repeated, "*Discos.*"

A look that conveyed both triumph and anticipation of what was to come crossed the soldier's face. He replaced the disks in the book and put it in the pocket of his field jacket. He licked his lips and motioned for Wylie to return to the front of the truck. He looked at Mercy, standing stiffly among other soldiers at the back of the nearest military truck, and smiled. The smile was short-lived.

An explosion occurred in front of the military vehicle farthest from him, cutting in half two soldiers chatting with the driver through an open window.

The Sendero Luminoso leader monitoring the events on the road had become puzzled and bored. He had no idea what the military wanted with those gringos, but was concerned they might all soon be loaded into the trucks and carted away, denying him his coveted targets. In addition, he was eager to fire one of the grenade launchers to see what it would do. The others had already selected their rifles and ammunition. He demanded that they fan out in the high grass in a semicircle so they could concentrate their fire on the enemy soldiers. He took up a grenade launcher and handed the second one to an experienced guerrilla who would anchor the northern end of the line of fire. He moved to the other end, and the men wiggled through the grass to get within one hundred meters of their targets. At that range, even the inexperienced members of his squad could do damage.

When they were in position, the leader raised the grenade launcher and sighted down the short, thick barrel. It was more like a shotgun than a rifle, and he did not know how accurate the aim was or, for that matter, how accurate it needed to be. He suspected he should aim high, which he did, sighting on the cab of the truck farthest north. He fired, watching the bulbous missile fly toward the target. The distance was correct, but the aim was off. The grenade exploded in front of the truck, ruining its front tires and killing the two soldiers standing there.

The next grenade clicked into place and he fired again, as did the man with the other launcher. The other men with small arms selected targets and engaged their very confused enemy. As bullets and explosives rained down on them, the soldiers milled around the trucks searching for muzzle flashes concealed by daylight and the tall grasses. Unable to see their enemy, some of the soldiers took cover under the trucks and on the roadway. Others disappeared into the high grass on the other side of the road, out of sight but useless.

—*Cobardes!* screamed the leader at the soldiers hiding in the grass as he awkwardly maneuvered behind the trucks, firing his own pistol in their direction. They quickly emerged to take positions with the others, firing wildly into the grass at their front. Return fire accurately began to pick off the soldiers, and explosions from the grenades injured some as gravel and debris from the roadway plunged into their bodies. In the chaos of what was becoming a killing field the soldiers' blood began to stain the dusty gravel of the roadway.

Larry and Pedro immediately took advantage of the distraction caused by the firefight. As their captors' attention was directed to their own preservation, they rose from their knees and ran to the pickups to find their hidden weapons—Pedro the assault rifle and Larry his automatic pistol. Santiago, Gaspar and the return drivers crouched behind the second pickup watching their guards look away from them, searching for another enemy. Gaspar reached into the bed of the pickup and found a tire iron, which he used to stun one of their guards. Santiago attacked the other with his beefy fist, sending him to the ground. Gaspar wielded his tire iron again to crown the soldier on the ground. Santiago saw an abandoned rifle and, surrounded by the ping of bullets hitting the earth, crawled to get it. As he stretched out his arm to recover the rifle an incoming round ricocheted on the road's surface and struck him in the shoulder. Suddenly he could not move his right arm and a sharp pain coursed from his shoulder to his fingers. Pushing with his left arm, he maneuvered back to the side of the truck, where Gaspar tried to stop the bleeding.

Larry dashed to the side of the pickup to the rear and surveyed the situation. Clearly, the military convoy was the primary target, but the lack of precision in the fire coming from the high grass gave no assurance their pickups would be spared. They needed to back up their trucks to avoid the kill zone created by those firing from the side of the road.

The moment the shell struck the first military vehicle, the soldier with the crutch spun clumsily toward the target, temporarily loosing interest in Wylie. When he swung back to focus on his captive, Wylie had disappeared, rolling under the pickup and pulling himself back toward the tailgate. The soldier cursed, looked toward the action and noticed some of the soldiers running into the tall grass on the other side of the convoy. Incensed, he pursued them and, as he did, another grenade struck the first truck, cut through the canvas covering the back, and ignited something. There was an explosion and a soldier wrapped in flames fell from the tailgate and rolled, shrieking, on the oiled pavement.

Larry ran to Wylie, helped pull him from under the truck, and told him to climb into the back and take cover. Instead, Wylie looked forward, searching for Mercy. He saw her, sprinted to the open door of the truck, reached for the rifle he had placed behind the seats, and ran pell-mell toward his daughter.

Mercy crouched next to one of the truck's large tires, dry mouthed, her heart pounding as little puffs of gray dust erupted around her. Her guard crouched on the other side of the tire, no less terrorized than she was. Wylie and Pedro were of the same mind and almost collided in their rush to get to Mercy. Her guard had only a moment to observe the near collision. Pedro hit the man in the forehead with his rifle butt and he toppled to the ground under the truck. Meanwhile, the grenades and small arms fire were arriving with greater accuracy. Although the impact of the grenades did not have the dramatic force of mortar or phosphorus rounds, they were powerful enough. Within the first few minutes, they incapacitated one military truck and a police car, and punctured the bodies of almost a quarter of the confused soldiers. Seeing their enemies concerned with saving their own skins, Wylie and Pedro picked Mercy up under the arms and propelled her to the first pickup, where all three crouched on the other side of the engine block.

The truck listed to the passenger side, and Pedro could see that both tires there were not only flat, but also shredded. An ominous puddle of oily liquid was visible under the engine. They looked to the other pickup where Larry waited, gesturing wildly that they abandon the first truck and run toward him. They closed the gap between the trucks like champion sprinters and arrived at Larry's side breathing hard and red faced.

They saw that Santiago lay on the bed of the pickup, a blood soaked rag wrapped around his shoulder, and that the two relief drivers had placed most of the bundles from the other pickup there as well. The drivers sat with their backs to the cab of the truck while Larry, kneeling on the tailgate, held an automatic rifle taken from one of the soldiers. As Pedro, Wylie, and Mercy arrived, Larry motioned them to the cab of the truck and Gaspar, who acted as lookout, clambered over the back to sit next to Santiago. Larry raised the tailgate and sat in the corner of the bed as Pedro and the others piled into the cab. Pedro twisted the ignition key.

Nothing happened.

Pedro frantically turned the key again.

There was not even a click or a grinding noise. Nothing.

Larry called from the back of the truck,

—Step on the clutch! Step on the damned clutch!

Pedro did. The starter clicked and groaned and the engine sputtered twice, finally coming to life. He slipped the gear into reverse and sprayed gravel from all tires as the truck backed quickly away from the other pickup. They were two hundred meters from the roadblock when the first military truck burst into flames, leaped from the roadway and exploded into an orange-and-black column of smoke.

The magazines of both grenade launchers were empty. Someone else had the satchel of ammunition, and the leader of the attackers was uncertain how to reload the weapons. He put the launcher aside and surveyed the carnage on the road ahead. One of the military vehicles was a smudged memory; another was burning brightly, both from the back and in the engine compartment. The police car was pockmarked with bullet holes and bereft of window glass. One of the policemen was slumped over the far fender, motionless.

All of the soldiers had found some sort of cover, even if only to lie prone on the surface of the road. It was difficult to tell how many were dead, but the wounded ones were writhing on the ground. A handful of soldiers were firing sporadically at targets they could not see.

It appeared that the smaller command vehicle might still be functional, but the third truck showed daylight through various holes in its skin. A pickup truck seemed undamaged, though oddly canted to one side. The other pickup made a fishtail turn and flew back down the road.

All told, not a bad afternoon's work for a group of mainly untested young recruits. It was time to go home.

An eerie quiet settled on the roadway. There was no more fire from the tall grasses to the east. Sunlight and fluffy clouds above contrasted with the burning vehicles and frightened soldiers waiting for further onslaught. Minutes passed. Cautiously, soldiers began to tend their wounded comrades and mourn the dead ones. Their frustrated leader organized a patrol to scout the position of their attackers, and five men crawled eastward through the high grass. After two hundred meters, they encountered no resistance, rose and walked back to the trucks. The enemy had evaporated.

In spite of its ruined appearance, the unburned truck functioned. The wounded and dead were placed in the bay, and three men joined them to help their injured comrades. Three more rode in front, and the truck passed the still-burning vehicles toward Cajamarca and medical treatment.

The leader's command vehicle suffered only minor damage. The radio functioned and he was able to contact their base in Cajamarca to report his present situation and alert medical teams. The dispatcher recorded the information and confirmed that their attack was one of many recently perpetrated by the emboldened Shining Path.

—*Mala suerte, jefe*, he added.

Bad luck indeed, thought the leader. We are not through with those bastard gringos yet.

—*Mira*, he said, they still want to reach the airport. Secure it! Do it now!

After two kilometers of coaxing maximum speed from the aged diesel engine of the pickup truck, Pedro followed the professor's suggestion and pulled over. They all disembarked, and Santiago, stiff with pain, pointed out water bottles they could use to wash off their accumulated dust and dirt. Their first bit of chatter involved guesses about the authors of their salvation.

—Classic ambush, said Larry. It was certainly the Shining Path. They specialize in targets of opportunity. I just wish they had started earlier to knock out the roadblock. We would be at the airport by now if they had.

He turned to Wylie.

—Sorry, man. After all that, you had to give up those disks. No other choice, of course.

He looked at Mercy, who stood with her arm around Wylie's shoulder. Wylie responded.

—Don't be concerned. When they finally get to look at the data on those disks, they will find old inventory lists of stuff in Don Weschler's warehouses. I arranged for the original disks to be couriered back to my office in New York. They should be in my office safe by now. I was planning to deal with this after a pleasant trek in these beautiful mountains. Shows how wrong a guy can be!

The looks of surprise among his companions gradually turned to grins. The irony of their situation was unmistakable. It cut through the accumulated tensions of the past hour or so. The grins turned to laughter, and Larry moved to Wylie and was about to punch him in the biceps, but thought better of it. The crutch had left some tender areas on his body.

—You son of a bitch, he offered. You might have shared that information with us before.

—Listen, Wylie said. You're the spook. Surely you appreciate the concept of "need to know." I couldn't see any benefit in explaining what had happened to the original disks.

Pedro, struck by a new thought, continued to laugh until water came to his eyes.

—*Coño*, but I would love to be there when they look at those files. A ruined helicopter, an avalanche, a bullet through the leg, and for what? A list of sacks of powdered milk and grain.

His laughter was infectious. When they all finally stopped, they sat on the shoulder of the road to recover and decide on next steps.

—The trucks will certainly still be there, guarded by some of the soldiers, so we can't take a direct route back, said Larry. Pedro, is there another way around?

The guide scratched his head.

—I believe there is an old dirt road at San Marcos, a few kilometers back, which skirts this highway to the south. I have never been on it.

—Do we have a choice? asked Wylie.

They all glumly shook their heads.

—At least we can find help for Santiago, offered Mercy.

As they returned to the truck, the two backup drivers, having experienced enough excitement for one day, said they intended to walk back to Namora. Larry peeled some greenbacks from a wad of bills that magically appeared, and rewarded them. They grabbed their blanket packs and walked on, relieved and very happy.

There was a man in San Marcos who healed animals and people. He promised to care for Santiago, and Gaspar assured his friend he would return for him. Gaspar, as a matter of honor, would not leave his employers until they were safely on their way home.

The dirt road to Cajamarca was little better than a mule trail, rutted and washed out. They had to ford so many streams that Pedro lost count. Finally, as lights from nearby villages began to cut into dusky shadows, they found the cutoff to the village of Jesús and the beginning of a paved highway. Fuel was low, so Pedro stopped at the first gas station, which, conveniently, had a telephone. Larry rushed to make a few calls as Wylie marveled at his ability to communicate with contacts almost anywhere in Peru. Wylie's tax dollars at work.

When they had reassembled after using the primitive facilities and succeeded in removing additional grime, Larry returned.

—There is no good news, he explained. A truck full of gringos will never penetrate the heightened security around the little airport. It makes no difference anyway. Our flight is now engaged in another mission. There is a high-level defector from Ecuador who has information about the plane crash in that killed President Jaime Roldós Aguilera. His escape takes precedence over ours.

Mercy let out a long sigh and looked at her father. Pedro kicked at the gravel underfoot.

Larry continued.

—We are directed to head to the Chachapoyas area, where there are three small airports. There is no rush. The town is about five hours away and I was told to make contact again two days after tomorrow.

Gaspar listened attentively, hoping to pick up the gist of the discussion through the little English he knew. He brightened at Larry's last comments, and said,

—*Chachapoyas es bueno*. Kuelap there. *Momias*. Many *momias*.

He pointed to Larry.

—You like. Many *momias*.

His train of thought interrupted, Larry did not at first grasp the meaning of Gaspar's outburst. Then the archaeologist understood. He had heard of the great fortress of Kuelap, a massive ruin that rivaled Machu Picchu, but he knew nothing of mummies there. They returned to the truck, preparing to find a place to stay that night. Wylie and Mercy rode with Pedro in the cab, Larry and Gaspar in back, sitting close together talking about mummies and the sixth-century fortress near Chachapoyas.

Lucho studied the report of the ambush near Namora. It was poorly written and reflected the verbal transfer of information before it was transcribed. A significant part of the report recorded appreciation for the newly available grenade launchers. He automatically reduced the estimates of damage done to vehicles and people; it was a universal element of military reports to exaggerate the prowess of the attackers. He focused on the two pickup trucks detained by the military. The report mentioned a few gringos and a woman but did not specify the exact number.

He consulted a map of the area. It was certainly possible that the Cypher group had crossed the Cordillera Blanca to the Río Marañón and found their way north to Namora. The timing seemed correct. He called two leaders in the Cajamarca area to alert them to the possible presence of his quarry.

The administration required hotels, guesthouses and the like to obtain and record basic information about their guests from either national identification cards or passports. The local police sporadically collected those reports. Given the porous corruption of lower-level members of the police, it was not difficult to obtain copies. Lucho's contacts in the Cajamarca region would certainly find a way to vet the reports, among other means of tracking the group of gringos.

There were, however, a number of routes out of Cajamarca. Luck would play a major role in discovering where the gringos were headed.

Larry was aware that operators of overnight accommodations were required to collect information about their guests, but also knew that requirement was honored more in the breach than in practice. Nevertheless, when checking in he always presented a Canadian passport identifying him as Harold Cummings, a fringe benefit of working for the CIA. After presenting his passport, he would nod to the others and tell the clerk they were with him. Usually that, and a few *soles* placed on the counter, preserved the anonymity of the others in his group. The past few days, however, the police were enforcing the reporting requirement very strictly, and the nod and the cash were not working. He hoped that they might avoid detection by staying in rundown places one night at a time. So far, that was successful.

23

The little cards with information about overnight travelers arrived daily at the Cajamarca main police station. The clerk who sorted, filed, and destroyed old copies was on an unaccustomed mission. On the right side of his sorting table was a stained card with two names written in bold print: Cypher and Kuitkowski. His urgent task was to see if either of those names appeared on the information cards filed daily. The names impressed the clerk, who was accustomed to filing cards with Spanish names. These were foreign and mouth filling. He tried to pronounce the second name to himself, and became tangled between the second and third syllables. He was filled with a great sense of accomplishment when, after his second break for coffee, Cypher appeared on a registration card. It was dated two nights ago from a small hotel in Enceñada, just off the only road north to Chachapoyas.

He reported this find to his superior, who sat in a proper office with windows and chairs. He grunted approval to the clerk, dismissed him and dialed the telephone number of the military office near the Cajamarca airport to make his report. He paused to light a cigarette and placed another call to a good friend and benefactor who was interested in those two names. In the space of a few moments, the military and Sendero Luminoso knew where the Cypher party had stayed two nights before.

Pedro and Gaspar were searching for a fan belt to replace the rapidly deteriorating one on the pickup truck. Mercy, Wylie and Larry sat in a little café that belonged to the roughshod hotel where they spent the night. Rested and showered, they had separately reviewed the events of days past and were discussing them without the influence of terror or adrenaline. Mercy was speaking.

—So, Daddy, you knew ever since we left Lima that the real floppy disks were on their way back to New York. Why did you even bother to keep the fake ones?

The professor also awaited Wylie's answer.

—Well, honey, in twenty years of lawyering, I learned that a little sleight of hand could be useful. If anyone looking for the disks believed I had them with me, they wouldn't be looking for them elsewhere. Also, although I did not know what value the fakes had, I assumed they would have *some* value. Since they provided a few moments' delay yesterday, I guess I was right. They were also handy bookmarks in the travel guide.

That comment amused Larry, but made Mercy frown. She sometimes thought her father took things too lightly.

They rehashed those fearsome events, emphasizing how lucky they were with the timely intervention of the attackers.

—Until that moment, there were no options other than to submit to that army guy, said Larry. Considering what happened on the mountain and the fact that Wylie shot him in the leg, it would not have been pleasant

Mercy had unanswered questions.

—Larry, you were sure that the attackers were Sendero Luminoso. Tell me more about that.

—They are a large group of Maoist communists who have taken advantage of the administration's failure to support or care for the poorest members of Peruvian society—the native people. In fact, the politicians in Lima seem to have a policy of purposeful suppression; the natives are actively discriminated against. So, as the gap between haves and have-nots increases, the seeds of revolt are easily sown. The organization has grown silently for years, and boiled over into guerrilla activities in 1980. They have accelerated since then.

—The Sendero Luminoso attracts people who will fight to improve their situation, and intellectuals who simply believe suppression is unfair or untenable. The young man who gave your father the disks was probably one of those.

—I see, interjected Mercy, but why were you sure those were the ones who attacked the roadblock yesterday?

—Who else could it be? Their tactics were taken right out of Chairman Mao's little red book. Actually, even though we were rather busy, I was impressed with those tactics. Smart—they withdrew after inflicting maximum damage with no apparent injury to themselves.

Wylie chuckled.

—Yeah. We owe those commie bastards our skins. Another one of life's little ironies.

Mercy continued.

—So, Larry, what does the CIA think the outcome of all this will be—if you can say?

—It's touchy. The government is a fresh democracy, elected after years of military rule. Corruption is rife and there is no indication that President Belaunde has the power or ability to pull together effective countermeasures. We will help where we can, but the outcome is unsure. It won't be the first time leftists have gained control of a Latin American country.

Larry paused to consider another thought.

—Insurrection and revolt are more common than we realize. It seems one government or another is overthrown every few months. We had our own shot at it in 1776. Never know—it might happen again.

Mercy regretted that her studies at Bryn Mawr had not included more references to South America. That was something she resolved to remedy, but not now. They needed to discuss plans for the next few days.

Wylie asked how they might fill the time until their departure by air from the Chachapoyas area. Larry had a few ideas.

—Gaspar believes he has an ongoing relationship with the goddess Pachamama, who has permitted him to observe things in the mountains not all can see. For some reason, mummies fascinate him. He has wandered these mountains all his life, and says he knows of a secret place on the way to Chachapoyas that he would share with us. I am not sure why, but I think he wants to show off the power of his ancestors and help us get closer to his goddess. We have three days to wait until I can make contact again. Perhaps we could have a look. The archaeologist part of me is fascinated with the idea.

Wylie agreed.

—We need to go in that direction anyway. But I think that by now, the soldiers have discovered that the floppy disks I surrendered aren't the ones they are looking for. The man I shot seemed very tenacious. I bet there's a good chance they will come after us again.

—You're right, said Larry, but they'd be spread thin. They need to know which way we're going, and there are many routes north. But there will always be risks until we are out of Peru. I was planning to take back roads and avoid the highway anyway. If we did that, we would be at the location Gaspar told me about at noon tomorrow. He says the place is not close to the highway.

—Have you talked this over with Pedro?

—Yes. He favors the idea.

Mercy and her father exchanged glances.

—Let's do it!

Pedro managed to smear his nose with grease while changing the fan belt; Mercy cleaned it with a baby wipe she carried for such occasions. The others loaded the pickup, creating a comfortable place for Gaspar and Larry in back. Pedro hid two attack rifles in places of easy access, and Larry carried a pistol in his belt. It was not as though the truck was bristling with armaments, but the Cypher group did not intend to be caught off guard during their continuing flight to freedom.

With Gaspar's help, Pedro repaired minor damage sustained during the attack at the roadblock and the truck was fueled and ready for rough travel. An extra spare tire served as a footrest for Gaspar in the back of the truck. They started north on the highway at midmorning, and Pedro turned onto a parallel side road as soon as he could. It was not quite as bad as the rutted mule trail to Cajamarca.

Gaspar pointed to various side routes that avoided the main highway, but a significant part of the way required travel on the only road through the mountains. Their objective was the place known as the Laguna de los Condores.

Gaspar laughed as he explained to Larry that the lagoon was now dry, and that all condors were farther south. However, the old name persisted.

Years ago, on his travels, Gaspar had learned from a farmer who employed him that there were underground limestone caverns near the old lagoon that were accessible by an almost perpendicular opening. He investigated and, by the light of a pitch torch, discovered mummy bundles and drawings on the walls. The torch burned out and he had to clamber his way out in darkness. He always intended to return.

Larry asked about grave robbers who often ruined or defaced such archaeological finds.

In deference to the spirits of the ancestors, the local farmers kept its location secret from outsiders. The entrance was hidden, and the passage was dangerous. So far as Gaspar knew, the caves were undisturbed.

This information intrigued Larry greatly. He studied all the archeological literature about discoveries in Peru as part of his professional obligations. There were numerous references to Kuelap and strange sarcophagi that resembled the Moai of Easter Island in nearby cliffs. However, no one ever mentioned mummy bundles either there or near the Laguna de los Condores. He hoped that Gaspar was not mistaken—or deluded.

Mercy held a map of the local area on her lap and helped guide Pedro along the side roads. Where none existed, they traveled along the main road. Wylie was content to observe the passing scenery—beautiful and rugged. The route Pedro and Mercy planned went from Enceñada to Balsas by way of the market town of Celendín. They would travel along a flat pass to the Marañón Canyon, more than three thousand meters deep. From the bank of the canyon, they needed to rejoin the main highway and follow switchbacks cut through the mountains to arrive at the lowest point between Cajamarca and Chachapoyas—the village of Balsas. In just a few hours, they would pass through high plains and a cloud forest to reach dry forest and jungle at the lowest point on their route.

The Cordillera Blanca had dropped away behind them the day before. Now Pedro pointed the truck east, toward the central mountain range of the Peruvian Andes. Their peaks were dappled with ice and snow, and the mountains rose like dragons' teeth from their misty foothills. Their predominant colors were brown and green, highlighted by silver streaks of tributaries flowing to the Marañón

River. The steep climb was still ahead. Wylie looked at the tall grasses waving on either side of the truck and understood how difficult it was to penetrate their golden camouflage. Larry was right: That had been an excellent ambush.

The thin air and physical exertion required to cross the high peaks in the Cordillera Blanca permitted only occasional moments to appreciate the raw splendor of the snowcapped mountains. Today, sitting comfortably in the cab of the moving truck, Wylie and Mercy fully experienced the rough beauty of their surroundings. Ahead lay the blue mountains of the Cordillera Central, closely ranked, with deep canyons separating individual peaks. They blended together in the distance like waves on the ocean's horizon, wisps of clouds simulating whitecaps. As they began to climb upward toward the rim of the great canyon, breezes turned to winds and the temperature dropped. The mists of the mountains consolidated and fogged the deep green leaves of surrounding trees. They entered the cloud forest, lush with vegetation, bromeliads, orchids and mistletoe cluttering the branches of the trees pushing into the road.

By the time they arrived in Celendín, their senses were so overloaded with the physical beauty of their surroundings that they almost forget the peril they hastened to escape. Pedro broke the mood by searching for a remote place to park in hopes of avoiding curious or dangerous eyes. He found a place behind a stable some blocks away from the central square.

As they walked toward the square to find *almuerzo*, Mercy noted the brilliant white straw hats worn by the villagers. The ones worn by women were like upside-down flowerpots, while the men wore wider-brimmed sombreros.

—I had forgotten, said Pedro. The people here make the best hats in Peru. They weave them from toquilla straw and work on a single hat for weeks or months.

Mercy was impressed.

—Is it okay for a woman to wear a man's hat? I think I would like to have one with a wide brim.

—They don't see many gringos here and will be very happy to sell you any hat you like. If you buy one, you can use it any way you want—even to shade a donkey's eyes.

Mercy bought a wide-brimmed hat and tied a green scarf around it. Pedro said she looked very pretty in her new bonnet.

Larry and Wylie talked with Gaspar. More correctly, Larry talked with Gaspar and Wylie scrubbed the corners of his brain to make maximum use of the Spanish words he knew. The mule driver was excited to be so near the place he had visited many years ago. He recalled the topography of the location and the place where an opening descended into the caves below. He was not sure how many mummies there were, but more than the fingers on two hands.

They consulted Pedro's map. Unless the roads were seriously bad, they would cross a suspension bridge over the Marañón River and be in Balsas just before nightfall. Overnight accommodations there were primitive, and Gaspar offered to sleep in the truck—for protection, he said. Celendín was a much larger town than Balsas, with a larger variety of needed items available. Wylie and Pedro went shopping for batteries, headlamps, candles, and rope. Pedro also acquired a shovel and a crowbar. They were not cavers, but Pedro had visited limestone caves before. He wanted to be prepared.

As they prepared to drive to the rim of the canyon, the men went over the proposed plans with Mercy. She was not thrilled with the prospect of exploring a dark cave full of dead people, but stoutly agreed to participate. There were, after all, no more attractive options.

The view from the top of the canyon was spectacular. From an altitude of more than thirty-three hundred meters, the seemingly endless Marañón River wound its serpentine way among the clustered mountains—twenty-eight hundred meters below. A distant sea of clouds obscured the far reaches of the valley. The group pulled on sweaters and parkas as they left the truck to enjoy the view. Gaspar pointed enthusiastically to landmarks only he could recognize.

—Laguna de los Condores, he said. Chachapoyas!

He beamed at the others. It was clear that he looked forward to introducing them to places he called home.

The road deteriorated as they began to navigate the switchbacks descending toward the floor of the canyon. The gravel was rutted, and many rocks placed as a meager guardrail had fallen off the edge. As Pedro drove the truck around another hairpin curve, Mercy saw a large yellow object in a canyon below. It was a school bus wedged on its side between two jagged outcrops. Pedro noticed her glance.

—Yes, he said. It was very sad. It happened two months ago and was reported on television and in the Lima papers. The bus fell off the mountain one morning. Twenty-seven little children and the driver died. It took almost a week to return them to their families.

Her eyes grew moist. She recalled a line from one of Shakespeare's sonnets—"Roses have thorns, and silver fountains mud." What else did this splendid landscape conceal?

The turns became more aggressive, and Pedro strained to manage the wheel. Wylie and Mercy dug their fingers into the plastic armrests and upholstery. Their hands ached when the truck finally reached the bottom of the valley and crossed the river. Larry and Gaspar were so involved in their conversation that they hardly noticed that the truck had arrived in Balsas.

The next morning a grumpy Wylie sat on the porch in front of the ramshackle "motel" where they had spent the night.

—Lumpy mattress, cock crowing all night long, a dog barking under my window. That's how well I slept, he responded to Mercy's inquiry.

She, on the other hand, looked clean and refreshed, had her hair pulled back and wore her new hat at a cocked angle. Pedro arrived a few moments before Larry and Gaspar, and one of the workers in the motel delivered hot mugs of instant coffee transformed with sweet milk. Coffee brightened Wylie's outlook; he told Mercy how pretty she looked.

—Gaspar says the lagoon is about a two-hour drive from here, noted Larry. Then we need to hike in a little way to find the entrance. If we are ready, I suggest we go.

Ten kilometers from Balsas was a flat area called Homopampa—oven plain—where, as advertised, they experienced a minor heat wave. The temperature quickly dropped as the road wound upward to the top of the eastern edge of the canyon, where they again saw the entire length of the river valley festooned with puffy clouds. They made another descent and continued toward the Laguna de los Condores, at an altitude of about twenty-seven hundred meters. Under ordinary circumstances, Wylie and Mercy would have been breathless a mile and a half high, but they were seasoned trekkers now, and felt invigorated as Pedro followed Gaspar's directions and pulled off the main road to a dirt path that pointed toward high cliffs in the distance.

Pedro managed to follow the path in the truck for half a kilometer, but then reached a washed-out arroyo he could not pass. Gaspar banged on the cab of the truck and said something in Spanish that Wylie translated as "close enough." They left the truck and followed Gaspar along the arroyo to the foot of rugged cliffs dripping with green vegetation. Gaspar carefully examined the base of the cliff face and turned to the right, beckoning the others to follow. Two hundred meters along, he walked toward the cliff as though to begin climbing it, but stopped short there and disappeared. Moments later, he reappeared, beaming broadly. He had found the entrance to the limestone caverns.

A wall of stone screened the opening. To enter they had to squeeze between two perpendicular rock walls and slip into a gap the size of a washbasin. Large rocks that had fallen from the cliff face surrounded the entrance. They prepared their headlamps and flashlights, and Larry wound rope around his upper body. Pedro carried the crowbar, and Gaspar secured the shovel to his back. Mercy easily slipped through the opening and found herself at the beginning of a long, sloping corridor, quite wide, but uneven, and bristling with stalactites and stalagmites that formed glistening curtains as far as her headlamp could cast its light. She moved forward, found a bench of rock and waited there for the others.

Larry soon entered, followed by Wylie, both cursing a too-rich diet that had expanded their waistlines and forced them to navigate the opening like corks pulled from a wine bottle. Pedro and Gaspar came next, and Gaspar took the large flashlight and illuminated the path downward. In the darkened echo chamber of the cylindrical entrance passageway, they felt their way along, suddenly warmed by the constant temperature of thirteen degrees Celsius.

After descending thirty meters, Gaspar flashed his light along the high wall to his left and showed an array of petroglyphs in ochre and red that looked as fresh as the day six hundred years ago when they were first painted: the sun with expanded rays, hummingbirds, monkeys, llamas, human figures with arms outstretched, spiders and square-headed people marched across the limestone walls. A row of beautifully formed but indecipherable symbols in red, yellow and black scrolled down the wall, leading the eye to a large chamber that dissolved into darkness. The ancient dust under their feet sent up puffs of powder as they made their way into the chamber. The only words spoken were exclamations of awe.

Gaspar walked into the chamber and shone the bright light against a row of large niches cut into the wall. Mercy gasped. Here were dead people arrayed like pins in a bowling alley. They even resembled large bowling pins: squat, pear-shaped, cream-colored bundles carefully wrapped in cloth. Mercy walked closer and played her headlamp over the bundles. Each one had an intricate symbol painted on its front, topped by crude features that resembled a smiley face.

Larry spoke.

—Absolutely fantastic! I have never seen anything like this. It is probably one of the best, most pristine group of mummified remains ever assembled. See, there they have painted a face that likely resembles the ancestor inside. And at the end there, that mummy has definitely been rewrapped. It supports the conjecture that their worship involved caring for their ancestors after they had been preserved. Very different from the Egyptians.

Gaspar moved about the large chamber, shining his light to highlight faces and paintings of warrior like figures that covered the walls.

—What do you think? asked Wylie. Are those warriors here to frighten intruders and ward off evil spirits?

—I don't know about you, but I am frightened by the whole thing, offered Mercy, as she illuminated one of the bundles to show the figure inside through the thin cloth. It was a fearsome sight.

The knees were drawn up to the chest, the arms positioned so the hands pressed against the cheeks. Cords of hemp held the hands in place. The climate of the cave retarded but did not eliminate the deterioration of mummified flesh. The lips and nose were gone, exposing a gaping mouth with bright and perfect teeth, drawn in either a grin or a look of horror. The shoulders and arms remained covered with fabrics of either cloth or leather. The hands were wrinkled and gray, but retained their original shape—with prominent fingernails.

Mercy looked at the figure as though transfixed. There was something familiar about the face in front of her. She remembered.

—My God! This looks just like the Munch's painting *The Scream*.

Wylie and Larry, who had also been examining the illuminated figure, agreed.

—Just like, they said. Extraordinary. A small world.

Larry pushed all other concerns away as he examined the group of figures assembled in the cavern. It was, he knew, a major archeological find. Undamaged by grave robbers and thieves, the wall drawings and the large number of figures located here would provide scientists with valuable material for years. Wylie joined him, and Larry shared insights with his companion. Wylie counted all the mummies he could see. There were twenty-three.

Pedro joined Mercy and they looked at the petroglyphs, which Mercy sketched in her journal. She'd had enough of dead people.

Pedro's dimming headlamp indicated that his batteries were wearing out. Mercy kept her light focused on his hands as he changed batteries. As they resumed their examinations, Wylie's flashlight also dimmed. He checked his watch and saw they had been in the cave for more than two hours.

Before he could suggest cutting their visit short, he heard, in the corridor behind them, the sound of a body crashing to the ground, followed by loud Spanish curses. Instantly exhilaration at their archaeological discoveries evaporated, and the Cypher group in the great chamber was on the alert. They dimmed their lights and looked in direction of the sound and curses. In the sudden darkness, the feeling of danger was palpable. Wylie and Larry bumped into each other, and Pedro felt his way to a niche, pulling Mercy with him. All remained quiet, listening.

The light from military issue torches stabbed into the darkness. The leader who Wylie shot in the leg and three soldiers were silhouetted against light playing off the marble walls. Those in the chamber saw that the leader held his pistol and the soldiers' rifles pointed haphazardly into the darkness ahead as they stumbled along the obstacle strewn pathway toward them.

How the hell did they find us? wondered Wylie as he and Larry shuffled quietly through the ancient dust, feeling their way farther into the chamber, along a wall, away from the soldiers. Wylie heard a click as Larry checked his pistol and kneeled in the dust, presenting a smaller target. Wylie thought that was an excellent idea and crouched beside his friend, wishing he still had his rifle, wishing he had shot the leader through the heart and not the thigh. Beams from the soldiers' flashlights penetrated the chamber, playing along the walls, showing the ancient mummies, discovering the outlines of fresh footsteps on the dusty ground.

Soon after their arrival in Cajamarca, Manolo, the leader of the soldiers charged with pursuing the Cypher party, proudly presented the disks recovered from his quarry to his superiors. It took some time to find a computer in their headquarters that could display the disks' contents, and more time to discover they were decoys. Manolo became apoplectic when he learned the disks were phony.

To be shot by him in the leg was a distasteful event, but an acceptable risk in combat. Managing to slip through his fingers twice in the course of their pursuit was embarrassing but, given the circumstances, the intervention of an avalanche and an ambush by the Sendero Luminoso, understandable. However, to gull him with bogus disks and cause his personal embarrassment at headquarters . . . that was too much. The Admiral apparently agreed; he personally authorized continued pursuit. Bloodlust was on Manolo; he wanted that damn gringo—alive or, preferably, dead.

Manolo knew they were on the way toward Chachapoyas. The police had spotted their truck in Balsas the night before. They hurried northward from Balsas in their military vehicle, not sure what to expect, but alert for any signs of the gringo and his companions. One of the soldiers spotted their truck parked on an access road near the highway. Their tracks led to the entrance to whatever this chamber was.

The soldiers aimed their lights toward the far end of the chamber, searching out the people they knew were there. One man picked out the figures of Wylie and Larry crouching close together. The two parted quickly, and the light followed Wylie. He recalled his old army training; he zigged and zagged, and the light did not follow him.

In his eagerness to capture these accursed gringos, Manolo rushed toward the last place he had seen the man who shot him. His torch provided but dim light and he stumbled over a round stalagmite on the ground and reached out to steady himself against the wall. Instead, he contacted one of the mummy bundles, which toppled from the limestone shelf and struck the leader on his shoulder. The fabric covering the mummy, gossamer thin after years in the cave, tore away. Ancient dust enveloped his face and the mummy's joints gave way, showering him with brittle bones. He stumbled and fell forward onto a rib cage, which broke into sharp shards—one of which penetrated his side. He howled, and one of his men ran through the gloom to support him. Blood oozed through his fingers as he kicked aside the mummy's bones at his feet.

He held his painful side and all the soldiers moved together toward the far wall, trying to herd their quarry to the end of the chamber. In the darkness, Wylie and Larry stumbled through the thick dust on the ground to the place where Pedro, still holding Mercy's arm, called out to them. The lights from the soldiers' torches occasionally revealed their locations. Shots rang out and bullets bit into the limestone above their heads and showered them with marble dust. They did not know where to turn as the soldiers advanced toward them.

Gaspar shouted to his compatriots.

—*Ven acá! Ven acá!*

He shone his light at a corridor that led from the chamber and, as the soldiers stumbled past the mummies and toward the far wall, the Cypher party slipped around a corner into another long corridor. As they did, more .32-caliber bullets smashed into the stone wall just behind them. They followed Gaspar's dancing light down the corridor, but not before Larry aimed a few shots from his pistol on the direction of the soldiers. He was rewarded by a pained scream of

—*Mierda.*

In what seemed like pitch darkness, they moved down the corridor, bruising themselves on stone outcrops and scraping their sides as they stumbled into lacerating shards of limestone. There was loud movement behind them. Random small-arms fire pock marked the stones above and beside them, made more threatening by the reverberation of the explosions on the high-ceilinged chamber. Pedro helped Mercy as they scurried down the corridor, following Gaspar's blinking light. They turned one corner, then another. The sounds behind them became faint.

Larry risked turning on his light and saw that the corridor they were on canted upward. Gaspar beckoned them forward, and they moved on, bent at the waist to counteract the steepness of the climb. Far ahead, a pinpoint of light pierced the gloom. In moments, they all stood next to Gaspar, who retrieved the shovel strapped to his back. At his feet was a small opening. Mercy reached toward it and discovered cool air blowing through the little hole.

He probed the opening with the tip of his shovel, loosening earth and pebbles. letting more light in. Pedro joined him with the tip of his crowbar. In minutes, the opening was large enough for them all to crawl through. They stood in the same arroyo they passed earlier that day. Gaspar tried to appear nonchalant about engineering their escape, but could not long contain an expression of glee that he had thwarted their attackers. He accepted the warm *abrazo* of the three men and a kiss on the cheek from Mercy. Nevertheless, they remained wary and vigilant. Their resourceful foe had tracked them this far, and they still had a few more days to elude that enemy before they could finally end their eventful trek across the high Andes.

Larry recommended they seal the opening they had created. Five more minutes with shovel and crowbar, the movement of some heavy rocks, and the opening was properly sealed. Larry asked Gaspar whether they should mark it, but Gaspar demurred. He would remember. They carefully retraced their steps of the morning to where they had left their truck. Larry took point, his pistol ready.

An unguarded military vehicle that resembled an eight-passenger jeep stood behind their truck. Their truck's hood was up, and a quick glance showed that all accessible wires had been ripped out and discarded somewhere in the brush. Gaspar and Larry exchanged glances. Gaspar grabbed Pedro and the three retraced their steps of the morning, returning to the entrance of the chamber. It, too, was unguarded. In his eagerness to deal with the detested gringo, Manolo had ignored basic precautions to be sure his entire squad was on hand to subdue Wylie. The gringos used shovel and crowbar to bury the entrance and pry large boulders from the surrounding debris to seal it thoroughly. For good measure, Pedro kicked some gravel against the boulders.

—Unless they have some C-4 with them, there is no way they can move these boulders from inside.

—We may have added some soldier mummies down there, added Larry.

Although at this point they were unsure how they would get to Chachapoyas, they all enjoyed a victory swagger as they made their way back to the military vehicle. Wylie and Mercy stood next to the elongated jeep, and Wylie jingled silver objects in his hand.

—My brilliant daughter looked under the sun visor and found keys to their truck. It is three-quarters full of fuel and seems to idle nicely.

Larry broke out in a grin.

—As they say, even a blind hog stumbles across an acorn every once in a while. It's about time we caught a break!

They transferred all their gear to the rear of the jeep and placed their weapons out of sight. No doubt, gringos in a military vehicle would appear odd. Then again, as far as the locals were concerned, gringos always seemed to do odd things.

Mercy insisted on taking a turn at the wheel. She ground the gears and accelerated too quickly over the bumpy track back to the highway, but by the time she headed the truck north, it was smooth sailing. They soon relaxed as the vehicle eased farther down from the top of the canyon toward lush jungle ahead. Pedro consulted his map, looked at the sun just standing at two o'clock, and estimated that they would be in the little town of Magdalena in less than two hours. Mercy was humming a little tune.

24

That afternoon Larry and Pedro took the side road that avoided Chachapoyas to the little airport east of the town. Larry monopolized the telephone in the corner of the waiting room for many minutes, and then joined Pedro, who was examining the planes parked near the flight office.

—We have confirmation. Finally. Day after tomorrow morning a twin-engine Beechcraft will pick us up. It's no executive jet, but it is a reliable plane—and roomy. Now, the question is—do you want an all-expenses-paid trip north, stopping in Ecuador, with us?

Pedro had already given that question some thought. Of his parents, only his mother was alive, and his two sisters and their small children often attended her. Given the demanding nature of his medical studies and his part-time employment by the CIA, he did not see her often. He had no romantic entanglements.

Clearly, the military authorities knew of his association with the Cypher group. There was no question about it. His tenure in Peru would be very precarious.

—There is not much for me in Ecuador. Do you think I could take a connecting flight to America?

—I am certain that could be arranged. You have burned your bridges here. The company takes care of its own.

Although there was past evidence that Larry's last statement was inaccurate, he was confident the agency would provide cover for Pedro. A native Peruvian would be invaluable in assessing activities by the Sendero Luminoso.

Pedro nodded assent. They sealed their agreement like Roman legion-naires—with hands surrounding each other's forearms.

Larry and Pedro joined Mercy and Wylie on the veranda of a tiny café where the Cyphers waited, eager for news about their departure. Yet, they accepted that information with a mixture of relief and skepticism. Their other attempt to make contact with CIA Air had failed. Lately, every time they thought they were either safe or about to depart, their hopes had been dashed.

—Well, Daddy, what do you think? Better to maintain low expectations and not be disappointed?

It was an expression Wylie used to tease his children—especially when it came to their prowess in sports. Wylie smiled at his daughter and shook his fin-ger at her in mock anger. Turnabout is fair play, he thought. This trip had turned into much more than reinforcing the bond between parent and child. This young woman, the fruit of his loins, was tough, brave, and even-tempered. With all they had been through, she still made jokes. He kissed her cheek.

Larry and Pedro ordered something to drink and conversation dwindled. They still had to survive in this isolated town for another forty-eight hours, with the threat of capture or worse always in the back of their minds. The possibil-ity of sitting and drinking bad coffee on a dirty verandah to fill the time was unpalatable.

Sensing their unease, Larry said,

—So, we have another day to get through before we will be on our way home. Consider the source, but I suppose we could visit the Fortress of Kuelap that Gaspar is so impressed with. I have read about it in archeological journals, and although it is principally in unrestored condition, it is supposed to be a splen-did fortress built by the pre-Incan Chachapoyas people, who were called "cloud warriors" by the Spanish conquerors. It is a relatively short drive from here.

—Any mummies there? asked Wylie, half joking.

—Yes, answered Larry. And they are very unusual. Gaspar calls them *purun-machus*. These are humanoid capsules made out of clay to resemble the person inside. We should be able to see the ones that rest on ledges protruding from cliff faces.

—Sorry I asked.

—Oh, Larry, I think Daddy is having you on. We definitely need something to fill the time and I want very much to see the ancient fortress.

Pedro shook his head.

—Sorry. But I must make many telephone calls before we leave. The clerk at the *farmacia* will let me use his telephone, but the connection is not reliable. It will take some time. I will probably be waiting for you when you return.

Mercy had parked the military jeep liberated the day before discreetly behind a warehouse on the eastern side of Magdalena. They relocated their baggage to a storeroom at the back of their motel and did not intend to use the jeep again. Larry hired a tourist bus and driver for their excursion to the Kuelap fortress. Since they clearly were not locals, acting the part of tourists was a good disguise. The portly driver seemed unduly proud of the decrepit Ford shuttle bus that he pulled up to their overnight accommodations. The body was rusty, the windows flyblown, and puffs of dust flew from the fabric seats as they sat down.

Gaspar was their guide, and he sat behind the driver. The three gringos spread out in the bus and checked the daypacks purchased the day before. Rain jackets, alpaca vests, water bottles and, in Larry's case, a pistol, plus "samweech-es" and hard candies provided by the manager of their "hotel." It was a bright, sunny day, but it would probably be cold at the fortress, which rose from its foundations almost three thousand meters above sea level.

The bus left Magdalena, followed the main highway for a short distance, and then climbed up to the flat mountaintop where the cloud warriors had built their ancient fortress. Wildflowers and grasses lined the hairpin road to the top, and they caught sight of the Utcubamba Valley stretching out below. Llamas grazed by the road and in the grassy areas surrounding the fortress. The creamy white twenty-five-meter-high wall of limestone blocks that surrounded the urban center of the compound suddenly came into sight. The immense size of the fortress city was apparent; the wall stretched for a kilometer toward bright green vegetation in the distance.

As they left the bus and walked toward the west entrance, Larry commented on the fortification's strategic location. Unobstructed views of the surrounding valleys and the Utcubamba and Marañón rivers below guaranteed no surprise attacks, and the massive defensive walls were almost impossible to breach. The builders had tapered the entrance walls, forcing attackers to walk through a limestone funnel—where the cloud warriors could pick them off one by one as they pushed toward the inner citadel. Gaspar led the way through the entrance and they emerged at the opening to the citadel itself. Before them were the ruins of scores of round houses, clustered together like lily pads.

As they walked toward another wall in the distance, Gaspar pointed to one of the few tall buildings —a tower. He explained to Larry that more than two thousand stones for slingshots remained there—ready to be released even now, six hundred years since the fortress was completed. They picked their way over and around the blocks of limestone that outlined the ancient houses and walked toward the wall holding an entrance to farther reaches of the old city. Larry paused there.

—Each one of these weighs at least two hundred pounds and the keystones must be upward of four hundred pounds. This rivals the construction of the pyramids in Egypt. Imagine the effort it took to quarry these stones and carry them up here. These cloud warriors were fearsome engineers as well!

Gaspar showed them a partially reconstructed round building, which showed how the circular houses were built—a circular second floor offset above a circular base with a conical thatched roof.

—It looks like a two-layer cake with a party hat, noted Mercy, who was seeing, in her mind's eye, what this city must have looked like: hundreds of high-hatted houses arrayed across the top of the flat mountain, protected by stone walls seventy-five feet high. Not for the first time on this trip, she wished she had Larry's understanding of ancient architecture and his ability to visualize exactly how things looked centuries ago.

Gaspar moved from spot to spot, demonstrating a guinea-pig run here, a granary there. Although the overall effect of the citadel was awesome, care had to be taken as they wandered through the ruins. Surrounding vegetation had invaded the fortress. Tree roots protruded through stone walls; moss disguised large stones; orchids and bromeliads ornamented trees threatening to enclose pathways. Larry was so enchanted by the surroundings that he stumbled over a tree root.

As the sun rose and penetrated the interior of the old city, the temperature increased and the visitors made clothing adjustments. Sweaters and jackets returned to their daypacks and they enjoyed the sensation of cool mountain air on their skin.

Larry looked at the top of the highest parapet in view and spotted intricate designs of smaller stones embedded there. He suggested to Wylie that they climb to the top for a better look. Wylie was not so interested in the designs. He wanted to experience the view from the highest point on the mountain. Mercy decided to remain on the grassy area below to write in her journal, and found a temporary resting place on what might have been a grand plaza. With her permission, Gaspar wandered to the next and highest level of the city to explore on his own. Larry and Wylie clambered over footholds and crude steps to reach the highest point on the fortress wall.

There were parapets on each side of the wall, great shelves protruding eight or nine feet below the top. Larry guessed they provided positions where the residents could launch offensive missiles at potential attackers. He stayed on the inner parapet examining diamond-shaped designs and strange carvings on the large limestone blocks—on his knees so he could brush away debris and encroaching vegetation. He was lost in his world of discovery.

Wylie climbed down to the outside parapet and allowed the mountain breeze to dry the sweat that accumulated during his ascent. He stretched out his arms and gazed at the river valley below and the myriad greens of the countryside. He decided to invite Mercy to join him so she, too, could enjoy the fabulous view. He turned to pick his way back to the top of the fortification where he saw a large man standing on top of the wall, looking down at the spot where Wylie had left Larry.

Lucho cursed his drooping foot as he worked his way up to the place where he had seen the two gringos. One, he was sure, was the man who had kicked him in the head at Fredo's house in Huaraz. The other seemed a healthier version of the invalid Claudia cared for: the mystery man, Dr. Cypher, the one who might have turned Raoul de Sousa over to the police. He had murderous intent for the kicker; for Cypher, he planned an intensive interrogation.

He had difficulty placing his flopping foot on the narrow holds leading to the top of the wall and had to support himself with his good hand when he stumbled. Nevertheless, the kicker was completely absorbed in whatever he was doing on the ledge inside the wall, and there was no sign of the other one. He reached a place above the kicker without being observed and balanced himself securely on both feet. He pulled the .38-caliber Smith & Wesson pistol from his pocket with his left hand and pointed it at the kicker.

—Hey, gringo, he called.

Larry looked up to see the silhouette of a large man holding a pistol standing on the wall above him. He seemed vaguely familiar. The daypack concealing his pistol lay beside him. It might as well have been on the ground below. The large man said, "Hey, gringo," again, hoping to see recognition in the man's eyes. It came.

—¿*Qué?* he asked innocently.

A string of curses, mainly involving his mother and private parts, came from the man above.

—¡*Puto bastardo!* offered Lucho, then took aim at Larry's right knee and fired.

From his place on the ledge below the stranger, Wylie saw the pistol pointing in Larry's direction. He did not know who the man was, but assumed he was another of the many Peruvians who wanted to harm them. He saw he could quickly climb a few steps up the wall and reach its top, but was uncertain how that would aid his friend. Then he heard the shot and saw the blast of fire from the gun's muzzle.

Meanwhile, the subordinate who had accompanied Lucho on his search for the detested gringos waited in the plaza below the wall. There he encountered Mercy sitting on a wooden bench, daydreaming about the ancient civilization surrounding her. The man poked his automatic rifle in the back of her neck as his introduction and motioned her to back up and stand against one of the massive walls.

Initially shocked and afraid, she dropped her journal and moved toward the wall, looking at her captor, almost overcome by a cocktail of conflicting emotions. Fear tempered by the hormones that prepared her for fight or flight. Anger at her captor and herself for letting down her guard with danger all around. Self-pity at being once again singled out for capture or worse. Fear. Frustration. Anger. Her eyes blazed as she took the measure of her captor.

He was a small, very young man, almost a boy, who looked like many of the Indians she had seen in Huaraz. He wore blue jeans, a checkered shirt, sandals, and had tied a tattered sweater around his middle. His rifle had a metal stock and a banana clip, and the man had the disconcerting nervous habit of keeping his finger within the trigger guard. He spoke to her in Spanish, unpleasant words.

In spite of the nasty weapon he carried, the man himself did not seem as formidable as the soldiers they had dealt with during the past few days. On more careful observation, she saw that her captor had no facial hair at all; he was just a teenager. As she lowered her eyes to avoid the boy's glare, she came to a decision. On this trip, she thought, I have twice been captured by men with guns, been threatened with gang rape, been shot at and scared half out of my wits. Enough is enough! I will deal with this little weasel myself. Overcoming her fear and anger, she developed a plan based on a primal human desire—sex. She sought to lower her enemy's guard by diverting his attention, a tactic taught in her martial arts classes and used by seasoned military commanders.

The noontime sun raised the temperature in the ruins, and Mercy fanned her face with her hands and wiped imaginary perspiration from her brow, rubbing her hand slowly across her breasts to wipe away nonexistent moisture. Startled by that motion, the boy watched her more closely. She leaned back against the massive wall stone, unbuttoning the top button of her blouse, fanning the exposed skin on her chest with her hand. She loosened the next button as well. Her guard relaxed his grip on the rifle, his finger slipped from the trigger guard, and his right hand gripped the stock. He leaned closer to his captive, who moved slightly closer to him, smiling and reaching toward the third button on her shirt.

As the pink edge of her right aureole appeared in the widening gap of her shirt, the guard gave a small gasp and lowered his weapon. He concentrated on a small area of her chest and did not observe that Mercy's other hand, now formed into a weapon with knuckles protruding, supported by her thumb underneath, was drawn back at her side. With all the intensity she could muster, she plunged the knuckles into the soft spot three inches above his navel. She heard air escaping his lungs as he bent forward in a painful reflex action, dropping his rifle, clutching his middle, gasping for breath. He fell to his knees, then his side.

Mercy dropped on one knee to retrieve the rifle, held it in both hands, stood, and looked down at the fallen boy curled into a fetal position at her feet. The anger and resentment she had felt during the past few minutes rose in her, inflaming her, drawing a curtain of scarlet mist across her eyes. Without thinking, she reversed the rifle in her hands and drove the butt forcefully into the side of her attacker's head. He was motionless, inert, making it difficult for her to roll him into a ditch beside one of the circular houses.

She was preparing to drop a large stone onto his head when Gaspar turned the corner of an interior wall. He was devastated when he saw that Mercy had rescued herself from another attack—while he was absent and without his help. He ran to her and helped dispatch the soldier. He was still offering apologies for having left her when they heard a shot ring out from above.

Although he was accustomed to firing his pistol with his left hand, the two-dimensional vision from his good eye occasionally caused Lucho to miss his target, especially when it was close. His bullet did not shatter this victim's knee-cap; instead, it passed through Larry's calf, a quarter inch below the skin. Larry grunted and clasped his wound. Lucho recovered his stance after the recoil from his pistol and aimed carefully again, this time for the larger target of the gringo's chest.

Suddenly a call came from behind him.

—Hey, asshole, Wylie shouted, causing the large man to turn toward the front of the wall, pointing his pistol toward the valley below.

Wylie had reached a spot directly below and facing the top of the parapet and, as Lucho turned, reached up and grabbed his ankles. He braced his feet and knees against the wall and pulled outward with all his strength. It was enough. Lucho's weakened foot gave way first and slipped off the edge of the wall. Unbalanced, he tried to place his other foot on a firm surface, but found only open space. He tumbled forward, clawing at thin air and firing his pistol as he fell, puncturing the limestone wall. The breeze whipped away the peculiar moaning sound he made and he landed headfirst on the grassy plain below, flipped on his back and lay motionless. He remained that way as a curious llama pulled her head from the succulent grass and wandered over to the fallen man, sniffing his hair. There was no movement. She lost interest and returned to grazing. Larry and Wylie looked down at the man who had threatened them. From a height of forty meters, he seemed small. After a few moments, other visitors to the ruins ran toward the downed man. It was quickly apparent they could offer him no help.

Gaspar and Mercy were waiting as Wylie helped Larry maneuver the path down to the bottom of the wall inside the compound. They saw Larry limping toward them, blood oozing from his calf. What had happened was unclear to Mercy and Gaspar, and Wylie described their activities as Mercy reached for the first-aid kit in her pack and Gaspar helped Larry to a stone seat. The wound seemed clean; bleeding was slight. She applied antibiotics and covered it with gauze and bandages. Larry grimaced as she tended to the injury, but noted he had had worse.

It was time to go. They helped their injured comrade to the bus. The driver reported that three men had arrived in a car after they entered the citadel, but just before the gringos returned, one had raced to the car and driven swiftly away. He pointed to a dust cloud on the hairpin road below.

—There he goes, he said.

—Damn it, said Larry. The one who left can report what happened here. They may know we stayed in Magdalena. We need to be on our way. Let's hope Pedro is finished with his calls.

On the way back to their hotel, they stopped at the pharmacy where Pedro intended to make his calls, but he was not there. Nor was he at their hotel, although much of his personal stuff was in his room. The owner of the hotel had not seen him since morning, and no, there was no message for them. They returned to the pharmacy, where Larry interviewed the wary clerk. The application of some *soles* encouraged him to recall where Pedro might be.

—The police made a visit, he said in Spanish. They had a question or two for me and for the man, Pedro, as well. They had an interest in gringos and said they had heard that this Pedro was with a group. They wanted to know about those gringos, so they took him away.

—Away? asked Larry.

—Yes. To the office of the police. It is not far—that way.

Larry thanked the young man and reported to Wylie and Mercy, waiting outside with Gaspar.

—Gaspar, he asked, would you help look for Pedro? I think he is with the police now.

Gaspar understood the current situation. Once again, the authorities threatened his gringos. He had failed them that afternoon; as a matter of pride, he would not let that happen again.

—*Por supuesto*, he said, and had a brief discussion with Larry.

Gaspar was the image of an obeisant peasant as he entered the police station. He shuffled up to the littered desk of the only man in the office with his straw hat in hand, making a little bow. He explained that he had heard his friend was visiting the police and wanted to make sure he received his dinner. Pedro, his name was—a tall man. Was he there?

The young officer saw no harm in letting this mountain man speak with their captive, and led him through a door in the back of the office to a room where Pedro sat in one of three metal cages. The cage had a chamber pot, a washbasin and pitcher, and a metal bunk. Pedro sat on the bed and rose to greet Gaspar, shaking hands through the steel bars of the cage.

The officer withdrew, and Pedro explained that he had been detained because of a vague direction received from Cajamarca that the police were interested in locating gringos. Apparently, junior officers checked the three little hotels in Magdalena and learned that Pedro was with three gringos. Since the gringos were not available, he was detained as the next best thing. That was his bad luck and an unusual demonstration of police resourcefulness. The officer in authority would not be returning until the following morning. Pedro was stuck in his cage for the night.

He ruefully pointed out that their passage out of Peru was also scheduled for the next day. He asked Gaspar to collect his things and have them ready— just in case. Gaspar promised to do so, and said he would return later with a meal for his friend.

All this he relayed to Larry, Wylie and Mercy, who gathered and packed Pedro's personal items.

—But what, asked Mercy, if he doesn't get away in time? We can't leave without him.

—Let's just hope we don't have to make that decision, said Larry. We still have about fourteen hours to get him out.

Gaspar was waiting at the entrance to the police station at eight in the morning when the young officer arrived to open the door. He asked to see the *jefe* so he could speak with him about his friend. That would be acceptable, but the *jefe* usually did not arrive until later—sometimes much later. Gaspar found a wooden chair by the entrance and waited.

Larry observed the police station from a little bodega down the block, drinking strong coffee, which did little to calm his frustration at this unforeseen delay. The Beechcraft was to arrive at the little airport about noon. Fortunately, the airport was only a short distance away. The portly driver from yesterday was waiting with his disreputable van a block away. Mercy waited nearby, but Wylie could not stay still. He walked up and down the street, pretending to look into shop windows.

Larry saw an elderly fat man who overflowed his police uniform enter the building. He looked like the boss, though Larry could not be certain. If so, it was now up to Gaspar to follow his instructions and arrange for Pedro's release. The gringos waited. A flea-bitten Peruvian dog walked slowly along the entire block, pausing three times to scratch himself. It seemed that a half hour passed with no other activity at the police station. Larry pushed away his fourth cup of coffee.

The door cracked open and the young officer guided Gaspar to the sidewalk. For a sickening moment, Larry thought the door was closing behind Gaspar. It swung open again, and Pedro appeared.

The *jefe* sat in his office looking at the little pile of greenbacks Gaspar had placed on his desk. It was stupid of his inexperienced young officers to delay that fine Peruvian citizen as they did. Fortunately, the officer was in a position to remedy the situation. He scooped up the bills and, with magical sleight of hand, made them disappear. He leaned back and sighed. Today, he thought, we should look for gringos. After lunch would be soon enough.

Gaspar directed Pedro to the waiting van, where Mercy, in her great relief, hugged him, and Wylie did the same. Larry immediately appeared and hopped in the van and they started for the airport. It was just before ten in the morning.

The distance to the airport was only a few kilometers, but there were delays. Construction of a viaduct detoured them through a mucky meadow, and they had to stop for a herd of recalcitrant sheep and jittery llamas. At a little after eleven the van turned onto the dirt road that ran parallel to the airfield, leading to the low building that served as lounge, office and control tower.

As they approached the building, a small airplane made its approach for landing. It was a single-engine Cessna Skyhawk painted olive drab with stenciled military markings on body and tail. The craft executed a bumpy landing and taxied toward a spot near the office building. Prompted by Larry, Gaspar put his hand on the driver's arm and asked him to stop on the shoulder of the dirt road. Gaspar and the driver went to the front of the van, raised the hood, and looked at the engine.

The Cessna came to a stop and the passenger door opened. The person on the front passenger seat made his awkward descent from the aircraft, almost falling as he searched for the first step down. As he reached the ground, the pilot passed a Lofstrand crutch to his passenger and pushed his seat forward to let two soldiers out. They paused for a moment by the aircraft and came into view of the people in the van. Larry, first to recognize him, cursed.

—It's the leader of the troops who attacked us on the mountain—that son of a bitch! How the hell did he manage to get out of the cave with the mummies?

He could waste no time wondering how the soldiers happened to be here. The gringos had to deal with a new threat, and time was running out.

Larry called Gaspar back to the van. He and Wylie conferred with the muleteer for a few minutes and Larry handed him his Zippo lighter and a bundle of greenbacks. If Gaspar survived his next interaction with their military tormentors, he was assured of a comfortable retirement.

Gaspar put his battered hat on his head, attached his machete to his belt with a string, and ambled down the dirt road in the direction of the office building, but with his sight set on an old, disused outhouse rotting away in the jungle a few hundred yards from the building. Mercy searched through the few things in their packs for brightly colored clothing—anything garish enough to become an attention-getting flag. She, Larry and Wylie kept their heads down in the van while the driver still puttered with the engine. Wylie raised his head enough to observe the pilot of the military aircraft removing packs and weapons from the cargo area. The two soldiers retrieved them and joined their leader, who was making his way to the office building. Wylie noticed a vehicle similar to the one they had abandoned in Magdalena parked at the far side of the building. Three more soldiers stood there.

The gringos waited.

Promptly at noon, Mercy noticed a dark spot on the horizon, which quickly materialized into a twin-engine aircraft making its approach to the Chachapoyas airfield. The approach was high, to avoid the tall shrubs and trees that ended only at the edge of the hardpan field. Larry recognized the insignia under its wings. It was their aircraft, the Beechcraft King Air sent to fly them to Ecuador. Larry and Wylie hoped that Gaspar recognized the airplane as well.

Just as the plane touched down, two things occurred: The rotting outhouse in the distance burst into flame, fueled by thatch, wood and two unused catalogs showing women's finery. Three gringos and one Peruvian medical student raced from the parked van to the edge of the runway unfurling a red sweater, green sweatpants, an orange blouse, and a blue backpack. They stood waving the garments. Mercy and Pedro jumped open-armed into the air.

Although the burning outhouse posed no immediate threat to the building by the runway, the dry grass next to the privy smoldered, and sharp orange flames encircled the little building and began to spread. Three soldiers jumped into the military vehicle, drove toward the burning grass, thought better of their action, and returned to look for a way to halt the blaze. Fortunately, the only one who then noticed the strange activity beside the runway was the pilot of the Beechcraft.

The moving plane braked, raising ochre dust that floated toward the office building. The wheel under the nose turned aside as the propellers gained momentum and the aircraft made a slow turn and began to cruise toward its intended passengers.

Now the attention of those in the office building shifted toward the Beechcraft and its unorthodox maneuver. The frantic display of colorful clothing beside the runway escaped no one's notice now. Someone with binoculars stood in the building's doorway and focused on the four waving figures. Moments later, soldiers poured from the back of the building like clowns from a circus midget car, a few clambering into the jeep, the others sprinting down the runway toward the airplane. Manolo stood next to the building, leaning on his crutch and shouting unheard commands. The jeep rounded a corner of the building and followed the soldiers already on the runway.

The plane slowed as it drew near the Cypher group and the door behind the wing on the pilot's side began to lower. Larry's injury prohibited running toward the plane, so Pedro half carried him along and deposited him at the bottom of the steps. Larry pulled himself up, and Pedro pushed Mercy up to a man who held out his hand from the opening above. Pedro jumped inside and Wylie rushed up the still-moving steps. As they began to close behind him, two dimpled openings appeared above the bottom step. Small-arms fire had nearly found him.

As the door sealed, the four quickly sat in the plush leather-upholstered seats in the aircraft. The pilot, a young blond man, twisted in his seat to grin at them, and the other man, copilot and steward who rode shotgun, nodded as well. As they strapped themselves in, the pilot revved the engines, but then pushed the throttle back. The pilot adjusted his headphones and turned to his passengers.

—Looks like there are two reasons we can't take off. Some army guy wants words with you, and the dispatcher says there is not enough runway for us to clear the trees. That and, of course, people are shooting at us. Guys, it doesn't get much better than this!

The two pilots looked ahead. The end of the runway was close. Pedro confirmed that the jeep with soldiers was closer, attempting to cut them off. The pilots exchanged a look.

—Fuck, yes! said the copilot, and the pilot swiftly pushed the throttle forward. The two engines roared to life and the plane leaped forward, quickly outdistancing the jeep.

Grit and dust blew into the faces of the soldiers on the ground. They watched the Beechcraft leave the runway and climb to the north, heading directly into the trees at the end of the runway. The nose rose upward as the front wheel began to recede into its compartment. One of the rear wheels caught on a tassel of green leaves before it could retract, but the plane continued to gain speed and altitude.

Moments later the pilot turned the plane northwest, cruising toward the Cordillera Central. The passengers could see, through the large round windows, the crenellated backbone of the mountains they had crossed. Silver threads of the Marañón River stretched through the sere Andes. They settled into their soft beige seats. The copilot stood in the front compartment.

—Anyone think it is too early for a drink of fine Scotch? he asked.

No one did.

25

Aside from minor turbulence as it coursed over the highest peaks, the Beechcraft made its way uneventfully to a small airport in southern Ecuador where the Cypher group disembarked, found a flight to Quito and stayed in a fashionable hotel while Larry spent time reporting their adventures, explaining the location of the missing documents, and managing their continuing transportation home. Pedro was included with the group and Larry provided him with a visa from the American embassy in Quito. The scope and reach of CIA influence continued to impress Wylie. Three days after leaving Peru, they were all on a LAN flight to Kennedy airport. Wylie had telephoned Mavis from Quito and told her of their impending arrival, and she arranged for a car to pick them up. Unfortunately, she had other plans for the afternoon.

Wylie and Mercy, after careful discussion, decided not to confide the adventures of their trekking vacation to anyone else—not Mavis, not Brooks, not Wylie's partners. Mercy's reasons were simple.

—Daddy, she said, I can't think of anyone who would believe what happened to us. A middle class father and daughter involved in a chase across the Andes—getting shot at and worse? Messing around with two guys from the CIA? Come on! That's the stuff of cheap thrillers. I would rather we keep it to ourselves.

Wylie agreed; he was sure his partners would greet tales of his exploits with skepticism, perhaps derision. Though unlikely that anyone outside the family would notice the loss of his toe, he and Mercy concocted a tale of how it was lost in an accident with a slamming door. Mavis did notice, heard the story, expressed her regrets, and moved on to another subject.

After a while, the adrenaline rush of the dangers surmounted faded, and Wylie and Mercy recalled the ethereal beauty of the mountains and the establishment of a strong bond that was undissolved by passing years. Perhaps the maintenance of their secret strengthened that bond.

When he returned to his office, he discovered that, as arranged, the disks were in a safe place. He had copies made and, with Larry's guidance, provided them to highly placed officials in the State Department and the CIA. He received profuse thanks for his valiant service and confirmation that the disks were of great value to the nation. However, because of the sensitive nature of the documents in question, it would not be possible to provide official recognition for his service. Unquestionably, he would be contacted about the disks in the near future. Time passed. There was no further contact.

In the months following their return, Wylie engaged in the most important negotiation of his life—arranging the dissolution of his marriage with Mavis. There was something about his active participation in overcoming the dangers and threats of his last visit to Peru, of discovering his dormant resources, of becoming a kick-ass warrior, that dissolved his feelings of sameness and lassitude—and fortified his resolve to strike out anew—without Mavis.

The divorce was neither contested nor particularly difficult. Wylie simply agreed to all of Mavis' peevish demands and concentrated on thwarting her desire to ruin him. In the end, the settlement assured Mavis of a financially comfortable life ahead. Wylie also looked forward to a more contented life. He plunged into his legal duties with fresh fervor. It was many months before either of them found it necessary to contact the other.

Larry and Wylie met frequently during the months following their Peruvian adventure, and their friendship strengthened. Now that he had revealed his double life, Larry was less on his guard and their conversations included things about his CIA role that he could divulge. Wylie was pleased to have a trusted friend with whom he could discuss personal matters—including the details of his divorce with Mavis.

Months after Wylie sent the damning disks to government administrators, Larry invited him for a drink at a fashionable bar in Washington. When Wylie arrived, his favorite whiskey rested on the polished oak table, and Larry seemed subdued as he greeted him. The conversation was stilted; they spoke of mundane matters. Wylie wondered what his friend was holding back.

As Wylie examined the last half inch of liquor in his glass, Larry leaned toward his friend.

—Listen, I'm not exactly authorized to discuss this with you, but I believe it is only fair to pass this on—considering what you went through.

That quickly gained Wylie's full attention.

—It's about the information on those disks. They have been reviewed carefully and vetted by all appropriate actors, of which there were quite a number, and a decision has been taken.

Larry moved uncomfortably in the leather chair.

—Well, the thing is, our people taught the Peruvian military a lot of the stuff referenced in those documents. At the War College and by our advisers on site. Not all of it, but enough to raise strong concern that inappropriate connections could be made if the material got out . You understand that everyone is very grateful for your participation. Overall, it is a good thing you got them to the right hands.

Wylie was not sure about Larry's meaning.

—So, how do they intend to make use of the documents, then?

—Oh, they have been classified with highest secret status. They are protected for twenty-five years.

Wylie looked at the remains of his drink. Suddenly his Glenmorangie tasted bitter.

Years later, the *Washington Post*, under the authority of the Freedom of Information Act, was able to obtain a heavily redacted copy of the information contained on those floppy disks. By then, there was nothing new about the revelations they contained.

AUTHOR'S ENDNOTES

For readers who demand tidier endings to their stories or are interested in future developments in the lives of the characters, I offer the information that follows. Fortunately, it is possible to be accurate about these matters, since I have kept careful notes about what occurred during the more than thirty years since these events.

For the romantics among us, I report that the strong friendship that blossomed between Mercy and Pedro remained only that. No messy passionate entanglements ensued; they remained good friends through most of those thirty years. But friendships wax and wane. By the early years of the twenty-first century, they were content to exchange Christmas greetings each year.

Aside from a continuing relationship with "the company," which I am not at liberty to discuss, Pedro completed his medical studies in the United States and became a renowned thoracic surgeon and professor at Johns Hopkins University. He is married with three children. Last year his first grandchild was born.

Mercy went to graduate school to obtain a Ph.D. in clinical psychology. Apparently, her adventure in Peru whetted her appetite for further escapades, which I will not report at this time, since they may well be the subject of a future novel. I can say that she married twice and had two children, one of whom went on to become a lawyer. That young woman's name is Portia, and more about her appears in a novel called *Master Gardener.*

Larry—Professor Kuitkowski—gradually diminished his involvement with the CIA and devoted his formidable energies to archeological pursuits. Once the political situation in Peru stabilized, he led numerous expeditions to remote areas of that country. His seminal work was the definitive narrative of the conquest of the Chachapoyas people by the Incas. He had many affairs with female graduate students, late in life marrying one who became pregnant. His friendship with Wylie and Pedro continued through the years. Larry and his young wife now have two children.

The Admiral gained power and authority in the years after Wylie and Mercy escaped from Peru. He was active in organizing and dispatching death squads that were responsible for numerous notorious massacres during the late 1980s and early 1990s. Years later President Fujimori was found guilty of authorizing twenty-five death squad killings and numerous forced "disappearances"—authorized just as revealed in the documents Wylie received. In the early twenty-first century, Peru's Truth and Reconciliation Commission estimated that the Admiral's death squads were responsible for killing more than seventy thousand people.

The Admiral himself was required to answer questions about the massacres. It was a time when Amnesty International was leading inquiries into the atrocities and abuses committed by the armed forces. Believing that his activities were soon to be disclosed, the Admiral prepared to take an extended vacation in Spain, where a large sum of money awaited. One day, however, as he was getting into his official car, an elderly man approached and discharged six .45-caliber revolver bullets into the Admiral's chest. He died instantly. The man was apprehended and discovered to be the father of two young men who were "disappeared." His sentence of fifteen years in prison is presently being appealed.

Lucho's death intensified Fredo and Claudia's disenchantment with the policies and principles of the Shining Path leadership. Some years after this story ended, Fredo managed to convert his experience as a teacher and administrator to fill an education department position in the Fujimori government. He is now retired, living in Ayacucho, and he and Claudia have five grandchildren living close by. He has a comfortable government pension.

Gaspar returned to his wife and children and lived out his years in his little village, journeying into the mountains each time he heard Pachamama's call. By local standards, he was a wealthy man, and he used his resources generously in aid of his village and its people. He never forgot his adventure with the gringos. As the light faded for him, he thought often of the little mummy he had rescued—and replaced. He died in 2002, and now lies in a grave lined with stones in the shadow of Huascarán Mountain.

Footnote: The group of Chachapoyas mummies located in a burial cave complex some eighty feet below the earth's surface was discovered late in 2006. It became known as Lyacyecuj ("enchanted water"). The team leader and archaeologist Herman Corbera who first examined the limestone complex remarked, "This is a discovery of transcendental importance. It is the first time any kind of underground burial site this size has been found belonging to the Chachapoyas or other cultures in the region."

There was no record of any bodies other than those of ancient mummies. However, among the many cave paintings and offerings to the ancestors, one item caused serious consternation among the scientists who exhumed the site. It was a Celendin straw hat adorned by a green silk scarf. The label on the scarf read "Bloomingdale's."

TRUE FACTS

Peruvian Politics
1980-2000

Under Belaunde's leadership as president of Peru from 1980 to 1985, economic problems due to natural disasters and a drop in international commodity prices led to severe inflation and great unemployment. As suggested in the novel, those conditions provided a breeding ground for social and political dissatisfaction. The Sendero Luminoso gained strength and created chaos throughout the country.

In 1985, Alan Garcia replaced Belaunde. His economic mismanagement led to hyperinflation (7,649 percent in 1990), and his presidency was tainted by numerous massacres by the military of those who were merely suspected of being involved with the Shining Path. The Peruvians are either very forgiving or have short institutional memories. Mr. Garcia, after years in exile, was reelected president in 2006, serving until 2011. Corruption and bribery were highlights of his last term.

In 1990, Alberto Fujimori became president. He instituted dramatic economic reforms that resulted in an almost immediate drop in inflation and effectively coordinated government actions against the Shining Path. That resulted in the capture and first trial of Professor Abimael Guzmán, the notorious leader of the Sendero Luminoso.

Fujimori orchestrated a coup of his own government in 1992, forcing the former president, Alan Garcia, into exile and firing many of the people who helped elect him. He ruled the country with an iron hand, somewhat rusted because of corruption. When details of the extent of government corruption finally came out, Fujimori fled to Japan in 2000 and faxed in his resignation. The Peruvian congress refused to accept it and fired him instead—through impeachment.

Fujimori stayed in Japan until 2005 when, misreading the popular sentiment for his return to power in Peru, he flew to Chile preparing for a grand return to his country. There he was arrested and deported to Peru for trial on charges of ordering illegal searches and seizures. He received a sentence to six years in prison. The Peruvian constitution is vague on issues of double indemnity, and Fujimori was retried in April and July of 2009 on charges of 1) human rights violations, murder, bodily harm, and two cases of kidnapping, and 2) embezzlement. The court levied sentences of twenty-five and seven and a half years in prison. During his fourth trial, two months later, he pled guilty to bribery and was given an additional six-year term. The court apparently ignored the prosecutor's demand that the defendant pay $1 million in damages to ten people whose telephones were bugged. All those years in prison seem to have been enough. Under Peruvian law, all sentences must run concurrently. Twenty-five years is the limit.

Recently, various attempts have been made to extract the former president from prison. His daughter, Keiko, ran for president in 2011; part of her platform was the promise to pardon her father if elected. She lost in a runoff to Ollanta Humala that year. Fujimori is in prison today (June 2014).

Fate of Guzmán

The antiterrorism unit of Fujimori's government was watching several residences in upper-class neighborhoods of Lima because they suspected terrorists were using them as safe houses. The agents routinely searched the garbage taken from the houses—including a residence operating as a ballet studio. A single dance teacher supposedly inhabited the house, but the agents discovered much more garbage than one person could account for. Careful examination of the refuse revealed discarded tubes of cream used in the treatment of psoriasis. Somehow, the agents knew Guzmán suffered from this condition. In September of 1992, they raided the second floor of the residence, and captured and arrested the terrorist leader and eight others, including Guzmán's girlfriend.

They also seized his computer. In spite of an organizational structure that emphasized lack of communication between units, the computer contained detailed lists of his armed forces and the weapons each regiment, militia, and support base had in every province of the country. Obviously, those lists were helpful in arresting many of the organization's supporters, but the Shining Path remained active well after its leader's arrest.

A court of hooded military judges tried Guzmán and sentenced him to life in prison. There were various appeals to that conviction, the latest in 2005. Nevertheless, he was sentenced again to life in prison on charges of terrorism and murder. He remains imprisoned at the Callao Naval Base outside of Lima.

www.ingramcontent.com/pod-product-compliance
Lightning Source LLC
Chambersburg PA
CBHW070851250626
47159CB00003B/1022